The Singing Bird

John Milton Oskison in 1900.
Courtesy Western History Collections,
University of Oklahoma Libraries.

The Singing Bird

A Cherokee Novel

John Milton Oskison

Edited by Timothy B. Powell and
Melinda Smith Mullikin

Foreword by Jace Weaver

University of
Oklahoma Press
Norman

Library of Congress Cataloging-in-Publication Data
Oskison, John M. (John Milton), 1874–1947.
The singing bird : a Cherokee novel / by John Milton Oskison ; edited by
Timothy B. Powell and Melinda Smith Mullikin ; foreword by Jace Weaver.
p. cm.
ISBN: 0-8061-3818-1 (pbk. : alk. paper)
ISBN: 978-0-8061-3818-3
1. Cherokee Indians—Fiction. 2. Trail of Tears, 1838—Fiction. I. Powell,
Timothy B. II. Mullikin, Melinda Smith. III. Title.
PS3529.S545S56 2007
813′.52—dc22

2006026451

The paper in this book meets the guidelines for permanence and durability of the Committee on Production Guidelines for Book Longevity of the Council on Library Resources, Inc. ∞

1 2 3 4 5 6 7 8 9 10

In loving memory of Ruth Moody, 1924–2005

—MSM

Contents

Foreword by Jace Weaver

When N. Scott Momaday's novel *House Made of Dawn* was published in 1968 and won the Pulitzer Prize the following year, more than one critic referred to it as the first novel written by an American Indian. Such proclamations reflected what Osage scholar and critic Robert Warrior has termed the "rhetoric of ancientness and novelty," the seemingly near-irresistible impulse to label any production by a Native American as the first of its kind. Other "first" novels were Elias Boudinot's *Poor Sarah* (1823—the only problems being that it is not a novel and not by Boudinot); Mourning Dove's *Cogewea, the Half-Blood* (1927); and D'Arcy McNickle's *The Surrounded* (1936). Although Momaday's text is indisputably a remarkable achievement deserving of its prominent place in Native American literature, behind this rhetoric of novelty lurks a scarcely veiled paternalism reminiscent of Dr. Johnson's fabulously patronizing—and, by our modern sensibilities, sexist—comparison of women preaching to dogs dancing on their hind legs: it isn't that they do it well, the remarkable thing is that they can do it at all. Other early Native novelists who apparently escaped contemporary recognition as the progenitor of the Native novel include John Joseph Mathews (*Sundown*, 1934), Sophia Alice Callahan (*Wynema, a Child of the Forest*, 1891), John Rollin Ridge (the seeming winner with *The Life and Adventures of Joaquín Murieta, the Celebrated California Bandit*, 1854). And John Milton Oskison.

These and other Native authors who toiled prior to 1968 have been swamped and submerged in the wake of the dreadnaught Momaday and the many fine authors (Silko, Welch, Vizenor, Ortiz, Harjo, and others) who saw print after him. The problem with the so-called Native American Literary Renaissance, as the post-1968 period was labeled, was that it confused critical awareness with literal presence. Natives published in English from the second half of the eighteenth century onward. There was a boom in such literature in the 1920s and 1930s. And, to take nothing away from the wonderful florescence of literature since 1968, although fewer actual books were able to find their way into print from the late 1940s through the mid-1960s, Native American literary production was in no need of a rebirth. It had never died.

Much—though far from enough—of the work that has gone on in recent years has been a reconsideration of pre-Renaissance writers, a kind of literary archaeology. Both Native and non-Native scholars have recovered Samson Occom, William Apess, and Peter Jones. They have restored to us John Rollin Ridge, Sophie Callahan, Mourning Dove, and Ella Cara Deloria. Not surprisingly, most of this salvage process has focused on the period from 1925 to 1945, which saw both an increase in political activity and a literary surge. The beginning of the two decades is marked by the acknowledgment that allotment from its inception had been bankrupt as a policy. The decades comprised the entirety of the Indian New Deal and ended with the backlash that led to Termination and Relocation.

This era saw a remarkable number of talented Native American writers move to the fore. The best-known of this group, Will Rogers, has never been forgotten. Yet this man who never considered himself anything but that oxymoron to Amer-European ears, an Indian cowboy, has only recently been restored to his rightful place in Native letters. Today, thanks to growing interest in Native American literature, works by Mathews, McNickle, Lynn Riggs, and Todd Downing have been reprinted. Dan Littlefield reminded us of Charles David Carter and Muriel Wright, among others. Robert Warrior devoted half of his important comparative study, *Tribal Secrets*, to Mathews. Dorothy Parker published a full-length biography of McNickle. Littlefield, Hanay Geigomah, Craig Womack, and I brought plays by Riggs back into print and gave him back his pride of position among Native writers. The odd duck out in all of this has been Oskison.

It is this major lacuna in an important Native American literary epoch that Tim Powell and Melinda Smith Mullikin seek to fill with the book you hold in your hands. This is more than the first publication of a literary artifact, the print equivalent of a Mississippian potshard or statuary effigy recovered through documentary excavation. Rather, it represents a vital step toward the full recovery of Oskison's work, not only for the crucial period discussed above but as a vibrant part of Native American literature in general.

John Milton Oskison shares many common traits with his contemporaries John Joseph Mathews and Lynn Riggs. Like both, he was a cosmopolitan man who went off to college and then traveled the world. Mathews and Riggs knew one another at the University of Oklahoma. Mathews went on to Oxford. Riggs lived in Paris.

Oskison knew Will Rogers as a youth at Willie Halsell College in Oklahoma but went on to attend Stanford and Harvard. He and Mathews both fought in World War I. All three produced works on non-Native subjects: Mathews, a biography of Oklahoma governor and oil magnate E.W. Marland; Riggs, the cattle-drive drama "Out of Dust"; and Oskison, a life of Texas hero and politician Sam Houston. None of them, however, forgot who he was and where he came from. In contrast to Mathews, who moved back to the blackjacks of Osage County and became deeply involved in Osage political life, and Riggs, who left Oklahoma in 1923 but continued to write about it though seldom returning physically, Oskison worked as a writer and editor in New York but made frequent trips back home to gather source material for his stories and books.

Oskison's image of and attachment to both Oklahoma and his Cherokee heritage were essentially nostalgic. This is evidenced in his novels and even in his best short stories with Indian themes, "Tookh Steh's Mistake" and "The Problem of Old Harjo." In his only book on an Indian subject other than *The Singing Bird*—the biography *Tecumseh and His Times*—he wrote:

> What stirred Tecumseh to attempt the formation of an Indian confederation was a hope as old as the races of man: that it might be possible in a changing and turbulent world to find permanent peace and plenty. Because we understand that longing, and because in all of us burns some spark of resentment at encroachment on our liberties, we know why Tecumseh has become, in the minds and memories of three peoples, a knightly symbol and an enduring symbol.[1]

He says of his subject: "More clearly than any other apostle and warrior of his race, he crystallized the red man's hope for a paradise regained which has stirred Indian dreamers and plotters from Hiawatha to the obscure Osage communicant in his peyote lodge today." He dedicates the book "to all Dreamers and Strivers for the integrity of the Indian race, some of whose blood flows in my veins."[2]

Despite such florid pronouncements, Oskison's politics were, though complicated, fundamentally assimilationist. This can be seen in his involvement in the Society of American Indians and the American Indian Association, both aggressively assimilationist organizations (affiliations usually glossed over in any discussion). It is evident in essays he penned such as "Remaining Causes of Indian

Discontent" and "Making an Individual of the Indian." Gretchen Ronnow calls this a "naïve reading" of his writings, saying:

> It is not at all clear which side he is on. In the texts of otherwise insouciant, apparently "assimilationist" articles, he often uses harsh phrases such as "destroy the Indian identity," "soiled relics" after white contact, "inglorious passing," "imprisonment," "stilling the voices of wise Indians." The harshness of these occasional phrases undercuts any naïve acceptance of assimilation. When he writes that the "new man" is "Indian only in blood" or that the red man is gaining a sense of personal responsibility or that young girls are learning to appreciate the household implements of the white culture, we do not know whether he personally applauds these directions or bemoans them.[3]

The deployment of these arguably ambiguous "occasional phrases" does not, however, deflect an overall assimilationist trajectory.

As Ronnow does with Oskison's essays, Tim Powell gives a close and generous reading to *The Singing Bird* in his introduction to this edition. He makes a forceful and eloquent case. In the end, I nevertheless remain skeptical that the text is really all that subversive. It can as plausibly be read as an assimilationist work (much like Callahan's *Wynema*), in which the white missionaries become redeemed and indigenized by their contact with Indians, even as the Indigenes adopt and adapt to "civilization" and Christianity. The paradigm in the novel is the faithful and virtuous Indian woman Catherine Swan, a character modeled on real-life convert Catherine Brown, who like the Mohawk Kateri Tekakwitha had the good grace to die young so that her words and image could be mediated by non-Natives for their own purposes.

None of my criticism here is meant to impugn the worth of this project. I may, of course, be wrong. As Ronnow concludes: "John Milton Oskison's personal complexity is evident. He wrote about national and international powers and their modes of production, but he was also compelled by the romance and history of the old days in the Oklahoma Territory, especially the roles and heritages of its Indian populations, whose whispers stirred his own blood."[4] Texts are polyvocal. That is the essence of scholarly disputation.

Oskison has received less scholarly attention than other Native American authors of the 1920s and 1930s. LaVonne Ruoff briefly discusses him in her *American Indian Literatures* and in her article in *The Cambridge Companion to Native American Literature*. Ronnow's essay appears in Andrew Wiget's *Handbook of Native American Litera-*

ture. As Powell points out, Oskison's most frequently anthologized short story, "The Problem of Old Harjo," was included in *The Heath Anthology of American Literature*. Dan Littlefield includes it, along with three others, in *Native American Writing in the Southeast: An Anthology, 1875–1935*. Bernd Peyer includes "The Problem of Old Harjo" and "The Singing Bird" (a short story that shares a title, but little else, with the novel) in his volume *The Singing Spirit*. Paula Gunn Allen anthologizes the same two pieces in *Voice of the Turtle: American Indian Literature, 1900–1970*. Before Powell's fine introduction to this edition, the most fulsome treatment of Oskison, including of *The Singing Bird* was Daniel Justice's analysis in *Our Fire Survives the Storm*, his book on Cherokee literature. That is pretty much the extent of it.

Why has Oskison been largely ignored while his peers have been revived? In the end, he is simply not the writer that McNickle, Mathews, or Riggs is. His short stories are clever. His novels, however, generally disappoint. Justice says that his "characters and plots leave much to be desired," with "forced drama and didacticism."[5] Ruoff points out that Oskison himself "perceptively evaluates" his first two novels, *Wild Harvest* and *Black Jack Davy*, when Henry Odell, the author's counterpart in the autobiographical novel *Brothers Three*, describes his first book as "a mess, misty, sentimental, badly knit, with impossible situations and caricatures of human beings" and his second as "amateurish" but accurately reflecting "the people and the country I knew."[6] Other than *The Singing Bird*, only *Brothers Three* is a fully accomplished fiction. This, again, does not mean that his relative dismissal has been justified. William Shakespeare is better remembered and regarded than Francis Beaumont and John Fletcher, Theodore Dreiser than Stephen French Whitman, Hemingway and Faulkner than James Farrell or Edward Dahlberg, John Cheever and Harper Lee than John P. Marquand or Sloan Wilson. Does that mean that "The Maid's Tragedy," *The Predestined*, the Studs Lonigan trilogy, *Bottom Dogs*, *The Late George Apley*, and *The Man in the Gray Flannel Suit* are not worth reading and their authors should be disregarded? Of course not. To even pose the question is to expose it as absurd.

The Singing Bird is ultimately about white missionaries as much as it is about Cherokees. In 1736, John and Charles Wesley, the founding brothers of Methodism, arrived in Georgia to minister to the colonists and evangelize the local Yamacraw Indians. They were spectacular failures at both objectives. A little over two centuries later, their spiritual heirs met to revise the hymnal of what was now a mighty denomination. As the revision committee concluded its work in 1938, one of the members shook his head and lamented the gross reduction in the songbook's Wesleyan hymns, saying, "Gentlemen, what have we done? Only 54 hymns by Charles Wesley and only 7 hymns by John. Gentlemen, what have we done?" Robert McCutchan, the dean of the Depauw University School of Music and a major force on the committee, replied curtly, "Improved their reputations immensely."

Posthumous publications rarely serve authors well. Discovery and publication of texts by Dickens, Twain, Verne, and Hemingway long after their deaths smack either of estates attempting to wring the last few pennies out of the sweat of their meal tickets or scholars desperate to burnish their own credentials, even at the expense of their subjects. The brutal truth is that unpublished works are usually unpublished for a good reason. Happily, this is not so in the instant case. Powell and Mullikin have done everyone interested in Native American literature a valuable service with this volume. Publication of *The Singing Bird* will only enhance Oskison's reputation. As Daniel Justice writes: "[T]he actual world Oskison creates in *The Singing Bird* is the most fully realized of any of his fictions, and the most devoted to representing the Cherokee context of Indian Territory with as much honesty, detail, and sensitivity as he brings to his biographies of the adopted Cherokee and politician Sam Houston and the Shawnee statesman Tecumseh."[7]

The famous putative Chinese curse runs, "May you live in interesting times." John Milton Oskison lived in very interesting times. Born in 1874, he grew up in a vibrant and thriving—if threatened—Cherokee Nation. His creative career stretched from Allotment and the dissolution of Cherokee territorial sovereignty until the eclipse of the Indian New Deal as World War II shouldered Native Americans from the public agenda. He died as Termination and Relocation became the policy of an American government that he always viscerally (and correctly) distrusted. Justice writes: "Throughout his work, Oskison provides neither easy answers nor grim predictions for an empty future; he simply shares the stories, neither optimistic nor entirely despairing, as certain of the righteousness of the Indian cause as he is of the inevitability of U.S. treachery and greed. Which will survive the longest depends on the willingness of people to be led not by their unquenchable appetites or base fears, but by their better ideals. And that, Oskison suggests, is a question still very much without an answer."[8] Six decades after Oskison's death, this question remains unanswered. Powell and Mullikin are to be commended for restoring his full-throated voice to us. Reentering the dialogue, Oskison reminds us that things—both literary and political—are always more complicated and nuanced than we think. The response is ours.

Notes

1. Oskison, *Tecumseh*, 237. *Brothers Three*, Oskison's best-known and most accomplished novel, deals with Native American siblings. As LaVonne Ruoff writes, however, "Although the major characters are part Indian, the novel focuses not on Indian life but rather on the importance of honesty, loyalty, hard work, and thrift and on the economic and social history of Oklahoma from the turn of the century through the Depression." Ruoff, *American Indian Literatures*, 71.

2. Oskison, *Tecumseh*, viii, v.

3. Ronnow, "John Milton Oskison," in Wiget, *Handbook of Native American Literature*, 272–73.

4. Ibid., 274–75. She says "Oklahoma Territory," but she means "Indian Territory."

5. Justice, *Our Fire Survives the Storm*, 115.

6. Ruoff, *American Indian* Literatures, 71.

7. Justice, *Our Fire Survives the Storm*, 115.

8. Ibid., 118–19.

Acknowledgments

Thanks to Lynn Smith (Mom) for tirelessly typing the manuscript while I was completing my thesis. Tim, when I approached you with the novel, you saw its possibilities—thank you for helping make this project a reality. Drake, though you're too young to know what a great help you've been, your reassuring narfs and uplifting turtle grins were (and still are) a godsend. As always, my greatest support comes from my husband, Chad, who took time off from writing his dissertation to help me conduct a double-read on the manuscript.

The folks at the University of Oklahoma Press have been very helpful, among them Pippa Letsky, Steven Baker, and Alessandra Jacobi-Tamulevich. And finally, thanks to the grandchildren of John Milton Oskison, Martin Olstad and Carolyn Somer, who have generously allowed us to print the novel. Martin, your willingness to talk freely about your grandfather has increased my understanding of Oskison, who can be, as you know, hard to characterize. I have found that because he is quite an enigma, he is often too quickly judged. In honorable memory of your grandfather, I have done my best to offer a fuller view of his writing.

MSM

Introduction

> Days in the saddle began before sunrise and ended after dark. . . . On those daylong rides, especially in the afternoons when hunger stimulated the imagination, I began recalling some of the characters in the fiction I had read. . . . Suppose I were able to write these stories? I might make a book of them, and call it "Tales of the Old I.T." I would let the world know about Indian Territory! Much later, some of the tales were written, and published in good magazines, but I never collected them into a book.

This passage from John Milton Oskison's unpublished autobiography, "A Tale of the Old I.T.," was written at the end of his life about his teenage aspiration to become the writer who would make the stories and characters of Indian Country known to the world.[1] Although he may have started as a cowboy, riding herd on his father's cattle farm outside of Vinita in the Cherokee Nation, Oskison would travel the world from Indian Territory to California to Boston to New York to Paris, France, before his death in 1947. A remarkable character in his own right, Oskison was the first Native American student to attend Stanford University (1895–1899). He later attended Harvard University for a year to study literature and subsequently married Nathaniel Hawthorne's granddaughter, Hildegarde Hawthorne.[2] Although well-known in the early part of the twentieth century, Oskison had been largely forgotten by the end of the century except for one or two short stories in anthologies.[3] Perhaps this critical neglect can be traced to the fact that *The Singing Bird*, his most historically interesting novel, was never published in his lifetime.

John Milton Oskison was born in 1874 on a small farm outside of Tahlequah, the capital of the Cherokee Nation, in what was then known as Indian Territory but later became the state of Oklahoma. Oskison's father, John, was born in England. Orphaned at age two, he accompanied his uncle to settle in Illinois. At seventeen, John ran away from his "tyrannical uncle" and joined a California-bound wagon train in 1852, thus beginning an itinerant life that eventually led him to Tahlequah, where he married Oskison's mother, Rachel, a "dark soft-spoken and sweet-faced daughter of parents whose Cherokee name, in English, was Buzzard."[4] Oskison wrote in his autobiography: "The Indians [my father] came to know in Indian Territory were not all like the nomadic hunters he had seen on the plains. They were farmers, stockmen, merchants. . . . Their chief was a well educated man, a graduate of Princeton. Among the tribal judges, senators, and councilmen were other graduates of eastern colleges, Dartmouth and Princeton. They published *The Cherokee Advocate*, a weekly newspaper printed half in English and half in the Cherokee characters devised more than forty years before by Sequoyah." This highly literate tradition, which extended back well before removal (1838), inspired Oskison to a distinguished life of letters and provided the historical motifs to which he returned, much later in life, when he composed *The Singing Bird*.

At age twenty-one, Oskison left home for Stanford. Although he never returned to live in Oklahoma, throughout his life he maintained close ties with Will Rogers and other childhood friends and returned to the themes of Indian Territory frequently in his short stories, magazine articles, and novels. Oskison first began writing at Stanford, where he published "Two on a Slide," a playful dialogue "between two of the microscopic playboys," an imaginative response to a biology lab where he studied "slides on which amoeba scuttled and divided." It was when he enrolled at Harvard in 1899, though, that Oskison began writing "short stories in every spare hour. They were Indian Territory tales, more 'Tales of the Old I.T.' which I had projected in my mind as I rode the prairies before going to college."[5] Oskison's writing career was launched in 1899, when his story "Only the Master Shall Praise" (a title borrowed from Rudyard Kipling) won a prize from the highly respected *Century* magazine, which convinced him to leave Harvard to pursue life as a professional writer in New York City. During this period, Oskison published a number of his most well-known short stories related to Native American culture—"When the Grass Grew Long" (1901), " 'The Quality of Mercy': A Story of the Indian Territory" (1904), and "The Problem of Old Harjo" (1907), which were published in high-profile magazines such as *Century*, the *North American Review*, and *McClure's*.[6] From 1903–1912, Oskison concentrated primarily on his journalistic career: he edited a daily newspaper, wrote for the *Saturday Evening Post*, and climbed his way up the hierarchy of *Col-*

liers until he reached the position of financial editor. The turn of the century was a volatile period in the history of Indian Territory, particularly with Oklahoma being made a state in 1907, which Oskison responded to with a significant number of political articles that criticized corruption and argued for the protection of tribal sovereignty.[7]

After serving in World War I, Oskison abandoned journalism and began writing novels. His first two ventures into the novel form—*Wild Harvest: A Novel of Transition Days in Oklahoma* (1925) and *Black Jack Davy* (1926)—are critical of both white and mixed-blood characters' corruption in the early years of Oklahoma statehood when many Native Americans were dispossessed of their tribal lands. A later novel, *Brothers Three* (1935), invokes the familiar tragic mulatto motif by tracing the story of three mixed-blood siblings who relinquish their traditional relationship to the land in order to chase the elusive American dream of individualism and capitalism. The biography *Tecumseh and His Times* (1938), seems to mark a turning point that may be related to a dramatic change in U.S. Indian policy in the mid-1930s, a complex historical moment (see below). Ideologically, *Tecumseh* is markedly more nationalistic than the assimilationist narrative of *Brothers Three*. Nevertheless, the narrative of *Tecumseh* remains haunted by the master narrative of the dominant society. As Oskinson wrote in the foreword: "[Tecumseh] was the dreamer of a hopeless dream . . . he followed it straightforwardly and courageously to the inevitable end—[he died] while battling for the right of his red brothers to live in freedom according to their own conceptions."[8] Although more nationalistic in tone, Oskison's depiction of Tecumseh's rebellion makes Indian sovereignty appear "a hopeless dream" and thus implicitly reifies the myth that Indians were predestined to assimilate or vanish. The book, however, in regard to *The Singing Bird*, is Oskison's first real venture into writing a counternarrative that explicitly argues for a distinctly Native American view of history.[9] "Tecumseh could not have undertaken the formation of the confederation he conceived . . . to change the course of Indian history in America," Oskison writes, "without a thorough grounding in the story of his own tribe and that of other Algonquin tribes."[10] This vision would be more fully realized in *The Singing Bird*, where Oskison reaches back to precolonial literary forms to explicate an interpretation of indigenous history that stresses survival and empowerment over removal and despair.

The date of *The Singing Bird*'s composition remains a mystery. What we do know is that Oskison's daughter, Helen Day Oskison (later Helen Day Olstad), donated an undated manuscript of the novel to the Western History Collection at the University of Oklahoma at the time of his death. Given that at the end of his life Oskison was in poor health and working on his autobiography, which he never completed, it seems reasonable to conclude that *The Singing Bird* may have been completed shortly before his death, leaving the manuscript without a publisher. Oskison published a short story entitled "The Singing Bird" in 1925, so it may have been around this time that he began to formulate the idea for the novel of the same name. Although this is more speculative, it can also be argued that there is an ideological progression from assimilation, to "hopeless" struggle, to a redemptive view of history in the sequence *Brothers Three* (1935), *Tecumseh and His Times* (1938), and *The Singing Bird*. This and many other intriguing questions about the novel remain for a new generation of scholars to consider.[11]

The Singing Bird

John Milton Oskison's sweeping novel *The Singing Bird* recounts the tumultuous period of Cherokee history between 1820 and 1865, when the tribe very nearly fragmented over issues such as removal, slavery, and the Civil War. Oskison skillfully blends fiction and reality, thoughtfully demonstrating how literature can rewrite the master narrative of "history" and bring to life moments in the past that remain outside the scope of the written records maintained by the dominant white society. Although the main characters—Dan Wear, Paul Wear, Ellen Morin, and Miss Eula—are invented, the historical circumstances and the people who surround them are real. The cast of historical characters include many of the most important members of the Cherokee tribe: Sequoyah, John Ross, Elias Boudinot, John Jolly, and Stand Watie. And although it may appear strange that a Cherokee author writing about Cherokee history would choose to see events through the eyes of white missionary characters, it can be argued that this narrative technique (more fully explained below) is part of a sophisticated strategy that allows Oskison to comment poignantly on both white and Cherokee culture at a critically important moment in their tangled histories.

Before examining Oskison's complicated narrative structure, it is helpful to review briefly the historical setting of the novel. One of the central themes of *The Singing Bird* is the reunification of the Cherokees in the wake of removal. The fragmentation of the tribe began as early as 1794, when small bands began moving west to escape white encroachment. *The Singing Bird* presumably begins just before 1820, when the first mission was established among those Cherokees who had already moved west and settled in Arkansas Territory. (This was the Dwight mission of the American Board of Commissioners for Foreign Missions.)[12] Conflicts with land-hungry whites forced the old settlers to give up their lands in Arkansas Territory and move to the newly created Indian Territory in 1828. Distrustful of U.S. treaties, a significant number of Western Cherokees set off for Texas, then part of Mexico, where Chief Bowl oversaw a community of eight thousand that included members of the Lenape (Delaware), the Shawnee, and other displaced tribes. In 1839, Chief Bowl was attacked by white settlers (the president of Texas declared that "the sword should mark the boundaries of the republic"), causing some Cherokees to return to Indian Territory and others to move further south into Mexico.[13]

Back east, Chief John Ross fought valiantly to retain what was left of the Cherokees' ancestral homelands. In 1832, the Chief Justice of the U.S. Supreme Court, John Marshall, ruled in *Worcester v. Georgia* that Georgia's attempts to extend its laws over the Cherokees were "unconstitutional, void, and of no effect."[14] As the Cherokees looked on in horror, President Andrew Jackson refused to enforce the decision, and Cherokee lands were raffled off to white settlers. Bereft of hope, a small group of prominent Cherokees known as the Treaty Party signed the Treaty of New Echota in 1835, whereby the tribe had to surrender its lands in the East and move west to Indian Territory.[15] The treaty flagrantly violated Cherokee law. Members of the tribe voted overwhelmingly against the treaty. The twenty Cherokees who did sign knowingly broke a law stipulating that any member of the tribe who sold Cherokee land would be put to death. The U.S. Senate ratified the treaty by a margin of one vote, amid a tempest of protests. John Quincy Adams denounced the Treaty of New Echota as an "eternal disgrace upon the country."[16] Three years later the Trail of Tears began. Approximately sixteen thousand Cherokees

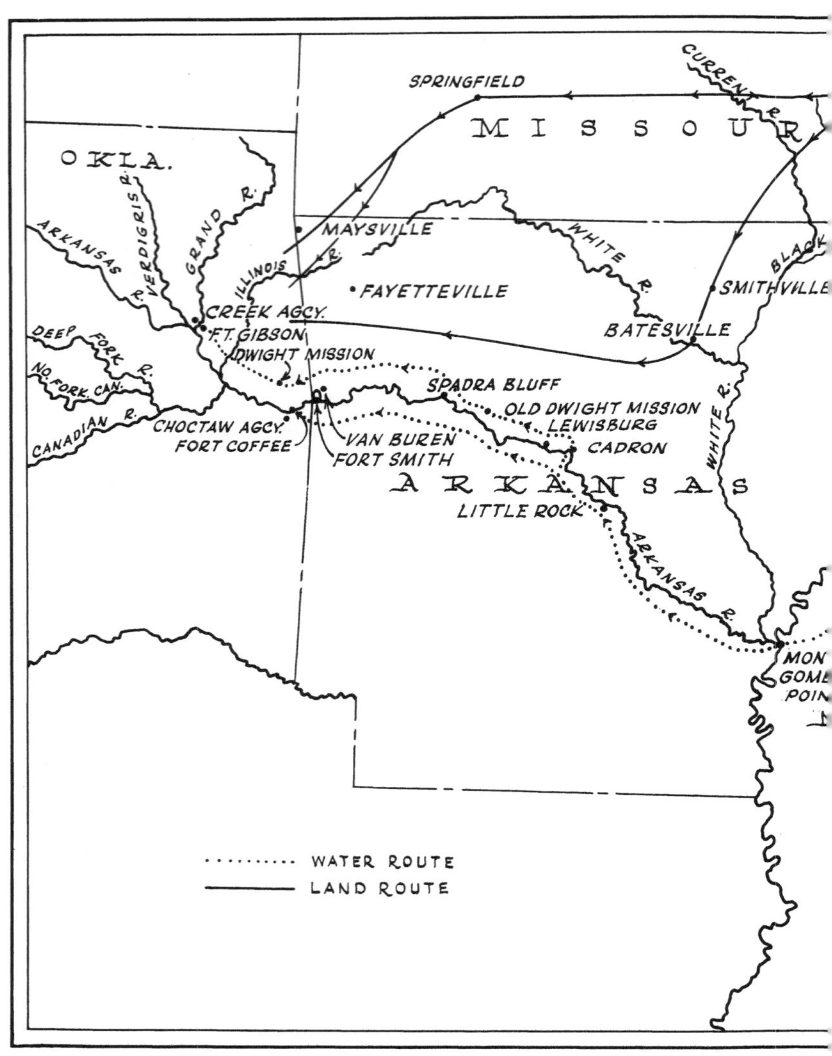

The routes taken by the Cherokees in their removal to Indian Territory, 1838–39. Reprinted, with permission, from Grace Steele Woodward, *The Cherokees* (Norman: University of Oklahoma Press, 1963).

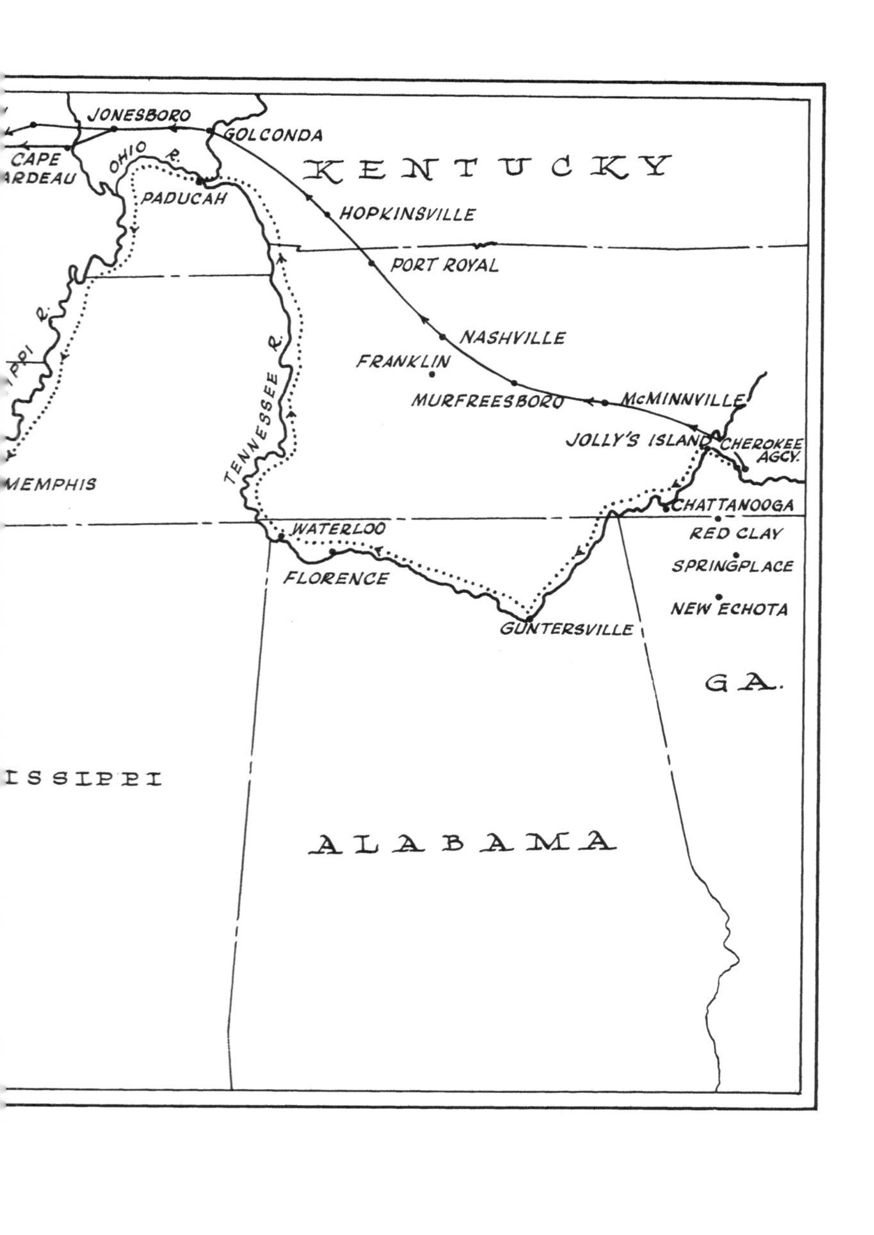

JONESBORO
GOLCONDA
CAPE
ARDEAU
OHIO R.
KENTUCKY
PADUCAH
HOPKINSVILLE
PORT ROYAL
NASHVILLE
FRANKLIN
MURFREESBORO
McMINNVILLE
JOLLY'S ISLAND
CHEROKEE
AGCY.
TENNESSEE R.
MEMPHIS
CHATTANOOGA
RED CLAY
SPRINGPLACE
NEW ECHOTA
WATERLOO
FLORENCE
GUNTERSVILLE
GA.
ISSIPPI
ALABAMA

were removed. Four thousand died on the long journey to what is now Oklahoma, while three or four hundred escaped and hid in the Smoky Mountains to form what would become known as the Eastern Band of the Cherokee Nation.[17] When thousands of displaced Cherokees descended upon Cherokee settlements in the West, dejected and homeless, tensions erupted between the old settlers and the new arrivals. The situation was further complicated when an internal civil war broke out after three members of the Treaty Party were assassinated by supporters of John Ross. The Treaty of 1846 finally reunified the old and new settlers. The animosity between the Ross supporters and the Treaty Party never really dissipated, however, and finally exploded with the onslaught of the Civil War. Slaveholding members of the Treaty Party, led by Stand Watie, sided with the Confederacy while the Keetoowah Society, a group of fullbloods who supported John Ross, formed militias and fought with the Union.[18] It is this bloody period in Cherokee history that Oskison depicts in the closing pages of his novel.

JOHN MILTON OSKISON'S NARRATIVE STRATEGY

Understanding the intricate structure of Oskison's narrative requires a kind of literary archaeology, where each stratum is carefully excavated and studied in relation to the layers above and below it. On its uppermost level, *The Singing Bird* recounts the deceptively simple story of a failed marriage between Ellen Morin and Dan Wear, the head of a mission first in Arkansas and later in Indian Territory. Beneath this tale, however, lie a number of narrative layers that reveal older, more distinctly Cherokee ways of explaining the past. This deeper story revolves around the character of Sequoyah, the inventor of the Cherokee alphabet, who embarks on a quest to find the ancient, sacred symbols of the tribe that had been stolen many years before by the Delaware Indians. Sequoyah's mission, before he dies, is to write a history of the Cherokee Nation that will record the oldest memories of the oral tradition in the new written form of the syllabary.

The goal of this literary archaeology will be to excavate the deeper discursive layers in order to demonstrate how Oskison's reconstruction of the removal period allows the reader to see both Cherokee and American history with a new sense of depth. One must be careful, however, of metaphors such as "literary archaeology," which may implicitly suggest that the older culture is now "extinct" or can be known only imperfectly through dusty artifacts. Rather, Oskison seems to argue that literature plays a fundamentally important role in keeping alive the most ancient memories of Cherokee culture and that these very old stories have not lost their power, for either the Cherokees or the white missionary characters in the novel.

The complex interplay between various levels of Oskison's multi-tiered narrative can be clearly seen in the opening chapters. The novel begins with an account of four white missionaries in 1818 who pass through Tennessee on their way to Arkansas. Their dialogue subtly calls attention to two of the most common problems that clouded white perceptions of Indians in the nineteenth and twentieth centuries: romanticism and racism. The narrator, Paul Wear, unconsciously articulates a kind of nativist fantasy when he dreams about a young Cherokee woman wearing "gay feathers in her headdress" and possessing "something richly barbaric in [her] bearing" (7). This discourse of romantic racialism, which viewed Indians as appealing because they were inextricably trapped in a prelapsarian past, grossly distorts the fact that the Cherokee were remarkably skilled in developing new technology to meet their needs in changing times (developing a sophisticated knowledge of medicinal plants, creating an alphabet or syllabary, writing a constitution, and publishing the *Cherokee Phoenix*, the first Native American newspaper in the United States).[19] The darker underside of this romanticism manifests itself in the novel's least sympathetic character, Ellen Morin. Oskison writes: "in truth she was disgusted by what she would call the odor of the savage occupants of the cabin" (13). This unbridled racism was all too real during the removal period, even among missionaries. As one Moravian missionary wrote just before the Trail of Tears: "For three nights the Indians held a Medicine Dance. . . . After dark we heard . . . savage whooping . . . [and] at day-break it appeared as if the vaults of hell had let loose the raving furies."[20] Oskison foregrounds these difficulties at the outset, as if to remind his non–Native American audience of the intellectual barriers that must be overcome in order to understand the Cherokee characters who appear later in the novel.

Oskison's depiction of white missionaries is complex, however. As he gradually exposes more levels of Cherokee society, the characters' (and the readers') understanding begins to deepen. It is significant to note, for example, that both Paul and Ellen undergo dramatic changes in the course of the story, after they come into contact with important members of the Cherokee community. Paul learns to listen carefully to the full-blood members of the Keetoowah Society, one of the most conservative branches of the Cherokee Nation, and his romantic fascination with feathered headdresses gives way to a firmer grasp of the political intricacies that confront the tribe after being twice removed—first from the ancestral homelands in the Southeast, and then from Arkansas to the newly created Indian Territory. Ellen, on the other hand, clings more tenaciously to her biased views, to the point where it eventually undermines her marriage to Dan Wear, who dedicates his life to helping the "Eastern and Western Cherokees to realize that they were brothers" (109). Embittered since the breakup of her marriage, Ellen turns first to Sam Houston (the young protégé of Andrew Jackson who married into the Cherokee tribe) and later to Tally Tassel, a renegade who opposes Chief John Ross in his struggle to reunify the Cherokee Nation.[21] Her affair with Tassel eventually leads to Dan's dismissal as mission head and exacerbates the internal battles raging within the Cherokee Nation. After Dan's death, however, Ellen seems to overcome her prejudices. She moves back in with the extended mission family, which Oskison describes as an "all–New England–Cherokee family" (170) wherein the two races intermarry and devote themselves to the betterment of the Cherokee Nation. Significantly, Ellen undergoes a profound change of heart just before she dies. Oskison writes of the "whirlwind of destruction" unleashed by the U.S. Civil War, which fissured the Cherokee Nation. A character named Wah-ti-ka threatens to take over the tribal government. In the closing pages, Ellen "with the swiftness of a striking rattlesnake, plunged [her] knife into Wah-ti-ka's back." Before Wah-ti-ka's men execute her, Ellen announces to Paul: "Tell Dan that he will know where to find me; I shall be waiting for him," and then, with her last breath, says "Oh, hello, Dan!" (175). In this sense, Ellen's transformation reveals the ideological structure of Oskison's novel—a difficult struggle to overcome white racism in order to preserve the integrity of the Cherokee Nation.

This same ideological pattern of development shapes the intellectual and spiritual growth of Dan Wear throughout the novel. Here again, Oskison begins by calling attention to the ethnocentric views of his white character. In the second chapter, Dan corrects his nephew Paul, who suspects that "the red men lived more sanely than the whites," by reminding him that "like it or not, the Indians must learn our language and adjust themselves to what we call Christian civilization" (22). This patronizing rhetoric, which implicitly assumes the superiority of the dominant white culture, caused many Cherokees to distrust the good intentions of the missionaries. As McLoughlin observes, "Missionaries were in low esteem because the Cherokees associated whites with their expulsion from their homeland and white Americans spoke of the United States as a 'Christian country'."[22] Dan's assumption that the Cherokee would be best served by learning the language and religion of the dominant white race typifies the benevolent discourse of the nineteenth century, which advocated extinguishing traditional Native Indian culture in the name of "Christian civilization." Oskison here is not criticizing Dan's Christian faith, but his blind devotion to the problematic rhetoric of "civilization." This notion that human history marches in a rigidly linear fashion from savagery to civilization constituted a master narrative of the nineteenth century—used to justify U.S. imperialism from President James Monroe's initial call for Indian removal in order to "not only shield [Native Americans] from impending ruin, but promote their welfare and happiness"[23] to the notion of the "white man's burden," which sanctioned the occupation of the Philippines at the end of the century.

As the novel develops, Oskison effectively challenges these deeply entrenched assumptions about the inherent superiority of Western society. He accomplishes this by exposing the violence that lurked just under the rhetorical surface of U.S. policy and by highlighting the Cherokees' own sophisticated sense of civilization. This process begins when Dan befriends Ta-ka-to-ka, the head war chief of the Western band, and witnesses white racism from the Cherokees' perspective for the first time. When the governor of the Arkansas Territory attempts to force the Cherokees to council with the Osages by sending the major general of the militia to meet with Dan and Ta-ka-to-ka, the general responds to the war chief's intransigence by declaring "if the old heathen refuses to attend the council, I'll hang him to the nearest limb!" (36). Ta-ka-to-ka responds, in turn, by shredding the general's "paper talk" and throwing it to the ground. This moment seems to transform Dan as he shifts his allegiance to the Cherokees. Gradually, Ta-ka-to-ka and other important members of the Cherokee community come to trust Dan. They invite him on a hunt and tell him "legends and tales" that recount some of the oldest memories and sacred beliefs from the tribe's oral tradition. The subtle contours of Oskison's narrative strategy thus become evident—by revealing the deeper layers of oral history and Cherokee political structure, Oskison makes the myth of white "civilization" appear unfounded, such that Dan renounces the "paper talk" of the dominant white society and recognizes Ta-ka-to-ka as a "philosopher worth knowing" (37).

The proverb of the Singing Bird, from which the novel derives its title, plays an important role in Dan's cultural evolution. The story behind the proverb is first told to Dan by one of his early Cherokee teachers, The Blanket. As Dan's marriage to Ellen disintegrates because of his devotion and her disgust toward the Cherokees, The Blanket tells Dan the parallel stories of the Beloved Woman and the Singing Bird. A "singing bird," The Blanket explains, is "a faithless wife, one who does not bear children . . . [and] sits in an empty nest, [where] her singing and preening cause the male birds to fight over her" (52). The telling of the proverb has a complex function in the overarching narrative, assuaging Dan's psychological wounds in the wake of his failed marriage and galvanizing him to pursue his work with Sequoyah. Although the story of the Singing Bird does not hold up very well on the other side of the feminist revolution, it is important not to lose sight of how the proverb works in conjunction with the Beloved Woman story (53). Historically, the Beloved Woman occupied a distinguished place among the tribe. Interestingly, it is Ellen who recounts the story: "Nancy Ward . . . took up a gun and stood beside her warrior husband to fight the enemies of the tribe and fell beside him and earned by that action the title and lasting renown amongst the Cherokees" (138), a role that Ellen would ultimately emulate in the novel's final pages (175).[24] In terms of Oskison's discursive strategy, the gift of the Singing Bird proverb initiates a turning point in Dan's life, which helps him divorce himself from Ellen's racist views and to discover the healing powers of the oral tradition while setting up Oskison's exploration of more traditional ways of recording Cherokee history in the second half of the novel.

Before we turn to these older forms of tribal history, it is well worth pausing to reconsider the question of why Oskison constructs his narrative such that the story of Cherokee removal is seen through the eyes of white missionaries. By documenting the white characters' evolution from romantic racialism to political empathy for the Cherokees, Oskison creates a unique literary environment in which the most devastating critiques of U.S. federal policy come from the white characters. In Chapter 4, for example, Dan says: "The Government at Washington is . . . hungry for more and more land. . . . Their hunger has grown keener as it has been fed with one enormous gobbling of Indian lands after another. It will not be satisfied, even when every tribe has yielded its last acre" (35). Oskison effectively subverts the racial hierarchy that supports the master narrative of white "civilization." This strategy manifests itself most clearly when Dan begins to work with Sequoyah. Oskison describes the moment with clear, Christian overtones:

> The man of the talking leaf [Sequoyah] was here with them, listening to the brief prayer of the Plain Talker [Dan], though he did not bow his head. . . . He was eating their plain supper of cornbread, hominy, and tea. It was the way, they had heard, Christ had come long ago to the white people. There was reverence [of Sequoyah] in their eyes. (76)

Here, in a brilliant satire of the missionary conversion narrative, Oskison inverts the role of teacher and pupil, savage and civilized, such that from this point forward it is Sequoyah's "own effective missionary work" (38) to which Dan devotes his life, rather than the idea that "Indians must learn our language and adjust themselves to what we call Christian civilization" (22). Finally, even as he sharply criticizes the duplicity of the federal government, Oskison does not give in to the despair of racial essentialism (that all whites are prejudiced, for example). Instead, *The Singing Bird* offers a hopeful depiction of a culturally diverse alliance of full-bloods and mixed-bloods, Eastern and Western Cherokees, Christians and traditionalists, whites and Indians, all working together toward a political future based not on the American myth of the melting pot but on traditional Cherokee values.

Sequoyah's Quest

Beneath the narrative of white missionaries struggling to help the Cherokees in the aftermath of the Trail of Tears lies another, more intriguing story of Sequoyah's journey to locate the lost "sacred symbols" of the Cherokees. This story first appears in Chapter 4 when "the century-old" Ta-ka-e-tuh discusses "the old beliefs that were passing, and the solemn rites that had degenerated into meaningless revels after the Delaware Indians had captured from the Cherokees their sacred symbols, their Ark of the Covenant" (38). James Mooney, an anthropologist who lived among the remaining Eastern Cherokees from 1887 to 1890, confirms that this story was part of the tribe's oral tradition: "The Cherokee once had a wooden box, nearly square and wrapped up in buckskin, in which they kept the most sacred things of their old religion. Upon every important expedition two priests carried it in turn and watched over it in camp so that nothing could come near to disturb it. The Delawares captured it more than a hundred years ago." Cephas Washburn, a missionary who lived among the Cherokees for many years, wrote in his *Reminiscences* that the old priests of the tribe ascribed the loss of the sacred "Ark" to the later degeneracy of the Cherokees.[25] The loss of "the most sacred things of their old religion" plays a centrally important symbolic role in the second half of the novel, as the object of Sequoyah's quest. These "most sacred things" also constitute an integral part of Oskison's strategy to recover an older form of Cherokee oral and written history in order to dispel the myth that Native Americans lacked "civilization." From a critical perspective, Oskison's sense of deep time works to dismantle the problematic idea that Indian culture before white contact was "prehistoric" and thus not part of American literary history.[26]

The existence of the sacred symbols and the meaning of Sequoyah's sojourn are ultimately ambiguous, presenting an enticing challenge to interpreters of the novel. It is perhaps best to begin by clarifying the interplay of the factual and fictional in Oskison's retelling of a story passed down through the oral tradition, which cannot be completely explained by either historical or archaeological evidence. Sequoyah's final trip to Mexico is real; the presence of a white missionary constitutes a plot device that allows Oskison to speculate on one of the great mysteries of Cherokee history.[27] Oskison approaches the meaning of the sacred symbols with a good deal of caution, calling attention to the fact that this was an important moment of tribal history that remains beyond the pale of Western historical records. The journey, for example, is described by Paul Wear based on information derived from Dan's notes, which are clearly limited:

> Dan wrote of Sequoyah's increasing absorption in his writing, about which he would say nothing. "I guessed, however, that it was a history of his people, and that he could not complete it without the material he hoped to find in Mexico. This is pure speculation, but I believe it has to do with the theft, long ago, of certain sacred symbols of the Cherokees by the Delawares. . . . Perhaps Sequoyah believes these sacred symbols—I have no idea of what they consist—are somewhere in Mexico, and that he may be able to recover them." (149)

This is an intriguing passage that deserves a good deal of scholarly attention. The idea of Sequoyah writing a "history of his people," beginning in the precolonial period and explaining the relevance of the Cherokees' ancient rituals to their postremoval plight, elicits many pertinent historical questions that are important to engage, even if they cannot be answered definitively. In what form would these sacred symbols exist: hieroglyphs, pictographs, wampum, or other material artifacts? What would this "Ark of the Covenant" mean to the Cherokees a century or more after it had been lost? How would Sequoyah's history differ from linear, chronological accounts that tend to emphasize the "progress" of Euro-American culture in relation to the "vanishing" of Native American culture?[28]

Oskison shrewdly employs the freedom of fiction to offer meaningful insight into these difficult historical questions. At one point Paul notes, he has "felt, since coming to know [Sequoyah], that a purpose even greater than his passion for teaching and for a reunion in peace of all the tribe dominates him. It is believable that he hopes to restore the faith of the Cherokees in their old god" (149). Manipulating Paul's conversion narrative, Oskison seems to suggest here that Sequoyah's writings and the rediscovery of the Cherokees' "old god" are interrelated, part of a communal healing process designed to bring about not just a reunification of the Eastern, Western, and Mexican bands of the tribe but a reconciliation of the ancient and modern as well.[29] Oskison, however, intentionally leaves many questions unanswered. When The Worm rides back from Mexico to report that Sequoyah had found the Lenapes (Delawares), Paul is left to wonder:

> Had Sequoyah and Dan found in that remote valley the sacred symbols? Had the ancestors of their present keepers fled with them to Mexico, swearing to hold them . . . until men should write no more of their daring in the Lenapi "Walum Olum," the record of the tribe's years on earth? Had they killed Sequoyah and Dan after refusing to listen to Sequoyah's plea for the return of the Cherokees' Ark of the Covenant? (153)

This series of questions points to the central interpretive challenge of *The Singing Bird*. On the one hand, it is possible to argue that the novel concludes on a dark, ominous note. The sacred symbols are never found. Sequoyah's history goes unfinished, then perishes. All of this can be read as a metaphor for a vanishing way of life—the symbolic death of the "old god." This interpretation may be supported by the fact that the novel ends with the bloody, intertribal conflict of the Civil War. On the other hand, it is also possible to interpret the conclusion as being an affirmation of Sequoyah's vision. It is interesting to note, for example, that Oskison ends the chapter in which Paul recounts Sequoyah's "passion . . . for a reunion in peace of all the tribe" by noting: "With the passing of time, peace between the Cherokee factions became a reality. Nearly all of the anti-Ross refugees returned and adjusted themselves to a regime that promised comfort for the people and education for all the children" (157). While "the most sacred things of their old religion" remain lost, what endures are the lessons that Sequoyah taught. Sequoyah's legacy can clearly be seen, for example, in Paul's memory of his teachings: "At least, Dan and I have not tried to stamp out their reverence for the old beliefs. We have not tried to discredit their god, nor to mold them in every thought to our pattern" (156). This is a striking contrast, at the novel's end, to Dan's earlier insistence that they must impose the English language and "Christian civilization" upon the Cherokees. Sequoyah's legacy is defined not only by the passion of his pilgrimage but by the invention of his syllabary. Thus, when Dan inquires about writing for the printing press that the mission purchased, Sequoyah answers: "Will you put the Jesus talk into Cherokee and save it with this machine?" To Dan's affirmative reply, Sequoyah insists that the publications will include "the old beliefs and the old stories of our people" (78). Thus, it may also be argued that, despite the horrors of the Civil War and Sequoyah's death at the end of the novel, Oskison never surrenders to despair but instead insinuates that the "old stories" can be preserved and passed on by modern technology.

Underlying these contrasting interpretations are two fundamentally different conceptions of historical time. The first, which sees the disappearance of the sacred symbols and Sequoyah's unfinished "history of his people" as an indication of the tragic but inevitable decline of traditional Cherokee culture, operates according to a linear conception of temporality. The second, which views Cherokee history as a continuum of loss and recovery, suggests a distinctly different sense of time. Scholars often note that Native Americans maintain a "circular" view of time, in contrast to the dominant white society's "linear" view of time. *The Singing Bird*, however, productively complicates this binary. Rather than a circular temporality (which suggests that the recovery of the sacred symbols would signal a return to the old beliefs), Oskison imagines a spiraling movement of time, where old and new combine to form a future society deeply rooted in—though not an exact replica of—the precolonial past. An example of this spiraling history can be seen in the following exchange. After Sequoyah's death, Paul asks: "Who among the Cherokees . . . [could] write the history of [their people], express their philosophy, put meaning into their old beliefs?" To which Catherine, a white missionary married to a Cherokee missionary, answers: "It might be that my own little son, Richard Junior, could do a good job if he will keep his eyes and ears open, go away to Harvard for his English, and come back a Cherokee" (156). Oskison here clearly insinuates that Cherokee history has not been lost, only that it awaits the right historian or storyteller. Catherine's hopeful statement might even be read as a metacommentary on Oskison's own project. That is to say that Oskison, himself a mixed-blood writer who studied literature at Stanford and Harvard, perhaps sees *The Singing Bird* as his own generation's attempt to fulfill Sequoyah's quest to write the history of the tribe and to give meaning to the "old beliefs." In keeping with a more complex understanding of time, the fragmentation brought on by the Civil War at the end of the novel does not necessarily symbolize the demise of the tribe but only the historical need for a storyteller to reunify the Cherokee once again.

The History behind the Novel

In *The Singing Bird*, John Milton Oskison uses the novel form to explore some of the most controversial and compelling questions of Cherokee history. While the panorama of tribal history he invokes extends well beyond the scope of this introductory essay, it will perhaps enhance the readers' appreciation of the novel if it provides some historical background for three of the novel's central themes—the role of missionaries in Cherokee history, the debate about the origins of Sequoyah's syllabary, and the question of how old are the "old beliefs." These motifs will obviously be of interest to scholars and students of Native American studies. Our hope, though, is that the novel will also raise meaningful questions about American studies, a field that has not yet fully acknowledged or explored the ways in which Native American literary history can be traced back well before European contact.

Missionaries played an important, albeit complicated, role during the removal period of Cherokee history. An illustrative example of this complexity can be seen in the case of Samuel A. Worcester, of whom Paul observes "he was so like Dan that I thought of them almost as blood brothers" (40). Dan procures a printing press and works with Sequoyah to publish Cherokee and missionary tracts; Worcester provided the Cherokees access to their first printing press in 1828. Working with Elias Boudinot, Worcester helped to publish the *Cherokee Phoenix* and translations of Christian tracts.[30] Worcester later courageously defied Georgia's demand that all whites sign an oath of allegiance, and he became the leading litigant in *Worcester v. Georgia*, the landmark decision in which Chief Justice John Marshall went beyond his earlier, derogatory ruling that the Cherokees were a "dependent domestic nation," to state: "The Indian nations had always been considered as distinct, independent political communities, retaining their original natural rights, as the undisputed possessors of the soil, from time immemorial."[31] Like a great many missionaries, however, Worcester accepted removal as inevitable, after Andrew Jackson refused to enforce the court's ruling in 1832. Three years later, he accompanied Elias Boudinot (a leader of the Treaty Party) to Indian Territory in the West. Worcester was later criticized severely by the Ross faction, particularly the full-bloods, for what was perceived to be his resignation to the unlawful treaty's legitimacy.[32]

Not all missionaries abandoned the Cherokees' claim to sovereignty so quickly. Dan's allegiance to the full-blood faction of the Cherokees is grounded historically in characters such as Daniel S. Butrick, an American Board missionary who refused to accept the removal treaty of 1835 and accompanied the Cherokees on the Trail of Tears in 1838. Like Dan, Butrick kept detailed journals that were later published as *Antiquities of the Cherokee Indians* (1884). The missionary who perhaps most directly inspired the character of Dan Wear is probably Evan Jones, a missionary for the northern Baptists who lived with the Cherokees from 1821 until his death in 1872. Jones worked closely with full-blood members of the tribe (particularly Robert Bushyhead) and is credited by historians with helping to form the Keetoowah Society in 1857, which supported John Ross and fought against the mixed-blood slaveowning faction of the tribe during the Civil War. Like Dan, Evan Jones was stripped of his position on the basis of a moral scandal drummed up by members of the Treaty Party (he later regained his post). Jones openly defied his own missionary board, which prohibited involvement in tribal politics. In 1865, the Cherokee council voted to adopt Evan Jones and his son John B. Jones (with their families) as full citizens of the Cherokee Nation, making them the only missionaries ever to receive this honor.[33] Although atypical of missionaries in general, Dan Wear's devotion to Sequoyah's vision does therefore have historical precedent, which productively complicates the predominant view of missionaries as being purely agents of assimilation.

The most intriguing, albeit elusive, historical question raised by Oskison's novel is the form and significance of the "sacred symbols." Three of the noted early historians of Cherokee culture—James Adair, Cephas Washburn, and James Mooney—all confirm the existence of the sacred "Ark." Its contents, however, remain unknown to Western historians; although stories are still told in the Smoky Mountains about ancient forms of writing that predate the invention of Sequoyah's syllabary.[34] With all due respect to the Cherokees' sovereign right to keep the sacred rites of the tribe secret, there are parts of the historical record that perhaps help to contextualize these symbols.

Although definitive answers are probably impossible, one source in particular illuminates the history that lies behind Oskison's depiction of Sequoyah's quest. In 1717, a Carolina trader by the name of Alexander Long wrote (with his own creative approach to English spelling) about a discussion he had with an unnamed Cherokee who related a migration story "from our ancestors [who] . . . brought it down from generation to generation /// [*sic*] the way is thus wee belonged to another land far distant from here." The migration story concludes with a captivating account of arriving in the Southeast:

> we are tould by our ancestors that when wee first came on this land that the prestes and beloved men was writting but nott one paper as you doe but one white deare skins and one the shoulder bones of buflow for severall yeares but the . . . young people being so grate thatt they would nott obey the priest . . . but lett thire minds rone after hunting of wild beasts that the writing was quite lost and could not be recovered againe.[35]

This oral narrative was recorded in 1717 and refers to historical events that had occurred hundreds of years earlier. We gain a sense here of the remarkable depth of Cherokee memory and the suggestion that some form of hieroglyphic "writing . . . on deare skins" may have predated Sequoyah's invention of the syllabary.[36]

It is important here to understand the terms "sacred symbols" and "writing" within the context of Cherokee history, as opposed to the Eurocentric assumption of an alphabetic text. Although neither Oskison nor the primary documents describe the sacred symbols in detail, historical examples exist of alternative symbolic systems utilized by the Cherokees long before Sequoyah invented the syllabary. In *Myths of the Cherokee*, James Mooney recounts such a story related, interestingly, by Sequoyah.[37] In 1768 the Cherokees and Iroquois signed a peace treaty ending a long and mutually destructive war between the two tribes. Three years later, an Iroquois delegation was dispatched to the Cherokee homeland to deliver the wampum belts and pipes symbolically encoding the terms of the peace. Becoming lost on the long journey, the Iroquois mistakenly ended up in the town of Tellico. The Iroquois entered the home of a local chief and asked for something to eat. The chief's daughter, respecting ancient customs of hospitality, set out food. The warriors of the village, upon learning of their ancestral enemies' presence, descended upon the house with the intent of killing the Iroquois. The chief, however, defended the Iroquois and offered safe passage to Itsati, the Cherokee capital.

Although not explicitly mentioned in the historical record, the pictographic text inscribed on the wampum belts undoubtedly played an important role in the local chief's decision to spare the Iroquois. These belts were later presented to the Cherokee chief Agansta'ta, to whom the Iroquois explained the symbols woven in wampum beads.[38] The translation of the pictographs revealed a long, complicated story about how the sudden clarity of water in formerly murky Iroquois well convinced tribal leaders that the time had come to make peace with the Cherokee. Mooney writes that the wampum, pipes, and feathers "made a considerable package, which was carefully guarded by the Cherokee keeper"—an analogous, though not necessarily identical, historical example of the sacred "Ark" that Oskison describes.[39] These wampum belts, along with the oral stories that accompanied them, were carried by Chief John Ross on the Trail of Tears to Indian Territory, where they were subsequently destroyed by the intertribal violence set off by the Civil War, much like the events that Oskison describes in the concluding pages of *The Singing Bird*.[40]

This story of the wampum belts offers a number of important insights into the semantic matrix surrounding the sacred symbols. It is interesting to note, for example, all the different functions the pictographic text plays in this brief story: as a treaty recognized by both tribes; as a symbol of true intent that protects the Iroquois peace delegation from attack; and finally, as an archive of tribal history, preserved long after the Cherokees and Iroquois had both been removed from the boundaries formalized in the treaty. Analogously, it is important to consider how these stories—the history of the Iroquois war, the Cherokee chief's hospitality, and the symbolic meaning of the Iroquois' well—come down, vividly intact, more than two hundred and twenty-five years later. These events are preserved by a discursive chain that begins with an oral interpretation of the symbols encoded in wampum beads, which is then preserved by Sequoyah's oral history, and subsequently passed down by Mooney's published anthropological account.

This literary paradigm provides insight into the relationship between the sacred symbols, Sequoyah's unfinished history, and Oskison's historical novel. Even though the sacred "Ark" and Sequoyah's writings have been lost, like the wampum in the previous story, the meanings associated with them have, in a sense, been preserved by the discovery and publication of *The Singing Bird*. This continuum, however imperfect, between ancient symbols, the oral tradition, and contemporary print culture offers an important lesson for Americanists, who continue to struggle with the fact that nonalphabetic forms of writing and/or material artifacts provide invaluable insights into American literary history before European contact. *The Singing Bird* offers a critically important counternarrative, suggesting that the origins of the Native American tradition (and American literature) can be traced back hundreds, if not thousands, of years before the colonial period, which too often marks the temporal border of "early American" studies.

The salient point here is the persistence of Cherokee traditions. Within the academy, the term "prehistoric" continues to be widely used—implying that "history" commences when the first white "discoverer" set foot on the continent and began recording his deeds in an alphabetic script. Given this truncated, ethnocentric conception of history, the continuum described by Oskison may be difficult to understand. Oskison's novel clearly strives to keep alive the memories of the Cherokees encoded in the sacred symbols and Sequoyah's history of his people—even though these two texts may be seen as "lost," like the tales encoded in the wampum belts that John Ross carried on the Trail of Tears. The term "lost," however, needs to be used carefully; just because memory is not recorded in the alphabetic form of Western "history," this does not mean that the Cherokees have forgotten. The tribe possesses hundreds of documents written in the Cherokee syllabary, which few Western scholars can read. Both the Eastern and the Oklahoma Cherokees are in the process of undergoing historic moments of revitalization, in which the language and syllabary are once again being widely taught in schools. Perhaps, then, the scholar who possesses the skills to interpret the meaning of the sacred symbols or to rediscover Sequoyah's writings among the tribal archives will emerge out of a high school classroom in Qualla or Tahlequah, to fulfil Oskison's vision of a young person from the next generation who will "write the history of his [or her] people, express their philosophy, [and] put meaning into their old beliefs" (156).

Situating *The Singing Bird* in Native American Literary History

The publication of John Milton Oskison's *The Singing Bird* will hopefully call attention to the fecund period of Native American literature written in and around the 1930s. While a great deal of scholarship has focused on the so-called Native American Renaissance (from 1968 to the present), this earlier period deserves recognition as a turning point in the development of modern American Indian literature and political consciousness.[41] This era, which arguably begins with the publication of Mourning Dove's *Cogewea* in 1927, includes such important works as Lynn Riggs's *Green Grow the Lilacs* (1930) and *Cherokee Night* (1930), John Joseph Mathews's *Sundown* (1934), D'Arcy McNickle's *The Surrounded* (1936), and Ella Cara Deloria's *Waterlily* (written in the early 1940s but published posthumously). The addition of John Milton Oskison's *The Singing Bird* (c. 1935–1945) to this list contributes significant historical weight and clarifies the relationship of this earlier period to the great works produced at the end of the twentieth century.

In order to understand the literature written during this period, it is necessary to situate these works within the broader context of Native American history. Compared to the self-assured manner in which Native writers now connect traditional forms of knowledge to contemporary issues, the authors from this earlier era seem haunted by the specter of cultural annihilation. This dark undercurrent running beneath many of the novels, plays, and short stories of this period undoubtedly derives from the implementation of destructive U.S. policies such as the General Allotment Act of 1887. The Dawes Act, as it came to be known, divided up lands held in common by Native American people into 80- or 160-acre individual allotments, with the goal of dismantling tribal sovereignty and assimilating Indians into the dominant white society. (The Five Civilized tribes were initially excluded from the Dawes Act; allotment was imposed upon them twelve years later.) The effect on Indian Territory was profound. In 1890, the Territory of Oklahoma was created from what were formerly tribal lands. After the individual allotments had been distributed, President Benjamin Harrison declared nearly two million acres of tribal land in the center of Indian Territory to be available for settlement. In 1898, Congress delivered another debilitating blow by passing the Curtis Act, which abolished tribal laws, schools, and courts. This legislation effectively ended tribal rule and paved the way for Oklahoma statehood in 1907. In the midst of this imposed hardship, Native people struggled to endure. As Wilma Mankiller, the former chief of the Cherokee Nation, wrote in her autobiography: "the Cherokee medicine and ceremonies continued despite everything that happened around us. . . . Tribal elders told me that when they were young and trying to make a go of it, no one ever gave up the dream of a revitalized Cherokee Nation. . . . They spoke of the old days of our tribe, and they told stories to keep our Cherokee spirit strong."[42] The devastating effects of boarding schools and allotment on Native people was documented by the Meriam Report of 1928, which helped create a period of reform known as the Indian New Deal. The Indian Reorganization Act (1934) and the Oklahoma Indian Welfare Act (1936) allowed Native Americans to adopt constitutions, administer tribal property, and elect officials. The effectiveness of this legislation was mitigated, however, by the Great Depression and by the severe cuts in domestic spending brought on by the beginning of World War II.

The Singing Bird can be seen as occupying a pivotal position within this historical and literary context. The novels written before the Indian Reorganization Act—*Cogewea*, *The Surrounded*, and *Sundown* —clearly reflect the psychological, social, and political upheaval inflicted upon Native communities by the U.S. government's failed attempt to implement a policy of assimilation through the termination of tribal sovereignty. All three novels focus on mixed-blood characters caught between two seemingly unreconcilable worlds at a historical moment when it appeared that federal authority might succeed in crushing Indian traditions out of existence. The Osage writer John Joseph Mathews captures this inner conflict vividly in his description of Chal, the mixed-blood protagonist of *Sundown,* watching a traditional dance: "Chal had an almost uncontrollable urge to go down on the floor and dance. . . . But he had never danced with his people. When he was old enough to dance he was in high school, and he hadn't wanted the people at the high school to think he was uncivilized." When Chal finally does dance at the end of the novel, the turmoil only intensifies: "He was in pain and he danced frantically for some sort of climax. . . . But he couldn't dance fast enough, and his singing lacked the fire to release his dammed up emotion."[43] The despair that seems to characterize *Cogewea, The Surrounded,* and *Sundown* is in large part the result of the historical circumstances in which they were written.[44] In the late 1920s and early 1930s, the dominant white society succeeded in imposing a paradigm of linear temporality on Indians (cloaked in the rhetoric of "progress"), which claimed that history marched inexorably in a straight line to either assimilation or extinction.

Whereas the novels written before the New Deal all focus almost claustrophobically on the post-Dawes era, as if the characters were suffocating in a historical moment from which they could not escape, Oskison's novel implements a much deeper and more hopeful historical paradigm. *The Singing Bird* works implicitly to assuage the despair of the allotment period by looking back to the nineteenth century, when the Cherokee Nation demonstrated a remarkable ability to survive despite a series of social catastrophes ranging from the Trail of Tears to the Civil War. Eschewing the tragic mixed-blood trope, Oskison focuses on how white missionaries, Cherokee full-blood nationalists, and their mixed-blood children work in concert to reconnect to deeply rooted tribal values. In sharp contrast to the linear logic of the Dawes and Curtis acts (that "progress" is attained by forgetting the past), Oskison looks back to traditional forms of Cherokee history to suggest that the problems of the present can be overcome by invoking tribal memory, in order to create future possibilities informed by the wisdom of ancient teachings.

Oskison's sophisticated experiment of infusing the novel form with a Native American vision of history can be seen as one of the earliest examples of a narrative technique that would reach fruition in some of the Native American Literary Renaissance's finest works. Although Sequoyah's great work remains unfinished at the end of the novel, Oskison clearly gestures toward the redemptive possibilities inherent in the deep memory of Native Americans. It is a narrative technique that writers like James Welch, Joy Harjo, N. Scott Momaday, Luci Tapahanso, Simon Ortiz, Leslie Marmon Silko, and many other contemporary authors have employed with great success. Leslie Marmon Silko's *Almanac of the Dead*, for example, utilizes a strikingly similar sense of spiraling temporality. The translation of the ancient almanac, which begins with pictographs and precolonial forms of Native writing, galvanizes Indians across the continent and foretells a future revolution to "take back the Americas." In a sense, John Milton Oskison's *The Singing Bird* anticipates a literary revolution that would not be realized in his lifetime. Perhaps now, in retrospect, Oskison's vision of using the novel form to recover the most sacred elements of Cherokee oral tradition can be said to constitute an important turning point in Native American literary history, from the despair of allotment to the hope of tribal sovereignty.

Notes

1. "A Tale of the Old I.T.," Oskison's unpublished autobiography, can be found at the Western History Collection, University of Oklahoma Libraries.

2. According to Oskison's grandson, Martin Olstad, Oskison's first wife was Florence Ballard Day. Their daughter, Helen Day Olstad (née Oskison), donated the manuscript of *The Singing Bird* to the Western History Collection. Oskison and Day divorced in 1920, the year he married Hildegarde Hawthorne.

3. The most frequently anthologized story by Oskison is "The Problem of Old Harjo," which can be found in *The Heath Anthology of American Literature*. The best resource for accessing Oskison's writings is the Electronic Text Center at the University of Virginia (http://etext.lib.virginia.edu), which includes "The Quality of Mercy: A Story of the Indian Territory," "Only the Master Shall Praise," "When the Grass Grew Long," "Diverse Tongues: A Sketch," "The Problem of Old Harjo," "The Man Who Interfered," "Young Henry and the Old Man," "The Biologist's Quest," "The Apples of Hesperides," "Remaining Causes of Indian Discontent," and "Friends of the Indian."

4. Oskison, "A Tale of the Old I.T." John Oskison later moved his family to Vinita, a town in the Cherokee Nation, where he ran a successful ranch during the period that John Milton Oskison lived in Indian Territory. Rachel Oskison was one-quarter Cherokee, making John Milton Oskison one-eighth. Despite the fact that his mother died relatively young, Oskison was an active member of the tribe. What are sometimes called the Five Civilized Tribes (the Choctaws, Creeks, Seminoles, Chickasaws, and Cherokees) were not included in the Dawes Act of 1887 but were later allotted lands with the passage of the Curtis Act in 1898. According to Bob Blankenship, *Dawes Roll "plus" of Cherokee Nation "1898"* (Cherokee, NC: Cherokee Roots Publication, 1994), a John Oskison is listed on Dawes Roll No. 29433, p. 356, as being one-quarter Cherokee. This contradicts Oskison's autobiography, where he identifies himself as being one-eighth Cherokee.

5. Oskison, "A Tale of the Old I.T."

6. See Littlefield and Parins, *A Biobibliography of Native American Writers*, for a more complete overview.

7. For a fuller account of the loss of Cherokee land in Oklahoma, see Rennard Strickland, *Fire and the Spirits*; Bays, *Townsite Settlement and Dispossession*; Hagan, *Taking Indian Lands*.

8. Oskison, *Tecumseh*, vii.

9. Oskison's fictional writing needs to be considered in relation to his journalistic writings, where he often dealt much more directly with Native American politics. See, for example, "Remaining Causes of Indian Discontent." At this point in his career, Oskison's politics were distinctly more assimilationist than his later writings. Cf. "Making an Individual of the Indian," where Oskison writes that the portraits of Native Americans from James Fenimore Cooper and George Catlin are outdated: "The point is that the modern Indian must be thought of as an individual, not merely as a unit in certain tribal groups." For more about the struggle of Native American writers to overcome the myth of assimilation to attain "intellectual sovereignty," see Warrior's *Tribal Secrets*.

10. Oskison, *Tecumseh*, 4.

11. There has been relatively little scholarship on the literary works of John Milton Oskison. Cf. Vizenor, "Native American Indian Literature"; Littlefield, "Short Fiction Writers of the Indian Territory"; Justice, *Our Fire Survives the Storm*; Arnie Strickland, "John Milton Oskison"; Ronnow, "John Milton Oskison: Cherokee Journalist Singer of the Semiotics of Power"; Ronnow, *John Milton Oskison: Native American Modernist*; Smith, *Singer of His People*.

12. It appears that Oskison has fictionalized the mission. The closest historical parallel to the Wears would appear to be Rev. Cephas Washburn, who established the first mission among the Western Cherokees in 1820 for the American Board of Commissioners for Foreign Missions. Mooney, in *History, Myths, and Sacred Formulas*, writes: "In response to the invitation [of Tollunteeskee] the Reverend Cephas Washburn and his assistant, Reverend Alfred Finney, with their families, set out the next year from the old Nation, and after a long and exhausting journey reached the Arkansas country, where, in the spring of 1820, they established the Dwight mission" (136). Oskison's novel states that the mission headquarters of Dan Wear was in New York City, whereas the headquarters of the American Board of Commissioners for Foreign Missions was in Boston. Other denominations with missions among the Cherokees at this period included Moravians (1799), Presbyterians (1804), ABCFM (1818), Baptists (1820), and Methodists (1823). For more on the missionaries among the Cherokees, see McLoughlin, *After the Trail of Tears*, and McLoughlin, *Cherokees and Christianity*.

13. Mooney, *History, Myths, and Sacred Formulas*, 145.

14. Marshall quoted from *Worcester v. Georgia*, 31 U.S. 515, 540. For more on the history of the Cherokees' removal, see Mooney, *History, Myths, and Sacred Formulas*; Starr, *History of the Cherokee Indians*; Foreman, *Indian Removal*; Perdue and Green, *The Cherokee Removal*; Wilkins, *Cherokee Tragedy*; Mankiller and Wallis, *Mankiller*.

15. For more on the Treaty Party's deliberations, see chapters 10 and 11 of Wilkins, *Cherokee Tragedy*. For an interesting primary historical document recounting Elias Boudinot's version of events, see "Documents in Relation to the Validity of the Cherokee Treaty of 1835 . . . " (document PAM012), and for the

nationalist perspective, see John Ross, "Letter from John Ross, principal Chief of the Cherokee Nation of Indians: in answer to inquiries from a friend regarding the Cherokee affairs . . . ," June 21, 1836 (document PAM017).

16. Wilkins, *Cherokee Tragedy*, 289, 292.

17. Duncan and Riggs, *Cherokee Heritage Trails Guidebook*, 29. This is an excellent resource developed in conjunction with the Eastern Band of the Cherokee Nation.

18. McLoughlin, *After the Trail of Tears*, 201–21.

19. The complete *Cherokee Phoenix* is available in digital form from the Digital Library of Georgia (under "Historic Newspapers") at (http://dlg.galileo.usg.edu).

20. McLoughlin, *Cherokees and Christianity*, 27.

21. For more on Sam Houston's relationship to the Cherokees, see Gregory and Strickland, *Sam Houston with the Cherokees*.

22. McLoughlin, *After the Trail of Tears*, 38–39.

23. Richardson quoted in Dippie, *The Vanishing American*, 61.

24. For more on the role of women in Cherokee society, see Perdue, *Cherokee Women*; Hill, *Weaving New Worlds*; and Johnston, *Cherokee Women in Crisis*.

25. Mooney, *History, Myths, and Sacred Formulas*, 397; Washburn, *Reminiscences*, 191, 221.

26. For a better sense of the temporal depth of Native American literature, see Womack's *Red on Red*: "Native people have been on this continent at least thirty thousand years, and the stories tell us we have been here even longer than that, . . . that we originated here. For much of this time period, we have had literatures" (7). The phrase "deep time" is borrowed from Dimock, "Deep Time": "I propose a more extended duration for American literary studies, planetary in scope. I call this *deep time*. This produces a map that, thanks to its receding horizons, its backward extension into far-flung temporal and spatial coordinates, must depart significantly from a map predicated on the short life of the U.S." (759).

27. Given the historical importance of Sequoyah, there is surprisingly little primary material recounting his life. As Jack Frederick Kilpatrick, one of the finest Cherokee ethnographers, observed: "There is much in Cherokee oral tradition and not a little in untranslated manuscripts that, were it available to scholarship, would surely enrich our knowledge of Sequoyah. It is indeed strange that although Sequoyah methodically kept journals . . . none of them have come to light." Perhaps the best primary source is "The Wahnenauhi Manuscript," written by a Cherokee woman who was at "Major George Lowrey['s] . . . house when George Guess (Sequoyah) left for the West, also when his companions returned without him." Wahnenauhi writes of Sequoyah's final trip to Mexico: "In all his journey, he had busied himself with writing descriptions of the country through which they passed." After he died, his companions buried Sequoyah in a cave, "placing his writing with him, they wrapped it in skins as securely as they could. They marked the place so that it would without difficulty be found." Kilpatrick, *Sequoyah of Earth and Intellect*, 211, 179, 210.

28. See, for example, Deloria, *God Is Red*, chs. 4–6.

29. For more on the importance of community in the Native American literary tradition see Weaver, *Native American Literatures and Native American Community*.

30. McLoughlin, *After the Trail of Tears*, 84.

31. Marshall, *Worcester v. The State of Georgia*, 242. For an interesting primary account by Samuel Worcester of the trials and tribulations he endured before he renounced the Cherokees' struggle to retain their ancestral homeland in the Southeast, see "Account of S[amuel] A. Worcester's Second Arrest, 1831, July 18."

32. McLoughlin, *Cherokees and Christianity*, 30.

33. Ibid., 104, 229, 108, 120.

34. Oskison here touches on a very sensitive subject. Because there is not much primary historical material detailing Sequoyah's life, the facts are elusive and opinions differ widely. Traveller Bird, a Cherokee writer from the Snowbird Reservation, wrote a controversial exposé, *Tell Them They Lie*, in which he claims that the man famously depicted on the cover of countless books holding the syllabary was not Sequoyah but a mixed-blood poser who appeased the white authority's claims that the syllabary was invented well after white contact. The real Sequoyah, Bird maintains, was a full-blood member of an ancient Cherokee scribal society that had long possessed the ability to write. For an array of perspectives on the subject see. Kilpatrick, *Sequoyah of Earth and Intellect*; Hoig, *Sequoyah*; and Kalter, " 'America's Histories' Revisited."

35. Corkran, "Cherokee Migration Fragment," 27.

36. The question of precolonial forms of writing really deserves a great deal more attention. The academic myth that Indians had no writing before European contact needs to be debunked. In Kalter's " 'America's Histories' Revisited," she cites two historical documents that suggest the Cherokees had some form of writing in the colonial period. In 1881, for example, Helen Hunt Jackson describes having seen, in Cherokee societies, "writ[ing] in black and red hieroglyphs on a dressed buffalo-skin" (Kalter, "'America's Histories,' " 339). For more on Indian writing systems, see Marcus, *Mesoamerican Writing Systems*, and Mallery, *Picture-Writing of the American Indians*.

37. Mooney writes that he collected the story from James Wafford of Indian Territory who, in turn, obtained it from Sequoyah and Gatun'wa'li. Mooney, *History, Myths, and Sacred Formulas*, 485.

38. For more on the interpretation of wampum, see Fenton, *Great Law and the Longhouse*, ch. 16; Speck, *Penn Wampum Belts*; and Robb, *Material Symbols*.

39. Mooney, *History, Myths, and Sacred Formulas*, 365.

40. Ibid., 353–55.

41. For an excellent overview of the intellectual history of the twentieth century from a Native American point of view see Weaver, *That the People Might Live*.

42. Mankiller and Wallis, *Mankiller*, 182.

43. Mathews, *Sundown*, 260, 297.

44. Not all critics agree that these three novels are characterized by despair. For an alternative interpretation of Mathews's *Sundown*, see Warrior, *Tribal Secrets*: "In *Sundown* the situation is dire, but not tragic in the way of McNickle's *The Surrounded*. . . . Matthews provides not so much an alternative as the possibility of an alternative. Drawing his lessons from . . . the land and from the resiliency of a community committed to resistance, Mathews offers a way to exercise what power of decision making is available, limited though the positive effect may be" (83). Jace Weaver has brought to my attention the intriguing insight that McNickle's original manuscript of *The Surrounded*, entitled "Hungry Genera-

tions," ended on a much more hopeful note. It would be interesting to explore in greater depth if the fact that "Hungry Generations" and *The Singing Bird* offer a more hopeful vision is in any way connected to the fact that both novels went unpublished. The publication of *The Singing Bird* will, then, perhaps offer new possibilities for scholars to explore these nuances in greater detail.

The Singing Bird

When the female becomes a singing bird,
the nest remains empty and cock redbirds
fight among themselves.

Old Cherokee Legend

One

The sun had risen high enough to shine through the treetops on Killbuck Ridge before I heard Ellen's sleepy greeting.

"Oh, hello, Dan," then, lightly, she accused, "No doubt you've been up and about the Lord's work for hours! Give me a kiss, and I'll struggle out of bed."

"Yes, my beloved," his voice was grave, "it is high time you were stirring."

I thought, Ellen has not yet realized what it means to be a missionary wife. Miss Eula, helping to pack for the long journey that lay ahead of us, looked at me with a hint of admonition in her clear grey-blue eyes, as if to say, We must be indulgent. But her words were, "You might start loading the household things, Paul; all is ready except a few breakfast dishes."

Dan came to check the stowing of kettles, bags of flour and meal, feed for our horses, the tent, and other heavy baggage, saying, "The nags have been harnessed, and we should pull out as soon as possible."

We three—Uncle Dan Wear, Ellen and I—had come out from New York to establish a missionary station among the Cherokees who were living in Arkansas Territory. We had stopped here at Kingslake Mission, near the Tennessee border of Georgia, in order to acquaint ourselves with the work. Our Mission Board had assigned to us as teacher Miss Eula Benson who, young as she was, had already served for four years at stations in the Eastern Cherokees' country. Now, after eight months of expert tutelage at Kingslake, we were setting off on what we knew would be a difficult task beyond the Mississippi.

All four of us were young, Dan, head of the expedition, only twenty-six, Ellen and I not yet twenty-two, and Miss Eula only a month older than I. At the Mission Board rooms in New York, Mr. Tilley, the secretary, had said to Dan, "You will be the youngest of all our station heads, but we expect much of you as a sound and vigorous descendant of the consecrated Vermont Wears," then to me, "You're a Wear, too, Paul, and I know we can depend upon you."

Turning again to Dan, with Ellen's hand in his, Mr. Tilley said, "Take good care of her. She's a New Yorker, to be sure, but we have high hopes of her."

He had gone on, as though to challenge Dan's competence, "You face a difficult assignment. Since the Arkansas reservation was set aside for the Cherokees hardly three years ago, some four thousand have gone out there from Georgia and Tennessee, a majority of them, I should say, are not contented in their voluntary exile; and already white settlers are crowding upon them and making trouble. They are in sore need of guidance, spiritually and materially. We should have had a station among them from the beginning of their migration, but until now have lacked the right man to send out."

Dan had said, "We shall do our best to jus[t]ify the Board's faith in us, Sir." His eyes had rested on his bride's lovely, rose-tinted face as he spoke, and I thought that a shadow of doubt clouded them.

As we three had driven on the fifty-day journey to Kingslake, I on the improvised back seat of our one-horse wagon, that shadow had deepened. Ellen maintained the holiday air she had assumed on leaving her wealthy father's home and a timorous mother's fears. As we ferried the Hudson River, she cried, "It's a good-bye to Ellen Morin! Now for the harvest of souls among the heathen. Dan, we'll gather them the way my grandfather Pierre gathered peltry from the Wyandots before Mad Anthony Wayne applied his trade on the Miami."

He had not liked her flippant tone, but smiled and said, "We will, my beloved, if the Lord so wills it."

Her friends had been amazed by the marriage. One said, "Imagine Ellen in the wilderness reading the Psalms and making broth for savages! In truth, that will be a new sensation for her!" What her friends could not realize was that at last she was completely and passionately in love with my straight shouldered, stave-thin Vermont uncle. And he with her, the spoiled darling and only child of doting parents. Yet they should have known, at least, that she would face with self-confidence whatever role she chose to live.

In the eight months at Kingslake, Ellen's holiday mood had changed. There she had found neither the savages of her friends' imagining nor the excitement of wilderness adventure, but the orderly routine of a successful mission station conducted in a peaceful setting by practical New England men and women consecrated as wholly and matter-of-factly to the Lord's service as Henri Morin, in New York, was to the business of shipping.

She had watched the workers at Kingslake in the schoolrooms

hearing lessons from Alden's reader, Murray's grammar, Worcester's geography; she had attended services at which Mr. King, Doctor Butram, Mr. Hicks, or Dan preached with no apparent realization that they were not addressing a congregation of New England farm folks, except that away from the Mission their words were interpreted into the Cherokee language by the convert John Bows; she had seen the chiefs, grave and courteous, in conference with the Mission staff, little different save in dress and tint of skin from the burghers of New York; she had seen the Mission men at work with their Cherokee scholars in the fields and at the shops and mill, and the women at the spinning wheel and loom, and in the sewing room instructing the quiet, dark-faced and alert girls.

The reality had been disappointing. She could not, or would not trouble to penetrate below the surface of this controlled life to the hidden zeal of the workers. Nor had she fathomed the current of Government policy that was steadily sweeping the Cherokees into exile. She could not realize how desperately these men and women were striving to prepare the Indians for uprooting.

At Kingslake, she had been by turns gay and unhappy, considerate, charming, irritated and contemptuous of the staff's industry and piety. When Dan said, as the period of our preparation ended, "I have profited beyond my expectations," she countered, "and I have been bored beyond endurance!" She was eager to move on, hoping, I thought, to find beyond the Mississippi the exciting existence she craved.

The big wagon obtained at Kingslake, and the light wagon we had driven from New York in which Ellen and Dan would travel, were loaded before Ellen finished her breakfast. Dan and I were waiting as she came out carrying her parasol, followed by Miss Eula with a hamper of tableware to be placed under the seat of the wagon. I was to drive. She gave her hand graciously to Mr. King, Mr. Hicks and Doctor Butram, kissed their wives, and waved to the silent group of scholars standing behind their teachers. We others had already made our adieux to the Kingslake staff.

Helping Ellen to mount to the seat at his left in the one-horse wagon, Dan led off on the long pull to Arkansas. As I swung my team in behind, with Miss Eula at my side, I knew without looking at her that her eyes were wet; and I heard her whisper, "Good-bye and God bless you and keep you, all you dear ones."

The road quartered southwestward; and as the Indian summer sun of November grew warm we saw Ellen open her parasol. O[n] our right the craggy heights of Lookout Mountain were a luminous brown rampart; at our left, blue haze tinted the forested slope of Killbuck. Miss Eula's eyes ranged slowly over the scene, as though she strove to fix in her memory every lovely detail of the swelling ridges and glades dotted with Spanish oaks she had come to know so well. "Paul," she said, "I should like just once more to climb to Lookout Point and gaze down on the looping Tennessee River, across to Walden's Ridge, and there say again the Cherokee word to describe what lies under the eyes, 'O-tullee-ton-tanna-ta-kunna-ee,' syllables that are more like a spring warbler's song than a name meaning mountains looking at each other."

"Yes," I nodded, "this Cherokee country is sightly; something like Vermont though grander."

"It is," said Miss Eula. "It is grander, too, than my own Far Cry Valley neighborhood in Massachusetts . . . I came out with the Kings when I was not yet eighteen, and it has been as though I've lived through a second childhood here. I've taught at three stations; and in vacation times I've gone nearly everywhere in the Cherokee Nation, to the Overhills and Valley towns, from Running Water to Creek Path to Etowah to New Echota to Oostanaula to Amoyee to Springplace to Red Clay to Candy's Creek to John Ross' home to the old John Jolly home on Jolly's Island where the Hiwassee tumbles into the Tennessee. I could pray that Arkansas might be as lovely as this homeland of the Cherokees."

To hear Miss Eula name over these scenes of missionary activity and the home regions of the scholars at Kingslake was like listening to a familiar loved poem.

She talked of John Jolly, now in Arkansas as chief of the western band, and his long friendship with Sam Houston, the protégé of Andrew Jackson who was making a brilliant career at the bar and in Tennessee politics. I told her what Ellen had said as we drove through Maryville, Houston's boyhood home, "I wish we might visit Nashville; I should like to meet handsome Sam—also, that awful red-haired white savage they call Old Hickory."

Miss Eula nodded. "I expect she would get a thrill from that."

Then, as though wishing to get away from talk of Ellen and back to the work that meant life to her, she began telling me about Catherine Swan, one of the first converts at Kingslake and the brightest jewel in the Mission's crown, whom we were to visit on the way to Arkansas. As Miss Eula talked, I wished that Ellen might hear her;

perhaps she could grasp something of the true significance of missionary work, feel something of the joy of gathering such an one into the fold. In Miss Eula's words I heard unrolled the story of Kingslake, of Etowah, of Springplace, of Elliott, of all the isolated outposts where, since 1802, valiant men and women had labored for the salvation of souls and the material welfare of the Southern Indians.

Her words took me back to the building of the first cabins at Kingslake, the clearing of the mission fields and the turning of the first furrows, the arrival of the first scholars, shy shirt-tail boys and weeping girls dressed in a single garment.

Catherine, however, had been quite different; and I could imagine the doubts and questioning when she came, at seventeen, to ask Mrs. King what the mission folks had for her. I could picture her, graceful and darkly beautiful, arriving with her rich, slave-owning father, she riding a fine young mare and he a tall roan horse, she decked out in silk and bracelets and rings, with gay feathers in her headdress like a lightminded singing bird, and he wearing splendid white knee-boots, a broadcloth coat, a blue and white shawl turban wound about his head, and hair so long that it flowed down upon his wide shoulders. There would be something richly barbaric in their bearing, as though a princess of Judea had sought the humble mission of our Lord.

She had wept when her father led away her mare. Then, smiling, said, "All right now, I belong with you. See, I speak English a little." She walked into their hearts at Kingslake as promptly and with as much assurance as she entered with Mrs. King into her cabin quarters, and put aside her finery without a word of protest.

In six months she was assisting the girls' teacher. Miss Eula said, "Catherine was the most brilliant scholar we have ever had, even quicker to learn than John Bows though no more devoted. All of us loved her, but to me she was especially dear, almost like a twin sister . . . Sometimes on spring days when she couldn't stand to be shut up in the schoolroom, she would beg me to go into the woods with her. 'Please, Miss Eula,' she would say, 'get us excused so that we can talk with God under the trees.' Outside, she would pray to be made worthy of His love, then rise from her knees to run with the swiftness and grace of a fawn. She sang then, sometimes the hymns we taught but more often Cherokee chants that are no more than expressions of delight in being alive. Once she said of her father, proudly, 'He is not William Swan, as the white people call him, but Yah-nu-gun-yah-ski. That means Man-who-drowned-a-bear, and that name he earned for himself. I love him very much!' "

In four years (Catherine was now just past the age of twenty-one) she had become a shining symbol of regeneration, a treasured first fruit of Kingslake, an Indian maid with the magic to stir the enthusiasm of all who met her, casual visitors, traders, members of our Mission Board, even President Monroe, and inspire them to try to express her charm and loveliness in letters, journals, and public talks.

"Dan has told me," I said, "that we shall see her in three days?"

"Yes, if she is not too ill to receive us."

As we went clanking along the rough but pleasant road across western Georgia and into Alabama, making two night camps near the cabins of Cherokees Miss Eula knew, my desire to see Catherine grew. I thought, If talk of her can rouse in Miss Eula's grey-blue eyes glowing stars in anticipation of seeing her again I want to learn her secret!

Before we came to the Cherokee town of Nocoy and drove to William Swan's plantation, Miss Eula told how Catherine's illness had come upon her. "I'm afraid," she said, "that we were to blame. We could not help petting and softening her, and when the time to leave Kingslake came and she went away with her father, they rode the hundred miles through winter rains and slept on the ground beside dead campfires in wet blankets. The exposure made her ill; she grew weak, and the cough never left her, but she would not rest from her work at the school she established and taught at Nocoy, nor from the direction of the temperance society she founded, nor from her visiting of the old and needy. But now," Miss Eula's voice was infinitely sad, "she must rest, for she cannot rise from her bed."

At William Swan's home we were met by Doctor Scott, who had come to take Catherine to his own house. He told Dan, "You and your lady and Miss Eula may see her, but only for a minute," then to me, "Young man, you may help me if you can be spared for three days."

"Of course, Doctor," Dan said. "Paul will do whatever you wish."

The doctor explained, "Catherine must be carried on a litter to the river, and floated down to the landing nearest my home. I need another pair of strong shoulders."

So while Dan, Ellen, and Miss Eula waited at William Swan's, I shouldered a corner of the litter on which the wraith-like Cherokee girl made her last journey, thinking, It's the procession of a living saint through this deep, browning Alabama forest. The other bearers were young Jared Leeth, white, and Roy Bascom and Henry Falling, half blood Cherokees.

We four stood at the doorway of Catherine's big room as her mother and Ellen padded the litter with fine quilts and shifted her from her bed. As we came forward to lift the poles to our shoulders, her smile and husky whisper greeted us. For me she had a special word, "I have not seen you before. You are my brother Paul, are you not?" and when I nodded, "They have told me of your loving kindness."

We followed the old Creek Path to the river. Roy and Henry walked in front, for they had often gone that way. I was at the left rear, and at times as Catherine moved her head I could see in her hollow, sunken eyes a fire that burned with increasing brilliance as she drew nearer to the grave. Her smile, as her eyes met mine, bathed me, made me tremble as though I were in the presence of my first sweetheart. Truly, I fell in love with her, as had all who came under her spell.

It was six miles to the landing. Behind the litter walked her mother, Doctor Scott, Cherokee neighbors, the children Catherine had taught, and two black women who wept shamelessly and moaned because they knew she would never come back to the Big House to be babied and scolded. Only her father refused to accompany us, saying, "I could not bear it."

Twice on the way to the river we put her down so that Doctor Scott might test her pulse and give her a sustaining draught. In these rest periods, we four bearers stood together to arrange how we would walk over the next stage. At the second, Jared said, "Me an' Paul best git in front now; the way's easy to foller, it's been beat plain by Creek war parties."

I thought, Like us, the Creeks have carried their wounded and sick over this trace. It is paved with sorrow, and glory, and I am honored to walk in it with this Cherokee girl.

We reached the Tennessee at mid-afternoon, and were on the barge and afloat by four o'clock. Jared, the best riverman, steered; Henry and Roy stood at the prow with poles to fend off lodged tree-trunks and drifting limbs; and I propped a square of canvas to shield Catherine from the sun. Her mother squatted beside the litter, and Doctor Scott sat at the stern, unmoving and silent except when he went to kneel beside his patient. He was an old, sorrow-stricken man. At his home, in his wife's care, Catherine had once come up out of the Valley of the Shadow to gladden their hearts.

Before pushing off Jared said, "It's forty mile to Limestone Landin'. We'll drift till sundown, then tie up till we kin see to navigate by the light o' the moon. Current's sluggish, so we won't git there much 'fore noon tomorrow."

Until sunset the course of the river was nearly straight, and we drifted for the most part near the south bank where overhanging trees made a cool shade. I went back to sit near the doctor, by turns watching his face, the reed-grown opposite bank, and the broken cliffs which rose above us. I could imagine Creek war canoes breaking out of the canes, all but hear the whoops of their warriors bearing down upon us although I knew that since the Cherokees had helped Jackson whip the Creeks at Horseshoe Bend in 1813, the two tribes had been at peace.

I had heard, too, that Catherine as a girl of twelve had run to hide in the woods from Jackson's foraging parties in order to save her chastity.

The woods were still full of birds, though they no longer sang. Once Doctor Scott said, "If you look sharp, Paul, you may see parakeets. Catherine used to prize their feathers for her hair." I believed I saw white herons and, remembering a passage from the mythology I had learned in school, imagined they were swans coming to draw the barge that was bearing Catherine to Valhalla. We drifted so quietly that at times I heard the barking of squirrels, and was reminded of the saying that at certain seasons they leave their accustomed haunts to migrate by the thousands, swimming rivers and scampering over mountains in response to some mysterious urge.

The sunlit hours of the voyage were a joy to Catherine, ill and weak as she was. But when sunset shadows stretched out to the barge she became fretful, and talked in broken Cherokee phrases with her mother. I went to stand beside Jared, who knew the language, and whispered, "What is she saying?"

He muttered, "It's somethin' 'bout her bein' just a little one still, how she ain't ready to die yit, but," his voice rose, "effen she ain't a saint on earth they's never been one!"

He began to look anxiously for a place to land, scanning eagerly the apparently unbroken growths of brushwood and canes that choked the muddy slopes, and calling to Roy and Henry, "Look sharp, you fellers; we got to tie up right soon."

Henry was first to discover a narrow lane between the canes, and called back, "Hard left!" The barge slid in to a mud ramp, Roy and Henry stepped down to tie it up, and Roy called, "They's a cabin yonder, I see a light."

We bore Catherine through the darkness, guided by shafts of firelight that rayed through the cabin's chinking. Her mother greeted the family who came out in answer to her hail, laying her palm in the offered palms of the father, mother and three children. We four bearers followed Doctor Scott inside, put down the litter on the earth floor, and went outside.

Presently the Cherokee woman came out bearing a kettle. I blew up a fire in the hot ashes of the cooking place; and when the stew of deer meat and corn was ready, she dipped soup into a bowl to carry inside. Then Catherine's mother brought out a big wooden bowl and a horn spoon, filled the bowl and gave it to us. It went around and was filled again before the doctor came out to eat.

Henry and Roy smoked, and Jared tore a hunk of tobacco from the same twist to chew; then we four set with our backs against the peach trees that grew close to the cabin to wait for moonrise. After a long time, Jared rose, peered eastward, and announced, "She'll be comin' up over Chattooga right soon."

And so she did, a lop-sided last quarter moon, and touched the ridgepole of the cabin with light. Henry knocked out his pipe, and roused Roy from a catnap. Doctor Scott came out to ask, "Can we start?"

Jared answered, "Time you git her wropped up, an' we push out into the current, reckon we kin see to navigate."

The owner of the cabin lighted a fat-pine torch at the cooking fire and showed us the way to the barge, and stood with his family to wish us Godspeed.

We drifted on down the glimmering streak that was the river. Catherine's mother lay down on a blanket beside her. The doctor returned to his place near Jared at the stern; and when he removed his hat his hair made a crown of silver above his sun-darkened face. There was an eerie stillness, a breathless faint radiance over the water. Tall, looming cliffs seemed to absorb the moonlight, and were immensely exaggerated in grandeur.

Roy Bascom motioned with his chin toward the right bank, saying (as though some human sound were needed to break the silence), "Over yonder's Chickasaw Old Fields.[*] Long time ago them Indians used there. They're all down Mississip' way now."

"Maybe I'll see them," I said. "We're going through Mississippi on the way to Arkansas."

Henry cut in angrily, "You mout's well wait till they git out there to where you're a-goin'. The Gov'mint's fixin' to boot 'em all outen Mississip' an' settle 'em tother side the Big River. Damn politicians!"

"Maybe not," I ventured. "They say at Kingslake—"

"You can hear anything," he interrupted. "But her old man," he turned to glance at Catherine, "he's fixin' to move west right now. Says the whites around Nocoy town air stealin' him blind already an' nobody lifts a hand to stop 'em. It's the way it's done, steal all they got in the way o' teams an' crops an' the Indians'll hafta go; they ain't enough game left to ration one out o' five among 'em."

With daylight we moved in a somewhat swifter current. Below, Jared said, was the long reach of Muscle Shoals, but we would get to Limestone Landing before reaching swift water.

Again I propped the square of canvas to shield Catherine from the stabbing rays of the morning sun, and she smiled as she said, "Thank you, brother Paul." I stayed beside her to make sure of the canvas' fastenings and trying to think of some casual words that might hearten her. I tried, "I heard fish jumping just at daybreak."

"Yes, Paul, I heard them," then, "You'll go gigging in the creeks of Arkansas; my brother Walter will show you how it is done."

Doctor Scott's carriage was at Limestone Landing when we tied up, but of course Catherine was not able to stand its jolting. In the group that had gathered were husky woodsmen friends of the doctor; and one said, "Doc., we figgered she'd have to be toted, an we—"

"Reckon not, friend," Jared pushed up beside the man to say. "Me an' Henry an' Roy an' Paul here aim to do the totin'."

We shouldered the litter again. Catherine's mother rode in the carriage, and Doctor Scott walked the seven miles to his home with one of Catherine's brown hands in his.

At the mansion, we marched up the wide mahogany-railed stairway and into a great high-ceilinged bedroom where the sun was picking out on spotless quilts the pattern of the lace valance on the four-poster's canopy. We lowered her to the level of the linen sheets, and held the litter steady as she was shifted to the bed.

She called weakly to us, "My brothers, come and let me thank you, Jared, Henry, Roy, and Paul. Take my hands." We clumped to her side, laying our hands on hers. I heard a great snort, Jared's explosion of grief, and then we were like four big babies crying. Catherine broke, too, for a moment, before she smiled and whispered, "God bless you all," and to me, "Brother Paul, you will do for my people what I have tried so hard to do?"

"I will—I'll try," I stammered, "and so will my uncle Dan."

"Good-bye, all of you, my dear friends," she murmured. Jared turned, took the litter under his arm, and ran from the room.

* * *

Driving on through Alabama within sight of Ellen's tilted parasol and Dan's straight back, with Miss Eula talking easily about Catherine's work at Kingslake and Nocoy, a picture of the dying girl filled my mind and sharpened my eagerness for the missionary adventure upon which we had embarked. Re-living those two vivid days, they seemed unreal, dream-like; and it was as though I had been awakened when I heard Miss Eula say, "Paul, we must do our very best to carry high the torch dear Catherine has been compelled to hand on. Her work was really so practical, you know."

I said, "Of course, she would have learned to be practical at Kingslake, wouldn't she?"

"Yes, it has been necessary. We have had to plow and sow and reap literally as well as spiritually. You helped to reap and stow our crop of timothy hay for horse feed this winter, so—"

"And a fine crop it was," I said, "thick and waist-high."

"Too," she reminded me, "we have had to deal with false reports that we of the Mission want Cherokee land, that we are in league with the white land speculators of Georgia who are determined to drive the Indians away from their homes . . . If our work is to succeed, we must be practical, and politic too."

Her words roused in me a memory. Why, I've heard them before; it's the way Dan talked after he had conferred with Mr. King and Doctor Butram. It pleased me that she had listened attentively to Dan.

That night, because of a drenching rain, we abandoned our tent to sleep in a roomy Indian cabin at the town of Nickajack. Miss Eula, who spoke fluent Cherokee, helped our Indian hostess with the supper while Ellen lay down to breathe smelling salts and complain that the jolting of Dan's wagon had brought on a severe migraine. I suspected that it was a polite evasion, that in truth she was disgusted by what she would call the odor of the savage occupants of the cabin. To me, as to Miss Eula and Dan, it had become a familiar and not unpleasant smell; here were nice people who dressed neatly; there were no lice in the children's hair, and their noses were clean.

Behind the blanket curtain where Ellen and Dan slept, I heard a steady flow of complaining until my uncle spoke sharply, "Ellen, my love, you will be quiet; the others wish to sleep." After that, there was only a muffled sobbing.

In the morning as we drove on, Miss Eula said, "Ellen is still new to this life and tires easily. We must try to be patient with her, and understanding."

"Yes, of course," I agreed shortly.

I had hated Ellen's futile protests in the night, as I had hated her for saying of Catherine Swan, "Why all the pal[a]vering about an Indian girl. Hearing you talk, one might think she was the Virgin Mary herself!"

Hearing her say that, Dan had rebuked, "That, my beloved, is an unfair and wicked thing to say," and to me, "Paul, you will forget the blasphemy; Ellen did not know what she was saying."

"Perhaps, Paul," she conceded grudgingly, "I spoke too strongly, but in truth your lyrical account of the girl's journey to Doctor Scott's home sickened me."

Two

As worked out with the men at Kingslake, Dan's plan was to cut the Natchez Trace, follow it through the Chickasaw Nation to a certain point, and from there work our way as best we could sixty miles to Elliott Mission station in Mississippi. There we would leave Ellen and Miss Eula while we rode on horseback to the Big River and proceeded thence by river boat to the site Dan would select for our Arkansas station.

Dan thought that by the new year he and I should be ready to set out from Elliott. Planning the journey in the comfort of our quarters at Kingslake, it had not seemed a difficult one, but its accomplishment, as we learned, was not easy.

Even before we turned into the Natchez Trace, persistent cold winter solstice rains came to chill us and turn the rough Cherokee roads into muddy rivulets and treacherous bog-holes. Through the quagmires Dan piloted his willing horse with the skill and patience of a Vermont farm-bred man, walking at times in slush half-boot-top deep so that he could spank Coley's rump encouragingly as he urged, "Just a few more heaves, old fellow, and we'll fetch terra firma!" At such times, Ellen sat tight-lipped and white about the mouth, as though she expected to become a human offering to the god of her fanatic husband. She loathed the experience, so much worse than she had anticipated, yet in spite of herself admired the courage, endurance, and self-control of the man she loved.

I was in luck to have Miss Eula as my companion. She could handle the team as well as I when I got out to put my shoulder to a wheel. Stretches of wretched road held no terror for her who had struggled over such traces on horseback and in carriages and wagons, even on foot, so often that she spoke lightly of our trials, "Paul, you should have been with us—the Kings and Doctor Butram—once when we journeyed to Amohe, to Red Clay, and down to Mr. Gambold's station at Taloney. You could have said then that you had traveled over bad roads!"

"We could stand it better," I said, "if Ellen wasn't so set on making a martyr of herself."

"Hush, Paul!" she rebuked me. "You should not speak, or think hardly of her. Dan loves her devotedly; and you must believe, as he and I do, that with seasoning she will become an excellent helper."

"The worst of it is," I could not stem back my words, "that he does love her so much, and she's not worth one of his little fingers!"

I believe Miss Eula would have slapped my jaw for saying that if I had been six years younger. Instead, she looked steadily at me as she said, "Paul, you're jealous of Ellen," then gently, "You must try not to be."

"What!" I shouted my indignation at her charge.

"Think it over," she said quietly, staring ahead to where Ellen was leaning forward to peer into Dan's eyes. I knew well that cozening mood, the wholly charming smile she was using to stir him and, too, the quizzical smile on his sharp-cut face. He was probably saying, "You're too lovely to be real, my beloved!"

Ellen could be maddeningly enchanting, glow with a flame of pure radiance—if that is the right word. But it was not like the radiance I had felt in the presence of Catherine Swan. Not at all like that. Ellen's appeal was wholly physical, the appeal of a highly colored, luscious beauty backed by wit and intelligence when she cared to use such re-enforcements, and the daring of the best—or worst—of the adventurous Morins. They had been conquerors, subjugators; it had long been in their blood to prevail. Yet thus far it had been my uncle's will that had directed Ellen's life with him.

What most roused my resentment was Ellen's persistent, though unspoken, determination to overcome Dan. He had shaped and ruled me, and I was proud to believe that he loved me enough to want to mold me to his excellent pattern.

But jealous of Ellen? How could that be? I was not a baby, to cry when my mentor and dearest relative took to himself a beautiful wife to fondle. I was not a pup, to fly at another when my master caressed it. I was a man, past twenty-one. Without straining, I could load a barrel of flour into a wagon. With Dan's help, I had earned my Bachelor of Arts at the College of Vermont. I was well enough grounded in logic, natural philosophy, and the Shorter Catechism, the foundations of a New England education. I believed in the importance of the missionary calling; above all, in the utter sincerity of my uncle and his consecration to the work he had chosen and for which he had thoroughly prepared himself.

I was hurt by Miss Eula's charge the more because, without quite realizing it, I had fallen in love with her. With young male vanity, I believed that I understood her. Was she not of the sound Yankee stock I had known all my life? Was she not clear thinking, loyal to an ideal, upright, unselfish? She had taken the Cherokees to her heart; their women and children, and their men too, were like members of her own family on the farms and in the villages of Far Cry Valley and the slopes [of] Benson Ridge in Massachusetts. Dan's sister Lydia was like that with her people in the Vermont hills. I believed that I could enter into the heart of everything that mattered to Miss Eula.

Actually, however, I knew precious little about her!

We came to the Natchez Trace after days of grief. At any rate, we called it grief in the early darkness of winter nights when we had managed to pitch the tent, feed our horses, tied shivering and stamping to the wagon wheels, and cook a supper of pork and navy beans on a smoldering campfire. Dan's prayers at these chill, wet camps seemed almost ironic. He asked God's mercy for them who walked in darkness, while the heathen Indians for whom he prayed smoked in front of log fires in tight cabins or slept, wrapped in warm blankets, on warm hearths. He begged for us the gift of humble unselfishness, knowing that he and Miss Eula (he might be doubtful of Ellen and me) would give all but a shred of clothing and a last crust of bread to any able Indian hunter who asked for clothing and food.

As she sat huddled inside the tent fly, groping for any faint reflection of heat from the cooking fire, Ellen's face sometimes revealed the measure of her contempt for Dan's "childish" petitions. I could imagine her springing up to cry, "If your God is all-knowing and all-powerful, ask Him to have pity on me! Can't you see that I am miserable and sick at heart? Get me out of this hell of rocks and bogs and bearded moss and rain and wind and cold!"

She never uttered such words, realizing that unless she fell ill Dan would not turn back on her account. She was beginning to learn in the hard school of experience what being a missionary's wife meant.

Then we drove into the Chickasaw swamps, where for miles the Trace lay under water, where all day long I left my team to Miss Eula's guidance so that I might walk ahead of Dan's wagon and, with a pole, sound the depths of bogholes, where it was sometimes impossible to find a patch of dry earth on which to pitch the tent and make a fire.

At one of these forlorn camping places, after we had tried in vain to light a fire, Dan said, "Paul, get on my Coley horse, ride back to that cabin we passed an hour ago, and fetch a firebrand while I search for wood that may burn."

I rode away through the drizzle, and from Chatti-nu-bi's fireplace borrowed a sizeable smoldering fat-pine knot. The Indian handed it up to me and, thinking of supper, I pounded Coley into a lope. Presently the wind of our going fanned it to a blaze that frightened Coley so that I had to cast it away in order to keep my seat on his back. I heard its sad sizzling in the slosh as Coley sped on.

Dan laughed at my tale of the mishap, and said, "It's too bad, Paul, but our supper will only be delayed. I'll go back on foot to borrow another brand, and while I'm gone you might scout around for more wood that will burn with some drying."

Miss Eula said, "I'll go with you, Dan. Perhaps I can help to explain what happened to Paul; I know something of the language the Chickasaws and Choctaws speak."

"Yes, come along," Dan said, and strode away without waiting to see whether or not she was properly wrapped. She ran to catch up with him, then they passed out of sight.

Ellen grasped my arm, shook me and cried, "Go after them, Paul, don't let her go with him!"

"Why?" I asked, astonished by her violence. "She'll be all right with Dan."

"Oh, well," she recovered herself and relaxed her grip on my arm, "perhaps she will be." She looked at me for a moment curiously, then, "Meanwhile you and I will hunt for sticks together, won't we, Paul?" She spoke my name caressingly.

"If you like," I grumbled.

She took my arm and cuddled close as I began to grope about on the motte on which we had pitched our tent so that I could feel her warmth. Hers was a body through which the heart pumped rich, hot blood; and I knew that she meant to show me how vital and desirable she could be. I loathed her for what I now realized was a senseless burst of jealousy, a gesture of disloyalty to Dan. I had been taught to believe that no woman should deliberately excite a man as she was exciting me until she comes to the marriage bed, and a wife must be to men other than her husband as a disembodied spirit.

Ellen's jealousy was wholly unjustified. Miss Eula and Dan were to one another only friends and traveling companions, not a man and woman in the remotest degree conscious of sex.

They returned sooner than I had a right to expect, yet the time of waiting seemed to me an aeon of agony. I was ashamed, and humiliated by the realization that Ellen's expert coquetries had shaken me profoundly. I was sure that she had meant to stir me to the pitch where I must show my desire to Dan's eyes. I thought, It is how she means to punish him, a wildly jealous woman's device. I believed that if I had yielded to my sudden hot impulse to hold her tight in my arms and kiss her lips savagely, she would have poured upon me a torrent of scornful reproach and pretended to be outraged by my presumption. So I had gone on stolidly searching for dry twigs, pine splinters, and bits of punk from the undersides of rotting logs, her hands groping with and touching mine, her body crowding close to mine, her breath on my cheek.

The fire going, Dan said, "Well, Paul, you have been busy! With all this wood we can be extravagant tonight."

"I helped a lot, didn't I, Paul?" Ellen looked at Dan as she spoke, and there was [a] spot of red in each of her cheeks.

"Good for you, my beloved!" he approved. "We'll make a pioneer woman of you before a bear cub can climb over the Green Mountains." It was a saying I had heard many times in Vermont. My heart was warmed by his refusal to read in Ellen's words the innuendo she had tried to convey. That, or his wholesome blindness.

It was late when we settled into our blankets, well fed and warmed, and I came awake reluctantly even after fire touched my stockinged feet. The tent fly and the bottom of my blankets had caught from a fat-pine slab we had used as a bridge from the tent to the fire. I scrambled up to tear away the blazing tentcloth, and stamp out the smoldering blankets.

Dan woke to ask, "Why the dancing bear performance, Paul?"

I answered, "A little blaze, that's all. It's out now."

As I sat down to appraise the damage to my feet, Miss Eula, in a woolen cloak and carrying a lighted candle, came to me with a jar of ointment. "You must let me rub this on your burns," she said. "We can't have you limping through the dismal swamps tomorrow."

"It's nothing," I objected, but she insisted. "Here, turn around so that I can get at your feet." She stripped off the blackened socks, and took my big farmer's boy feet in her lap, saying, "I saw you dancing; it wasn't funny," and presently, "Stand up, and see how the feet feel now."

"They're all right," I said, stamping.

Her competent fingers and firm palms as she rubbed the ointment into my feet had been as unexciting as though it had been Dan who doctored me; and I reflected with pride on her unthinking rectitude, the pure spring of her impulse.

From the pillow of Dan's shoulder, Ellen called, "When are you two going to sleep again?"

"Soon," Miss Eula answered. "As soon as Paul is comfortable. I'm sorry you were awakened."

In the morning, as I started to walk ahead, Miss Eula suggested, "Why don't you drive Ellen, and let Dan explore?"

"No, I'm all right," I said. Not blistered feet nor parched hands, had they been even worse than they were, could have driven me to the spring seat beside Ellen and the sly taunts I was sure I would hear about Miss Eula's ministrations.

Near the first deep stream marked on our rough map, we became trapped in a bog of stiff clay. My wagon stuck in it, and Dan and I spent laborious hours unloading, getting the wheels free, and reloading. Then, coming to the stream, we found it distinguishable from a vast spreading overflow only by a swifter current that made a winding lane among the trees.

Dan suggested that I should cross first, "Your heavy load will prevent the wagon box from floating off if you get into swimming water." He was right; Miss Eula and I crossed without wetting our feet. Dan followed, and as the light wagon reached the current its front wheels dropped away from the body. Coley and the front wheels went on while Ellen and Dan, who was compelled to drop the lines to prevent drowning the horse, floated crazily down stream to lodge against a tree.

Their situation would have been laughable if it had been less perilous. Ellen was hysterical with fright, gripping Dan's arm with the desperation of a drowning person[.] (I saw the purple marks made by her fingers on his bicep as he and I cleansed mud from our bodies at the night camp.) From the uncertain perch where he and Ellen sat, Dan shouted, "Paul, get out that length of bedcord, tie a hammer to one end, and throw it to me." When he had the stout cord in his grasp, Miss Eula and I hauled away in the slippery overflow and slowly brought the odd craft to land.

Ellen broke into wild sobbing as we helped her to the trunk of a fallen tree. Her words, when she could speak, were unintelligible to me, and Miss Eula explained, "I believe she is crying in French for her papa." Dan held her tight in his arms, soothing, "There, my beloved, you're safe. With God's help, I will always keep you safe."

"Will you, Dan! Will you, lover! Oh, love me always this way!" She kissed him with tear-salty lips avidly, passionately.

At the next swollen bayou, after I had put my wagon across, Dan found two bankside trees growing close together and felled them with an axe to make a crude bridge over which to carry Ellen and then, when the trunks had been trimmed and adjusted, to roll the light wagon across on its hubs. Dan was resourceful, clever with his hands and tools.

In the last sixty miles, after leaving the Trace, snow added to our misery. Now we came to know the real meaning of grief, sodden bedding, moldy food, chilled and stiffened hands and feet, ice-coated clothing, bleak and seemingly endless stretches of Mississippi swampland, frequent chopping and spading down of steep banks, an awful weariness that took hold of our bones. Dan and I bristled with beards that throve on our exhaustion; we were gaunt slime-caked scarecrows. The deep hem of Miss Eula's dress, too, was sodden and filt[h]y. Only Ellen preserved some semblance of a lady in distress.

We marveled that we did not come down with a malignant fever, though I heard afterwards from long hunters that winter exposure and short rations never hurt them as long as they were in camp. Only after they returned to beds, hearths and plentiful food were they stricken by colds, chills and fever.

After leaving the Trace, Dan estimated our best day's travel as seven miles; and one day we made no more than a mile; "hardly worth breaking camp this morning," Dan said cheerfully, sitting down on a wet log to relax as completely as though it had been a couch in the parlor of his Vermont home. He was beanpole thin, but all the heaving and grubbing and chopping and hauling he had done could not dull his spirit. I saw his eyes following the movements of Miss Eula as she juggled pots and skillet to prepare the best supper she could from our meager supplies. I knew he was thinking, There's spunk for you!

Fortunately, it was not until we were within five miles of Elliott Mission station that the front axle of my wagon broke, letting Miss Eula and me down with a sudden bump. Dan looked the wreck over. "We could probably repair it ourselves in a day, but I believe one of us," he looked questioningly at me, "should push on to Elliott with Ellen and Miss Eula, and send back the blacksmith."

"I'll stay and look after the team," I offered.

So they left me beside the brush-hidden stump that had caused the mishap; and for twenty-four hours I had rest, and opportunity to think soberly about the business of being a missionary helper in the wilderness.

I had heard Dan say that the Cause demanded only the able and resourceful among the hardy breed that New England was sending to the far corners of the world with axe and Bible, with stout hearts and the Mission Board's flaming tracts. I had thought, It is an honor to be chosen for an outpost soldier of the Lord.

This I believed. Yet I know that except for my resolution to follow Dan I should now be flinching from such ordeals as we had suffered and might face again. Except for Dan, I would be planning how I might most quickly escape from Elliott and get back to the familiar snow-covered fields and the indoor comforts of the old Bennington farm, the winter frolics, next March's sugaring off, next summer's haying, Aunt Lydia's brown bread and crisp doughnuts. Save in my brief contact with the dying Catherine Swan, I had felt no martyr's zeal for the task of teaching the Indians the story of Christ crucified and a knowledge of the white man's way of living.

Like others who had come to the Cherokees from a world troubled by politics, ranting religious hypocrisy, and greed for land, I had thought that the red men lived more sanely than the whites. They had held more firmly to their tried beliefs and customs, had been more diligent in putting first things first. I had thought sometimes, Perhaps we are the heathens.

Yet Dan was right when he said that, like it or not, the Indians must learn our language and adjust themselves to what we called Christian civilization. English-teaching schools must be opened to them, and shops and mills provided. The white man's knowledge of farming must be theirs. He had added, with fervor: "However men twist, travesty, or ignore the teachings of Christ, they will prevail. Always remember, Paul, that upon no other foundation can a people live securely . . ."

In the afternoon I built two roaring fires, lugged water to heat in our big iron kettle and, standing between the fires on a strip of clean bark, scrubbed myself with lye soap, then washed my mud-grimed clothing. The bath made a new man of me; and when I had painfully razored the thick growth from chin and cheeks and put on clean dry garments, I felt like the Paul Wear of a year ago going out to hitch Grey Lady to the pung for an evening of fun. I wondered what Abbey Wheeler, who had looked with favor upon me before I joined

Dan, would say if she could see me now? Probably, "Paul, your clothes are a sight, wrinkled like Granny Sanders' face; and you are sadly in want of a hair-cut." Well, I would get the hair-cut and have my coat and pantaloons ironed smooth at Elliott. Then Dan and I would start for Arkansas as good as new.

Miss Eula and Ellen would have some quiet months with the families of Mr. Orr, Doctor Pride, and Mr. Hitchcock. The women at Elliott would be grateful for Miss Eula's practical help, but what of Ellen? How she would endure Dan's long absence I could not guess. She might be a trial to the ladies, as she had been at times at Kingslake, or she might determine to show them how charmingly efficient she could be. I thought, She is unpredictable.

The Mission smith came out with Dan the next morning; and our big wagon pulled up before the main log house of Elliott station at sunset of the last day of the year.

Mr. Orr came out to shake hands, and say, "Brother Paul, you are indeed welcome. In time for our New Year's turkey, too!"

Three

In early February we heard that Billy Patton, a trapper of Okolona, would pass Elliott Mission on the way to the Walnut Hills with peltry, and we made ready to join him. To the two saddles with capacious leathern pockets closed by bearskin flaps already provided, we added ample saddlebags. We learned how to roll our blankets tightly and tie the rolls to our saddles so that they were protected from rain by the skirts of our cloaks.

We carried such food as could most easily be prepared, including tom-fulla, the Choctaw ration of parched cornmeal sweetened with boiled-down berry juice. We carried also the customary circuit rider's leathern cup and horn spoon, a medicine kit, a Bible and tracts wrapped in waterproof cloth.

The slow pace of Billy's pack train sometimes irked Dan, but I liked taking eleven days to cover a distance we might otherwise have made in six. We both liked long-haired Billy's windy stories, his comments on Indian character, and his arguments as to the credibility of Bible stories. Once he said, "Ye caint tell *me* a woman was made outen a man's rib. I'd ruther hold with the Injuns that say she was made outen the tip of a man's tongue, she talks so much an' caint keep a secret!"

It was diverting, too, helping Billy to unload and load the bales of skins, learning how to secure them firmly on cross-buck pack saddles, driving the horses to water and watching them roll in the dirt when relieved of their burdens, shooting squirrels from treetops and skewering their plump dressed bodies on sticks to roast along with biscuit dough to bake to a tasty brown.

Our ways parted at the junction of the Mississippi and the Arkansas rivers, Billy waiting there for a down-river boat that would take his cargo to the New Orleans market, and we embarking with our horses on a side-wheeler for Montgomery's Point. We took the steamboat captain's advice to land our horses there, to be taken across country to Arkansas Post. "Thereby," he said, "you'll be saved a hard trip with the animals through cypress-knee swamps. You can hire a skiff at Montgomery's, row across the White River cut-off, then take an Arkansas River boat at the Post.["]

Waiting at Montgomery's Point for the skiff promised "any day now" by the innkeeper, Dan's thrifty instincts were outraged by the charge of a dollar a day each for the dirty, lice-infected room we shared and the food reeking of rancid fat. There, we had our first close-up view of the institution of slavery. A Louisiana planter bound for a new plantation he was stocking in the Territory of Arkansas, was there with a fine stallion, a pack of hunting dogs, and a black "boy"; and kept them all chained in a filthy shed.

The mistress of the inn was absent when we arrived, and the master spent his nights gambling with army men and his days sleeping. His nearly naked blacks ran the inn with wild disregard for cleanliness or the guests' comfort. The morning after our arrival we saw from the window a huge mud-coated hog overturn the kettle in which, at an outdoor fire, milk was being warmed for the breakfast coffee. The hog gulped at the contents until a negro woman beat it off; and then she merely righted the kettle and added more milk.

Grinning, Dan said, "I don't believe I shall take milk with my coffee this morning; what about you, Paul?"

"The thought of it makes me want to puke!"

The next day the inn's hostess landed from a Cincinnati boat, a loud blowsy creature hung with more gauds than I had ever seen on a Christmas tree. She brought home with her a widowed daughter of twenty-two and a grandson of four. The child spent his first evening at the inn in the card room, leaning against his grandfather's shoulder and commenting on the poker game. At supper, his vivacious mother had said, "I aim to learn him to talk like a man. Andy, what do you call Gran'ma?"

He shrilled, "A damn ole bitch!" A roar of laughter went up, and loudest of all was the grandmother's shriek.

Dan muttered angrily, "The boy's probably right, but it sickens me to hear such words from a baby's lips."

I said, "Why go farther if we want to enlighten the heathen?"

"I know, Paul, we might try to sweeten the bitter grapes in our own vineyards. But this is not our work. May God help those who have the responsibility to realize its seriousness."

Both of us were remembering a Tennessee camp meeting we had visited while at Kingslake. It had been an astounding orgy of slavering exhortation, wild shouting, piercing screams; of a strange hysteria that struck so hard that men and women fell to the ground, rigid, to be carried away and laid in rows until, hours later, they came to life, rose, and began screaming again that they had been saved; of drunken rowdies riding at a gallop through groups of praying women; of boys and girls taken by "the jerks" bobbing insanely faster and faster, throwing themselves backward until their heads almost touched the earth then forward so that their hair swept their toes; of an ape-like exhorter swinging through the air on a long grapevine as he thundered, "I'm a-goin' to drap right daown on the ole devil's back, folks, an' ride him clean back to the gates o' hell! Oh, brothers an' sisters, watch him buck an' snort an' break wind when I drap; an', oh, brothers an' sisters, look out, fer I'm about to drap!"

"Hallelujah!" they screamed; and we saw women so crazed that they tore off their clothes and ran, jerking their heads with such violence that their streaming hair cracked like whiplashes.

As we went about the meeting ground at night with two elders of the vigilance committee, we came upon a huddle of men under a platform fighting to get at the strumpet who lay in their midst laughing. We heard from another group the gusty gibe, "Ole Ben Rowe's Betty'll shore be big-bellied six months from now, but Rile Petty says he'll be damned to hell afore he'll wed her . . ."

Rowing away from the mud, the rooting hogs, the lice and fleas, the raucous bawdiness of the landlady, and the concentrated profanity of her drunken husband, Dan blew out his breath in relief. "Phew, Paul, I'm thankful that Ellen and Miss Eula did not have to endure Montgomery's Point!"

I must not forget the monstrous blood-sucking mosquitoes that had swarmed around our faces by day and besieged us, under the torn netting of our beds, by night. Over the still water of the cut-off, we found them at their worst. During the three days and two nights of our passage to Arkansas Post we could neither rest from fighting them off nor sleep even in the smoke of smudge fires beside which we lay.

Except for those pests, we would have enjoyed our rowing, by turns, through the flooded forest ringing with early spring birdsongs, alive with chattering squirrels, ech[o]ing the thunder of wild pigeons in flight, and pleasantly creepy at night.

We came to the Post with faces pocked by mosquito bites, and aching for sleep, to find lodging in a paradise of cleanliness: snow-white and fragrant linen sheets, gossamer-like untorn netting over our beds, excellent food, and a motherly welcome from the Methodist wife who kept the house. Our horses had come through the cypress swamps uninjured. We waited cheerfully for the boat that, we hoped, would carry us the four hundred miles to Hebron Creek landing.

Dan yearned for Ellen, and talked about her with Mrs. Bevers, showing her the miniature of his wife which he wore next to his heart. She listened sympathetically, saying, "I don't wonder you're lonesome for such a lovely lady. I just know I'd love her myself. She would be so welcome, too, for it has been two years since I've known anyone you could rightly call a lady."

Hardly less acutely, I longed for the brook music of Miss Eula's voice, her cool loveliness, the comfort of her presence. I told myself that she was like a dear sister. That was true, and it was true also that I imagined her affection ripening into a love that would find consummation in my arms. I thought, It's so logical, too, for the missionary's helper to marry the female teacher.

Dan worked at the planning of the station we were to establish (he hoped on Hebron Creek), using information the Board had given us and other facts and hints picked up from Billy Patton, the river captain, the planter from Louisiana, and Mr. Bevers. He would sit for hours figuring the New York prices and shipping charges for necessary house furnishings, school supplies, plows, hoes and axes, clothing and books, estimating the amount of flour, sugar, tea and coffee we should probably require. Concerning coffee, he asked, "Paul, don't you think we might get along without it?"

"The Indians like it," I reminded him.

"Yes," he agreed, "and of course we'll have other visitors who will expect it. Our station must be a welcome port of call for all, red, white, or black."

I ventured to suggest, "Since there's certain to be more household work than Aunt Ellen and Miss Eula can do and attend to their own duties, we might buy a black woman for the kitchen."

"Paul!" Dan's sharp word was a rebuke. Then he explained, "It is not politic for us to condemn slavery openly among people, Indians or whites, who take it for granted, but we won't countenance it in our own establishment. If we require a black, we will purchase her freedom, but we must never forget that we are under obligation to labor as diligently in the fields and kitchen as any hired man or woman."

"You and I have done that, Dan; and so has Miss Eula."

"But not Ellen, Paul? You're thinking that she has shirked many hard tasks? True, but she will learn our ways; she chose me and my way of living freely and gladly."

"So she did," I said, but I thought, A woman like Ellen can change her mind easily, and justify herself in a hundred ways.

On the Arkansas river boat, when at length it pulled away from the Post, the one vivid passenger was a hugely fat, graying man called Colonel Pease. He was the one man I ever knew who could outcurse the host at Montgomery's Point. He blasphemed with marvelous fluency, with an extraordinary power of invention, in a voice that all but shattered the walking beam of the boat. Once I observed Dan listening to a burst of profanity with the fascinated horror of a child gazing through the bars at a crazed and obscene baboon. The Colonel became aware of his staring, and roared, "You don't like my language, Sir?"

"I do not," Dan answered.

"Then god-damn your sniveling soul," he made as if to charge Dan, "I'll throw you off of this hellfired floating pigpen and whores' nest like I would a hunk of maggoty pork!"

"I shouldn't advise you to try it," Dan said quietly.

The big man halted to trumpet a question, "Are you, Sir, one of those damned sanctimonious Bible-totin' preachers that sow weakness and corruption among Indians that wouldn't wipe their feet on you if you didn't toll them in with grub for their bellies?"

"I'm a missionary, if that's what you mean," Dan answered.

"Well, try to convert me, you—" he broke into a flow of language so utterly foul that Dan, who had heard plenty of obscenity, grew pale. I begged, "Let me stop his filthy mouth with my fist."

"No." Dan held my arm, and smiled at the Colonel as he said, "Try to convert you to decency, Sir? No, thanks; I know my limitations."

As the boat churned its difficult way toward the new settlement of Little Rock, where the blasphemer deabarked, he lost no opportunity to display in Dan's hearing his awful virtuosity, but Dan's only comment was, "He is talented, Paul; I should like to know him in a saner mood."

"If he ever has one!"

"Of course, he has; he has been drunk ever since we first set eyes on him." I thought Dan the world's greatest optimist.

We had gone only a few miles from Little Rock before the *Mary C* stuck on a sandbar. The captain contrived to crawfish her off, and when the boat was a quarter of a mile back ordered full steam ahead in the hope that he might rush her over. But the try was fruitless.

Now stuck fast, the captain explained, with smiling river philosophy, "It's a matter of time, ladies and gentlemen. We'll stay here until there's a rise in the river, and that depends upon the melting of the snows in the Rockies. We may not move for a week, or a month."

Dan said, "If we may, we will unload our horses and push on overland." That was easily managed, and from the captain and others we received careful directions for reaching Hebron Creek. We loaded our horses heavily with provisions from the boat's reserve stock, and walked. That night we camped in a pleasant wild meadow.

Next day the going was so easy that we covered twenty miles, and discovered that our feet were blistered; and Miss Eula was not there with her ointment! Bathing helped, but on the following day of humid heat we were hobbling like two aged and crippled men and made hardly ten miles, camping at night beside a rainpool covered with green scum. Dan mentioned the word malaria as we skimmed the scum aside to dip water for cooking; and through the night we fought mosquitoes.

Three days later, still limping, I was taken by a strange chilling rigor. I grew dizzy, and felt that my bones were bursting from an agonizing pressure. Dan made camp, then went to his saddlebag for the Peruvian bark which he had been advised at Kingslake to include in his medicine kit for the treatment of what Doctor Butram called bilious and remittent fever.

I had a bad night, but in the morning felt so nearly normal that we pushed on. On the following day, however, another severe attack disabled me.

So it went, alternate days finding me chipper and bone-shaken by what we learned later to call fever and ague. I could take but little food, and grew progressively weaker. I was tortured by a thirst which could not be appeased. My face was drawn and haggard, like that of a very old man, and my clothes hung on me like the flapping dress of a scarecrow. Dan continued to dose me with Peruvian bark, saying, "If I recall Doctor Butram's words correctly, Paul, the cure is certain provided the patient survives the treatment. You should ride tomorrow; I'm sure I could pack the equivalent of your present weight."

"No," I objected, "I won't ride until I'm compelled to."

At the edge of the Cherokee country, a settler urged us to stay until I was rid of the shakes, but I insisted that we push on to Tahlon-tees-kee's town, saying, "We've been too long on the way already." However, Dan secured another horse and hired as guide a

Cherokee who could speak English, and our situation seemed decidedly more cheerful as we went on, I on the new horse and Dan laboring to extract from the guide as much information as he could about the location of the Arkansas Cherokee towns.

Perhaps the Indian suspected Dan's motive in questioning him, for he left us without explanation at the end of the day. Before going, he pointed to a distant ridge beyond which he said we would find John Looney, a Cherokee who could direct us farther.[*] He refused an offered dollar for his service.

We had come into a dry, hilly region, and camped beside a water hole from which we had our first taste of alkali. Dan had developed an alarming thirst, and going to drink found a water snake at the edge of the pool. It slid away, and he called to me as he raised his head from the pool, "Paul, do you suppose the snake could have poisoned the water? It tastes very bitter."

I warned him against drinking, took a canteen and rode away in search of sweet water. But I returned too late to save him from the griping pains brought on by the draughts he had not been able to resist taking. To add to his misery, he was seized by the shakes—a worse attack, if that were possible, than mine had been.

We remained at this camp twenty-four hours, Dan lifting his head from time to time to take liberal doses of the bitter powder that was curing me. On the second day he was able to ride in comparative comfort, and we set out for the ridge. To our camp near a Cherokee town that night an Indian who spoke broken English brought the head man. He looked us over critically, and talked at length with the interpreter, who rendered the words as a jumble of conflicting directions for finding John Looney. "Good man, that John Looney," he said, "most white. Best you go so," he pointed, "maybe so four, six mile, turn it that way, an' soon you come his house."

I drew a rough map in the dirt as he talked, and the head man, stooping to examine it, nodded. Then, abruptly, they left us.

Next morning, we found the interpreter waiting to put us on the way. It turned out to be a tortuous trail, but to Dan's protests that we were being led around Robin Hood's barn, the Indian only said, "This good road, follow it all time."

Early in the afternoon, the guide vanished. One moment he was going on ahead of us with his easy sliding gait, and the next moment he was not to be seen. Dan halted, and exclaimed, "Why do [you] suppose he did that!"

"Perhaps," I suggested, "he has led us into an ambush."

"Don't be silly, Paul. This is no story-book expedition through hostile country." After looking at the sun, and studying the outline of a timbered hill toward the west, he said, "We may as well move on; we can't assume that he has led us astray."

Near the top of the long slope the trail ceased to exist; only radiating deer runs indicated exits from the small glade in which we had paused. Dan said, "We'll make camp, and sleep on the problem. I feel a chill coming on."

I rode off to find water, but as darkness fell I had discovered no trace of it, and I was in doubt as to the direction of our camp. I shouted, and waited for a response from Dan, but it was only after I had sent up a dozen loud cries that I heard, faintly, a metallic clang, and I said to myself, "It's Dan beating on our camp kettle."

When I came in he was lying beside the kettle, too weak to rise and unable to speak above a whisper. Sick at heart, I shook my empty canteen, and Dan whispered, "Never mind, Paul, we'll find water tomorrow."

During the night he wore out the worst of the attack of ague. Next morning, however, staggering from the ordeal, he was just able to mount; and he rode with an awful set look on his face, chewing a twig in the effort to keep his mouth damp, never once mentioning water. I, too, was agonizingly thirsty; and the horses chewed their bridle bits and tossed their heads incessantly to advertise their terrible thirst. I suggested that we turn back to the Indian town, saying, "That fellow may have made a mistake in directing us."

"No," Dan shook his head. "I know now that it was not a mistake. We must go forward, find our own way."

These were desert mountains, utterly new to us. Gravelly ridges, one after another, their slopes unbroken by living streams, came to loom like monstrous cairns marking the graves of travelers unused to them as we were. In a bone-dry ravine, near sunset, the horses stopped, and refused to budge though I beat them with all the strength that remained to me. Dan signed to me to stop, being unable to speak, and slid from his saddle like a half-empty bag of meal. I somehow removed the packs and saddles, but did not tether the horses, believing that they lacked life enough to stray.

The day had been scorching hot. Dan's face, hands, and arms (he had rolled his sleeves to his shoulders, as he had used to do in the hayfield in Vermont) were blistered to a yellowish red. That night he became delirious, passed beyond the reach of any possible comfort words of mine might give. I tried again and again to get through to his understanding, "Don't you see, Dan, we've got to keep our heads for the sake of Aunt Ellen and Miss Eula? We love them too dearly to desert them. Likely you don't know, but I love Miss Eula. I want to live for her."

Thrashing about, sometimes on his blankets and sometimes wallowing in the gravel in an agony compounded of thirst, the torture of blistered skin, and a bone-shattering ague, he muttered only unintelligible words thickly. Yet at times he seemed to strive mightily to fight through the fog that blanketed his mind, forcing himself to lie still, and grinding his teeth as if to crush out the life of a devil pitchforking a way down his throat.

Daylight showed me that our horses were gone. I felt like breaking into tears and yielding to the madness that had taken Dan and might bring me merciful release from conscious agony. Then I thought, Perhaps the horses scented water, and gained strength in the night to find it.

I got Dan to his feet, telling him in the words we had used as youngsters on the Vermont farm that we must follow our teams to water and fetch them back if we were to get any plowing done by noon. "Plowing?" he croaked weakly. "Yes, yes, plowing."

Half carrying him, I followed the snake track made by Coley's trailing stake rope. When Dan stumbled, and swayed forward to fall, I braced myself against his weight and prayed for strength to hold him upright, for I felt sure that I could not again lift him if he went down.

At mid-morning, as we stood propped against the trunk of a scrawny pine tree, I heard faintly the sound of human voices. I listened intently, thinking, If I am not delirious and hearing things, there are many voices, and gay. I saw Dan's head lift; he, too, had heard.

I could not shout, but the sound of voices did give me the power to help Dan across a last incredibly difficult ridge below which scores of Cherokees were camped under a great gushing spring preparing for a ball play.

None saw us until we [were] quite near, then there was a rush of young men to carry us to the spring. Mercifully, they held us from the water, to squeeze drops only from clean soaked cloths into our mouths and upon our parched lips. As the awful thirst abated, there came upon us, to judge from Dan's expression, such relief as a sinner, pictured by a ranting evangelist as snatched from the pit of hell, might feel as he walked in the flowery fields of Eden.

By nightfall, with Dan rational again, we were permitted to drink freely; and the women fed us a thin stew of bear meat, spoonful by slow spoonful, until we were no longer hungry. Our horses were found the next day on the stream which flowed from the spring, as we were told by the young man Da-tsi-da-hi (The Runner) who came to talk with us, and men had been sent to bring in our saddles and camp gear. The Runner told us that he had gone to school at Springplace, in Georgia, where that fine Moravian missionary Abraham Steiner had taken him in. He said that the head man at The Boot's town who had undoubtedly sent us into the waterless hills to die must have taken us for agents of the Governor of Arkansas Territory who was actively scheming for the removal of the Cherokees from that region.

I recall from The Runner's talk this harsh outbreak: "That white man would make our people like unto the Ishmaelites, and it is not strange that some of our war chiefs like The Boot want to kill such an enemy, and die in battle themselves against those who would rob us. So would we all willingly die if by dying we could bring peace and security to our children."

"Of course," Dan said, "but the sacrifice would be useless. The Cherokees must learn the ways of the whites, and prepare to meet them as equals at their own game."

"And you have come to help us prepare," The Runner said. "I know that you have a good heart. When you are able to ride, I will take you to John Jolly; he is now head chief of the Arkansas Cherokees in place of his brother Tah-lon-tees-kee. If you wish then, you may go to the agent of the United States to make whatever further arrangements are necessary."

Dan thought it politic to visit the Government agent at Round Rock first; and though he was still feeble, haggard, and jaundiced, and I proposed that we should stay for the three days of ball play and feasting, he insisted on leaving our new friends at noon of the following day. The Runner led us to the agent's house.

His wife came to the door in answer to Dan's hail, telling us before she had a good look at his face that Mr. Coppege would not return for ten days from a trip through the Indian country. Then, as her eyes took in Dan's haggard yellowed face, she started back, gasped, "Yellow fever!" and slammed the door. She would not touch the letter to her husband which Dan carried, but when she had listened to its reading through a crack in the door, she said we might occupy a detached cabin until the agent came home.

It was fortunate that we had shelter now, for Dan was called upon to endure days of such concentrated misery as Job must have known. He became a mass of suppurating blisters; he could not sleep, and to lie down was agony; he could take no more than a taste of the food Mrs. Coppege sent out to us by a black woman whose mouth was stuffed with tansy as a precaution against contagion.

As doctor and nurse, I was not a shining success, though I could somewhat relieve Dan's shakes with our dwindling supply of Peruvian bark, managed a change of clothing and scrubbed the garments he had worn.

Gradually he came back to life, the scabs fell away from his clearing skin, and his appetite returned. With something of the old quizzical twist of his lips, he said, "I can understand now, Paul, why I took the trouble to rear you from a cub!" It was his expression of gratitude for my care.

"Both of us know now that you're mighty hard to kill," I said.

"And we know, too, the meaning of real grief, don't we?"

Four

Our credentials inspected by the Arkansas Indian agent, and Dan fit to ride again, we went on to visit with John Jolly in his comfortable cabin home and learn from that able civil chief the situation facing the Western Cherokees.

Through no fault of their own, they were at war with the more numerous Osage tribe, and they were being harassed by the white settlers of Arkansas Territory. Jolly explained it this way: "White men wanted Osage lands 'way up north, so the men at Washin'ton tell them to move south to Missouri an' Arkansas an' make treaty with them that say they can stay in these new place forever. Forever mean twenty year! Then Washin'ton set aside part of Osage lands in Arkansas for Cherokees if they will come west out of Georgia an' Tennessee, but Washin'ton make no new treaty with Osages an' don' tell Cherokees they have no right to Osage lands. Four thousand of us have come here, an' Osages say we mus' get out. So we mus' fight for our homes an' stock and fields.

"At same time, white settlers of Arkansas want Cherokees an' Osages too moved out. There is no peace for us."

"Why," I asked, "has the Government done this?"

Dan answered for Jolly, who nodded assent as he spoke: "Paul, the explanation is as simple as A B C. The Government at Washington is a government of the people, and the people are hungry for more and more land. They, or their land-hungry fathers, came from England, and other countries across the water, where land is hard to come by and is man's most valued possession. Their hunger has grown keener as it has been fed with one enormous gobbling of Indian lands after another. It will not be satisfied, even when every tribe has yielded its last acre, for then the land-hungry will fight one another until they are destroyed, or until the envy and scheming in their hearts are resolved by the power of Christ's teaching. You and I will never know that peace, but we can hope and pray for it honestly, work for it with all our heart and strength. Here is our field of labor, and I thank God that it is a promising one."

Jolly said, "Your words are good; we are glad you come to work with us. Now, you go an' talk with Ta-ka-to-ka. He is head war chief of Western Cherokees."

We found the old war leader bitter, not only against the whites but against the Osages whom he called liars. Through his interpreter, he said that they made promises of peace which they did not mean to keep, raiding Cherokee towns after saying they had no quarrel with their people. "One time," Ta-ka-to-ka said, "any man can deceive me by lying. But two times, no! The Osages lie to us many times, so they must get out of the road."

Later, the Governor of Arkansas Territory sent a major general of militia to persuade Ta-ka-to-ka to council with the Osages. He came to our mission to secure Dan's help. In dress uniform, to impress the Indians, his sword clanking on the puncheon floor, he railed against the Cherokee war chief's stubbornness, and ended his tirade by saying, "By God, Sir, if the old heathen refuses to attend the council, I'll hang him to the nearest limb! I'll tell him so. Don't you agree that would fetch him?"

"I'm afraid it wouldn't," Dan answered. "I know the old man well; I believe he would laugh at your threat."

Dan was right, for when the general deemed it more prudent to send by us a paper talk, the war chief spat upon it, threw it to the ground, ground it to shreds with the heel of his moccasin, and without a word strode to his cabin. An unholy light came into Dan's eyes, and he said, "Paul, we have been talking with a man! I wish he were one of us."

But it was months after Ellen and Miss Eula had reached Hebron Creek, making the journey without mishap, that Ta-ka-to-ka came to us, saying through an interpreter, as he flashed his black eyes on Dan, "John Jolly wishes me to talk with this man. He says this man has a straight tongue. I did not know he came to me that time only as messenger bearing that paper from that man who want us to talk with the Osages. Now I will listen if he will tell me why he is here."

Dan said we were there to teach Ch[r]ist and His love. The war chief nodded, "Yes, that is what John Jolly and other good men say. But I do not understand why if the Christ man was a good man and showed the white people the right road they killed him. We would not do that."

Our plans for instructing the Cherokees in the ways of the whites he thought illogical, "If that Great Father the President wanted the Cherokees to follow your road, why did he send us to the west with a blanket and a rifle gun instead of with a hoe and a spelling book?"

Dan shrugged, and after Ta-ka-to-ka had gone said, "There's a philosopher worth knowing."

Ellen gibed, "I believe you prefer him to your college teachers."

"Perhaps," Dan admitted.

The way Dan had talked about religion evidently stuck in the war chief's mind, for when our school supplies arrived and Miss Eula was preparing to receive the first scholars he came to us again, saying, "As you have told me about it, and I have studied about what you have said, it is like what we believe. What your priests say about the creation of man and the coming of sin is nearly the same as we have always believed."

In that talk, Ta-ka-to-ka asked Dan to explain the daily appearance and disappearance of the sun. In the discussion, Dan took him to the spring, filled a bucket and whirled it around his head without spilling the water in order to show how the earth could rotate completely each day without tumbling everything off into space. The old man nodded, and said, "I see now that you are right. I was never satisfied when our priests told us the sun went down through a hole in the ground and came up through another. Such big holes, I believed, would weaken the earth's foundations too much."

Touching the schoolroom globe, he asked, "What big bird laid that egg?" As Dan explained, launching into elementary astronomy, the movement of planets, and the reasons for changing seasons, Ta-ka-to-ka listened to the interpretation intently. Turning away at length, he said, "I will come again, and when I am able to understand more I will take that thing so that I can show the truth to the people."

From Ta-ka-to-ka we heard more of the Cherokees' belief in witchcraft than any one had told us before. "I do not believe in witches," he said. "I have tried to stop the people from killing them. I do not believe what the conjurors say. One time I watched one stop the pain in a woman's tooth by touching it with the ends of one finger and a thumb. I saw that first he rubbed them hard against his shirt. I said, 'I can do the same thing,' and for another one with pain in the tooth I did. So they said I was a conjuror, but it was not so. Do you know why I could do that?"

Dan answered by feeling the horn-hard tips of the old man's finger and thumb and saying, "Of course, you generated enough electricity by the hard rubbing to drive away the toothache for a time." When he understood the explanation, Ta-ka-to-ka laughed and said, "You see, it is easy to be a conjuror!"

In the healing power of herbs, however, as some of the medicine men and wise women prepared them, the old man had faith. He had seen scrofulous ulcers cured with poultices of bean leaves, and slippery elm bark swabs, soaked in cold water, used successfully to disinfect bullet wounds. He told of a man who had been cured of cholera by his mother, who heated stones for blistering his feet, covered him thickly with scalding corn meal mush mixed with clabber milk, and dosed him with an infusion of red peppers. Listening, Dan smiled and said, "Yes, I believe that treatment would either cure or kill!" Then, "I see why she used clabber instead of water to cook the mush poultice; it would hold the heat longer."

Dan and the war chief became close friends. They were alike in their desire to know the truth, and in their scorn of lies and hypocrisy. I saw Dan nod with understanding when Ta-ka-to-ka told how he had at last been persuaded by the eloquence of Chi-kil-leh to treat for peace with the Osages. "I allowed myself to be overcome. I cried like a woman, and I spoke for the Cherokees at the council before I slept, after Chi-kil-leh ended his talk at sundown."

"Why," I asked, "didn't you change your advice next morning when you were no longer under that man's spell?"

He answered, "A man speaks only once."

Dan said, "That is so," and said to me afterwards, "That man has great power among his people because there is in him no shadow of vanity or insincerity."

There were others among the head men we came to know who measured up to Dan's exacting standard: Ta-ka-e-tuh, the war chief's aged uncle, Dik-keh the Just, The Blanket, John Looney, Black Fox, Flowers, and Sequoyah, who was doing his own effective missionary work by teaching his way of writing the Cherokee language to all whom he could reach, and that meant nearly the whole of the tribe in Arkansas and the East.

"Some day, Paul," Dan once half promised, "I may write down what I know of the great ones of the tribe"; and because he did find time during the years that were crowded with work to jot down in his journal many pages of clear brief notes, I am able to tell the greater part of this story.

It was the century-old Ta-ka-e-tuh who talked most about the old beliefs that were passing, and the solemn rites that had degenerated into meaningless revels after the Delaware Indians had captured from the Cherokees their sacred symbols, their Ark of the Covenant. "No," he insisted, "these things were not idols; it is foolish to worship idols." However, he would not say what the lost symbols were;

it was enough for us to know that when they had proved vulnerable the faith of the people was shaken.

"Well, why not?" Dan said. "It has happened again and again; and only faith in the everlasting power of Christ to redeem man can survive the accidents of fate."

Miss Eula's faith was as simple and deep as Dan's, but she spoke with more diffidence with the old men. Only in the schoolroom was the resourcefulness of her language revealed. She had as many ways of explaining, in English and Cherokee, the meaning of words in Webster's Speller and Cumming's First Lessons in Geography as a woods cat has for catching birds. She made the scholars laugh with her at their attempts to pronounce the difficult consonants of our language. She would say, "It is just as hard for me to speak your words, for I must keep my lips apart while you must learn to close your lips and teeth on many of our words. Now, you, John Knox Witherspoon, say your English name very slowly, then I will try to say the name of the boy next to you, Uh-lah-gah-ti . . . See, I can do no better than you! We will try again."

As the children lost their shyness and began to look upon the schooling as a game in which it was honorable to excel, she undertook to teach grammar, and the history of America. Under her coaching, they spoke dialogues, one based on the story of Joseph and his brothers, and recited pieces from the Columbian Orator. Sometimes a father visiting in the schoolroom rose to express his approval, and, as Dan said, proved himself a true orator by speaking what was in his mind in simple words and stopping when he had said it.

Ellen's duties were those of housekeeper and hostess. In her good moods she created an atmosphere of charming hospitality the fame of which extended to the limits of the Cherokee settlements. But she was often resentful of demands upon her time, and scornful of our Indian visitors. She did as little work with her hands as possible, saying, "It's much better to have the girls scrub, wash, iron, and cook than to send them back to their homes with only a little book learning and parrot talk about Jesus."

Ignoring the gibe at his faith, Dan agreed, but suggested, "Perhaps we ought to talk with the girls' parents before we try to make cooks and housemaids of all of them."

"Nonsense," Ellen protested. "It's the best possible training we could give them!" The wisdom of Dan's caution was shown when Wolfcatcher came to take away his daughter because, as he said proudly, he could buy slaves to do the work in his house. To cover Ellen's angry resentment of his words, Dan said, "If you are rich enough to do that, we should be glad to have you pay for your girl's lessons. Here, we are so poor that we must all work, like your slaves, with our hands in the field and the garden, care for our horses and oxen, and toil in the shop and forge."

Wolfcatcher considered Dan's words, stayed to watch our daily routine and, before riding away, not only agreed to leave his daughter but to send money. "Unless," he offered, "you would rather have my blacks haul corn to your crib, or fetch cotton for spinning and weaving."

When he had gone, Ellen sniffed, "It appears that we have a rich landed aristocracy among our savages!" However, she treated Wolfcatcher's girl thereafter with a new consideration.

Reports reached us of Mr. Worcester's ambitious plan to establish a print shop for the Cherokees of Georgia and Tennessee. He proposed to have types cast to reproduce the eighty-six characters which Sequoyah said were adequate to express the Cherokee language in writing. Printers were to be trained to set the type, and Cherokee translators found with sufficient English to render the meaning of the Scriptures and something of the news of the world to the literate tribesmen. With the press, a bindery was to be set up. When we first read of the project in the *Missionary Herald,* Dan said, "We must find out how this is to be done; if young Sam Worcester says it is practical, I believe it is."

We both knew Worcester, for he too had been reared in Vermont, at his father's parsonage not ten miles from the Wears' farm, and had worked at the same tasks we had performed. Seven generations of preaching Worcesters had preceded Sam, and like his missionary uncle he had prepared himself at Andover and Harvard for labor among the Indians. He had carried to the Eastern Cherokees, along with the Bible, extraordinary manual skill. He could slaughter a beef, cure pork, shoe an ox or a horse, keep accounts, do very well as a carpenter, sing and teach singing, and had learned the printer's trade. He was so like Dan that I thought of them almost as blood brothers.

Dan asked me, "How would you like to go back to Georgia and help Sam, learn to set Cherokee type, study the language, then come back to us and help us set up a print shop of our own?"

I did not want to go, did not want to leave Dan, from whom I had never been separated since I had been taken into his mother's home as a small child, nor Miss Eula. I could think of no convincing reason for refusing, however, until I remembered Sam Worcester's piece in the *Missionary Herald* about the enormous difficulties experts had met in attempting to make a grammar of the Cherokee language. There were, it seemed, a bewildering multiplicity of tenses and numbers, and a definiteness of meaning that made English, and even Greek, ambiguous by comparison. Only a young and exceptionally apt scholar, far apter than I, living in year-around contact with the Indians, could hope to learn it well enough to undertake putting the Scriptures into Cherokee.

Dan listened, and said, "Of course, Sam would know. We shall have to wait for some young Cherokee like Boudinot, educated in the East, although we may be able to train one. I suppose, too, it would be well to put off making plans until we are sure of the means to set up and maintain a shop. Sam is lucky to have the backing of Chief John Ross and funds of the tribe; and he is canny, too, in proposing to issue a newspaper and distribute it free to all who can not pay for it. Ross has a passion for enlightening his people, the better to resist their removal by the Government from Georgia and Tennessee."

So I stayed where I wanted to be, at his side and within hearing of Miss Eula's voice at meal times, at prayers, and at times in school vacations when I went with her to visit the families of her scholars.

On one such journey, more than a year after her arrival at Hebron Creek, I dared to tell her that I loved her and wanted her to be my wife. She let me come to the end of my limping declaration, then leaned to kiss my cheek and say, "Paul, I do love you dearly, but not in the way you desire. I feel towards you as I do towards my own kin. I have wanted to tell you this because I have known what was in your heart."

I cried, "I shall always love you, and want you!"

"I hope you will always love me, Paul," she said, and her words were a comfort.

Inevitably, we talked of Ellen and Dan. There, if I had known it, lay the key to my happiness. There was married love, revealed at times, as I thought, shamelessly by Ellen. It was far more passionate and demanding than the usual love relations of a missionary pair. Had I contrived to remove Miss Eula from association with Ellen and Dan, I am sure she would have married me. But she was, unconsciously, judging herself by Ellen; in her mind were memories of passionate scenes she could not help witnessing, and intimate loverly words Ellen had spoken in her hearing.

I remember Ellen saying once, when she must have known Miss

Eula and I were near, "Dan, I will not have a child! I want every drop of your blood, every ounce of your body, every shred of your affection for myself, as I've given you all of mine. I mean to keep myself as lovely as I can for you, I won't risk spoiling whatever beauty I have and keeping myself out of your arms for months while I am big with child. I won't have a child to share your love with. I won't coarsen my hands with work. My whole world is you, loving you is my only occupation, and will be as long as you want me that way."

The words must have struck deeply into Miss Eula's mind. She had, of course, made no sign that they had impressed her, and they probably seemed wild, but she knew they were spoken straight out of Ellen's heart. From them she could understand what hot physical love between a man and a woman meant. They may have been in her mind when I made my rather formal avowal. She may have asked herself what she could offer to a man of Dan's blood who loved and wanted her. True affection, companionship, submission of her body, children, with only the possibility of an aroused passion? Not enough; a vital man needed more. He needed the raptures of love that consumed then exalted him. He needed to spend himself utterly with his mate, so that he might be re-born to a more glowing life.

I may be wrong to believe that these thoughts ran through Miss Eula's mind, but I know she was sensitive and apt to catch the implications of Ellen's passionate outbreak.

What had stuck in my mind, as an ominous warning, had been Ellen's concluding words, "as long as you want me that way," and her cry in the Mississippi swamp, "Oh, Dan, always love me this way!" Would Dan always put her first? As he became more and more absorbed in the details that meant success in the work to which he had dedicated himself, as more and more difficult human problems were brought for solution by the people who were depending upon his wisdom and resourcefulness, could he continue to satisfy Ellen's avid appetites? She could not subjugate him, but she could hope to make a paradise of her arms that would give her the illusion that she was necessary. But what if he should tire of her raptures, her kisses, the eager pressure of her full breasts and rounded thighs?

To me, when she had yielded to the angry impulse to make Dan jealous, she had shown something of her equipment of seduction. Would she use it again, on me or another man, if Dan's fire should cool?

Below our casual talk about Ellen and Dan, I thought, ran currents that neither Miss Eula nor I dared to hint in words.

Five

The picture of our Hebron Creek station, and of the ordered life we led there for seven years, is clear in my mind. Pictures, rather, for the scene changed with the seasons and the years.

When Dan chose the site, he was remembering the swamp evils he and I had suffered, mosquitoes and the shakes. It was high ground on which he built, below a great spring which the Indians rightly assured us would never fail. Between the station buildings and Hebron Creek lay a sloping meadow dotted with trees, oaks, hickories, and black locusts, enough to supply timber and shade for our stock. Dan said, "We'll save the upper half of it for pasture, and use the creekside half as plowland." Above the spring rose the loamy timbered steeps of the Hebron hills where deer and wild turkeys used [*sic*].

I recall the first night Dan and I spent under our own roof. The first cabin was not finished, but we could set up the stove and beds that with other furnishings had come by slow stages from New York.

At dusk, Dan called in the Cherokee builders, lit candles and held a service of prayer. Then he and I filed out behind the workers, saw them go to their blankets under the trees, and stood for a time at the doorway exhilarated by the sweet air blown to us across the flowering meadow. The stars seemed incredibly near.

Dan said, "There's little really good farm land in the area the Arkansas Cherokees occupy, white land seekers have seen to that, yet in their way the hills and dales of Hebron are an Eden. The people have come to love them."

"This section," I said, "is something like that in Georgia between Springplace and New Echota."

"Yes," he nodded, "and let us hope that it may prove a welcome refuge."

By the time Ellen and Miss Eula arrived, Dan having gone to fetch them from Elliott, the Cherokee builders had added another cabin, set eighteen feet away and in line with the first, had roofed the intervening space and under the roof made a loft that would serve as sleeping quarters for me and any other single men who should spend the night. The newer cabin was for Miss Eula; and would serve also as a schoolroom until we expanded the station.

It is only fair to give Ellen's account of the place as she first saw it, taken from a letter to her father which later came into my hands:

"In my last, which I sent from the miserable huddle of cabins and dramshops called Little Rock, I told you of the trying journey from Elliott. It was much worse from Little Rock to the muddy, desolate landing of Hebron Creek; and I am unable to convey in words the filth, stenches, profanity and drunkenness of the ruffians—traders and soldiers—on the way to distant frontier posts.

"Dan left the river boat, at the urging of two savages who paddled out to it in a canoe, before we reached the landing at dusk, leaving Miss Benson and me to the *tender* care of the captain who assured us that he would provide shelter and protection until my husband returned to 'carry' us to the mission station.

"We stepped off into the light of flaring torches, to see only Indians and a few of their black slaves. The men wore pantaloons which might have been made from striped bed-ticking and gingham hunting shirts, with no covering for their heads save their long hair. The woman wore tight basques of calico, very full skirts of some drab woolen material, and leggings that were merely extensions of their deerskin moccasins. Looking upon the heathen, with my ears assaulted by the oaths of men discharging cargo and the revels on the boat, I thought, How can I dwell among such as these. I said to Miss B., 'I will not stir from here until Dan returns!'

"She said, calmly enough, 'It will not be necessary. The captain has arranged to have us conducted to a cabin nearby where we are to wait for him.'

"Presently a black woman tore herself away from the *fascinating* scene at the landing to lead us to the cabin and light candles. It was, of course, filthy. There was no window, only a door swung on leathern hinges which we must leave open lest we smother from the humid heat.

"It must have been midnight when Dan and Paul appeared, on horseback and with Indian ponies for Miss B. and me, accompanied by the two Cherokees who had taken Dan from the boat (why they did that Dan has not explained except to say that it was an emergency). The two Indians were to act as our escort to the mission station, then return to their homes with the borrowed horses. I was truly thankful for Dan's reappearance, although he laughed when I told him of my fear of the group of drunken men who passed near the door of the cabin. He said we had been as safe from molestation as though we had been in our drawing room in New York!

"We reached our wilderness *palace* just at daybreak, after hours of riding Indian ponies astride on rude Indian saddles. But as we traveled slowly, I got on well enough as we wended our way through the forests on trails that seemed to me no trails at all. Arrived at 'home, sweet home,' I simply fell off my pony. Of course, Dan must pick me up in his dear arms and carry me over the threshold, saying that otherwise I might not feel properly installed as chatelaine. I wonder if I shall ever feel at home here! It is no more than two rude huts, yet Dan and Paul, and even Miss B., believe it is the beginning of something quite grand."

Ellen was right about that; we others were proud of our clean-smelling cabin home. Our delight in it grew as we watched it expand to an ample U of buildings, with a bell fixed at the top of a tall post in the middle of the U playground. Detached from the main building were the later additions of kitchen, shop, barns, cribs and granary, storehouse, and quarters for the increasing number of workers we required. We took satisfaction in the sight of stock in our pasture, fields of silking corn and yellowing wheat, and the grist mill squatting over Hebron Creek for the slow grinding of our grain, and the wheat and corn our Indian neighbors brought in.

At times, Ellen seemed content, then her fear that she might be losing some crumb of Dan's devotion made her angrily exacting, although her tantrums seemed to pass lightly over his head.

One half of the three-sided main building included quarters for Ellen and Dan, Miss Eula's cabin, the schoolroom and dormitory for the girls, and the commons where everyone ate, Miss Eula at the top of one long table, Dan at the second, and I at the third. The other half of Main (as we called the integrated cabin units) was for the boys, who always greatly outnumbered the girls. My room was the dividing line between the sexes, the limit beyond which the boys could not go except at meal times.

Heaven knows I had enough worry over the boys, who had increased in numbers to seventy before we were compelled to give up the station. Yet I was thankful for the opportunity to help prepare them for what lay ahead.

Many came to us wild and scantily clothed, more especially after white depredations on Cherokee communities increased. In Arkansas, as in Georgia, the technique of "stealin' 'em blind" had been expertly developed. The boys hated the whites; and to make them realize that they must learn to walk in the white man's road, however hard it seemed, was a straining job. Without Dan's tact, patience, and resourcefulness, and the example of Miss Eula's firmness and her unshakeable faith in the girls, I'm afraid I would have bungled my job almost as miserably as Ellen did hers.

I carry in my mind a clear portrait of Miss Eula of those days in stout high-laced shoes, wearing a good black alpaca dress with a deep collar of fine cambric closed at the throat by a gold and ivory cameo brooch, her abundant chestnut-brown hair parted in the middle and drawn smoothly down and back to cover her ears and in some fascinating fashion folded under a round comb. Always mindful of her duty to be an example to the girls in the schoolroom, at table, on the playground, or on her rounds of the dormitory where they slept in clean blankets on scrubbed floors, she was never old-maidish.

Girls came under her care who were old enough to think about sweethearting, and with a conception of sex freedom utterly foreign to a lady bred in New England. Yet she was not outraged by their ideas and stratagems, saying, "We must be understanding, as I'm sure they try to be with us. They want to do right." Once I saw her face go white in anger, although she held her tongue, when Ellen jeered, "All these precious female savages above the age of twelve are bawds, or want to be!"

It was Dan who spoke sharply, "Ellen, what you have said is unfair and stupid. You will please never repeat it."

Ellen broke out, "Oh, you're fools, all of you, fools and hypocrites. With your praying and psalm-singing and sugar tits for the little beasts that laugh at you behind your backs, I'm sick of the whole dreary pretense!"

Dan said only, "When you come to your senses, Ellen, I will talk with you. Now go to your room." He spoke as to a child.

That night, I know (their room was next to mine) she wept in Dan's arms, kissed him wildly, and begged, "Darling, take me away from here before I go mad. I love you so much, want you and need you so much that it's killing me to lose you to those who care nothing for what you're doing for them."

His answer was, "I am doing the Lord's will, not my own. You must know that, my beloved." But she did not cease from complaining until he had given her the sedative of passionate love she craved.

In another letter written in those early days Ellen described for her father the visit of three Osage Indians who had come to talk with Dan after seeing John Jolly: "The four, Dan and the savages, sat in a circle on the floor surrounding the interpreter. It was warm, and soon the Osages threw off their short buffalo-skin cloaks, and I was horrified to see that they were stark naked except for necklaces of bears' claws and bits of cloth about their loins! What next must I endure . . . ? Dan told me, after I had fled the room, that they had wanted him to go in the interests of peace to prevail upon the Cherokee war chief to council with them, for it seems that my husband and that chief have become as thick as thieves because of some of Dan's childish demonstrations of his superior wisdom."

After she had lost the brief glow of missionary fervor which illuminated her when she fell in love with Dan, our routine was worse than dull for Ellen. It was deadly. She pictured it with bitter detail in another letter to Mr. Morin:

"Imagine, Papa, we are all out of bed before dawn, and breakfast is prepared by candle light (how many gross of candles are molded and burned in a year I would not dare guess). We must *all* partake of this Spartan repast of hominy and tea, then join in a service of song and prayer. Until nine, the girls work at household tasks and the boys in the stables, shop, or fields. At that hour a bell calls them to the school benches where Miss B. and Paul labor to cram down their throats the startling information that 'c-a-t' spells cat, that New York is a large seacoast city, and that four times six is twenty-four. Also, of course, the dear children must be taught not to wipe their noses on their sleeves nor spit upon the floor.

"The scholars (what a travesty on words thus to describe them!) are given from twelve to twelve-thirty for cleaning and prettying themselves for a dinner of pork, beef, or venison, cornbread and spring water. Afterwards they change to work clothes. The girls, under Miss B's direction, grind corn, spin, weave, sew, make quilts, while Paul, often assisted by Dan, keeps the boys from mischief by finding employment out of doors for their hands.

"Supper is served between sunset and dusk; tea again, hominy, cornbread and milk, sometimes butter (and once I recall how delighted Dan was when Miss B. provided doughnuts). Then comes a short play period and prayers before our precious charges are sent to their blankets.

"Saturdays, all are excused from classes, and spend the morning at what Dan and Miss B. call redding up. The afternoon is theirs to use in whatever games they choose, doll dressing or noisy play party riots for the girls, noisier ball play for the boys, or bow-and-arrow hunting expeditions to the Hebron Creek woods. Sunday is visiting day for parents; services in English and Cherokee; and, in the afternoon, singing and Sunday School.

"Month after month, we tread this round. Our young victims come and go, the unpronounceable names of our visitors change, but we go on forever—at any rate, we have followed this program so far. Sometimes I wish so hard for a break in the monotony that I would welcome the news that Miss B. and Paul were meeting under the rose, and that she was to have a baby—which I shall take care not to do as long as I can remember Mama's excellent instructions.

"As you know, Papa, I prefer to live and love rather than become the traditional missionary wife-martyr. You may have heard it said that one missionary wears out three wives, and buries six children for every one he rears to maturity. That, I have come to believe, is scarcely an exaggeration."

Dan spoke to me only once of his desire for children, "Paul, I have the vanity to want the name carried on. I am confident that I could give children of mine the care and education the Wears have always had. I should want them to carry on our tradition of service, as you and I are doing . . . But I must respect Ellen's wishes."

I was tempted to cry out, "Oh, Dan, why didn't you find Miss Eula before you were bewitched by Ellen's beauty and spirit!" For now I believed that Miss Eula would not marry me because I failed to measure up to Dan's stature, that without acknowledging it to herself she was in love with him. I imagined her in Ellen's place, with Dan's children to love and care for, little ones who would, when they grew old enough, tag around after me and pepper me with questions, "Uncle Paul, what makes the big wheel turn around in the creek? Uncle Paul, is Miss Eula (I would teach them to call her that) your mother, too?" When the boy was seventeen and the girl sixteen I would contrive to assist Dan in sending them East to Harvard and Mount Holyoke for the final touches of education and then glimpses of the world beyond to which we believed the Wears were entitled.

More and more, as he became known among the Cherokees as a man who spoke with a straight tongue and could keep a still tongue in his head, Dan was called to council with them. Their troubles with white neighbors became almost as grave as those of their Georgia brothers, as Dan explained to me one evening after supper as we rode to a meeting of fullbloods known as the Ki-tuh-wah Society:

"These Western Cherokees would be as hard pressed as those in the East except that there are fewer whites out here. But the men we are to meet tonight know that more will come. Their Society is founded upon resentment of white intrusion. It embodies the hopes of older Indian leaders like Pontiac and Tecumseh of stopping the white flood. Some of its older members fought with Tecumseh, and they want to fight now to preserve their homes. Ta-ka-to-ka, however, is now against fighting, for he knows that the whites of Arkansas would welcome an 'uprising' that would justify the militia in raiding and burning, and forcing the Cherokees to leave their fields and cabins and mills and shops and go farther west.

"They want me to approve resistance, and try to bring influence to bear at Washington to protect them. I would do so willingly if there was a chance to succeed, but there isn't. I shall advise them, instead, to turn the other cheek. A hard counsel, Paul!"

Dan pledged me to secrecy before we rode in to the secluded winter camp where two great log fires lighted the faces of the closely ranked men who sat between them. As we came among them, they greeted Dan by touching their palms to his. They questioned me with doubtful glances until Dan said to The Runner, who was to be the interpreter, "You know he will not talk."

I was surprised to see that nearly all were young men, for I had thought the Conservatives, as the haters of the whites were called, to be old men who yearned to go back to the life of the hunter.

As the long night session went on, it was made clear to me why they wanted to fight. It was to drive back white thieves who stole their horses and cattle, to hunt down and kill white ruffians who violated their women, to drive beyond the Cherokee borders every white whiskey runner who debauched their youth, to remove forcibly every brazen intruder upon their lands. They knew that armed protest would be costly, but as one of them said, "If we die and our children are made safe because we fought, it will be good. A man is not afraid to die."

Dan chose that moment to ask, "Is it not true, also, that a man is not afraid to live?"

It was a new thought, and they wrestled with it, demanding from Dan further elucidation. I believe his words were in their minds when, at daybreak, they scattered to their homes. The Runner's last words were: "They say they will think about all that you have told us. If we make up our minds to go on the war road, against your counsel, we will tell you in time for you to take your people from Hebron Creek to a place where they will be safe from the white soldiers."

"Why," I said as we started to ride back to the station, "they seem to think of *us* as Cherokees!"

"Yes," Dan was pleased by the thought, "I believe they do."

On our return, Dan was immediately occupied with the problem of repairing our battered one-horse wagon so that it might carry Ellen to the river, for she had said with a glow of excitement, "Oh, Dan, I have just received a message from Colonel Acton's lady at Fort Gibson—you met her in New York; she was Kate Buell, remember? She invites me to visit her at Fort Gibson. I *must* go."

"Of course, my beloved," Dan said, kissing her cheek. "You shall go and be gay, be the belle of the Post."

"As though an old married lady like me could compete for a handsome officer's attention!" But Ellen flushed as she spoke, knowing quite well the havoc her coquetry could create.

Dan drove her to the Arkansas River steamboat, watched the boat out of sight, and came back to us happy in the belief that Ellen's "spree" would raise her spirits.

Six

Within two months of the Ki-tuh-wah meeting, the last legal barrier to the banishment of the Arkansas Cherokees to a newly created Indian Territory was removed. Agents of the United States came to give them notice that they must go, either voluntarily or under escort of soldiers.

That meant, of course, the end of our Hebron Creek station. Dan said: "The Board has already secured permission for us to remove with the Cherokees to the new Territory, and have authorized me to select a site agreeable to the Western chiefs. Paul, you will hold the fort while I am away. Gather everything together that we can transport by land or by river. Send the scholars home. Tell them that, God willing, we shall welcome them at our new station."

I felt that his decision to go at once was affected by his longing to see Ellen, and that he meant to bring her back to assist in our transplanting. She had written only once, a brief note saying that she had borne the slow voyage better than she anticipated, that the Post at Gibson was jolly, and that Kate Acton had been overjoyed to welcome her.

Miss Eula made it possible for me to carry out creditably his instructions concerning the children. It was her idea that we should go to their homes with them, talk with their parents, and ourselves give them Dan's promise.

When the last scholar had been delivered and we were back at the lonely-seeming station with only the staff to direct, she began at once on the cleaning, bundling, and ticketing of blankets and other household gear. Then whatever school furnitu[r]e could be taken apart for more convenient haulage fell before our screw-drivers and hammers. We estimated that three trips of our big wagon would suffice to remove enough to re-open the school.

"But where can we put it?" I asked. "You know, buildings—"

"Surely," she interrupted, "we shall be able to manage some sort of schoolroom. I recall the beginnings at Kingslake and other stations in Georgia where in winter inkwells sometimes froze in makeshift quarters, and the wind whistled up between the rails first used as flooring. There were weeks when none of us was warm. On the playground I saw little girls squat to cover their feet with their skirts in the hope of warming them."

I had heard it said of young Mark Hopkins, a teacher at Williams College, that a good school need be no more than Hopkins sitting on one end of a log and a boy on the other. I would amend that to Miss Eula sitting on a log under a brush arbor with a group of Cherokee girls and boys on the ground before her, for later at our new station, Oak Hill, that was how she resumed teaching.

Before removal, however, our pressing problem was not the salvaging of Mission property but helping as many poor families as possible to get out of Arkansas. Our wagons and horses, stores of food, the blankets Miss Eula had cleaned, farming and shop tools we loaned or gave to the old, the crippled, and the widowed. On his return, Dan said, "Well done; I'm proud of you!"

He spoke briefly of Ellen: "We thought it best for her to remain with the Actons until we are settled at Oak Hill . . . Yes, she is well, and asked about you." That was all; and I knew that he was glad to have thrust upon him a multiplicity of duties to keep him driving day and night and in some measure divert his thoughts from the loved one who had failed him.

I recall him loading corn into the light wagon, and driving away at dusk with The Blanket beside him on the spring seat. On top of the corn they had piled as many hoes and spades and axes as they could find. When they had distributed this load, he told me, they would go on to beg another load from Wolfcatcher, saying, "I know he has more corn than he can carry away, and wouldn't want to leave it to fill a white man's crib. We shall try to find other supplies, and if we succeed it may be two or three days before I return."

It was like Dan not to speak of their loadings and unloadings during the three days of his absence. Rather, he talked about the legends and tales The Blanket had told. One was a long recital of the Cherokee version of the Creation, the fall of man, and the god Oona-luh-nuh-heh's promise to restore to the Indians their old earthly paradise. Another explained the inferior status of women: They do not stand beside men in battle, and do not sit with men in council because they are unable to keep a secret. Rarely, however, a woman shows that she can do both. "To her," The Blanket had said, "we give the power of life or death over captives. We call her 'Beloved Woman'; among us none is more honored. Such an one, long ago, was the wife of Kingfisher."

As Dan talked, his eyes were upon Miss Eula. I felt a sharp stab of pity for him whose beloved woman was arrantly shirking the tasks which were wearing him down and taxing Miss Eula's strength. I despised Ellen for her desertion.

"I asked The Blanket," Dan said, "why Indian mothers are given control of the children until they are men and women. He answered, with a glint in his eye, that every mother knows who her children are, but fathers have no such certain knowledge . . . He said that a faithless wife, one who does not bear children, is called a 'singing bird.' She sits in an empty nest, and her singing and preening cause the male birds to fight over her. The Blanket was once married to a singing bird, and was not pleased with her. He left her and went back to live in his old town with his own clan. When I asked what became of her, he said, 'It may be that she put away her fine feathers, stopped singing, and is now a good wife for some other man.' "

I was sure that Ellen was not in his mind as he told this, but certainly she was in mine.

I would not have it thought that Dan's whole time, in the years we had spent making Hebron Creek Mission a considerable establishment, was given to practical work and advising the Cherokee leaders. He was a preacher as well as a minister. His sermons were as carefully prepared, and as long—sometimes an hour and a half—as though he addressed a congregation of Bennington townsmen and neighborhood farmers. They were sound, as they must have been coming from an honor graduate of Andover Theological Seminary. Into them was written the zeal and hard sense of those young men who, a quarter of a century before, had met in the lee of a haystack near Williams College in Massachusetts to plan for spreading the Gospel of Christ throughout the world. Like them, he would have died a martyr to his faith as willingly as he had chosen to endure the hardships of living and laboring for it.

If I have written overmuch of the material things that concerned us and drew the practical minded Cherokees to him, it is because my duties had been almost wholly secular, and I could understand that phase of his work better than I could estimate the effect of his preaching. However, I know that the converts who came, slowly at first and then in increasing numbers following their periods of probation and Dan's conscientious examination of their understanding of the step, remained his brothers in Christ through every trial. Above all, he was a soldier of the Lord, and had no place in his company for deserters—backsliders we called them.

After we had sent off a few of our scholars to be prepared for work among their own people, Dan listened critically to their first sermons on their return. I recall seeing him make a note in the midst of young Cornelius Huff's first sermon, "Speak to him about hell." Huff had remembered too well the old picture of hell as a pit in which the unrepentant sinner was seared by flames and gnawed upon by the dreadful worm that never dies. It was a picture reminiscent of those drawn by the Tennessee exhorters we had heard, and was especially repugnant to Dan.

But he liked Huff's account of Christ's sacrifice of Himself for mankind when of His own accord He came down from dwelling in felicity in His father's house to endure the agonies of the cross. Even better, Dan told the young preacher, he liked that part of the sermon in which he said that the Saviour while on earth made rules by following which a man "may arrive at his own residence in heaven," and the saying that "these rules are excellent, without any mixture of evil." Language like that, direct and simple, pleased Dan because it spoke to the reason rather than to the emotions of listeners. I heard him flare out once heatedly on hearing an evangelist rebuke a Cherokee mother because she said his exhortations frightened the children. "Oh, my sister," the hell-fire-and-damnation shouter cried, "it would better become you to tremble before the terrible wrath of the Almighty than to doubt His purpose to cast even babes into that eternal fire unless they be cleaned by the blood of the Lamb!"

Dan liked camp meetings, saying, "They're in the Indian tradition. If our white evangelists had the good sense to preach as convincingly as Dik-keh the Just or The Blanket talks about Oo-na-luh-nuh-heh, the meetings would indeed be refreshing and fruitful."

Any Friday-to-Monday after the last spring frost to late fall might be chosen for the meeting; and I have seen close-wrapped Indian sleepers shake snow from their blankets on rising at daybreak. Fires would be built from the big piles of wood cut and brought in the day before; cooks would put on two-gallon pots of coffee to boil, and kettles of meat and corn to stew; on peg-leg tables under brush arbors were set out for all corn bread and iron pots filled with skinned-corn hominy, with long horn spoons thrust into the sourish food.

As the sun climbed, the women sat in circles, blankets down about their waists in order to free their hands for knitting, sewing, plaiting baskets or riddles, decorating beaded moccasins. Men gathered at the hitching ground to feed their horses or shift ground pegs to which picket ropes were attached. Boys eagerly beat brier patches with sticks, and when rabbits scurried out sent after them flights of arrows from their small bows. The girls rolled hoops made from slender willow twigs adroitly plaited and bent into circles.

At mid-morning, a cow-horn trumpet summoned the people to the brush arbor under which they sat in close-packed rows to listen to a service conducted by Dan or Cornelius Huff. A prayer was followed by singing in which all joined, some doing well enough with the English words of a hymn, the rest using Cherokee words which, Miss Eula said, rendered its sense with surprising accuracy.

No congregation could be more attentive. Dan, of course, spoke in English, two or three sentences at a time, then his interpreter, standing impassive at his side, put the words into the native tongue without emphasis or gestures. Dan had picked up from Cherokee speakers certain intonations and mannerisms that brought throaty chuckles: a trick of rubbing one palm quickly across the other, thrusting out his chin, and sometimes putting a period to a sentence with a grunting "hunh!" They had given him a nickname that meant Plain Talker; the one they gave me meant Strong One.

Saturdays and Sundays were full: morning and twilight services each day; horse racing by the young men; children's games; shifting groups of men talking and smoking; women visiting with one another and attending the cooking fires. On Monday, a brief sunrise service ended the meeting; and we watched the homebound Indians set off on foot, on horseback, and in wagons.

Before she went away to stay with Kate Acton at Fort Gibson, Ellen sometimes attended the camp meetings, but more often stayed at the station, saying to Dan, "I see no reason for boring myself with your Presbyterian Indian tea parties." If Miss Eula failed to attend, it was because she must stay to watch over girls and [boys] whom she judged too ill to go. At times, too, I was kept at home for the same reason. In these cases, Dan would, on his return, bring us up to date on what the people were thinking.

* * *

Then the long drawn out months of the removal.

I have lately been turning over the pages of an old ledger in which are recorded claims for losses and damages suffered by the Arkansas Cherokees.

We know well the widowed Martha Bird, with nine children to provide for, who had so successfully met her obligations that she was compelled to abandon two sound cabins, thirteen acres of rich bottom land "fenced and well tilled," a good stable, six milch cows and twelve young [m]eat cattle, and such house furnishings and farm tools as chairs, pots, cedar buckets, plows, trace chains, saws, drawing knives, and clothing. The furnishings, tools, and clothing, she said, had been taken from her forcibly by the white intruder who came to appropriate her home before she got out; and when she had sent men from the new neighborhood in Indian Territory to recover her cattle, they had been driven away and threatened with death unless they gave up the search.

The United States Government had given Martha Bird one hundred and fifty dollars to cover her losses, and was resisting her claim for five hundred more! Hundreds of other claims like hers filled the pages of the old ledger. Miss Eula, Dan and I helped list the possessions of scores whom the whites brazenly robbed in face of Washington's promise to guard their property and forward it safely to Indian Territory.

As Dan said, "We dare not protest the looting because politicians would brand us as meddlers and have us expelled from among the Cherokees." How right he was became evident later, in Georgia, when Sam Worcester and Doctor Butler were arrested and imprisoned for two years because they joined Chief John Ross in resisting in talk and writing the forcible removal of the Eastern section of the tribe.

We saw frightened Indian children run into the woods to hide from white men who fought with their fathers to prevent them from loading their household goods in wagons for transportation to Indian Territory. We saw mothers going in search of these children, and saw the wagons pull away with scant provisions, the women weeping and the men staring straight ahead in stony silence.

At long intervals, in the months during which we did all we could to allay the hardships of the removal, Dan received letters from Ellen. In one which he read to Miss Eula and me, she wrote: "Kate Acton is annoyed because her colonel must do something at once to prevent a body of starvelings from Hebron Creek going on a raid against thieving Osages, and his absence, with that of other officers, will cause Kate to postpone a very gay party she has planned." She said nothing about coming back, but (as I guessed from elisions as he read her letters to us) was impatient at what she thought of as his stubborn refusal to leave Hebron Creek station until all who needed our help had gone. In a letter to her father at this time, she wrote,

"Dan will not acknowledge the truth that his work in the west is finished, but insists that it shall go on at the new location some twenty-five miles from Gibson that he calls Oak Hill—which is nothing more than a name . . . Why will he not quit this hopeless tilting at windmills, and give thought to making a life for us that is tolerable to me!"

She lost Dan in those months. Afterwards, he could not believe [it] in his power to make her a true helpmeet. All that remained of his beloved woman were the beauty and fire and flame of sex that burned strongly in her.

I read in his face, in evenings we spent at Indian cabins while families prepared for the journey to Indian Territory, the disappointment of a man denied the importunate clutch of his own children's hands. By the light of an oak-log fire in a wide fireplace, one evening I recall, set three small boys and an elder sister half buried in a pile of cotton from which they were picking seeds. As they worked, they spoke to one another in low voices in order not to distract their parents and us. The girl and the eldest boy had been scholars at Hebron Creek; and he, without stopping his work, would half turn his head to interpret the words his mother and father wished to say to us. Once it was, "My mother he (English genders bothered the Cherokees surprisingly) say he goin' to make warm quilt out of thees cotton."

We watched the mother expertly tease the fluffy lint into foamy battens with the cards, then with dark swift fingers conjure firm threads out of which, if fortune should provide a loom in the new home, would be woven garments for her brood. From time to time, a handful of cotton seeds was thrown on the fire to light the father's task of attaching a sole to a home-made shoe with seasoned maple-wood pegs. Tap-tap-tap! his light hammer drove the pegs into the holes made by his big-handled awl. His words were interpreted by the boy, "She goin' to make that shoe good for thees one," indicating his sister by a gesture of his chin. "Maybe so he got to walk to thees new Indian country."

Thus singled out, the girl lowered her head shyly, and scolded the boy for drawing attention to her.

Now and then one of the children rose to go to the water bucket and fill a gourd dipper, always offering it in order to Dan and me and the mother and father before drinking. Or dip from the kettle hanging in the fireplace a spoonful of meat and corn, blow upon it until it was cool, then take it at one mouth-filling gulp.

Dan found it hard to leave an evening scene like this, hard to restrain his longing to take in his arms the sleepy littlest boy, hug him to his breast and kiss his clean brown cheek. Confessing his longing to me after riding away one night, he said, "I know I must not do that, for Indian parents do not fondle their little ones." But he could smile upon the boy who had been our scholar when he came to offer his palm as we rose to go, and say, in his halting Cherokee, "Ya-nu-usdi!" (little bear); and to the girl, "Agi-usdi!" (little woman). At the door, he said, "Na-hwun-yu-ga-i," (I am going.) The words drew from the children half suppressed giggles, then the boy, with a glance at his father as though apologizing for playing host, answered, "Hwi-la-hi" (go then) and "hi-lu-nu" (go to sleep).

Riding away through the chill night, Dan discussed our plans for next day, then took up previous discussions concerning the layout of the new mission station at Oak Hill. He had pictured the site, on wooded land that sloped steeply on the west to the fast-flowing Illinois River, much bigger than Hebron Creek and just as clear. Eastward, he had said, "our land eases gently down to what they call a prairie which in summer will be lush with tall grass and flowers; and there will be wild roses in our fence corners."

Then, "Paul, I believe it might be best to build detached cabins, in a convenient pattern, clustered about the church."

"Church?" I was surprised. "You're surely looking a long way ahead. It's a luxury we haven't been able to afford here."

"Yes," he said firmly, "I am looking ahead and dreaming of grand things. I hope that at Oak Hill all the rest of my life and strength will be spent in our Lord's work."

His words were not a rhetorical gesture. I was sure that with them he was saying good-bye definitely and for always to Ellen.

After that night, both Miss Eula and I found in him a new cheerfulness. It heartened her immensely, for she had been so sensitive to his moods, knew so surely that Ellen had hurt him terribly, that her own courage had been tried.

Seven

We were now a team of three working as one. Dan's dreams for Oak Hill became for Miss Eula and me plans on which to build. With him, we should somehow transform them into solid realities: a chapel for his preaching, schoolrooms, shops, a mill, cribs and granaries to contain the produce of the new fields, and what he wanted most, after the chapel, a printing press.

When our teams and wagons had been returned to us by the last emigrant borrower, we closed Hebron Creek station and set off for Oak Hill over roads rutted and churned to frozen slush by Indian wagons and foundering pack horses.

I thought of our departure from Kingslake, and Ellen's tardy appearance that morning, half expecting her to stroll out when all was ready and climb to the spring seat beside Dan. But he had explained briefly, after his visit to Fort Gibson, "She will not come to us until we have completed suitable living quarters at Oak Hill. Until that time, the Actons have graciously asked her to stay with them."

Along the way we had abundant evidence, other than the nearly impassable road, that we followed a trail of sorrow: a path broken through stiff dead weeds to a shallow grave beside a stream now icebound but promising, to some Cherokee mother who chose the spot for the burial place of her child, friendly springtime chatter, flowers, and summer warmth; stacks of household goods, a stove, an extra kettle, a cedar chest packed with treasured dishes abandoned at a stream crossing where gaunt ponies could no longer pull overloaded wagons up steep and muddy banks; dead and dying horses and mules, bones of calves slaughtered and eaten when they could no longer stagger at the heels of their mothers, and bodies of dogs that lay like ghastly deflated toys cast aside by children, and hungry domestic cats that had taken to the woods after being thrown out of wagons that must be lightened of the last possible superfluous ounce of weight.

We saw where women had hacked crude mortars in logs in which to pound corn for cooking. Once Miss Eula said, "I have looked to see if I could find one wasted grain, but haven't. What hunger they must have suffered!"

We had been on the road a week, and had pitched our tent early because a sleet storm beating into our faces made the going bad. Our fire was roaring high, throwing welcome heat into the tent, when a booming voice across the blaze startled us, "Evening, Sir! May I share your fire for a minute?"

"Of course," Dan rose to greet the stranger.

"Well!" and Colonel Pease strode forward, holding out his hand. "I've been wanting to meet you again, Sir, all the years since I made a braying jackass of myself in your presence, and offer my humble apologies for that performance."

"And I," Dan smiled, "have thought of you more than once." Shaking hands with the Colonel, he turned to me, "Of course, Paul, you remember our friend," then presented Miss Eula.

"Madam," the big man bowed over her hand, "if Mr. Wear has told you of our former meeting, I prostrate myself at your feet in shame and beg your forgiveness, if you can find it in your heart to forgive the beast that was in me then."

"Of course, Colonel Pease," she had taken her cue from Dan, and smiled. "I have heard something. I hope you will share our supper?"

"With pleasure, Ma'am."

Beaming upon Dan as we ate, the Colonel said: "Sir, you made a new man of me on the boat when you answered my foul challenge by saying, 'Try to convert you to decency, Sir? No, thanks; I know my limitations.' You were like a tiger, Sir, that is too much of a gentleman to pounce on a crazy man. I'll swear I tried to put you out of my mind, and I was beastlier than ever until I left the boat. But I could not forget your words, and I'm a triple-dyed son of Belial if I have allowed an oath or a drop of liquor to pass my lips since that day.

"That is what you did for me, Sir, and more than once I have resolved to tell you, but it was only six months ago that I found out where you were and what you were doing for the Cherokees. Then the Government's order went out for the poor devils to move, and I said to myself, 'That missionary fellow will be so busy helping them that I must not waste his time.' Then I said to myself, 'Maybe I can do something to help, too.' So I've been going back and forth along this road that is paved with suffering carrying whatever I and my blacks could manage with teams to make the journey easier for them. I saw the last of the exiles into Fort Smith four days ago, and I'm carrying my black Cato back to the plantation. No doubt, Sir, it was Providence that directed my eyes to your fire, although I admit," he laughed, "that I have been hoping to see one, readymade, for some hours."

"Colonel Pease," said Dan, taking advantage of the first full stop he had made in his talk, "our fire is no more welcome to you than your presence, and what you have just told us, is to us. We are indeed well met again!"

"Now, Sir, I presume you three are bound for the new Cherokee country to carry forward your good work?"

"Yes," Dan answered. "We hope to re-establish our station there, and do whatever we can for our friends."

The Colonel said that he knew the Oak Hill site. He had hunted, with officers from Gibson and Fort Smith, all over the region in which the exiled Cherokees were settling. "I like the name you have chosen for your station, Oak Hill. It's a fitting, plain-sounding name that will stick in the mind—like all the words I have had the pleasure to hear you utter, Sir, if you will pardon me for being personal."

"I'm flattered," Dan laughed.

After the Colonel had gone to his tent, which Cato had meanwhile pitched nearby, his voice boomed across to us, "Sir, I hope you will allow me to build for you at Oak Hill some useful structure you have set your heart on as a kind of tribute to your work from a heathen that, unlike the leopard, was able to change his spots."

"What about a chapel, Colonel?" Dan called back. "A log chapel with a fireplace in it as big as your heart. I'll call it Pease Chapel."

"Right, Sir; it shall be built. Now, good night to you, Sir."

"Good night, Colonel," Dan answered, then in a low voice, "Paul, do you remember that I said I should like to meet that man again, in his right senses?"

"Yes, and I thought then that if you hoped to find anything worth saving in him you must be the world's prize optimist."

* * *

On the way to Oak Hill, Dan came back in talk again and again to the possibility of setting up a press at Oak Hill, and we reviewed at some length what Ellen had once called "L'affaire Panther-Decker," and attempted to estimate practically the promise it held.

Among the older boys who had come to us while we were new at Hebron Creek was a brother of The Runner, a lad of sixteen with keen intelligence and eagerness to please us and reflect credit upon his brother whom he adored. Without his helpful understanding of some of the small boys—their outbursts of furious resentment against schoolroom discipline, their hours of desperate homesickness, their flights into the woods, their amazement at certain of our sanitary arrangements—my task would have been far more difficult than it was.

We dubbed him Richard Panther, a fairly literal translation of his Cherokee name Tlun-tuski, and panther-like was also a good description of his movements. He took to Dan's ideas, ideals, and system as a duckling does to water; once he said to me, his eyes on Dan, "That one, she is a whole man!"

At twenty-one, he had pumped us dry. Dan said, "We must somehow manage to send him east to a good school, give him a glimpse of our world, and bring him back to help us. He may perhaps be the one to realize our hope of finding an adequate translator and editor when we are able to establish a press."

It had been Ellen who suggested, "Let us ask papa to pay for his education? Tell him the savage will agree to change his name to Henri Bonaparte Morin if he will pay the bills."

Mr. Morin wrote asking Dan to send Richard to New York (enclosing a generous bill of exchange to pay his travel expenses) "in order to determine for myself whether or not you and Ellen have mistaken a crow for a thrush," then, after he had talked with Richard, "The young man impressed me favorably by his modesty, his good sense, and good manners." At the end of his letter, he wrote jestingly, "You need not fear that I shall insist upon his changing his name as a sop to my vanity. The one he bears pleases me."

Dan had been elated, saying to Ellen, "My beloved, you are priceless." He believed that two years at Lakeside College, then a year or two as apprentice in a Boston print shop would equip Richard for the work he was eager to undertake.

Lakeside was a small college in an old and wealthy Massachusetts community. Richard was the first of several Indian youths to sit under its able teachers; and when it became known in the village that he was not only an excellent student but a Christian gentleman he found a cordial welcome in Lakeside homes. His letters to Dan, written each week but usually coming to Hebron Creek in batches of four or five, reflected the keen pleasure his reception by Lakeside afforded him. Reading one, Dan interrupted himself to say, "Paul, this is a perfect description a such a village and such people as we knew. Wouldn't you like to know the Deckers?"

"I would indeed," I said, "especially Catherine."

"Yes. Do you suppose they're falling in love, as Elias Boudinot and Harriet Gold did? Or is it just your imagination?"

I protested, "I've not suggested the possibility, but since you mention it I do suspect something of the sort. And if it's true?"

"I don't know, Paul. Perhaps Lakeside would not be as horrified by the notion of one of its young ladies marrying a Cherokee as was Cornwall when Harriet Gold battled her own family and the people of the village for her Elias."

Then had come the urgent call to Ellen from her father: "Some one of us Morins must set a watch on that affair. Your mother cannot go to Lakeside, and I am fully occupied with matters which I understand far better. If Dan will permit, you shall come at once, talk with Mme. Maman, then go to Lakeside. I assure you that you are needed."

Dan, of course, agreed, and Ellen had been glad of the opportunity to visit in New York and also to observe an "amusing" situation. In her first letter, she wrote: "I do believe Lakeside is more *boulversé* (upset to you, Paul) than Cornwall was about Harriet and Elias, if what I have heard about that mésalliance is the whole story. The good people with whom I have talked would have Papa withdraw his patronage and return young Mr. Panther to the forests of Arkansas forthwith for daring to look with desire upon the fair Catherine (she really is a lovely girl).

"But what to do about her, for she is deeply in love with Richard, they don't know—except to send her most pious relatives to beg her not to disgrace the village, the township and, I doubt not the noble Commonwealth of Massachusetts. One must believe, I suppose, that the State of Connecticut can never be the same since two of her daughters, Harriet Gold and Sarah Northrop, have married and gone to bed with Elias Boudinot and John Ridge, both brilliant youths of unexceptionable manners whose families, as you have told me, are of the Cherokee aristocracy.

"I have entertained myself by pointing out to the good folks of Lakeside that it is illogical to civilize, educate, and equip the savage to live as we do, then deny him the only privilege which if exercised would make him and his children one with us. And why? I have asked. Only because of the tint of his skin? Certainly Catherine Decker does not find that objectionable; and she has rebuked with proper spirit a smug uncle who asked her with sarcasm intended to wither how she could endure to be kissed by an Indian, and how she would feel on bringing into the world a black baby. 'Why,' she answered, 'I certainly prefer to be kissed by Richard, whose mouth is sweet and whose teeth are sound, than by some Lakeside swains whose whiskers annoy and whose breath—' well, you can see that Catherine is able to speak plainly. 'As for black babies,' said she, 'you are mistaken. Richard's and mine will have skins like beautiful burnished copper, not the pale unwholesome hue of members of my own family.'

"So much for Uncle Obadiah. Hearing Catherine stand up so stoutly for Richard, and sing his praises as a lover, I am almost sorry I did not refuse you, Dan, and wait to marry a savage!"

A month later, she wrote: "My coming to Lakeside, it seems, has brought matters to a crisis. Catherine's mother has been compelled by the pressure of her brothers to say that if her daughter marries the Indian she will disown her, and Mr. Decker, who is by way of being the tail to his wife's kite, has said the same. Then the uncle pressed to have Catherine sent away to her New Hampshire kin to reflect calmly upon the outrage she proposes to commit upon the community. To that the spirited Catherine said, 'I will go if mother and father command me to go, but in that case I shall not return.'

"Learning of this contemplated ukase by the Deckers, Richard took upon himself to quit the college. He is now in Boston, employed as you would have him in a printery owned in part by my Uncle Raymond (I suspect Papa's hand in this, bless him!)[.] Before leaving Lakeside, however, he told Catherine's parents that he meant to marry her if she would have him, and at whatever time she chose. And he said, also (as Catherine proudly repeated to me) 'She shall, if necessary, go with me to Arkansas and be one of my own family.' Meaning, of course, that Catherine and he would do this if all of us—her family, Papa, and you—should fail him.

"Catherine has consented to wait for him a year, or until he has finished his apprenticeship at the printery. So we are at the beginning of a truce. I shall go back to New York tomorrow, and leave for Hebron Creek toute à l'heure."

But two weeks later she wrote again from Lakeside, saying: "Here I am in the middle of the third set of the drama of Catherine and Richard. He had just started to work at the printery when a blundering fellow apprentice let fall upon one of his legs a heavy piece of machinery, injuring him quite seriously. Catherine was frantic to go to him, and could be stopped only by her father's promise to bring him into his own home, by carriage and with a surgeon attending upon him if that was required.

"Back to Lakeside, therefore, has come our savage, to be installed at Catherine's insistence in a room next her own so that she may more conveniently wait upon him. She is with him at all hours, seemly or unseemly, quite as though they were already married. Scandal upon scandal! The village is seething with—

"Last night this letter was broken off when I looked from my window at the Inn to see a strange procession of men and women file upon the common, lighted by torches and lanterns and bearing two objects which at first I could not identify. They stopped on the bare-earth space where the villagers are wont to gather around the town crier; and as the church bell began to toll as for a death, a torch was applied to a hogshead of tar. Then into the leaping flame were cast the objects I had not been able to identify, straw-stuffed effigies of Catherine and Richard! And between the strokes of the bell there came to my ears such a chorus of amens that I became frightened lest the anger of these saints mount until it should get beyond control.

"I ran as fast as I could to the Deckers', and begged Catherine to come with me and hide from them at the Inn. At first, she would not listen either to me or to her parents, but when Richard said firmly, 'You will go at once, dear!' she took up her cloak and returned with me to watch the ghastly scene on the common and listen to the slow, incessant tolling of the church bell. I was able to quiet her fears for Richard by saying that even New England barbarians were not apt to snatch a wounded man out of bed and burn him at the stake. 'At least,' I said, 'they will wait until he is sound enough to run the gauntlet of their prayers.' That made her smile, and she said firmly, 'I shall take care to have him out of their reach before he is well.'

"Now, whether I approve or not, I am commit[t]ed to assisting this romance. One day soon, if my plan does not miscarry, Papa's carriage will swing into the Deckers' driveway, after taking me up at the Inn, and we three will depart of New York. In our home, I doubt if anyone will censure Catherine for attending upon Richard as intimately as she will; and we shall find a clergyman who will not believe he is offending God by marrying them.

"The surgeon says that Richard will be sound again in six months. What do you advise him to do then? I believe Papa will arrange for whatever you suggest."

Dan wrote to Ellen, applauding her skillful management of L'affaire Panther-Decker. To Mr. Morin and Richard he suggested that the young man should take his Catherine to Boston and complete his term in the print shop. He added a paragraph addressed to Catherine:

"My dear, you have proved yourself a spunky girl. You will be a wonderful helpmeet for Richard, and a treasure to be cherished by us at Hebron Creek. Come with him as soon as he is ready. I trust we shall be ready by that time to use his talents in the way we have planned."

In that business, Ellen had been at her best, acting wisely and generously. It had been such a complication of love as would engage her interest, and the practical Morin in her led her to the right solution. Dan, of course, was elated, and I had felt a renewal of pride in her and an affection I had believed gone forever.

Yet it had been hardly a month after her return to Hebron Creek that she went to Kate Acton and the gai[e]ties of the frontier post at Gibson.

Hearing of the impending removal of the Arkansas Cherokees, Richard begged leave to return and help us. Dan, however, bade him remain in Boston, writing, "You will be far more useful to us, and to the people, if you complete your apprenticeship. Here you could do only odd jobs. I believe your Catherine will agree with me, and I am sure that Mr. Morin will."

Ellen's father had written, "I have become greatly attached to both the young people, and would like nothing better than to keep them in New York. But Richard shall have his chance to do the work with you upon which he has set his heart."

Dan ended our discussions by saying, "God willing, it will work out just right. By the time they return to us, we should be well settled at Oak Hill, and have a building ready for the print shop."

If only he could have added, "Ellen will be so proud of it!"

Eight

Winter ended with our removal to Oak Hill. One of those incredibly early springs, about which Catherine was to write later, came to Indian Territory. Frogs began to pipe early in February, and before the month was out corn was being planted and buds were swelling on the Judas trees.

Because cabin homes were urgently needed, and gardens and corn fields must be planted in newly turned sod, we would not ask our Cherokee friends to help us build. Our buildings must wait until fall. Meanwhile, we lived under canvas; and constructed Miss Eula's brush-arbor schoolroom ourselves in the most sheltered nook on Oak Hill. She made the rounds of Indian families living near enough to send their children as day scholars. Surprisingly, there were twelve boys and girls in attendance at the opening, and the number increased as older children could be spared from spading, hoeing, and planting.

Dan and I, with the millwright and the stockman and "Uncle Frank," the one black who had followed us from Hebron Creek with the final load of equipment, used the daylight hours in getting a station garden and a first cornfield into cultivation. For breaking the ten acres of raw prairie, Dan found at the Agency a sod plow and two idle yoke of oxen he could borrow. We had, of course, worked oxen on the stony, friable soil of Vermont, but when, with Dan prodding and gee-ing and haw-ing, I let the share of this ponderous plow into the sod I discovered that my previous experience helped me very little. The grass growing on the long eastern slope of Oak Hill had roots that were veritable devil's shoe-strings, so tough and matted that they popped like a whip-lash as the steers strained against the yokes. I fought grimly to keep the plowshare at the right depth, three to four inches. In and out the plow jumped like some live bucking monster. Dan spelled me at the handles, but could do no better until he thought to rig a wheel under the front end of the plowbeam to prevent the share from plunging too deeply into the earth.

The others followed us, and with axes cut holes in the upturned sod into which they dropped kernels of corn, covering them by grinding dirt into the axe-holes with their heels.

Fortunately, we found twenty each of young apple and peach trees to start an orchard; and between the rows we labored with heavy one-eyed hoes and spades to pulverize the sod for planting beans, potatoes, yams, onions, squash and, at Miss Eula's suggestion, a square of salad plants and herbs.

Before the corn and garden plants became tempting to hungry deer and woods-roaming hogs, we made a fence around our ten acres. With axes, wedges and mauls, we became rail splitters; and it seemed incredible the number of ten-foot rails required for a proper stake-and-rider worm fence. When we were ready to build it, we called in as expert Jim Redbird, who said that the bottom rail should be laid in the light of the moon; otherwise, it would rot within a year. He also advised setting peach and plum trees in the angles of the fence, saying, "When that fruit drop outside hogs come an' eat, root, keep fence line clear so brush fire don' burn it rails." He pointed out, too, that fruit trees so placed would be protected from the danger of being "barked" by plow equipment as the corn was cultivated.

Miss Eula somehow found food and cooked it for a plain noon dinner for the scholars and us; and I helped her with breakfast and supper. I liked working with her in the dusk of spring evenings. More often than not, Dan was in a hurry to eat his evening meal in order to start off on what he called his parochial duties before the Indians went to sleep.

We never spoke of Ellen's absence. Miss Eula and I, though we never expressed the thought, believ[e]d that we got on better without her, and that it was good for Dan to exhaust himself in hard labor. He showed no sign of the longing he must have felt for her. Sometimes, casually, he spoke of her, as when a joint letter came from Catherine and Richard, who remembered her with gratitude, or when a brief, infrequent letter arrived from Gibson. As the pressure of work somewhat relaxed, I wondered that Dan did not fetch her. I wondered, too, why she did not come of her own accord, if only to satisfy a natural curiosity about Dan.

Colonel Pease wrote reminding Dan of his promise, saying that in August he could conveniently send blacks to build the chapel under Dan's direction, adding, "The great pleasure of hearing your first sermon in the new House of God is something I have promised myself if you will have the goodness to inform me of the date."

Dan answered: "We will be ready to welcome the builders in thirty days. If you approve, we will make the chapel a one-story, four-room log building with a big chimney at the center and a fireplace in each room. I want it to be Indian, a spiritual home for the Cherokees, familiar and friendly. We will seat the old people near the fireplaces so that as they smoke they may spit in the ashes. On weekdays, the chapel will serve as a schoolhouse. The bell, as at Hebron Creek, will be hung at the top of a tall post.

"You may be interested, my dear friend, to know that between the chapel and the site of our own cabins, the sleeping quarters of our scholars, and commons will lie a broad, almost level playground which we shall call the 'chungke yard.' Here boys can roll their stone disks and 'shoot' them with lances. I will have a wooden 'fish' placed on top of the bell-frame as a target in their ball play. At the edge of the playground will be the range for 'stalk shooting.' It might astonish you to see experts of fifteen and sixteen, their arrows tipped with fifteen-inch iron points, with bows of bois d'arc requiring a thirty-pound pull, fire away from a distance of one hundred yards at a target of cornstalk bundles, piled between stakes, that present a surface the size of a deer's body. The winner in this game is the boy whose arrow penetrates the greatest number of stalks."

Dan and I became fair chungke players and bowmen after we found that control of the boys was made easier by joining in their games. At blow-gun making and shooting, however, we proved inept because we lacked the skill and patience required to fashion the long, light tubes of cane and the finely balanced slender darts with which the boys often killed squirrels, rabbits, and birds.

In winter, either Dan or I went out with the older boys on Saturday night coon hunts. Following the Indian dogs through the timber by the sound of their trail music, we would come upon the treed animal. The boys would build a ring of small dry-wood fires around the tree in order to "shine" the coon's eyes, then the arrows began to fly. Next day the shooters returned to recover their marked arrows.

With luck, we came back from the hunt laden with meat. Then, fetching potatoes from the storehouse to be roasted in hot ashes, we prepared a feast.

For the boys this was real living! For us, too, yet Dan never forgot the purpose of the station. The zeal that had sent him to the Indians burned steadily; and the children followed his lead as willingly in singing "How firm a foundation" as they did on the playground.

They believed that his God spoke to Dan with a straight tongue, whatever some of their bitter and disillusioned elders said of His helplessness to assure justice for the Cherokees.

Uncle Frank's cabin, in which he lived amid an orderly confusion of tools, harness to be mended, brooms and axe-helves in the making, his home-made chair bottomed with rawhide as was his one-legged bunk in the corner, was a favorite resort for the boys. In a curious medley of Cherokee, Georgia English, and gestures, he told them his own story of the origin of races: First to be created were three men, all black. Setting off together to explore the world, they came to a stream tired and dusty. One went into the water, washed himself all over, and came out white. Another, washing himself in the roiled water, came out a reddish hue, and became the father of the Indian race. The third merely dropped his palms and the soles of his feet in the water and except for these muddy-white parts, remained black as the Creator intended all men to be.

He delighted the children by fashioning a crude travois and strapping it on our patient old Coley horse. When his load was light, he permitted three or four small girls to pile on. When it was heavy, and they attempted to pile on, he stormed at them, "Wha fo yu-all wan' a bu'den dis Jesus hoss ontel he moan an' blow? Yu-all got two feet, same as me, to walk de glory road."

Due to a sprained ankle, in our first summer at Oak Hill, Miss Eula conducted school for some days from an improvised couch under the arbor, with fourteen-year-old Betsy Wolfcatcher beside her as monitor, maintaining discipline with a delicious imitation of her teacher's manner. Betsy insisted, too, on staying to tend the cooking fire, then sat in Miss Eula's place at the head of table at the noon meal and called soberly on Dan to say grace. We were indeed one big family!

Until the chapel was built, Dan's fair weather pulpit was one end of the arbor dining table. On rainy Sabbaths, he sent round word that he would hold meetings in the roomier cabins, Wolfcatcher's, the Redbird's, or The Runner's. The people who came made a day of it, fetching their cooked food in time for eleven o'clock service, attending a song service in the afternoon, and listening to Dan again after supper.

Evening meets at the cabins Dan thought especially refreshing. They were truly family sessions, with the small children and dogs going out and coming in at will, but quietly, with a group of older girls and boys sitting close to him as he held a candle in one hand

and a pocket Bible or song book in the other. Nearly always The Runner was in the company and, at Dan's request, lined out the songs in Cherokee. In a liquid natural tenor, he would begin the Cherokee version of

> "Sow in the morn thy seed
> At eve hold not thy hand,"

and the group beside Dan repeated the lines. Then on to

> "Angel reapers shall descend
> And heaven sing harvest home."

Among the voices singing the Cherokee words I always listened for that of Miss Eula, sitting on the floor with the women at one side of the shadow-haunted cabin and following Dan's moving lips with her eyes.

Such cabin meetings were not new. It had been after one such service near Hebron Creek that Ellen referred to Dan's work as childish make-believe. She had come away with a stitch in her side from sitting on the floor, complaining, "I have an odor in my nostrils that I'm afraid I shall never get rid of, and I'm famished." She had refused to eat the good conutche (corn prepared with nut meats and sweetened with wild honey) our Indian hostess had served.

As we rode back to the station, she had broken out, "Dan, when will you cease to play at being God! I can understand why you should teach them cleanliness, good manners, farming, carpentry, and the like. But you say they have a god of their own; well, let them keep and worship him."

Dan answered calmly, "I wonder, my beloved, if you're right? Tomorrow, a witch may be put to death within ten miles of Hebron station. I can't think that it is child's play to try implanting in their hearts faith in a God of kindness and mercy."

Then came Colonel Pease's crew of blacks to build our Oak Hill chapel, bringing their own food, camping equipment, oxen, log wagons, heavy chains, axes, adzes, hatchets, mauls, frows, and a stock of hard wrought nails and door latches. Their women came, too, with cotton to be seeded and spun. All was under the direction of the Colonel's trusted Cato. For choice eighteen-foot logs with which to make the walls, they cruised the woods for miles around. While axemen and adzmen cut and shaped the logs, the reavers of shakes for the roof found great white oaks to fall, saw into four-foot lengths and split to proper width and thickness. A mason and his helpers quarried and sledded to the chapel stones for the massive chimney and the four huge fireplaces.

Dan thought this a fitting time to call on our Cherokee neighbors for help in building our first cabins. We had a small building fund, obtained in part by the sacrifice sale of the Hebron Creek building and what equipment we had not been able to remove. It was sufficient to feed the workers and pay them something besides. The Runner found for us the expert builders who could be spared from their own work; and he became for the crew of shifting builders what Cato was for the Colonel's blacks, a foreman and disciplinarian. Keeping illicit whiskey sellers away from them was one of his chores.

We were under roofs on the same day the first fires were lighted in the chapel to dry the plaster-like daubing between the logs. Cato could send home all but two door and window fitters, with Dan's invitation to the Colonel to come to the dedication services late in September.

Then he said, "Now I shall fetch Ellen."

She returned with Dan, very becomingly dressed, riding the young mare he had led to Gibson on which Kate Acton's silver-decorated saddle, which she had preferred to the plain saddle Dan had provided, made a fine showing. She was as cordial and smiling, as a Vermont saying had it, as a selectman seeking re-election. I grasped at the hope that she meant to stay until I saw on Dan's face the serenity which meant that he would no more be troubled by her caprices and exactions. I could not know, but I guessed that they were still passionate lovers; and I felt sure she had not been unfaithful. But if they were lovers again, Dan's delight in her beauty and sensual appeal was no longer confused with a burning desire to make her in all respects his helpmeet; a vital part of the mission establishment. He had brought her because it was seemly that she should be there at the dedication of the chapel.

She saw at once that Dan had no intention of ousting Miss Eula from the role of hostess and housekeeper. She had the wit to recognize that Dan had discovered in himself no sentimental interest in Miss Eula. However, in the weeks of open house following the dedication, Miss Eula kept in the background and thrust Ellen forward to play the gracious hostess. Ellen did it well, accounting for her absence by inventing family and business matters that she said had kept her at Gibson so long.

She was charged at first by Colonel Pease. His gallantry, springing as he said from the fact that he had arrived at the age when only the essentials of life, literature and the ladies, interested him, pleased her vanity; and she could follow him in his quotations from Shakespeare and Sir Walter Scott, which he produced to show that literature for him did not mean altogether Byron's Don Juan. His elegance, self-assurance, and wealth appealed to the snob in her.

But the Colonel's extravagant praise of Dan puzzled her; and she resented it when she realized that it was as genuine as was Dan's liking for him. She was annoyed because she was unable to wedge herself between them, that she could bring the Colonel to her feet only in words, and that she could not convince Dan that Pease was only "a vain, senile echo of a plantation aristocracy marooned in the wilderness."

Almost as impressive as Colonel Pease was the stout middle-aged Peter Hummingbird, a clan brother of Chief John Jolly, who came as Jolly's substitute, explaining, "That John Jolly must go to Washin'ton; she is sorry she can't come to see new church." Hummingbird's arrival was impressive, riding a splendid stallion in advance of an elegant barouche drawn by two fine bays, with a black coachman and footman, and a negro maid to wait upon his wife, a friendly woman who spoke good English and at once began assisting Miss Eula. Hummingbird and Dan beamed upon one another, the Indian recalling for the benefit of the little group around them, "This man my frien' long time. One time meet him in Arkansas, an' he got no pony. So I give it him pony to ride home. Dam' fella he send it back that pony. Maybe it ain't good enough that pony?"

"No, Peter," Dan denied, "it was not like that. It was damn good pony, but I think maybe if I send it back you will give me two big stout horses."

Peter chuckled, "Sure smart, this fella. This time I mus' give him them bays, make it my ol' woman walk home, huh?"

Dan asked, "Peter, how did you get away from Arkansas with so much of your property?"

He answered, "Me, I know long time we all got to go, so I commence takin' my stock to this country, buildin' my house on river, sendin' my blacks to open up farm. They don' catch Peter asleep!"

Later, in less crowded days, Dan and I sometimes enjoyed the hospitality of Peter's considerable establishment on the Arkansas River. There, he had his own steamboat landing and a store; and on sharply rising ground some two hundred yards back from the river below, a fine spring he had built an enormous two-story mansion of logs with a verandah across its front. From its big front door a double row of walnut trees led to the Fort Smith road a mile away. His slave cabins were dotted on the slope between the mansion and the river; and his thousand acres of rich cotton and corn land spread fanwise from the house.

Once Peter talked to me of Catherine Swan, saying, "She was blood kin to me. When she is little girl, I see her many times. Smart, always full of fun. I feel bad when she die, an' my ol' woman he cry, Jesus girl, that one, an' good ever' way."

Our celebration ended, we began to push our plans for resuming at Oak Hill the busy life we had lived at Hebron Creek. Dan wrote to Boston to hurry the printing press makers and the type founders who were to send out duplicates of Sam Worcester's Georgia equipment, paid for by Mr. Morin. We built a cabin for the print shop, with wide windows in the north wall for lighting the type cases.

Nine

One whom we hoped would come to the dedication of our chapel but did not was Sequoyah, who lived as neighbor to Hummingbird. Peter brought word, however, that Sequoyah would visit Dan as soon as his corn and pumpkins were stored in the loft of his cabin, and before the opening of the season for coon hunting.

We had the chapel school under way, and had been notified that the press and type, along with a hundred reams of print paper, would soon arrive, before Sequoyah dismounted from his pony in front of Dan's quarters and looked about for some one whom he could ask in Cherokee for my uncle. Fortunately, Miss Eula was near. She called a boy to take the pony, and with an air of pride led the lame man to Dan, saying, "Here is our long-awaited visitor." Dan asked her to stay and serve as interpreter, and the three were in earnest talk when I went to call them to supper.

As I first saw him, this Cherokee Cadmus was not impressive: a short, somewhat stout, shabbily dressed man of fifty, with a blue-and-white striped shawl turban wound about his thick long hair, already showing grey. As he walked beside Dan to supper, he thrust a Cherokee pipe—burnt-clay bowl and reed stem—into the woolen belt-sash he wore around his striped-cloth hunting shirt. To the belt-sash was attached a wooden-handle hunting knife in a stiff cow-hide sheath. His patched pantaloons of faded yellow jeans were thrust into the tops of the plain moccasins that showed signs of stirrup wear.

At that time he was obsessed by the importance of teaching his syllabary to the people. Ellen called him "a crackbrained, untidy old man." In a sense, she was right. What she could not comprehend was that his obsession had become a light in the darkness to the Cherokees at a time of doubt and distress, a standard around which they could rally their pride of race. As for the clothes he wore, they were like those he had always worn as a worker in silver since being lamed in his youth, the proper garb for a poor man going from cabin to cabin explaining his magic.

As he took a chair beside Dan in the dining hall, the children's eyes fastened upon him, and whispers ran about the tables. The man of the talking leaf was here with them, listening to the brief prayer of the Plain Talker, though he did not bow his head. He had come as one of them, he spoke as they did with the liquid intonations of Cherokees of the lower towns. He was eating their plain supper of cornbread, hominy, and tea. It was the way, they had heard, Christ had come long ago to the white people. There was reverence in their eyes.

Through Miss Eula, Sequoyah made clear his opinion of the mission, saying to Dan, "I do not like your preachers' Christ talk. We cannot believe in a Saviour who tells us to do good, and then says it is all right to be wicked and do injustice if we will only say we believe in the power of that one you call Jesus to clear us of blame by dying for us. That cannot be true.

"But I like what your Jesus talkers do to teach us out of the white man's books, and what they tell us about using good tools and raising better cotton. Peter Hummingbird has said that you are to bring here a machine to put on paper what is written in Cherokee so that all the people can keep it to read. I have come to talk with you about that. I will help you to do that if I can."

"I will be glad to have your help," Dan said. "As for our beliefs, a man follows the light that is in his own heart," and Sequoyah nodded in understanding.

I have heard many accounts of Sequoyah's life, and of the long period of experimentation through which he labored before discovering that eighty-six syllables are used in the Cherokee language, and that writing it would mean merely setting down symbols to represent the syllables.

His personal history is vague. He knew that a white man, about whom he was never told however, was his father. Perhaps that man's name was Gist, as some said, and had been a Virginia gentleman sent by President Washington to recruit Cherokee warriors to fight the British. His mother may have married this white man, or it may have been only a woods romance. To Sequoyah, as to his people, that was not important; all such talk about who was whose father was only sound. He was all Cherokee; he did not know, nor would ever learn, any other language or way of living.

Dan spoke to him of Sam Worcester's discovery, on setting up his press, of the complexity of the language and its fine shades of meaning. Sequoyah nodded, and said: "We have always liked to talk, and to say exactly what is in our minds. While I was a boy, I listened to the head men and saw how they took care to find the best words. They were like a singer who makes up something he wishes the people to remember.

"I found out," Sequoyah went on, "that the white man could save his words by putting them on paper. I began to wonder how we also could do that; and I spoke to some of the young men about it. They told me I had a foolish idea, for the Indian is made different from the white man. The Creator of men had offered the book to the Indian, whom He created first, and the bow and arrow to the white man. But the Indian was slow to take the book, so the white man stole it. The Indian must take the bow and arrow, and make his living by hunting. But, of course, that was only a story.

"So I began to think about how to save Cherokee words on paper. Maybe I could make a picture, the way I had learned to do, that would mean a word. But too many pictures would be needed. Maybe just a mark for each word would do; but soon I had so many different marks that no one could remember them all.

"I studied about this a long time, while I was working in silver at the bench, or in my garden, even after my wife Sally came to keep my fire, even after my little girl was old enough to talk. All this time, the others said I was thinking foolish thoughts. Sally said the same thing until I began to think about writing in syllables, and found out that there were not many. Then she helped me. We both listened carefully to the people's talk, and put down a sign for each syllable—any kind of sign, a letter out of a white man's book I had, a bird track, a cross, just anything easy for us to remember.

"Still I had too many signs, and I tried to cut some out. That was all right; Sally and I could say everything without many of them. When I had only eighty-six left, I found out that I could not throw away any more. Then I got some paper at the trading post kept by John Ross and Mr. Meigs, learned how to whittle a pen, and make ink out of boils on the oak trees. Then I said to some of the young men who had scoffed at me, 'Now I am ready to show you how to write.'

"Sally helped me, and so did my little girl. At first, the people said it was a trick when I sent my daughter clear away, wrote down words that were said, and went away myself before my daughter came back and read on the paper what they had said. I asked for a few young men to teach. They learned fast, and could meet any test. Then all the people believed, and the head men wanted to learn. Then everybody wanted to learn, for John Ross and Hicks and Jolly, and even Pathfinder, said I had found out something our people ought to know; and John Ross fixed it so that I would get two hundred dollars a year to live on, and I was able to spend my time going among the people and teaching them to read and write. This I did in Georgia and Tennessee, and in Arkansas; and when the people had to leave Arkansas, I came with them. They gave me a salt spring to work to help make my living, and I built my cabin in the neighborhood where many are living.

"Washington has not paid me for the property I lost in Arkansas, but I get along all right. Sometimes I yoke my oxen to my old cart, load my bedding and things to eat, and drive to my salt spring to camp for two or three weeks. I start the fires under my salt kettles, chop wood and trade salt for more, and talk to all who come about reading and writing in Cherokee while we watch the kettles.

"In cold weather, we go to hunt coons at night. We sit by the fire while the dogs are working, and the others listen to what I have to say. The people in Georgia have sent writings to me about this printing machine at New Echota, and have also sent the newspapers that go out to the people. That is something the white Jesus-talker Worcester and the young man Boudinot have done back yonder. And now," Sequoyah tapped Dan's knee with a hard brown forefinger, "you will do the same thing for us here?"

"I mean to try," Dan nodded.

We went to the cabin erected for our print shop, and Dan explained as well as his limited knowledge of printing permitted the process of setting type, locking it into forms, putting the forms on the press, inking them, and impressing white paper upon them.

"Ho," said Sequoyah, "so that is the white man's magic. It will make my work go fast, like the spreading of dung on the plowed field before the beans are planted."

He refilled his pipe from the worn buckskin pouch in which he kept a mixture of tobacco and fragrant powdered sumac leaves, lit it, and stood for a time looking out upon the northern slope of Oak Hill, then asked, "Will you put the Jesus talk into Cherokee and save it with this machine?"

"Yes," Dan answered, "and other writing also, such as the laws which the Cherokee have made to govern themselves in an orderly manner, and advice about what to plant in this country and the best way to care for crops."

"And," Sequoyah suggested, "the old beliefs and the old stories of our people?"

"Yes; such things as I have heard from Ta-ka-to-ka and Ta-ka-e-tuh and Dik-keh the Just. They are as important as our Jesus talk."

"Good. Maybe this Jesus talk is not all lies, and maybe some of the old beliefs of the Cherokees were wrong. The road to the truth ought to be plain, but it is not always that way. We will both look for it."

"That will be good," said Dan. "Now you shall come with me to see the boys and girls at work; and then you will tell me the best way to save our pumpkins and squash through the winter."

Sequoyah was for cutting the pumpkins into thick rings and hanging them to dry on wooden pegs driven into the rafters, saying "It is the old way, and we like their fragrance in the house."

He went on to say that a whole man wishes to please all of his senses. "His eyes are pleased when he looks at truly-made ornaments like the bracelets and gorgets of silver I hammer, or the feathers of a pretty bird. His ears bring him pleasure when they hear the first redbird in the month of budding willows. His tongue is pleased with the taste of wild honey, or well mixed tobacco in the pipe. His nose—but I have already spoken of drying pumpkin rings; and as we travel through the woods we sniff for pleasing scents like hunting dogs trailing a fox. When we are very old and blind and deaf, and unable to taste good things very well, there is left for us the pleasure of touching soft and smooth things like the faces and fat legs of our little grandchildren."

"And the heart?" Dan prompted.

"It is that room in a man's body where he sits alone; and if it is pleasant to sit there, we say he has a good heart. Also, you and I know that no pleasure is altogether enjoyable that is not understood by the mind. Best of all is what we think about first and then turn into something we can see or hear or taste or smell or touch."

"You are thinking now of your syllabary," said Dan, "and the press which we hope to use for the people's pleasure and profit?"

"Yes, these thoughts are filling my mind all these days."

Sequoyah's visit lasted a week. In that time he spoke often with the boys and girls, coming into the classes at any time he pleased or gathering them about as he limped slowly across the playground. He found Uncle Frank, and sat in his crowded room talking with the old negro and stirring him to eloquence, in all but unintelligible Cherokee, on the subject of Dan's ministry. Only in Ellen's presence did he appear uneasy. He sensed her indifference to his syllabary and his passion for teaching it. Also, he felt and resented her contempt for Dan's work. He himself might scorn Jesus talk, but he believed Dan to be as honest and as devoted to his mission as he himself was to educating the Cherokee to read and write their own language.

Seeing them together so much, Ellen gibed, "Wouldn't you know Dan and that old crackpot would be chums!"

Once Sequoyah said to Miss Eula, half seriously, "In the old days, when it was permitted to take more than one wife, I would have asked my uncle to go to your mother and arrange for you to keep my second fire—as you are doing for the head man here."

Miss Eula was shocked, and resentful, "No, no, that is not true!"

Sequoyah smiled, and explained, "Not in the old way, I know. You do not lie with him, but in a way of your own you are his woman."

Grasping his real meaning, she interpreted the words to us, and turned to say to Sequoyah, "If I can help this man to keep alive the fire of faith in his work, you may call me what you will; I am flattered that you think of me as his second wife!"

Sequoyah joined in our laughter when Miss Eula told us what she had said. Ellen's mirth, however, was forced, and after our guest had gone off to sleep she said, "I should think even a more ignorant savage than Sequoyah would know that we don't share our husbands with other women. At any rate, I don't!"

"But," Dan defended Sequoyah, "don't you see how he meant the words, my beloved?"

"Perhaps," she said coldly, "I see more than you would admit to seeing."

"I know; you're very clever, Ellen." It was the first time I had heard Dan speak to her with a tinge of sarcasm in his voice. Infuriated, she broke out, "The old man spoke the truth. You *are* living with two wives, although neither you nor she," her anger-flashing eyes shifted to Miss Eula, "would admit it."

I rose to go at the same moment Miss Eula did, but Dan begged, "Please, both of you stay; we are all concerned with what Ellen has said. Now," he asked calmly, "will you tell us your reasons for saying it?"

"Dan," she cried passionately, "it's because I love you so much that I can see the truth. She," Ellen would not use Miss Eula's name, but put into the pronoun an accent of insult, "has taken my place here as though—"

Dan interrupted, "You must know that some one has to do the woman's part in our work. Since you have been unable, or unwilling, to carry that burden, Miss Eula has shouldered it; and I thank God that she has proved competent to carry the extra load."

"You love her, Dan, and she loves you," Ellen said bluntly.

"That," Dan said hotly, "is a wicked untruth, and I ask you to apologize!"

"Apologize for opening your eyes?" Ellen laughed as though a small boy had flared out at her. "Dan, I don't mean that she has slept with you while I was away. I don't believe you have held her in your arms, or kissed her. I don't believe she would have permitted you to love her in that way if you had wanted to. There you have, both of you, the only apology I can offer."

"Then why," Dan insisted, "do you believe you spoke the truth just now?"

"Because, as you have told me," she smiled, "I am a specialist in the matter of love. I know a woman's heart; and, my dear, I know you. I know that in you and in her, in all of your kind, the passion for serving God is stimulated by the desires of the flesh."

"I believe," said Dan, rising, "that you have made yourself quite clear."

"I'm glad if I have," Ellen said. "Tomorrow, if it can be arranged, I should like to go back to Kate Acton for a time—until I can see my way more clearly."

"Of course," Dan said. "Paul will ride to Gibson with you, and bring your horse back."

I wanted to say, "Dan, you should go!" I knew, however, that the suggestion would be fruitless, that the journey would be a bitter experience for both. I went off to bed hoping that by the morning Ellen and Dan would have made their peace. Perhaps she would use her love magic, her contrite kisses and the exciting surrender of her body, to convince him that she had spoken out of a passion of unreasonable jealousy. Perhaps Dan still loved her too much to permit this definite break.

Wakeful, I began to reconstruct the scene; and, to my surprise, could not recall a single word spoken by Miss Eula. She had sat rigidly in her chair, her eyes shifting mechanically from Ellen to Dan. The faintly rosy hue of her face, however, had changed to white, and she walked stiffly as she left the room.

I asked myself, Must Dan now lose both Ellen and Miss Eula? How can Miss Eula stay if Ellen goes? Always between her and Dan must stand the ugly spectre Ellen had raised. Then the question rose in my mind, Can there be any substance to Ellen's charge? But, I said to myself, there can't be. I have seen them together in close association nearly every day for seven years.

They were of the same breed as myself—on my father's side, I mean. Of my errant mother, who disappeared out of my life, after my father's death, before I could remember more than a tinkle of gaiety and a soft and fragrant breast, I know nothing. I was sure that Miss Eula and Dan were capable of maintaining the impersonal relations of fellow workers all their lives.

Yet Miss Eula had not added her denial of Ellen's accusation to Dan's, and I thought, What if I have misjudged her all these years? What if, in her heart, she has confessed her love for Dan, and has given herself to the work with all of her strength and devotion because she must be near him. What if she had determined long ago to supplant Ellen.

I thought of what this might, if true, mean to Dan. If she could work with heart and soul with him because of her secret love for him, that love might prevail over him, might be a more compelling love than Ellen's. My mind went on to another thought, Suppose Dan awoke to a physical desire for Miss Eula? It might be that the thought of children, with her as mother, would grow so compelling that he could face divorce and the consequent inevitable separation from missionary work which would follow.

In a moment of protest against that certainty, I said to myself, Why must a worker for the Lord be required to remain immune from human desires unsanctioned by some Board made up of men who cannot possibly know, cannot possibly foresee every situation that might arise?

Then I thought, Of course Dan gave himself into the power of the church missionary organization with full knowledge of its requirements. The Board's support had been, however, almost wholly spiritual, for I know that he had never received from it as salary and station expenses more than the two hundred dollars a year which the Cherokees were paying Sequoyah. For that, he had given the Board overall supervision of his work and final judgment on his personal conduct. He had not thought of the Board's authority, however, as restrictive. He had made the station self[-]supporting with a self-sacrificing zeal that was as deep as that of the men in control at the New York Mission rooms.

In my mind, I went on, Dan's work for the Cherokees would not be less effective if he should divorce Ellen and marry Miss Eula. I remembered hearing The Blanket say that he had put away a wife who became a "singing bird" and gone back to his own clan. Certainly The Blanket had not lost the confidence of his people, nor his influence for good because he would not marty[r]ize himself by cleaving unto that unworthy woman. I thought, The Cherokees are a reasonable, understanding people.

I thought of Sequoyah, secure in the knowledge that the importance of his work was everywhere acknowledged, whose personal life was no concern of his people. His Sally, now proud of his prominence, had been nagging, shrewish, had berated him for wasting time on what she called the profitless juggling of words; and it was said that he had taken a second wife to console him. In a moment of unhaltered fancy, I pictured Dan adjusting himself to life as the Indians did.

But that would mean sanctioning immorality! Then, for the first time, I put to myself the question, What is morality? And after that no hope of sleep remained. I heard the early morning gobbling of wild turkey cocks in the Illinois River timber before abandoning such speculations and banishing the fancies they generated. I dressed, and went to ask Dan if I should groom and saddle my gelding and the mare Ellen was to ride. He came to the door at my knock, and I knew that he, too, had not slept.

"Yes," he answered, as calmly as though I had asked for a geography book for one of my classes. "Be ready to start whenever Ellen is. Try to make Wolfcatcher's place before sunset, and sleep there. You should be back in three days. I will take your school work while you're gone. Ellen's things, except what she will take with her, will remain here until they're sent for."

There it was, all in a breath, the answer to my question as to the finality of their separation. My heart went out to him, but I knew that I must not utter a word of sympathy. I said only, "It's good weather for traveling."

Ten

Sequoyah was standing with Dan and Miss Eula, who seemed hardly more constrained than usual, when Ellen and I mounted to ride away, offered his palm and, through Miss Eula, wished her a pleasant ride. Then he said something at which Miss Eula flushed and shook her head.

Ellen's parting words were casual, spoken cheerfully, as though she were going only for a short visit; and as we rode out of Dan's hearing, she said, "Paul, I believe my farewell to Oak Hill was seemly, as befits a lady?" I said nothing. Then, smiling, "Did you understand what Sequoyah said that your dear Miss Eula would not interpret? I'm sure it was something about me."

"Yes," I said, "but I caught only a few words; something about a singing bird."

We rode in silence until we forded the river. Then, with affected gaiety, she exclaimed, "There, I have crossed my Rubicon; now let the Gauls beware!"

"You will never come back?"

"Never is a long time, Paul. At this moment, I can think of no reason why I should."

"Don't you love Dan?"

"Yes, and always shall. But you ought to know by now that I cannot go on paying the price he demands for living with him. I have found out that he is a luxury I cannot afford."

"Dan is a fair man, and he loves you."

"It is not enough to be fair, according to one's own conception. Paul, am I a dull, plain woman?"

"No, of course not, Ellen. You're lovely, brilliant; and fascinating when you care to be."

"I've wanted to be that to Dan, but have failed. I am not young; I shall soon be thirty. I can no longer hope to persuade Dan to give up the unreal life he is leading, his play-acting pose as a humble regent of Christ."

I resented her words, "Dan is not play-acting; I know the work he's doing is real and important!"

"And I know," she flared, "that I want him to live among the people I like, and succeed among men, not among these childlike savages. I want him to leave what you call his work to the emotional fanatics who like to preach and pray and sing themselves into orgasms of ecstasy. Dan is not their sort."

"No, thank God, he is not; and what he does to help the Cherokees has been, and always will be, sane and practical. It will be remembered."

"And what he will not do for me, if I should wear out my life for him—will that also be remembered, Paul?"

"You should not have married him."

"How could I help it? I loved him, desired him so, and knew so well that otherwise I could not have him—"

"Hush!" I almost shouted. "You're talking like a light woman."

"No; I am only telling the truth, Paul, and you hear it so seldom that it shocks you. When we three drove from New York, I had no intention of living as a missionary's wife. I counted on weaning Dan from his praying and hymn singing within a year, and taking him back to New York. My father liked him, and still does; he could have done so much for him. We should have had children, a normal happy life together. Paul," she turned a dazzling smile on me, "if it had only been you that I fell in love with!"

"Yes," I, too, tried telling the truth, "you could have overcome me."

"You could be a wonderful lover, Paul; you have the loins of a Samson, and you would be tender and considerate." She smiled at my obvious embarrassment. "Once, you remember, I was tempted to find out."

"Is that true? I believed you were tantalizing me only to make Dan jealous."

"Not altogether. I was desperately afraid of the wilderness, and even then I was beginning to doubt that I could cure Dan of his obsession. I wanted to escape from the swamps he was facing so inexorably. I wanted to get away from your courageous and pious Miss Eula, too. I felt small, and so damned inefficient, in her presence."

"You hated her, I know."

"I did, and you would have come to hate her if you had married her, as you hoped to do then. No," she held up a gloved hand to stop me when I tried to say that I preferred not to talk about Miss Eula, "you would have lost her to Dan, as I have lost Dan to her. You and I would have been a better team. You were hardly more consecrated to missionary work than I was. I was sure of that, and I thought of using you to get me away from the wilderness. I might have gone back to New York with you. My father would have forgiven me if I had loved you, wanted to divorce Dan and marry you; and he would have managed Mama. He would have helped you along in the world, as he would help Dan, as he has helped Richard Panther. And if you grew tired of me, or I of you—well, I considered all that. But you were so self-righteous and loyal to Dan that I had to give up that plan of escape."

"I supposed it was only Miss Eula's going off in the darkness with Dan that made you tempt me."

"That, too, of course. I *was* jealous of her. I knew that there was no fire I could help Dan to keep burning in the swamps except that which I could fan with my love; and now that no longer warms him. He would not come into my bed last night . . . So you were tempted, Paul?"

"Yes, I trembled as you touched me, yet I hated you for what I thought was your cheap device for hurting Dan. I hated you, and wanted to kiss you. I felt a physical hunger for your lips."

"Well," she cried, "now we *are* telling the truth! Why didn't you kiss me?"

"You have answered that; I was loyal to Dan, and am still. I believed, also, that you would have been outraged had I taken you in my arms."

"No, although it would not have been easy for me to pretend to love you when my heart was full of Dan."

"Will you go back to New York?"

"Who knows! My father will give me enough to live anywhere and anyhow I like. He will think I am foolish to leave Dan, but he does understand and love me. Paul, my father is the greatest man in the world!"

"And your mother?"

"You have seen her, Paul. I have always loved her for her sweetness; and have had my way with her since I could talk. It is she who needs protection. She is a lady in the Continental sense, a mannered, old-fashioned lady; I have laughed at her when she said that being a lady is the highest possible calling for a female. But she is sincere; she ha[s] worked at her calling, and is as truly consecrated to caste, as Dan is to his God."

"Don't you believe in anything, Ellen?"

"Of course. I believe in making the most of myself, getting the greatest possible satisfaction out of life. I love love, and want it in the most convenient and civilized surroundings. I want it with one man whose body and mind please me. Dan was everything I wanted for a time. The months of our honeymoon in New York, while you were waiting to come as his helper, were glorious. Every one liked and admired Dan, and I was insane with love for him."

"Isn't it always true," I asked, "that passionate physical love dies out, and—"

"And, you were going to say, Paul, that only the love of Jesus lasts? Well, you don't believe it any more than I do, or your pious Miss Eula does."

"I wish she had married Dan."

"Perhaps it would have been best, yet I'm egoist enough to believe that I gave him something of more value than she could have given. I made him feel; in his human, not his missionary heart he understands his problems better because of me. I know that I've hurt him, but he's more of a man—"

"He was always that," I broke in. "I ought to know; I've been with him all my life."

"You!" she shot the word at me and then, bitterly, "You haven't seen him break down from disappointment, haven't heard him weep in my arms and beg me to love him in his way and to believe in his God. I have; and my scorn has humanized him. He has realized that to some of us God is only a word, and Christ an impossible paragon of perfection. So many of his dear Cherokees are like me that he's a better missionary for having had the truth from me."

"I can't believe you, Ellen."

"No," she spoke quietly now, "for you don't really know him. You tight-lipped men of New England prefer to believe in an ideal. Dan has been yours. What has moved him, under the surface, you haven't seen. I wish I were like you. I wonder if you could make me over? Perhaps with you—"

"With me!" I broke in. "Now? You're saying wicked words."

"Wicked?" she challenged me with her eyes. "Are you then outraged, as you believed I would have been had you kissed me in the swamp? Remember, we are telling the truth. The truth is that Dan and I are separated. My future is in my own hands, and you are as free as I am to make your own future."

I attempted to speak, to protest, but she stopped me, "Let me finish what I was about to say. I believe that with you I could be reasonable, and yielding. You would not want to make me over according to your own pattern; and Paul, I believe I would be content with you as a lover."

"Good lord, Ellen!" I was amazed. I had not believed it possible for a lady to utter such words.

Before I could say more, she went on: "It is perfectly practicable for us both. While I was with Kate Acton I wrote to father asking for money. I have it here," she touched a visible mound that swelled her riding skirt over her thigh, "enough to take us to New York, and to keep you until you could place yourself. We could turn at this moment toward the Arkansas River, and take the first downriver boat on the way to the Mississippi, New York, and a new life. It could be a good life for us both. In our hearts nothing has changed since that night in the swamp, except that I know I am free of Dan. You could send word to him that I changed my mind about going to Gibson, and that you were escorting me to New York—and let him think what he likes. You could come back if you want to, if you were not satisfied with me."

It was so cool, so starkly realistic and, as she said, so practicable! It was utterly, outrageously impossible, yet I had let her go on. I was sickened and ashamed, but I had let her go on. She looked at me appraisingly, as though to measure my power of resistance, and continued: "I'm not forgetting your loyalty to Dan; I forget nothing that concerns the heart. I, too, have been loyal in act. I have not allowed any other man to possess my body because I hoped to save Dan. But now I want a lover, another husband, as decent and satisfying as I believe you would be, Paul. I have been starving for love. You, too."

"I?"

"Of course, although you wouldn't admit it. I believe you are a virgin. You have waited for your Miss Eula, or some other godly virgin to share your bed for the first time; and you're becoming slightly wizened. Already, and you're not yet twenty-nine! Paul, your Bible says that it is not good for man to live alone. Your Bible tells how Naomi and Ruth contrived so that Ruth might have Boaz. They were realists in those days, as you and Dan say the Cherokees are today. Well, so am I."

I blurted, "These are crazy thoughts. I should be ashamed even to think of Dan after—" [I]t was impossible to put a confession of my temptation into words.

"Oh, say it, Paul, 'after deserting him and going off with his wife.'

Go on being honest with yourself. Does Dan really need you? No; he can get another helper who will do as well as you. Would you be going away with his wife? No; I am his wife now in name only. You would be going to make a life of your own with a woman you have already desired and will learn to love. Is that not true?"

"No!" I denied hotly. "I hate you, Ellen. I have hated you since we left Kingslake, ever since I realized that you were set against following Dan and helping him."

"Yes; but you've desired me, and would love me. That is true, isn't it?"

"You could make any man desire you," I said.

"Well, my dear," she spoke in a whisper as she leaned close, "shall we find a warm, sheltered place soon where we can make a fire and prepare our food. You may kiss me, and we can—" [N]ow it was she who could not complete in words the thought that was in her mind. Then, "We could know then whether or not I have only dreamed of you as the lover to satisfy me, whether or not I have been thinking and talking nonsense."

I was trembling as I said, "You know you can have your way with me."

But the strain had become too great for Ellen; and in the very act of urging her mare close to my mount and offering her lips for a foretaste of bliss, she burst into laughter, wild and frightening laughter. I had never before seen anyone taken by that sort of hysteria. Out of the discordant cackle, after a time, words emerged: "Paul, it's comic . . . Imagine me making love to *you* . . . I don't love you, or want you . . . I don't want any damn man but Dan . . . And you hate me . . . Oh, you're so damn comic, so damn—why am I cursing like a damn strumpet! But you're so solemn, Paul, as though you were going to your doom . . . It's so comic, so damn comic!" Her voice rose almost to a shriek.

"Stop it, Ellen!" I seized her arm and shook her roughly.

"Yes, hit me, Paul, knock this devil of mirth out of me! Oh, I don't know what to do!" She dropped the reins, put her hands over her face, and broke into a fit of weeping. I pulled up, held the reins of her mare until it was passed, until she said quietly, "Forget it, Paul. I'm not worth thinking about, not even worth lying with for an hour in a pile of these golden autumn leaves. Will you believe that, Paul?"

"No!" I was aroused now. "I do want you, although I hate you—and love you, too. You're right, I've never been with a woman, and I want you."

She began to weep again; and I knew that if I should thrust all thought of Dan from me I could have her. We could have our hour, then turn south from the Gibson road. My life would thenceforward be passed in New York, and she might mother my children. But I could not put Dan out of my mind. I said, "Yes, let us forget it."

Perhaps I was wrong; I shall never know. At the time, I knew only that I was thankful for the strength that had been granted me to resist the temptation.

"Yes, let us forget it. Here is the truth, Paul: losing Dan drove me insane. As I talked to you, I imagined that he was listening. I wanted to hurt him as terribly as I could. I imagined that somehow he would see us lying together, see me giving you the pleasure of my body, the delight I had sworn never to give any man but Dan. I wanted to kill his faith in women. I would have lain with you if you had really wanted me, but you know that I'm not worth the sacrifice of your loyalty to Dan."

"You will come back to him," I said.

"No, he doesn't want me. He never needed me. Why did you say that?"

"Perhaps because I know Dan better than you think I do. I'm sure he will always love you, and I believe that anyone he loves can never escape from him."

"But you're wrong, Paul; he doesn't love me, I tell you! Haven't you seen that for yourself?"

"I have thought so, yes," I said, "and then, a little while ago as we were talking I tried to imagine him hating me and putting me out of his mind and heart when he found out that I had gone off with you. I couldn't. His love of me, and of you, would not be killed; some day we should both beg to be taken back to his heart."

"Paul, Paul," she whispered pityingly, "I have been blind. I should have seen the truth, but you two Vermont men have been so close-mouthed; and perhaps you didn't realize the truth yourselves. Let me try to say it now, decently and in the right words, for this love that binds you two together is decent and right."

"Of course; how could it be otherwise?"

"It's a stronger bond," she went on, ignoring my question, "than could ever exist between a man and a woman; to break it might mean death."

"It might," I said.

"And I was so blind that I believed I could come between you. I have believed that some day he might send you away, with your

Miss Eula, and I would no longer have to hear his 'Paul, what do you think of this?' or, 'I'll see what Paul and Miss Eula say about that.' "

There flashed into my mind Miss Eula's accusing words as we were pulling away from Kingslake, "Paul, you're jealous of Ellen!" I quoted her words now.

"You see," she said. "Your New England Miss Eula would know. She understands you and Dan; and she would have shared you with Dan if you had married her. I couldn't, and really, Paul," she laughed, "I'm the comic one, thinking a little while ago that I could take you from Dan!"

We slept, as Dan had suggested, at Wolfcatcher's home. They found a bed for Ellen to sleep in alone, though it was in the room with the parents and two of the children. I wondered if she would complain the next day of the crowding and the "stuffiness", but she did not. I shared the blanket of a son of six, who lay quietly at my side until, just before he slept, he crowded close as though seeking the comfort of an arm about his shoulders. He was a clean, shy child; and as he lay warm against me I thought of the consolation Sequoyah had said remains to the aged and blind, the feel of a child's soft, sweet flesh. I touched the chubby arm of the boy thrust against my face, and said to myself, This is good. For such as this child Dan is giving himself. It is worth while.

I had no more than a glimpse of the curiously gay, uneasy, cosmopolitan life of Gibson post. The officers had come from service in many quarters. Some of the older ones had fought with Mad Anthony Wayne against the Indians of the Ohio territory. One had been with the vainglorious William Henry Harrison at Tippecanoe and had seen Tecumseh. Another had been attached by Jackson to the Cherokee regiment that had helped him to defeat the Creeks. Their families were in Virginia, Pennsylvania, New York, and New England. They were poised here on this outmost frontier, ready to move out swiftly under Colonel Acton against whatever bands of Indians, Osages, Cherokees, Pawnees, or Comanches, the Government thought required chastisement.

Kate Acton, a slender, nervous blonde, was older than Ellen and, like Ellen, childless, intent on making life as easy and diverting as possible, and seriously occupied in the struggle to preserve her good looks. She was in a flutter over a letter that had lately come to her husband; and Ellen was scarcely off the mare before the Colonel's lady exclaimed, "My dear, you have come in the nick of time. We are to have a visit from Mr. Irving within the week!"

"Who is he?" Ellen asked, unhooking and dropping her riding skirt.

"Why, the great Washington Irving, of course."

"Oh, the writing man. Mother doesn't like him. She thinks that he's not quite a gentleman because he wrote that comic Knickerbocker's History of New York."

"Your mother may be right. At any rate, he's coming with something of a retinue, a Commissioner sent by the Government to treat with the Indians, an English gentleman, a Swiss nobelman, and a galliard Frenchman. He proposes to go out with the Osages on their fall hunt, and Dick may have to supply an escort of troopers for a tour on the prairies beyond the Verdigris River. I believe Mr. Irving means to write a book about his experiences. Until he leaves for the country of the Pawnees, where Commissioner Ellsworth is to treat with the savages, I shall have to entertain him. I hope you have read his works. I haven't; I never read."

"Fortunately," said Ellen, "I have. I named my first boy doll Ichabod, it looked so gawky and solemn—and nearly as dull as Paul here. Oh, but you are not acquainted with Dan's nephew, Paul Wear."

Kate Acton gave me her hand, then sent a questioning glance toward Ellen. I flushed, wondering if women like Mrs. Acton and Ellen could read one another's thoughts. "I'm sure," she smiled at me in a very friendly way, "you have taken excellent care of Mrs. Wear. Your uncle, of course, is so busy at Oak Hill that he could not come?"

Ellen answered for me, "Yes, he's like Dick; and, like you and Dick, he has a distinguished guest to entertain, the great Sequoyah."

"I've heard of him. The chaplain has told me something of his wonderful Cherokee alphabet; and that reminds me, probably Mr. Irving would like to meet him. I'll have Dick send for him."

I was tempted to say that if Mr. Washington Irving wishes to know Sequoyah he would have to visit his cabin, go with him to his salt spring, and travel with him among the people as Mr. John Howard Payne had done at Chief John Ross' suggestion—and had himself arrested for his pains by the Georgia militia, along with Ross.

Mrs. Acton asked me to stay overnight, sharing the chaplain's quarters, but as it was only a little past noon I declined. I stayed to bait the horses, however, and sit down with Ellen to a whipped-up luncheon. The Colonel came in before I left, a tall, thin man of forty-odd who wore his calvary officer's uniform with an air, to greet Ellen warmly and me civilly, and ask about Dan with such real interest that I dismissed from my mind the suspicion that it was he, not Kate Acton, who drew Ellen to Gibson.

I rode fast on my return, to reach Wolfcatcher's home before the family went to bed. As Dan once wrote, "The Indians go to roost with the turkeys, unless they have cotton to warm and pick by firelight. Darkness is apt to find them in their blankets, ashes raked over the coals in the fireplace, and the dog curled up in its nest of rags at the door."

As I sat before Wolfcatcher's fire between sunset and dusk, cross-legged on a worn blanket spread on the dirt floor, with a dish of meat and corn in front of me and a spoon and a sheath knife as my only eating tools, Wolfcatcher's wife spoke to her man and gestured toward me with her chin. He laughed, then interpreted, "He say this one here," he touched the lad of six, "wan' to sleep by you."

"Good," I grinned at the boy. "Tell him I will be glad."

The boy hid his face in his mother's lap. But presently, as Wolfcatcher and I talked of the report he had read in a copy of the *Cherokee Phoenix* that the Georgia Cherokees might soon be forced to emigrate to Indian Territory, he came to stand beside me. He was like a half tamed young deer, wanting to be touched but shying from an unfamiliar hand. I pretended not to be aware of him until I felt his hand on my shoulder; then, until we went to our blanket, he sat in my lap quietly playing with the sheathed knife I unhooked from my belt.

Wolfcatcher said, with unexpected directness, "That woman don' come back to Plain Talker's cabin, I think."

"No," I said, seeing no reason for evasion.

"She marry now with that other one?"

"I don't know. Maybe no woman will keep his fire now."

"So? Well, our Jennie—he is marry now to Gu-le-ga of the Aniwadie clan—say that one is good woman, make fire good, wan' baby—ever'thing," and Wolfcatcher smiled as he told his wife in Cherokee what he had said. She nodded vigorously.

Riding on to Oak Hill, I strove to put out of my mind what had passed between Ellen and me. I tried to believe that she had been playing on my imagination with words; and I recalled Dan's tribute, "My beloved, you are more expert with words than I could ever hope to be. I suppose it's the Gallic strain in you." I thought, She will always experiment, with words, with men, with love. But as I passed the drift of brightly colored leaves in which she might have lain with me as a final gesture of defiance of Dan and his unyielding purpose, I knew that in our hearts we had both been disloyal.

I dreaded facing Dan, answering the questions he might ask, possibly seeing him break down, as Ellen said she had seen him, if I should have to tell him that she had no intention of coming back on his terms. I slowed the horses to a pace that irked the mare I led, and I thought, At least there's one creature anxious for the comfort of Oak Hill.

Dan's questions, however, were concerned only with the commonplace details of the journey and "What's the news at Gibson?" He smiled at my report of Kate Acton's flurry over the coming of Mr. Irving, and said, "I will do what I can to bring him and Sequoyah together, for Irving might help us in the East to find support for our press."

He had not yet seen the copy of the *Cherokee Phoenix* which had given Wolfcatcher warning of the imminent removal of the Eastern Cherokees, and he said, "It is probably true. I don't believe Sam Worcester would have allowed it to be printed if it was only a rumor. Jackson, and the Georgians, are becoming desperately impatient to send them west. We must prepare to serve them in every way we can when they arrive, for they will be even more demoralized and destitute than the Arkansas Cherokees were; and they are thrice as numerous. Paul, we have work to do!"

Eleven

By no word did Dan betray his unhappiness at the loss of Ellen, and the only difference in his routine of work and planning was that he seemed to lean more heavily than before on me. I noticed this more quickly because of her saying that the bond of affection between him and me was unbreakable.

We had more problems to solve in after-supper discussions, into which Miss Eula was gradually drawn. Dan's attitude towards her seemed to have been affected in no way by Ellen's accusation, and her self-consciousness in his presence soon disappeared.

Certain stark figures formed the foundation of our planning. By now, there were six thousand Cherokees in Indian Territory, and an estimated sixteen thousand in Georgia, Tennessee, Alabama, and North Carolina; all those in the East who were to be swept up and deported to Indian Territory. How many of the exiles would survive the hardships of the journey we could only guess, but the removal would certainly mean that there would be three times as many who would need our help than we now served.

Getting ready for the greater task meant putting all of our land that was fit for cultivation under the plow and fencing it; finding means to pay for the plowing and fencing and hiring another farmer; building additions to the dormitories, dining hall, barn, cribs and granaries; acquiring more tools and shop equipment. The Mission Board in New York supplied a few of our needs, but we must rely for most of them on contributions from friends in the East who knew of our work. Mr. Morin was among the most generous.

The printing press, a printer from Cincinnati, and Catherine and Richard Panther came. Since The Runner had already built and furnished a cabin for his brother, Richard was free to help Mason, the printer, and Uncle Frank set up the press and make cases for the Cherokee and English type. As might have been expected, parts of the press had been lost on the long voyage from Boston to New Orleans and up the Mississippi and the Arkansas rivers. Between them, however, Mason, Richard, Uncle Frank, and the blacksmith hammered out workable substitutes. Also, twenty reams of precious print paper had been exposed to rain and damaged so seriously that they could not be used until, much later, Dan and Catherine together worked out the project of printing on the splotched and faded paper a farmers' temperance almanac which proved to be one of our most popular publications.

Dan chose a four-page tract telling about missionary work in the Sandwich Islands as the first publication, saying, "I believe our readers will be interested to learn something of the problems of folks in a distant land." He wrote a sparing introduction in the form of a greeting to the readers, and quoting, as a spur to the imagination, some words from John XXI: 25 : "And there are also many things which Jesus did, the which, if they should be written every one, I suppose that even the world itself could not contain the books that should be written."

Catherine was puzzled by Ellen's absence, for the Morins, hoping that she would go back to Dan, had said nothing about their separation. Her questions were answered brusquely by Dan, Miss Eula said only, "You must ask Dan," and she came to me, saying, "There is something amiss, and I think Richard and I should know." I told her, as truthfully as I could, and she said, "I can understand; I suppose Ellen will always be the spoiled child. I'm sorry, because she was such a help and comfort to Richard and me. I loved her spirit, and have looked forward with pleasure to being here with her."

Catherine was too far gone with child to help Miss Eula in the schoolroom, but in Miss Eula's quarters it was deemed proper for her to talk with the girls in preparation for her future work as teacher. Her radiant, plumped-out face reflected her hope that her baby might be a little brown replica of Richard. She was fair, wholesome, solid—but far from stolid, as her defiance of Lakeside had shown. Miss Eula and I liked her at once, and to Dan she was both young sister and daughter.

She became a welcome member of Richard's family, and wrote, to reassure her own people at Lakeside: "I have come to love my Cherokee mother and father as though they were my own. They, and my Indian sisters and brothers, are amiable, considerate, and affectionate in their restrained fashion. My sister Susan has told me that before Richard and I arrived her father spoke of me, saying that they must all be friendly to me because I would be far away from my kin; and Richard's dear mother has made me happy by saying that I am like an own child."

One by one, she named and characterized her Cherokee brothers and sisters: "Eldest is called The Runner, a talented, serious man, and a devoted Christian, who has always had a special fondness for Richard and whom Richard adores. Susan is nineteen, very quick in her movements, smart for business, and a member of the church. Fifteen-year-old Henry much resembles my nephew, Jonas Becker, and is as full of fun as a pumpkin is of seeds. Martha, a sweet girl of twelve, is quick, bright, and when not at her lessons at Oak Hill assists Miss Benson. Betsy, eight, is our prettiest sister; she is in school, and spells English very well—she will be a smart woman; next is a brother of seven who has taken the name of a gentleman in Baltimore, Mr. James Fields, who has promised to bear the expenses of his education in the East when he is ready to go, so you can see that he is an ambitious boy; and last is precious Rebecca, the baby, sweet and grave, whom we all adore."

In another letter (Dan had me copy many of her letters, with her permission of course, to send to friends who might be moved to assist us by contributions of money) she told of the food served at her Indian mother's table: "When Richard and I go to his family for meals we have bread, made of flour or cornmeal, pork, veal, venison, squirrel, wild turkey, quail (not all at one time, of course!), butter, home-made cheese, a variety of pickles, and preserves made from wild fruits (plums and grapes.) We are served coffee or tea, and there is milk for the smaller children. When I found there a quantity of sugar, currants, and rice I made rice pudding which they all liked so much that Mother has learned how to prepare it.

"The bread is baked in an iron oven in the fireplace, which is a sort of household altar, as used to be, and I doubt not still is, the case in many New England homes. They have a variety of food-dishes made from corn, the most delicious of which they call 'conutche.' One day soon, I will write out and send you the recipe for it and other good things."

In February, she wrote, "The climate is far milder than in Massachusetts. The frogs have been piping for the last three evenings, and last evening we sat with our doors open."

Of Richard's work, she wrote: "He is absorbed with Uncle Dan (so we have learned to call Mr. Wear) in studying the Cherokee language as a grammarian would. Richard, of course, has always spoken it, and writes it easily in Sequoyah's characters, but to translate its subtleties into English is a baffling task. He and Uncle Dan have found in all verbs at least twenty-nine tenses in the indicative mood alone; and the verb form 'to tie' has no fewer than one hundred and seventy-eight variations of the present indicative! I wonder that any one could master the language. Uncle Dan says it is only a question of time, however, and quotes the Arkansas River steamboat captain who said that his vessel always arrives *in* time, if not *on* time."

She and Richard fitted into our life, our work, and Dan's plans as perfectly as Ellen's expensive gloves ever fitted her shapely hands. In the spirit of Ruth, she wrote to her mother, "I am content. The place of my birth, of course, is dear to me, but I love this people and with them I wish to live and die."

Catherine could not remember when she first began to write. "It's a secret vice," she confessed when Dan found two pages of foolscap on his desk, "to which I have been addicted since I used to take my dolls and scraps of paper under the bed, and hide my scribblings in the attic of my doll house. Honestly, Uncle Dan, I didn't mean to leave this here as though hinting that I wanted you to read it."

He passed the pages to me, saying, "I'd like your opinion, Paul." The piece was in the form of a story-tract, more or less like two that Sam Worcester had printed for the Cherokees, "Poor Sarah," and "Patient Joe." She had chosen to tell the life story of Catherine Swan; and though she felt obliged to underline the moral significance of the vivid Cherokee girl's brief time on earth, the writing was vital and warm without being sentimental. In my bungling fashion, I tried to say something of the sort to Dan. He cut me short, "Yes, it's decidedly worth printing," and called Catherine back to say, "So you're a writer, Kit! With your permission, we shall print this, and look forward to other contributions."

Dan sat back from his desk, took off the spectacles he had begun to use since being compelled to read and write so much by candle light (sometimes he was at it until three o'clock in the morning), and said, "Paul and I have agreed that something of Catherine Swan that was more than an echo of what you've heard got inside you and set you afire. I suspect that you ought to write only when you're at the boiling point."

I wanted to urge her to write her own story since Richard's appearance at Lakeside, but said nothing because such a piece would involve Ellen and we no longer spoke of her in Dan's presence.

It seemed to me that Miss Eula had deliberately withdrawn a little from us, as though she had said to herself, "It must not be thought that I have more than a friendly interest in Dan, or could in any way have turned him from Ellen." The truth was, of course, that from the moment, at Kingslake, Dan chose her to go to Hebron Creek she had influenced him. For more than seven years, she had been showing up Ellen's deficiencies by her own competence. I could understand why Ellen hated her. The wonder was that by now Dan had not seemed to realize how important she had become to him, or that in her love of the work he directed smoldered the passion of a whole woman craving completion.

What Ellen had said of me—that already I had become somewhat wizened for lack of a woman in my bed—recurred to me as I watched Miss Eula graduating into the sort of spinsterhood I had known in Vermont. She would never be the acid-sharp, frustrated old maid type, but I could believe that while Catherine was blooming in the enjoyment of Richard's love, and Ellen was finding with a lover or a second husband the passionate experiences which fed the springs of her beauty, Miss Eula's lovely face would be taking on a pinched look, and her eyes would reflect unsatisfied yearnings hard for me, who loved her, to watch.

She had not been without suitors. Missionaries from the East, widowed workers from western stations, and single men in charge of mission schools had ridden hopefully to Hebron Creek and Oak Hill to pay court to her. Correct, formal advances they had been, such as "Miss Benson, will you do me the honor of walking to evening service with me?" and "Miss Eula, may I hope that you will consent to be my wife?" She walked with them, and smiled at their turgid wooing. She was interested in their problems, questioned them searchingly about their school routine. Driven to answer their vital question, she had said firmly, "I am sorry, but I trust you can see that I am well satisfied here." In her way, she could be as chilling as a February sleet storm.

* * *

In small contingents, Cherokees from the East began appearing in Indian Territory. The first few hundreds who came were the families of the three score and ten signers of the farcical treaty negotiated by President Jackson's agents. Although a two years' grace had been written into that spurious agreement, in which time all Eastern Cherokees were required to remove, the Indian signers had come at once lest the others whom they had betrayed should invoke against them a tribal law which made alienation of Cherokee land treason punishable by death.

By the time they reached Indian Territory, these Treaty Party exiles had ample cause for bitterness against the Government. They had not been paid for their abandoned homes and possessions. They had found that the responsibility for conducting them to their new homeland had been entrusted to contractors who had proved incompetent and venal, willing to sell the lives of a band of emigrants for a share of the food contractors' thieving.

It was from Crowheart, who settled nearest to Oak Hill, that we had the story of the making of the infamous treaty. For more than twenty years, Georgia had been putting increasing pressure on the Federal Government to remove the Indians from the state. At last Georgia's land-hungry whites had put into office a Governor who dared to tell Jackson and the Congress of the United States that if the Federal Government did not expel the Cherokees the Georgia militia would.

Spurred by that threat, Jackson had sent two men with peremptory orders to make a treaty of removal. One was an honest Tennessee gentleman who soon discovered the hopelessness of the task and resigned his appointment. The other was known as "Old Hickory's last resort" when dealing with Indians, an ex-preacher untroubled by scruples or conscience.

Dan's face grew hard as he listened to Crowheart's account of the ex-preacher's attempts to bribe the Cherokee head men[;] his denunciations of Chief John Ross who was fighting with words, at Washington and in New York and New England, grimly and eloquently to save their homeland for his people[;] his lies, and his angry threat that if the Cherokees would not go peacefully they would be driven away by the sword.

Crowheart said that this agent had called upon the Cherokees to meet with him in council time after time, but at Chief Ross' urging, they refused to appear until at length a few among them argued that it would be better to make terms than to suffer forcible removal; and when still another council was called by the ex-preacher two hundred and fifty of the sixteen thousand Eastern Cherokees came to talk with him. Of these, only seventy signed the treaty of removal.

Crowheart said, "I signed only because I saw that we must go anyway. I and my family joined the first party sent off. We went first to a camp on the Hiwassee to wait until the boat was ready for us. There was not enough to eat, but the whiskey boats came and they allowed some of our men who liked to get drunk to trade everything they had for whiskey.

"We stayed there a long time. Then it was winter, and then we went down the Hiwassee and the Tennessee and the Ohio and the

Mississippi till the boat got to the mouth of the Arkansas River. Then in another boat we stayed a long time till we got to Fort Smith. It was still cold, and there was little to eat and no clothes and blankets for them that had only moccasins and cloth hunting shirts and thin pantaloons to wear.

"In that party when we came to the camp on the Hiwassee were sixty-three; only forty-two landed from the boat at Fort Smith. The others we buried in the ground, or put under piles of logs if the ground was frozen or swampy, when the boat tied up at night.

"That man who persuaded us to sign the treaty told us that it was the will of God that we should go. He told us that he was our friend and would look after us. He told us we would have everything we need in this new country. All he said was lies. We have nothing to eat except what our brothers who came here from Arkansas give us. We have no tools except what they lend us. If that man who lied to us is your God's man I don't want to hear any more about your God."

Dan asked, "Are there no deceivers among your medicine men?"

"Yes," Crowheart agreed, "but they do not speak for John Ross the way that man spoke for the President. John Ross tells us the bad medicine men are cheats. We have nothing more to do with them, except a few old women among us and some men who want to do mischief."

"Will you send your children to us?" Dan asked. "They can be day scholars, and we will give them a meal at noon."

"My woman he say no, but I think yes. Ever'body tell me your place is good place, an' you do not lie to them people."

Sally and William Crowheart became day scholars; and Miss Eula heard from Sally how sorry she and her brother felt when her father took their littlest sister away from the boat at night and left her sleeping under the ground. Other children, too, had tales of crowding into steamboat engine rooms for warmth, of puking when they ate the rancid meat supplied by the contractors, of a terrible cholera that attacked them on the Arkansas River boat, of drunken men of the boats' crews coming to frighten their mothers, slap them and make them cry when they would not lie down with them.

A boy of fifteen told how a party, ravenous for something besides bread made from wormy flour and fat salt pork, came one evening upon a field of green corn and an orchard of half-ripe peaches: "We ate and ate till our bellies stuck out, and when we got back on the boat we got terrible cramps and we could not help doing nasty things on the boat. We rolled and puked and did other nasty things and nearly everybody was screaming because they hurt so much; and there was no medicine and no doctor. It was such a smell! We did not get clean, in our hair, for a long time; and seems like I am stinking now."

Another child told how the doctor, who was aboard the boat before the people ate the green peaches, was attacked by the cholera. "He was good man, and came to help my mother when he was sick himself till he just fell over and died."

Then there was the story of the kind-hearted army officer, in charge of exiles forced to leave a stranded boat and travel two hundred miles on foot: "He found a horse to ride, then went off to find horses and wagons for our old ones and our blind and crippled ones when he was sick himself. Then a white man stole his horse."

Another of our new scholars remembered: "Way back yonder, they took us off of a boat and put us on the railroad cars for a while. We got scared when the cars started. My uncle's hat blowed off, and he jumped off to get it back and the cars hit him and mashed him. But they did not stop to see if he was dead." Contractors, paid for the number of exiles they set out with, stopped for nothing lest their profits be lessened by delays. Burials of those who died on the boats must take place only after a boat tied up for the night. Sometimes a mother must carry her dead baby in her arms all day.

Another said of the time before they embarked: "The soldiers came to our house. They said we must go to the river as soon as my mother cook for them; and they would not wait till my little sister find her doll. They say they are damn tired of roundin' up the people, an' they stuck gran'ma in the behind till she bleed with the knives on the end of their guns because she could not walk fast."

Another said of the concentration camp on the Hiwassee: "When we run away an' try to go home, soldiers come through the woods to find us. They swear at these god-dam Indians an' say why don't they let us shoot all the sonsabitches. My mother cry, my father tell them she don't like such bad talk, so they knock him down with a gun an' leave him like he is dead; an' they say, Why you run away, you dirty bastard. But my father was not dirty because we had been in that camp only one day."

Time after time, I came upon these still-frightened children on the playground as they talked to groups squatting close around them and listening intently. They rose reluctantly when I told them that it was better to play than to talk too much of the evil days of the past.

For other thousands, however, the evil days were to come.

It was Catherine who, as the tide of immigrants swelled to overwhelming proportions and the tales of suffering became a continuous wail, somewhat restored our perspective by saying: "After all, we are not hearing anything new. Remember the Children of Israel; read Kings I and II, and learn what cruelty and treachery prevailed. Read Esther, and find out how the women were taken and prepared for concubines. Surely the Cherokees have suffered terribly, and will suffer more; and others of the tribes to be removed will suffer as they have. It is a never-ending tale."

It was difficult to be philosophical, however, with the ragged thin-bellied and frightened children under our eyes every day; with shrunken-cheeked barefoot old women coming on cold nights furtively to rake with feathers a few kernels of corn out of the cracks of our cribs, not knowing that we would gladly fill their baskets as long as our supply lasted; with young women hiding from us, before we entered their cabins, the bastard half-white babies begotten by raping roustabouts on the river boats; with parties of young Cherokee men, who believed that some sort of wild anarchy had been loosed upon the world, drinking themselves crazy and robbing and killing—and laughing at us at Oak Hill for Jesus-talking fools. One of the diversions of these young men was to race their ponies around the chapel during Sunday services, whooping and firing pistols, another to fling stones on the roof of the girls' quarters, then laugh insanely at the sounds of panic inside. They would be gone before Dan or I could dress and help Miss Eula to quiet the children.

We never spoke of our fears for our own safety, but I know that Richard watched vigilantly over Catherine, that I felt uneasy when Miss Eula was out of my sight and I did not know where she was, and that Dan kept us as close to the station as he could without acknowledging his fears. Also, he sought out John Jolly and the other head men of the western Cherokees, Sequoyah, The Runner, Hummingbird, Wolfcatcher, and old Ta-ka-to-ka—all the men of influence who had become his friends—and asked for help in taming the desperate young men.

Their practical answer was to secure from the Council authority to organize troops of light horse police, some of whom were always within call of Oak Hill.

Twelve

The notes left to me by Dan after our last journey together, which have enabled me to tell the greater part of this story, refer at fairly frequent intervals to Ellen in the years following her farewell to Oak Hill. None of us, however, was aware that through trusted friends he was keeping himself informed of her actions, although we might have known he would.

The journal entries were mere jottings, but from other sources I have been able to make a fairly complete story:

After Mr. Irving went off on his tour of the prairies beyond the Verdigris River, Ellen found Fort Gibson dull. She had not made any notable impression on the celebrated author, who later referred to her merely as "one of the ladies who made our stay at the post pleasant." She had not cared to bring her fascination to bear on any of the Irving entourage, saying that the men were so eager to get to the buffalo range, and so busy preparing their horses and guns for the chase, they were bored at Kate Acton's ball, and actually yawned in her presence! "They love the smell of powder," she noted, "but not in a lady's hair."

Coming into Tennessee on our trip from New York to Kingslake Mission, Ellen's imagination had been stirred by talk concerning young Sam Houston, Jackson's latest and most brilliant protégé, and she had said, "I wish we might have the opportunity to visit in Nashville and know him." For Jackson she had no respect, only admiration of his ruthless march to power. She had said of him, "In a way, he is like my grandfather, who did not pretend to be a gentleman."

We in Arkansas and Indian Territory knew little, of course, of the swift rise in law, in policies, and in the social circles of Nashville of the humbly born Sam Houston. His notable court battles, his energy and pomp as the incredibly young major general of Tennessee militia, his duels with adversaries of social and political prominence, his short career in Congress, his successful whirlwind campaign for Government, his swift wooing and winning of the lovely young girl who, as his wife, brought him to the peak of social eminence, then wrecked his happiness with a word—all these developments had been for us only faint echoes.

But when, at Gibson, Ellen was told that Houston was living in a cabin not ten miles away, she remembered her early interest in the youthful soldier-statesman of Nashville. From officers at the post, and letters from Washington and New York, she pieced together his story. It was exactly the sort of romantic life history to capture her imagination. She might have phrased it, "A great man wrecked by a beautiful and heartless woman; or, the tragedy of love unrequited."

With the facts of Houston's Tennessee career in her possession, Ellen wished to know why he was here in Indian Territory, living like any obscure renegade among the Indians. The only explanation she could get, from Colonel Acton, was that in his boyhood Sam had often run away from his mother's home in Tennessee to spend months with John Jolly at his Hiwassee Island home and with other Cherokee families. In his distress, after flinging away the Governorship, he had instinctively taken his broken heart and blasted career to the Indian friends of his boyhood.

Ellen's mind began to dwell upon the thought that it might be her destiny to rescue Houston from this obscurity. She said to Kate Acton, "Why, the man is still young, hardly past thirty-six. With his talents, he is capable of making a still greater career than that which he renounced. If only—" she left the thought dangling.

Mrs. Acton knew more of Houston's present circumstances and mode of living than she deemed prudent to tell Ellen lest (should his eclipse prove to be temporary,) her report be magnified by gossip and return, by way of Washington, to prejudice her colonel's future. She knew army posts.

Ellen saw no reason why she should not ride to Houston's cabin and, on any excuse as valid as asking for a drink of water, estimate her chances. She would arrive at noon, when he was most likely to be at home. It was early April, unseasonably warm, and she rode through grass fetlock high and mottled with prairie flowers. A caressing wind blew from the south, bringing pleasant scents from the woods bordering the Arkansas River. In the fringe of timber along Thirteen-mile Creek, which she forded, redbud and wild plum blossoms were past their prime. Lone quail called from the tops of ragged last-season sunflower stalks, the Cherokee hunter's sign that the buck deer's horns are nearly full grown. The day promised romance.

As she first saw him, Houston was sitting on a split-log bench beside the door of the cabin's kitchen room, dressed in a tattered undershirt, sagging pantaloons, and moccasins. His hair was long, his beard uncombed; and his eyes were greatly inflamed. On the bench beside him was a nearly empty gourd dipper that had been full of whiskey. In spite of his sordid appearance, however, there was more than a suggestion of power in his huge frame and large head. In his eyes Ellen read a truculence that befitted a half-mad genius trying to drink himself into permanent forgetfulness.

As Ellen described their encounter later, he rose and came to hold her horse as she slid to the ground and asked for water. Turning his head, he called in Cherokee to some one inside the kitchen. A woman's voice answered, then Talahina came out with a cup and a china pitcher full of spring water. Ellen looked at the Indian girl in astonishment, for she had not been told of her presence at Houston's cabin. Talahina might have been twenty or thirty; Ellen saw only that she was mature yet carried herself with youthful grace. Houston said shortly, "My wife." Ellen gave her own name, and the big man nodded, "Madam, I knew you at once. If you care to rest yourself, I will look to your horse. We dine presently."

With Talahina at her cooking fire, Ellen sat on the bench to wait for Houston to return from the shelter of poles and hay that was his stable. He finished the whiskey before speaking, then, "You should know, Madam, that you risk your reputation by coming to see me; I am not a respectable man."

"I am afraid, Sir," she took the tone he liked, "that I don't greatly care whether you are respectable or not. I find the water refreshing, and this bench well placed for one who loves the spring sunshine."

He went inside to talk with his wife, then reappeared, saying, "Talahina will set a table for us out here. I am like a bear that can't be shut inside after a winter of hibernation. As soon as spring comes I sleep out of doors except when it rains—or when I am too drunk to manage a bivouac under the sky."

"Unfortunately," Ellen said, "liquor makes me ill, and I must deny myself the pleasure of taking it."

"Madam," he laughed, "say rather that you are fortunate. I have taken the stuff so long that I am copper-lined; and the best I can manage is a mild glow until I fall insensible. I shall give it up some day. It's a poor remedy for what ails me; and my wife doesn't like it."

Talahina made the table ready, brought the stew of venison and corn, and sat on a stool opposite Ellen. Houston offered, "If you are accustomed to any grace before meat at Oak Hill, you have our permission to say it here."

"Oh," Ellen said, "I believe that when you are in Rome, et cetera. I have always left the saying of grace to my husband."

"I have heard," he said as he filled a plate of good English ware that was one of Talahina's prized possessions and passed it to Ellen, "nothing but good concerning the station at Oak Hill. My Cherokee friends like your husband. In my way, I too am trying to help my red brothers. God knows they have done, and are doing, all that is humanly possible for me. Officially, they have made me a member of the tribe. They feed me when I am incapable of finding food for myself. Talahina came willingly, and with her people's sanction, to keep my fire. On my part, I use my sober hours in an effort to thwart the scoundrelly contractors who are mistakenly believed to be rationing the immigrants and supplying them with tools for farming. It may seem improbable to you, but I am not quite forgotten in Washington and Nashville; and Jackson is still my friend."

"The President," Ellen suggested, "must be a strange, contradictory sort of man, Mr. Houston."

"I know what you mean, Madam. I have hated him for his course towards the Cherokees, although I know he could have taken no other unless he cared to sacrifice himself politically. Yes, I have hated him, but loved him more, Madam, he is a great man."

Now and then, as they talked, he put into Cherokee the substance of what was said, and Talahina smiled, nodded, and spoke a rapid sentence or two. Once Houston laughed, and told Ellen, "My wife is pleased that you have come, and hopes that your husband will also come. I'm afraid there is a vein of conventionality in her, as well as a strain of the evangelist."

"Then she might be disappointed in Mr. Wear."

"I think not, Madam. I know the Yankees are no great shakes as exhorters, but neither are the Cherokees. If I were a praying man, I would ask the Lord to make men reasonable so that workers like Dan Wear might move them with logic. But we ranters, I fear, will always be top dogs. I hate the ranter and demagogue; and, God help me, there's something of both in me.

"One reason for coming back to my Cherokee friends was that I might be quit of such cattle. In these last two years, I have enjoyed the luxury of denouncing them, and the liers and falsifiers also. Let me show you," and he brought from the cabin pages torn from the

Arkansas Democrat and the *National Intelligencer* containing his fiery yet amply documented letters on Cherokee affairs. "If you can obtain further circulation for my fulminations, you may take these pages. I assume you also are a friend of the Indians?"

"I will send them to my father," she promised. "He has friends who write for the *New York Evening Post* and the *Commercial Advertiser*, and knows one or two of the Boston pamphleteers."

"Excellent! You and I, Madam, shall see more of one another."

"Houston became a changed man," Ellen said, "even in the brief time of my visit. His drunkenness passed, and his angry bitterness faded. I could not believe that his heart needed mending, but that he did need something to do besides drink and scold, something to try his enormous strength of body and mind."

Mrs. Acton warned Ellen, "If you do see him again, you will risk getting yourself talked about and, possibly, having Dan brought upon the carpet by his Mission Board on account of your interest in the man. However—well, I wish you luck, but remember the Indian woman!"

Ellen laughed. "My dear, I'm not thinking of him as a possible lover, so you may rest easy on that score."

She saw Houston often after that. With her father's approval, she took a house in Little Rock, the growing capital of Arkansas Territory, engaged a companion and cook, and contrived to have Houston sober and properly dressed when he came to talk with the men she brought in to listen to his budget of facts concerning the venality of contractors and agents for the Cherokees.

She was, of course, talked about; and the letters to Dan from the Mission Rooms in New York became persistent in their carefully worded criticism of her conduct. Dan could answer only that he had no power to control his wife's actions and point out, in fairness to her and to Sam Houston, that both were striving for the good of the Cherokees.

Then, almost as suddenly and secretly as he had come for sanctuary with the Indians, Houston disappeared. Going home to her family to await his call to join him, Talahina said only that he had ridden south, taking saddle bags full of writings, a few extra clothes, and a meager camping equipment. She believed he was on the way to the Texas province of Mexico, perhaps to visit the band of Cherokees who had settled on the Trinity River.

One report was that Ellen had gone to President Jackson and told him of Houston's restlessness and his desire to undertake a private survey of sentiment in Texas for secession and union with the United States. It was said that she convinced Jackson of Sam's fitness for the mission, and gave her promise not to f[o]llow him to Natchitoches, not to reveal or in any way hamper his movements.

Ellen learned why Houston's Tennessee bride turned against him. In the battle against the Creeks at Horseshoe Bend in 1813, he had received a serious wound in the shoulder which had never healed. On occasion, the suppuration from the wound produced an offensive odor; and it was this stench that caused his wife to hurt him beyond forgiveness by shrinking from him and crying out that he stank.

When Ellen told this to Kate Acton, the soldier's wife said, "What a fool that girl must have been! Imagine a soldier's wife shrinking from an open wound."

Ellen said to me once that she had no expectation of being called to Texas. "Sam Houston was never my lover. So far as I know, he remained true to Talahina, and would have sent for her after he defeated Santa Anna and became President of the Republic of Texas had she not died of a quick consumption in the meantime. I should have enjoyed watching him force Talahina upon the Indian-hating Texans as their First Lady. That would have been more amusing than 'Old Hickory's' struggle at Washington on behalf of his wife, the innkeeper's daughter.["]

With Houston's disappearance the Mission Board ceased to question Dan. He was able to concentrate on the difficult and delicate problem of bringing Eastern and Western Cherokees to realize that they were still brothers.

There was bitterness in the hearts of the twelve thousand who had survived forcible removal against the handful who had signed the bogus treaty and those who had abandoned the fight to save their homes in Georgia and Tennessee; and when they found that the six thousand already living in Indian Territory expected them to submit to the Western Nation's laws and tribal officials, their anger flared out against them. At councils called to debate the question of government for the reunited Cherokees few Westerners attended. Quarrels between the factions led to violence. Pitched battles were prevented with difficulty by the Light Horse police. Assassinations were reported.

Dan rode often to talk with John Ross, chief of the Eastern Cherokees, John Jolly and other head men of the Western faction, nearly always accompanied by Sequoyah. In his absence, Oak Hill was in my charge, and it was I, ably assisted by the advice of Miss Eula and the nimble pen of Catherine Panther, who must frame replies to the letters from the Mission Rooms in New York questioning the wisdom of becoming involved in tribal politics. Impatient with the men of the Board, Dan gave me a free hand.

Miss Eula, Catherine and I managed to justify our conception of Dan as a peacemaker working under the banner of Christ, but the Board still feared that if he should become openly partisan he might be killed. "Such a tragedy," we were reminded, "could not fail to destroy the station's usefulness, and lead to the expulsion of all missionaries."

Reading that admonition, Dan laughed and said, "If Jesse Bushyhead can ride everywhere among the Western Cherokees armed only with his Baptist Bible and his love of his people, I certainly am in no danger. John Ross and the three Johns who are holding out against control by the Westerners are all friends; and if I need further protection Sequoyah supplies it, for both factions honor and revere him.

"Paul," he went on with a faint glow of the fanatic's fire that was later to burn high in him, "I am becoming more and more convinced that Sequoyah is the greatest man I shall ever know. In this time of strain, he is our main reliance in bringing peace. He is wise, and patient beyond belief. He will sit through a turbulent all-night council smoking as calmly as though it was a session of antiquarian gossip, then rise at dawn and say, 'Now we will eat; afterwards, if you wish, we will talk again.' He seldom speaks. I believe it is his purpose to exhaust the hotheads this way and, by force of example, bring them to reason. He can do it because it is the way he has taught hundreds of them to read and write. Patience and calmness are great qualities; I expect Socrates had them."

A tired smile softened his thin face as he continued, "I suppose I ought to deplore the fact that Sequoyah is no nearer to accepting our God than when he first talked with me. But I can no longer think of him as a heathen destined to fail of salvation. I accept him on his own terms. He is committed as surely to an ideal, as wholly consecrated to a noble purpose, as our Christ was. What do you say to that, Paul? Is it apostasy?"

"What can I say?" I answered. "You know that I will follow your lead. What troubles me is what I shall say in my letters to Mr. Tilley, at the Mission Rooms, beyond reporting that urgent matters have called you away from Oak Hill."

"Temporize, Paul. Fill your letters with figures showing the number of tracts turned out from our press, the amount of corn given to the needy, the progress of the temperance society that Catherine and Richard have established, and tell Mr. Tilley of the attendance at chapel when Cherokee preachers conduct services. I can rely on you. After a while the soreness of the people will be cured, and I shall leave Sequoyah to his teaching and come back to the useful routine of Oak Hill."

It struck me then that the work of the station seemed less important to Dan than it had before he knew Sequoyah. An odd thought came to me; both Ellen and Dan had been diverted by a strong man. I recalled her dismissal of Sequoyah as a crack-brained, untidy old man, and wondered how Dan would characterize her find, the huge, fanatic, hard-drinking and profane wreck that had been Sam Houston. I wondered how much he had known of her frequent visits to Houston's cabin, of his visits to her at Little Rock, of his gradual emergence from his sordid lethargy, of the Indian wife's fear of her as a rival for his love.

After Houston had gone off on his greatest adventure, and Ellen's home in Little Rock had become a port of call for Jackson's agents shuttling between Washington and Texas, and a clearing point for information about the progress of the stimulated insurrection against Mexico, Dan came back to Oak Hill one evening looking drawn and spent, and with a tragic tale to tell.

He had Miss Eula, Catherine, Richard and me in his quarters with doors closed as he said: "What I have to tell you may bring serious trouble on us. I want you four who are closest to me to think it over, carefully and prayerfully, then say if I am right.

"Last night I slept at John Ross' home. After breakfast, I walked a quarter of a mile to talk with Sam Worcester. As you know, I hoped to borrow for a time Elias Boudinot, who has lately come from Georgia, to go over with Richard the Cherokee version of the Eighteen-twenty-eight Constitution, and the tribal laws, we are to print.

"As always, Sam was engrossed in details of his own work, and said, 'Go and talk with Elias; he will know better than I how urgently he is needed here. He is building a house quite near us,' and he showed me Boudinot perched on the rafters of a new frame building nailing on shingles.

"The new house is on the slope between Sam's new establishment and Ross' home. As I went towards it I saw four Cherokees appear below Boudinot, and one called up to him. Elias came down, and as soon as he stepped from the lowest rung of the ladder, they closed in on him. One flashed a hatchet from under his coat, the others drew knives; and before Elias could have divined their purpose and attempt to escape he was struck down and killed.

"It was a matter of seconds. I had seen John Ross come out of his house to mount a horse that was held by a slave, and I shouted to him to come as the assassins turned to run to a fringe of trees where other men were holding their horses. There were nine or ten of them; I could not be sure of the number as they dashed off towards the river.

"Ross was the first, after me, to reach Elias. He looked hard at me, when he knew that Elias was dead, and said, 'If only he could have told me who did this!' But he did not ask me if I had recognized the killers."

Dan paused for a time, then went on: "Before I turned for home this afternoon, I learned that two other prominent men of the Treaty Party had been assassinated at the hour Boudinot was attacked, Major Ridge and his son John, the young man who had gone to school in Connecticut with Elias and married Sarah Northrop of Cornwall.

"We know, of course, why the three men were killed—perhaps 'executed' is the better word. It was because they had signed that spurious agreement to cede the Cherokee lands in the East. They had been found guilty of treason, according to the Cherokee laws which we have been preparing to print, by some secret council of Eastern Cherokees. The men who did them to death carried out the decree of that council; of that I feel certain.

"Now listen, and try to realize the importance of what I have to decide. *I recognized the four men who killed Boudinot*. I did not volunteer to tell Ross their names. You, Paul," he turned to me, "have heard them talk within the last two months."

"On Sallisaw Creek?" I asked, and he nodded. It had been another secret meeting, like the one Dan and I had sat through when the Kituh-wahs admitted us to their council in Arkansas. At the Salisaw council, however, the matter of exacting blood vengeance from the treaty signers had not been raised.

Dan went on, "I must decide whether or not to reveal the names to John Ross, the Government Agent, and the military authorities at Gibson. If I do, I must also tell why I know them so well as to be able to identify them at a distance of fifty yards; and I must tell about all I have done, alone or in company with Sequoyah, to help close the breach between the factions. I will certainly be branded as a meddler in Cherokee politics."

"Would that—would it mean," there was a catch in Miss Eula's voice, "you would have to leave us, leave Oak Hill?"

"Undoubtedly," he answered, "it would be the end of me as a missionary of the church. It might mean the end of Oak Hill, also. These killings—assassinations or executions, however you choose to call them—will bring about others, then reprisals, and a feud that is bound to last a long time. If in any way, John Ross can be shown to be responsible by the powers that be in Washington the Federal Government will do everything possible to unseat him, for he is hated because he thwarted so long Jackson's attempts to get the Cherokees out of Georgia.

"If I speak, I shall become the center of a storm. If I remain silent?" He turned his head slowly to look intently at each of us in turn.

Catherine was first to speak. Pressing the tips of her forefingers to her ears, she said, "I find that I am quite deaf, I have heard nothing; and, Uncle Dan, I know that your eyes have troubled you a great deal of late."

"Why, that's true, Kit," Dan rose with a grateful glance at her, "and if you others are as deaf as Kit—"

We assured him that we were.

"Then," he ended the session, "I have seen nothing. Now, if you don't mind, clear out; I have work to do which I don't feel at all like tackling."

Thirteen

Dan's prophecy of an outbreak of violence that would destroy any hope of peace between the factions for years proved all too accurate. The Cherokee Nation, inflamed by feeling aroused by the killings, became more than ever a house divided against itself.

It may be that some individuals among the missionaries of the various churches at Dunster, Park Hill, River Point, Will's Prairie Union, and Hope Haven were able to steer clear of the storm. At Oak Hill, however, we could not ignore it. We could not teach Christ crucified without relating our words, by implication at least, to the tragic killings and their terrible aftermath. In our school, boys would have fought one another with knives, Easterners against Westerners, if we had not been vigilant; and in spite of our diplomacy, four scholars from Western families were taken away by fathers who believed that Dan was too friendly with Ross.

A first result of the killings was the rapid assembling of warriors, the old tribal title for fighting men revived after fifty years of disuse, sworn to avenge their leaders' death[s]. The rumor of their purpose had hardly gone abroad, however, before Ross' friends had gathered six hundred young men, armed them, and established them in camps surrounding his house. They allowed no one to pass in, even army officers from Fort Gibson, until Ross gave the word.

For Catherine, who asked what lay behind this threat of armed strife, Dan sketched its background: "Ever since Jefferson proposed in 1803 to make the Louisiana Purchase a dumping ground for all Indians, Government agents have striven to create factions in the tribes favorable to removal. They petted those who yielded to removal propaganda, and promised them fat rewards—which were seldom paid. Poor Boudinot, for instance, lost everything he owned in Georgia; and Sam Worcester's press that had been in his charge and was most precious to him was confiscated by the Georgia militia. Now he has lost his life to men who believed him to be a traitor.

"Those who believed the Government's promises and removed to Arkansas twenty years ago, as well as the treaty signers, are frantic to save something for themselves as their justification. They believe

Washington will support them in their purpose to rule the Cherokee Nation. But they are building on a false hope. Washington will not try to establish by force six thousand as rulers over the twelve thousand. Ross has told the military at Gibson to keep hands off, and he means it. Washington will send the order, for the Government could not justify to the people of the United States a war against Ross.

"The Government will, however, continue to make promises to the Westerners which will not be kept, and harass Ross. It has sown the dragon's teeth and must needs harvest the terrible crop. Sequoyah and Ross say, 'Unite and grow strong,' but the Government's policy is to divide and destroy.

"It is incredible but true that men's emotions can be distorted to hate him whom they have wronged, as the Jews hated Christ. By its acts the Government, ever since the first Colonists obtained land from the Indians at the musket's muzzle rather than by fair negotiation, has chosen the evil way. Penn, of course, was the one exception."

Dan was greatly moved, and confessed to me that he had been won definitely to Ross, saying, "I can't believe that he and the twelve thousand were wrong or foolish to struggle against removal from their homes and a way of living that was as civilized as that of their white neighbors. I believe it is right to resist thieves. A man is not admirable who throws up his hands to a robber; the best you can say for him is that he may have been prudent. Christ could have saved himself from crucifixion by prudence of that brand."

He had not been drawn into the inquiry concerning the killings because, as he said, "Ross has been able to carry his point that it is a matter to be settled by the Cherokee themselves, and he has not questioned me."

Then he said, "I have opened my heart to you, Paul, because you will not repeat what I have said. Now I must seal my lips again. I wish I had a pipe like Sequoyah's, and a deep buckskin bag of sumac-flavored tobacco, so that when I was tempted to speak or act hastily I would light up and say to myself, 'I will neither say nor do anything until I have finished this pipeful.' "

* * *

Among Dan's notes, dated some six months after Boudinot's death, I found this: "The Runner says Ellen is still at Little Rock, her house used as rendezvous and refuge by T—, H—, W—, & other anti-Ross leaders. E— much interested, especially in T—."

It was characteristic of Ellen to ally herself with the enemies of

Ross, whom she called the anti-Christers. Her antipathy to Ross was due in part to her scorn of the pious; to her pious, right[-]living men and women were dull. The leaders among the anti-Ross faction, designated by Dan in his notes only by initials, were certainly not dull if judged by her standard. The "T—" in whom Ellen was most interested was Tally Tassel. He was forty, tall, robust, aggressively handsome, half white. He wore his thick black hair in the fashion of a Daniel Webster. He was one of those who had been educated at a New England college. Unlike Boudinot and Richard Panther, he had returned to his people with no desire to give himself to the unselfish service of his fellows. With no deep convictions, an oratorical flair, a fondness for frock coats, strapped fawn-colored pantaloons, black Ascot ties, and tall beaver hats, he proposed, in his own words, to "follow the legal profession." He let it be known that his goal was the chieftainship of the Cherokees. As chief, he would, he said, collect for the people their claims for the millions lost when they were compelled to abandon their homes and property in the East and in Arkansas. How much of the money he might collect would stick to his own fingers was a matter of speculation among those who knew him best.

He was a Westerner, had come to Indian Territory with the Arkansas Cherokees. An opportunist, however, he had probed the possibility of becoming tribal attorney under Ross. But Ross wanted nothing to do with him, seeing through his hypocrisy, despising his bombast, and doubting his integrity. Ellen said of him, long after their affair ended: "I was never quite convinced of his reality." She gave him credit for being a wonderful lover, only less vital than Sam Houston might have been "if he had not consecrated himself to Jackson's ambitions."

At the beginning of their close association, Ellen thought of Tassel as a more magnificent Richard Panther, physically. But when he pressed for marriage, she said, "I don't love you in the way a wife should love a husband; I don't want to bear a child by you; and I don't love you enough or trust you sufficiently to face the scandal involved in a divorce action—which, by the way, would hurt you more than it would me."

Her enjoyment of Tassel's love was genuine enough. She was stirred, in spite of her distrust of fine words, by his fervor, the grandiloquent rhymes he fashioned to describe her ripe beauty. She hoped that she might become his Egeria. And when she was sure that Dan had gone over to Ross, the situation gained added piquancy. She had not been able to master Dan. She would always love him—and hate him more for the hard integrity he would never lose. She might hurt him through Tassel; and that would be a keen satisfaction.

Ellen and Tassel were seldom seen together, but when they did drive out, he in tall hat and she in Baltimore silks, he dark, and grave in manner, she vivid, with touches of artificial color on her cheeks, they were sensational. He drove her fast-stepping pair the way an Indian youth rides his pony, to the limit of their speed.

Tassel resented Ellen's cordial welcome to other anti-Ross leaders who came to her house for secret councils, good food, and better liquor than they could find in the dram shops of Little Rock; the solemn bull-like Wah-ti-ka, the sunny-mannered Hoo-leh, the cat-like Suneater with the shrewdness, controlled hatred, and icy eyes of a killer. They were, she believed, essential to Tassel's purpose to rid the Cherokee Nation of Ross, by vote or by assassination.

The elimination of Ross would mean proof to Dan of her power if he knew of her liaison with Tassel and her dominance of Ross' chief enemy. Surely he must know, though doubts troubled her. Perhaps he knew, and no longer cared enough to make a sign? The thought was infuriating.

Tassel and his followers whipped up the movement for vengeance by repeating over and over again the charge that Ross had instigated the killing of Boudinot, Major Ridge and John Ridge, although they knew it was not true. They knew that John Ross had cordially welcomed Boudinot to Park Hill to resume his work, with Sam Worcester, as editor and translator. They knew of Ross' long friendship with Major Ridge, and his admiration of young John Ridge's ability.

Had Ross wanted the three out of his way, he could not have chosen a means of removing them more certain to cause trouble for himself; and even his bitterest enemies did not believe him a fool. They knew that he was a fighter, but only with words, with brain and heart; at the crisis of the struggle against removal from the East, when he could have sent every able-bodied man in the tribe into battle against the Georgia militia and Jackson's troops, he held them firmly to a course of peaceful submission to the inevitable as only a wise leader could have done.

I give this explanation as I had it from Dan. Rightly, he said that the fortunes of Oak Hill must of necessity be linked with the tribe's political fate; however much we wished to remain neutral, we could not stand entirely apart. His problem was to steer our course to survival through the turmoil until Ross became in fact as well as name chief of a re-united and peaceful Nation.

We others gave ourselves wholly to the work of the station. We saw our influence wane for a time. Then, as we held to the course Dan mapped, the deserters from our classes and chapel returned, bringing others; and we were pressed to find room for all the scholars and time to minister to the older people. Dan conducted services in Pease Chapel when he could, and when that was impossible because of engagements with Ross or Sequoyah or Hummingbird or Jolly or The Runner, he found able substitutes like Jesse Bushyhead or the Moravian Steiner from Wild Horse Mission.

Gradually, our station expanded, and became almost altogether self-supporting. Aside from Pease Chapel, the building of which we were proudest was our new Main, an impressive two-story structure of logs. It was so big that Catherine suggested stating its dimensions in cubits rather than in feet. In fact, it was twenty by eighty feet. Designed by Dan and Richard, half of the lower floor became ample kitchen and dining room. Miss Eula, her older girl monitors, and the rest of the resident girls occupied the remainder of the first floor and the second floor. Three big chimneys carried into the air the wood smoke from twelve great fireplaces. As I write, I can all but smell the strong fragrance of burning blackjack, hickory, and hackberry logs, and see the long piles of fuel corded against the north wall by our wood-cutting details.

Eventually, we had erected twenty-two buildings of various dimensions; we cultivated three hundred acres of fertile land for corn and wheat, our food staples, besides twenty acres of garden that yielded richly staple vegetables, potatoes, beans, squash, beets, turnips, cucumbers for pickles. Our orchard supplied enough fruit for our tables, fresh or dried. Our milch cows amply met the enormous demands of our own staff, the fifty day scholars who had a noon meal with us, and the hundred and ten boarders. Our station staff grew to twenty. Tales went out about our wealth, and the comparative luxury of Oak Hill. Our modest output of tracts, portions of the Scriptures, Cherokee law books, and Farmer's Almanacs increased in the telling to prodigious proportions.

Once, in a letter to New York accompanying a request for "an extra large cloak which will better protect my shins from sleety winter blasts as I ride; also, two pairs of pantaloons, one for every day, for Paul Wear," Dan wrote: "I suppose we could exist on a far more modest scale than we do. We could supply bare tables with bread made from corn grown in our fields and ground in hand mills, but all of us, workers and scholars alike, prefer linen cloths on the tables, and wheaten bread as a frequent change from cornbread. Molasses, which we make by the barrel from our own cane patch, is a good food served in moderation, but, as we used to say at Andover, if eaten three times a day it is apt to replace the blood in our veins! Our effort is to make our God, our conduct, and our manner of living desirable to a people driven by circumstances to renounce their old gods and slump into spiritual and material lethargy.

"I suppose we might do without books, of which you may believe we have asked for more than might seem to be justified, but we regard them as essential for our own stimulation and for lending freely to all others who can read English."

Before sending off that letter, Dan smiled and said to me, "Paul, do you know what Ross said once to Sam Worcester and me? He said that we must both be certain that God is a Yankee. I answered for myself, 'I won't insist that He is, but I do believe that the New England conception of God as One who cleanses, purifies, and readies the body as well as the soul for salvation is altogether sound.' "

Slowly, because of Dan's insistence that candidates for membership should be tested through adequate periods of probation, our church roll grew.

Catherine it was, somehow finding the time from station duties, who went oftenest among the cabins in which lived the parents of our scholars. She went to give material help, of course, but more to offer friendship. She brought back from her visits tales that made us laugh as well as pictures of heartbreaking tragedies. The Indians loved to have her at their fires, and joked among themselves over her valiant attempts to talk with them in Cherokee. They welcomed her as one of themselves, too, because she had married Richard and (at the time of which I am thinking) borne him two bronze-tinted babies over whom the women exclaimed lovingly.

Once, in an after-supper gabfest, she told us of her welcome at The Bullfrog's cabin: "Now there's a family that is coming up in the world. They would have me stay for supper, and Mrs. B[.] did not serve it directly from the kettle in the fireplace, but dished the meat stew first into a rose-decorated chamber pot from the bedroom and passed it around with all the pride Grandfather Decker used to show in exhibiting his Pilgrim rocker. Of course, it was thoroughly clean."

Again, having just returned from the funeral of Flying Crane's wife, she told us: "He was sorry that Polly was gone, but, as we knew, he would have her again to keep his fire in heaven. Meanwhile, however, as Polly neared her end he had been thinking of some one to stay in his cabin [u]ntil they were re-united. A week before Polly passed away, he told her that Susan Starr would succeed her. Polly said it was a good choice, but begged him to destroy all of her things because she believed Susan would not want to use them.

"So, in preparation for the smashing of dishes and the burning of clothing and so forth, he hitched up a team and drove to Fort Smith to buy the new things Susan would require. Also, he bought a coffin for Polly and, with the coffin packed full of new store goods and tableware, came back in time to comfort her in her last hours. And you know, watching him help dig her grave, then stand bareheaded at the burying, it didn't seem funny."

Another story I have remembered well because it occurred to me that I must have known some such experience in Vermont, where our families are by no means demonstrative in our affections.

In school as a boarder was a boy of eight, Luke Plowman, so homesick that it was difficult to interest him either in books or play. One day, at his worst, he broke away from the other children on the playground and ran to the gate of East Field. Catherine said: "I thought he was running away, and ran to overtake him and try to persuade him to come back. But he stopped at the gate, and I had almost come up with him when his father appeared.

"Luke's father just came up to the gate, reached through the bars and laid his arm across his son's shoulders. Neither said anything. I didn't know what to do, and stood there like a stump. After five minutes perhaps, the father turned to walk away into the woods. Luke watched him until he was out of sight, then came to me smiling. He chatted happily on the way back to the playground, and explained, 'She is my father, an' I am knowin' she will come.' I asked, 'Were you glad to see your father?' and he said, 'Oh, yes, we is both glad.' Then I said, 'But you did not speak; why was that?' and he answered, 'Oh, it is how we do; what for we talk?' I asked 'Who told you your father would come to the gate?' and he said, 'Nobody tell me; I just know it she will come.' I am sure he was telling the truth, and if any of you will tell me how Luke knew his father would come to the gate at that particular moment to comfort him I shall be obliged."

Once The Turtle's boy became ill. He had a high fever, but Dr. Butram, who came from Dunster to see him, said that with the care we were giving him and the medicine he left he should be back to normal in ten days. Then The Turtle came on horseback, saying that he knew the boy was sick and that he had come to take him to a Cherokee medicine man. We tried to persuade him to let the boy stay until the fever left him, and promised that when he was well enough to be moved he might go home for a long rest.

But The Turtle could not be turned from his purpose and, since we could not forcibly detain him, he took his son from the bed, bundled against a winter storm as well as we could manage, put him up in the saddle in front of him, and rode away. Five miles from Oak Hill, and a mile from home, the boy died in The Turtle's arms.

After news of the boy's death came to us, Catherine accounted for Richard's absence from supper by saying, "It is the first time I have seen Richard really angry. He was so angry that he cried, and broke out at me, 'What are we doing here, anyway! Are we playing at this work?' and then went off into Cherokee fireworks that I am sure wouldn't bear translating. He probably won't speak for two days, and then he'll be all right. Sometimes, when things go wrong, he will not speak for a long time, only to say when I prod him with questions, 'No, I am not angry with you; I just don't want to talk.' Afterwards, he is as cheerful and loving to me and the babies as any one could be."

Moodiness was a trait he shared with many Cherokees, the survival of an old savage instinct to go off alone to cure a sickness of the spirit. Once he said to me, "We ought to be sent off into the woods sometimes, the way our people used to send the young women when their monthly sickness came upon them, until we are cleansed of the evil in our hearts and are rid of the sadness we feel."

I was reminded of how fortunate we were to have with us two such understanding women as Catherine and Miss Eula by a sermon Dan preached in that time of uncertainty. His text was Philippians IV: 3: "And I entreat thee also, true yokefellows, help those women who labored with me in the gospel, with Clement also, and with other my fellow laborers, whose names are in the book of life."

I could not help thinking, as he read the text, that Ellen was in his mind, although she had deserted him and he would be justified in believing that she walked with "the enemies of the cross of Christ, whose end is destruction, whose god is in their belly, and whose glory is their shame."

The sermon was Dan's tribute—the only one I ever heard him pay except for occasional words and his general attitude of complete reliance—to us, his yokefellows. That day he named us all, one by one, to his Cherokee listeners who grunted approval when he paused. Then he went on, "Without the women who have labored with me, I should be as a man with only one eye, one arm, one leg, and a dry heart." Catherine wept at his words, "I am without children of my own, as you know, but she who has come to share our work, our life and yours, who married your Richard and brought into the world Cherokee children to share the destiny of your children, is like a dearly beloved daughter." Of Miss Eula, he said, "She is my sister and holds up my hands."

Then, more generally: "We are one family, these fellow laborers and I. You have made us also members of the greater family of the Cherokees; with you we must labor to restore the peace without which we stumble and lose the road." He did not speak Ross' name, for in the congregation were members of both factions, but put special emphasis on the tribal schools which were the chief's special concern[:] "Before the persimmons ripen this fall, there will be eighteen schoolhouses open to your children which you have provided for yourselves, and the teachers will be Cherokees. And one day not far in the future there will be built at Tahlequah, your capital, seminaries for the higher education of your boys and girls."

To us of the station, Dan told of going with Sequoyah to talk with Ross about the tribal schools, and especially about the male and female seminaries Ross was determined to establish. "He is hoarding every possible dollar to add to the education fund. Already, he is in correspondence with friends in Boston and New York who may find for him an architect to draw plans for the two seminaries. He has written to Mount Holyoke, Dartmouth, and other colleges in the hope of finding good teachers who might be persuaded to staff the seminaries at the meager pay that could be offered. His Scotch-Indian eyes glowed when he talked of the need to prepare the new generation for the future. He is certain that the present rift in the tribe will close, and there will come a time of peace and plenty for his people—*his,* although he is only one-eighth Cherokee by blood. He is indomitable; I love him!"

It was Ellen who suggested, for the use of Tassel, the title "White Chief" to describe Ross. He seized upon it instantly to magnify in what he called his "address to the real Cherokees." She said of him later, "Of course Talley is no more Indian at heart than I am, but professional[l]y he is all savage."

He was also a professional exile from Indian Territory, spreading abroad the fiction that if Ross' assassins should find him within the boundaries of the Nation they would kill him. He was wont to say, "The people would make me chief tomorrow if they were not overawed by the despotic Ross." That was a catch phrase he had picked up from the ex-preacher whom Jackson had sent to bludgeon a treaty from the Eastern Cherokees.

Although Ellen did not take Tassel's poses seriously, she was genuinely apprehensive for his safety whenever he crossed the Arkansas border into Indian Territory; she said, curtly, "He talks too much." For her reassurance, he told her how he foiled "Ross' assassins." He would cross the border at Will's Prairie, almost within sight of Eben Wright's mission station, then go to the nearby "Fort Wah-ti-ka" where that belligerent enemy of Ross had established a garrison of fifty or more "warriors" (really idlers who were glad enough to trade a promise to fight the Ross men for free shelter and food). At the fort, Tassel would pick up a body-guard, then go on about his business of spreading anti-Ross propaganda and soliciting spoliation claims against the United States Government.

As a matter of fact, Tassel could have moved safely among the people. If necessary, Ross would have insured his protection against any danger save that arising from his intemperate speech when, more than half drunk, he uttered insults which Ross' friends found hard to ignore.

The Runner told of seeing Tassel and his guards ride to a district courthouse on the Sallisaw, impressive in long-tailed coat and tall hat, one saddle pocket containing a law book and the ledger in which he entered the names of claimants for reparation, with details of their losses, and the other bulged grotesquely by a jug of whiskey.

In his address to the crowd gathered for a court session, he had exhausted his usual anti-Ross routine without stirring the listeners. Then he produced a new charge. He said that Ross was now taking orders from Dan, and demanded heatedly, "Do you intend to submit to the rule of this Christer who is not man enough to keep his own woman? I will tell you—" At that point there was a movement in the crowd that caused Tassel's guards to close in on him and hustle him to his horse. "That man would have been killed," said The Runner, "if he said what was in his mind to say because all the people know about that woman. All the people know a man cannot keep a singing bird at his fire."

Although Tassel's attack could hurt either Ross or Dan very little, it brought into the open Ellen's liaison with the anti-Ross leader;

and now it would almost surely mean that the Mission Board must take cognizance of the situation. I feared that they would, out of regard for the good name of missionaries everywhere, be obliged to dismiss Dan.

After all, Ellen might succeed in her purpose to wean Dan from the work which she believed to be unfit for a real man.

Fourteen

Then, as though fate were playing into Ellen's hands, came the unsavory Otis Janes to pry into the scandal and attempt to smear Dan's name. The man and his background deserve illumination.

Before setting up the press at Oak Hill, Dan had to secure permission from the Cherokee Council. At the time, it meant the Council dominated by the Western Cherokees from whom Janes, representing himself as a missionary of an obscure evangelical sect, had secured authority to establish a press and a grant of funds from their scant treasury to assist in that laudable enterprise. Janes had spent the money, but produced no results, only thin excuses for his failure. Until Dan had made it clear that he was in no way connected with Janes, and that the press would not require Cherokee funds for support, there was opposition.

Then Janes attempted to insinuate himself into Dan's project, saying that he was experienced in the printing and publishing business. Dan investigated, and reported to us that his statement was untrue. "The fellow is a cheat, a windy hypocrite," Dan said. "I wish it lay in my power to remove him from the missionary ranks."

Ironically, it was Janes who undertook to remove Dan from the missionary ranks. After being dropped by the Council, he had allied himself with the anti-Ross refugees in Arkansas. In pulpit appeals for money with which to support their cause, he called them "martyrs of an intolerable despotism." But when talk about Ellen and her lover became public, he chose to abandon Tassel and hit at Ross through Dan. In a letter to an Arkansas newspaper which had become an anti-Ross organ, he demanded that "the winds of truth be permitted to blow through Oak Hill, where infidelity and who knows what cankers of moral degeneration exist." His demand was taken up by a refugee rival of Tassel who, with the newspaper's assistance, organized a commission of inquiry that made Janes its agent.

Dan answered the commission's request for "light on Oak Hill's teachings" by saying that the station's activities were open to scrutiny by anyone. Janes took this to mean an invitation, and notified

Dan of his purpose to come to Oak Hill accompanied by a newspaper representative. Before the date of his arrival, Dan talked with Ross, Sequoyah, and Hummingbird.

I saw Dan's lips tighten as Janes, beginning the inquiry, suggested, "Since I have come on behalf of many Christian congregations perhaps we should for their information make a record of the proceedings?" Dan assured him that there would be no objection.

"Fortunately," said Janes, "Mr. Crater of the *Little Rock Palladium*, who accompanies me, is a rapid writer and is willing to serve as recorder."

Sighing, Janes prefaced his inquisition by saying, "I wish to assure you, Brother Wear, that our commission have entered upon this inquiry reluctantly. Only our sense of obligation as ministers of the Gospel and fellow missionaries could excuse us for touching upon so delicate—er," he began to grope for words, "so—"

Dan smiled, and offered, "You mean, of course, the report that my wife has left me and is living with Talley Tassel. It is true. What more would you like to know?"

Janes was confused. I felt sure that he had expected, before getting to the point of the inquiry, to expose for Mr. Crater's pen a considerable budget of gossip about Ellen and Miss Eula, and by innuendo suggest that a three-cornered affair had been going on. Dan's bluntness, however, led him to plunge at once into accusation, "Knowing this, you have nevertheless remained in charge at Oak Hill and thereby condoned your wife's conduct."

Dan said quietly, "I have remained in charge, certainly, and will stay here as long as the Missionary Board of my church believes I am fit for the place."

"What of the tender souls entrusted to your care by their Christian parents?"

"Our scholars? They have known for a long time that my wife has not been interested in the work at Oak Hill. They are able to distinguish between us."

"They must know that 'ye are of one flesh,' and—"

"I'm afraid they don't," Dan cut him off. "The Cherokees are realists; they do not judge the husband of an unfaithful wife by her standards of conduct, nor hold him responsible for them in all cases."

"You do not admit your responsibility for her conduct?"

"Only so long as she is with me. I can not compel her to stay with me, and would not if I had that power."

"So your conscience is untroubled by the fact that the woman you promised in God's sight to cherish is living in adultery?"

"Far from it," Dan said. "I am distressed. My point is that I can do nothing about it that would be both effective and reasonable. It has not occurred to me, for example, to shoot Tassel or lock up my wife."

"I must say," Janes spoke in an outraged tone, "that to the Christian mind your views are indeed shocking."

"That," Dan objected, "is undoubtedly a matter for argument. I have never heard of a universally accepted type of Christian mind. However, let me admit that you are shocked, then perhaps you will be good enough to answer certain questions about your own personal life which in some aspects shocks me."

"My conduct, Sir, is not in question!"

"I believe it is, Mr. Janes." As Dan said this, the softness went out of his voice, and I recalled him as a lad of twelve tensing himself for a battle with the school bully. He went on, "I have been glad to reveal my belief that a wife has an individuality and a power of action apart from her husband's. May I ask if you believe it Christian to make a drudge of your wife?"

"Sir!" Janes sputtered.

"It is true, I believe, that she does all the work at what you call the Janes Missionary Orphanage."

"My wife is a true Christian helpmeet."

"That means she is required to teach as well as cook for, sew and do the washing for the ten children at your 'Refuge'?"

Janes flared, "I repeat, Sir, that I am not under investigation. Mr. Crater, you will take no notice [of] these questions."

"Whether he does or not," Dan said, "is a matter of indifference to me. However, if Mr. Crater's newspaper should print your questions to me and my answers and omit mine to you, I shall have the pleasure of sending them to the *Arkansas Democrat*.

"With that understood, let me ask you if the children under your wife's care are not half starved, clothed in the cheapest and shoddiest garments you are able to purchase, and worked in your fields beyond their strength?"

"I will not listen further to your impertinent questions!" Janes rose.

"Oh, but you will," Dan promised, turning to nod at me, "even if we must detain you by force . . . Now, isn't it true that in the fifteen years during which you have collected money on your preaching tours throughout the country, ostensibly for the support of your orphanage, you have banked in St. Louis in your own name and now have in that account more than fifteen thousand dollars?"

"I will not deign to answer that insulting question."

"For Mr. Crater's record, then," Dan went on, "let me say further that out of money collected for your orphanage and now on deposit in a Little Rock bank you are building a house for yourself. The house will be completed within six months, at the time you expect to be retired by your church authorities with the usual retirement allowance granted after twenty-five years of preaching, although you are ten years short of the age at which your church pensions its ministers. That is true, isn't it?"

Janes fumed, but made no coherent reply.

Dan turned to the amazed Mr. Crater and said: "I believe that you will find the facts as I have stated them if you care to verify them. You might also find out what proportion of the funds this man has collected to assist the anti-Ross refugees in Arkansas has reached them. You might verify the fact that he has been forbidden by the Cherokee Council to conduct a mission in the Nation. You might discover how he contrived to swindle many Cherokees of their cattle and hogs when they were compelled to remove from Arkansas. You might talk to the Indians who helped to remove his orphanage equipment to his present location after promising to pay them and then refusing, saying that the Lord will provide for their destitute and hungry women and children."

Crater, who had written nothing after Dan's abrupt acknowledgement of Ellen's infidelity, turned his eyes on Janes and said, "Well, I will be damned! If what Mr. Wear says is true, and I believe it is, may I say that you are the most arrant scoundrel it has been my ill fortune to know!" Then to Dan, "My apologies to you, Sir, for appearing here with this man. I doubt that my editor could be induced to print a friendly word about Oak Hill, but you may be sure that nothing Janes has said or insinuated will be written by me; and I promise myself the pleasure of back-tracking him, as you evidently have done very thoroughly."

"Yes," Dan nodded, "it is sometimes necessary to fight fire with fire. It is one of the jobs a missionary must learn to do." He turned again to Janes, "You have our permission to go."

The man gathered up his papers, stuffed them in his saddle bags, and flounced out. Before Crater left, Dan said, "Whatever happens to me, I believe we shall all have the satisfaction of knowing that the Janes nuisance is suppressed."

"That you may count upon," said Mr. Crater, and shook hands with Dan and me.

I asked, "Dan, how were you able to gather such a budget of scandal about Janes?"

"From Peter Hummingbird, mainly," he answered. "Peter is a very enterprising man. Sequoyah gave me the facts about his wife's servitude, and Ross those about his swindling operations . . . Be prepared for the hypocrites, Paul."

"I?"

"Yes; I'm afraid it will be your problem soon."

* * *

Cephas Wear brought the news of Dan's dismissal. He was an old man, this uncle whom Dan had looked up to all his life as a great missionary. On arriving by carriage from Fort Smith without notice, he said, "This tour of Indian missions is the last service I shall be able to render. You know, my boy," he glanced up at Dan quizzically as he walked to his room leaning heavily on Dan's arm, "I bulldozed the Board into sending me. I'm superannuated, and have been so classified since my seventy-fifth year. I'm eighty-two now . . . My, my, Dan," he paused to look around, "it's good to see a station that has the Wear brand on it, clean and thriving!" Then, turning to me, "Paul, mind that you keep it worthy of us Wears."

"So you've brought the Board's verdict, Uncle Cephas?" Dan asked.

"Of course. I wouldn't have you hear it from anyone but me. I had them delay writing out your dismissal until I could fetch it. But we'll not talk about it until tomorrow; now I need food and rest." As he went inside, sank into a hickory-bark-bottomed rocker from Uncle Frank's shop, and ran his nearly bloodless hands over its solid arms, he looked appraisingly at Dan and said, "My boy, you're wearing well. It's good to see a man who meets life with head up and eyes lifted to the Throne."

"It's good to hear you say that, Uncle Cephas."

"This is a fine, comfortable chair, Dan. I wonder if Richard's Catherine could fetch a bite for me here? I've not seen her since they came out."

"I'm sure she could," Dan said, going off to find her.

The old man said to me, "Paul, this is the hardest task I have ever had to perform; and harder because I believe the Board could have made no other decision. We are caught in strange webs of fate sometimes. Who was it, in Greek mythology, that was supposed to be weaving such nets so industriously?"

"Ariadne, I believe, Sir. And the Cherokees tell of a grandmother who is busy up yonder making a net to be let down some day to gather in all who are worthy to sit at the fire with their old god Oo-na-luh-nuh-heh."

"Yes, a fine conception . . . And they believe that Dan will be dredged up amongst the worthy?"

"They haven't a doubt of it, Sir; they know him."

"Good . . . Ariadne, eh? The name is something like Ellen, Paul." He was doing his best to keep to the outwardly casual tone in which we Wears spoke of matters that touched us deeply.

"Have you seen her, Sir?" I asked.

"Yes; and have talked with her father, too. Morin says that neither he nor I can judge her. That may be true, but we know she has made a pretty mess of Dan's career, don't we?"

I said nothing, and he went on, "Fortunately, the Board is taking nothing from Dan that he cannot replace; he has many years of usefulness ahead of him. Do you know his plans?"

"No, Sir, except that I can't imagine him leaving the Cherokees."

"Oak Hill is yours, Paul, if you want it."

"I should like first to talk with Dan. If I could rely upon his counsel and support—"

"That," Mr. Wear interrupted, "I'm sure you can count on, and can in no way concern the Board."

"I couldn't ask him to sacrifice any plans of his own."

"Would you refuse Oak Hill if he should ask you to join him in another enterprise?"

"Of course. I have never been away from him, and don't want to be. As the Indians say, I am not a whole man apart from Dan."

"I expect, however, that you would do very well."

Richard came with Catherine to sit near Mr. Wear; [t]hen Miss Eula; and then, one by one, our whole staff. All suspected the significance of his visit. He took each one by the hand, and gave each a word commending his work that showed how thoroughly he had acquainted himself with the affairs of Oak Hill. To Uncle Frank he repeated, "This is a fine, comfortable chair; if I were ten years younger I should have you make its twin for me." I thought, He is like a patriarch of old among the people of his household.

Next day, from the bed in which he rested, he talked with Dan and me about the future of Oak Hill, about the seething political stew into which the Cherokees had fallen, about Ross and Sequoyah, about the attitude of our staff towards Ross. At the end, he said, "Dan, I suppose it will be a considerable chore to make your final accounting to the Board?"

"No, Uncle Cephas," and Dan put a hand on my shoulder, "Paul has proved so expert as a balancer of the budget that I expect we can have the figures prepared for you after two or three nights of work by candle light."

"Don't hurry; I find Oak Hill an excellent place to rest."

It was as though Cephas Wear had come home. When he wrote for the Board his certification of the correctness of Dan's accounting he enclosed a letter with the figures to say that if he was not required to report in person on his tour of the Indian missions he would stretch out his visit to us. Then, during succeeding days, seated in the rocker or on still days (for he could not endure the booming early fall wind) walking on the playground on Catherine's arm, he dictated to her an account of all he had seen.

Looking up from the desk at which she was turning her notes into clear, round script, Catherine said to me, "What a memory that old man has! Listen," and she read: "At the Creek busk grounds on the sixteenth of August, two miles south of Mingo's Town, I was privileged to talk with Mr. Akwright who took me later to the 'New' Tyner Mission. They had begun their labors for the Lord on the twelfth of April, 1835, by assembling a sufficient number of able men, who brought their families, to cut the timbers and lay up the first cabin of two rooms of an overall dimension of twenty-four feet by sixteen. The next day, they rove shakes with which to roof it, laid up the greater part of the chimney, cut out two doorways and four windows, split puncheons for the floors, and smoothed the logs inside. On the third day, they chinked the house, completed the roof, and lighted the first fire for drying the chinking. The fourth day was the Lord's Day, and seventy of these good people came to attend the services.

"One week later, Mr. Akwright opened school with eleven scholars, and by the fifteenth of May thirty-seven were crowded on the benches. Among the last to come were two brothers of twelve and eight, sharing a new suit of clothes. The elder wore the pantaloons and the younger the coat and waistcoat. Mrs. Akwright was able to supply acceptable garments to make up the deficiencies . . .

"On arriving at Tyner, I was able to verify Mr. Akwright's statement that the school now has an enrollment of ninety, including thirty-one day scholars, and Tyner Chapel a membership of thirty-eight."

Catherine said, "He is as definite as that about every station he visited—and he made no notes!"

"It has been his life," I said, "and the Wears have good memories. I believe Dan could describe the events of every day in the history of Hebron Creek and Oak Hill without looking at the station diary."

"Yes, and farther back, I expect," Catherine added.

I thought, Yes, even to the day at the Mission Rooms in New York when Mr. Tilley took him to Henri Morin's house to exhibit him as a candidate for the Arkansas assignment and he first met Ellen.

With the Board's approval, Cephas Wear stayed on, and turned over to me his small retirement allowance, saying, "Use it as you see fit, Paul, but if Dan is in need of anything—"

"Of course, Sir," I agreed. "I believe, however, that his income from the family properties in Vermont is adequate to meet his needs. He has been using it, as he says, to add to our luxuries."

"You must remind him," the old man's eyes twinkled at thought of the innocent deception, "that I am a lonely old codger, and must rely largely upon him for companionship." It was, I knew, his device for holding Dan near to guide and counsel me, for his time at Oak Hill was a happy one, and it was not in his nature to feel lonely.

In order to be near his uncle, Dan built a cabin close to The Runner's home. Legally, he became The Runner's tenant since no white man might own land; and each year he paid the fee required of every white person not a teacher or missionary living in the Cherokee Nation.

Nearly always when Dan rode to Oak Hill he brought Cherokee friends with whom he believed Mr. Wear would like to talk. One day an old man of seventy on seeing Mr. Wear broke into a broad grin and let his hand linger in his grasp as he recalled, "Long time now I know this man; she comin' one day Dah-lo-ne-ga."

"Yes, Dah-lo-ne-ga in 'twenty-five." Mr. Wear's fingers went to his beard as a sign that he was casting back in his memory. "I saw you the last time at Candy Creek, in 'Thirty-seven, talking with Stephen Foreman about the people Stephen was to lead to Indian Territory. My, my, now we meet again, my friend, and I find you looking younger, and fatter, than ever!"

Mr. Wear did not make a joke at meeting Sequoyah, but settled down, with Miss Eula acting as interpreter, to question him at length about his work and his plans. It was in Sequoyah's mind to make a pilgrimage to the Cherokees in Texas, and to others who, he had been told, had pushed on over the Rio Grande into Mexico. For various reasons, but principally to escape white domination, they had gone south in clan and family groups; and to them Sequoyah wished to carry his syllabary, a plea for their return to Indian Territory. Also, I had heard, his mission involved some mysterious business of which I believed Dan knew something but said nothing.

Cephas Wear was puzzled by Dan's almost reverent attachment to Sequoyah, and tried to understand the reason for it. However, I don't believe he did completely because he lacked that grain of mysticism which sometimes made Dan unpredictable and which drew him close to Sequoyah. I wondered if Mr. Wear thought of Sequoyah as the sort of zealot who, as we used to say in Vermont, went on whipping his horse after he had won the race. I recalled Ellen's question, "Hasn't he already taught the people to read and write his silly hen-tracks?" and Dan's answer, "Yes, and there are others who can teach his syllabary as well as he, but there's more to the man that that. He has a message of far greater importance to the people." Pressed by Ellen's questions, however, he confessed, "It's not quite clear to me, but I feel its urgency."

* * *

Dan's dismissal Ellen regarded as her triumph over him. Now her hope rose that the men who fought Ross would prevail. She wrote to her father: "Dan's God did not save him from the discipline of the Board. How then can He save the pious Ross and such Christers as Bushyhead, who is chief justice of the Cherokees under Ross? Talley Tassel and Wah-ti-ka, who represent practical statesmanship and armed force, are the logical leaders in a realistic era. They have the ears of Washington and the support of the Government's agents; they are obviously best fitted to bring order to the Nation. You will see that I am right, that I have not been wasting my time."

She failed to realize, however, that Ross, in his way, was firmer even than the belligerent Wah-ti-ka, and a far shrewder politician than Tassel. Also, he was honest; and his sobriety, his uprightness, kept him fit for the task at which he toiled six long days each week. Schools, his reliance for survival in the long run, supported by the tribe's own funds which he managed to obtain from Washington, grew and throve.

Ellen expected Dan to quit the Cherokees. In her mind was revived the old hope of joining him in the East and, united with him again, helping him to make a place in the world that she understood. She could not believe that, unlike Sam Houston, Dan had committed himself unalterably to the Cherokees.

I found in Dan's notes a brief account of the first visit she paid him after riding away from Oak Hill with me. It was when he had been settled in his own cabin for more than a year:

"Ellen came, by boat and carriage, saying she had just heard of my dismissal from Oak Hill and professing concern for my welfare. Talked about Tassel as though I knew nothing of her relations with him. Puzzled to know why she had come until, on the point of leaving—I could not keep her over night—she wanted to know if it was true that Ross was dying. I said he had been ill, but is now sound as ever, and advised her to stop crediting rumors . . . She seems little changed in appearance, but is more restless, seems even more discontented, harassed."

In a letter to her father, Ellen pictured the non-committal Dan who sat on the other side of the fireplace from her that day:

"He was so damned polite, and so anxious for me to cut short my visit, that I was tempted to scream—or faint, so that he must touch me . . . Papa, I wanted him back so much that I cried all the way to Fort Smith in the carriage, and slept not at all on the boat that carried me on to Little Rock. You may be pleased to know that he is well, and that he asked after your health and that of Maman.

"I have not the smallest idea of what he means to do; he was more tight-lipped than ever, but I shall try again. I am becoming tired of my life in Little Rock, and somewhat doubtful of certain ambitious ones who come to me there. I wish that you might come out and advise me, but as you have said it is I who have taken the ox by the horns and must manage it or get free the best way I can. Nevertheless I adore you for your understanding. I love you more than any one else in the whole world, for I still hate Dan even as I long for his love."

The next time she came to Dan's cabin he was not at home. The Runner told her that he was at Oak Hill, and she came on to find him in one of our frequent staff councils. Besides Dan and me, there were Miss Eula, Catherine, Richard, Mrs. Ryan the housekeeper, and the farmer, Will Farley; also, at my insistence, Cephas Wear had joined us.

The matter under discussion was how to divide the time of the older boys between the schoolroom and the fields which, as I have already written, had been greatly expanded. Dan had risen, after proposing to go with Farley to look over our hundred and twenty acres of young corn and estimate the number of days that would be required to hoe them free of weeds by stretching out the older boys' work period an hour each day and adding to the field work force eight of the older girls who, Mrs. Ryan had said, were willing to help, when Ellen walked in. She made a motion to withdraw, saying to Dan, "If you're busy, I'll wait outside."

"I can put off what I was going to do," Dan said politely, "if you want to talk with me."

We others rose. I shook hands with her, and went into the next room. Miss Eula said, "How are you, Ellen?" then, "You must come and see the girls before you leave." The others spoke to her with obvious embarrassment, save Cephas Wear who invited, "Sit here for a while with me, Ellen, you and Dan."

Through the open door I heard her spirited reply, "I shall be glad to if you can induce him to look at me as though he had really known me once!"

That visit, too, became the subject of one of her letters that Mr. Morin sent to me later, with the notation, "Perhaps they will assist you to understand Ellen; and now that Dan seems to have got beyond our reach I must beg that you keep your eyes on her."

Ellen wrote: "We came at least to plain speaking, thanks to Dan's old uncle who, you will remember, visited me at Little Rock and asked me why I had chosen to wreck my husband's career, and only laughed when I told him that it was no concern of his.

"This day, at Oak Hill, the old man put another blunt question, 'What do you want from Dan now?' I answered, 'Nothing; I only want Dan.' Then he asked, as though Dan were not present, 'Have you got rid of the other man?' When I said that he was being insulting, and that I would not answer such a question, he shook his white head and chided, 'You and I, my child, are past being insulted by honest talk; and, whether you like it or not, I am Dan's kin and well wisher. We Wears stick together, and I've never heard of a Wear who played second fiddle to such a pumpkin-head clothes dummy as you took up with.'

"I was so angry that I cried; and then I came out with the truth, saying (you know, Papa, how sometimes I swear, but without blasphemous intent), 'To hell with that man! I'll drop him instantly if Dan will be good to me.' The old Christer wasn't shocked, as I expected he would be, but only rubbed his beard and said, 'I don't like that if, my dear.' Again I swore, 'I don't care a damn whether you like it or not! I came to talk with Dan, not to listen to a sermon.'

"He said to Dan, 'She's right, and I'll get me hence.' But Dan stopped him, saying, 'Don't go, Sir. I seem to be getting the whole truth from Ellen at last,' then to me, 'Why should you think I would drive such a bargain with you?'

"I tried to make him see (what you have understood, Papa, bless you!) my need for a man of warm flesh and blood in my life. I spoke plainly, God knows, but I said nothing that both of them did not already know. Dan listened with maddening calmness (how often have I wished that he would storm at me, or beat me even!) and then Cephas Wear produced chapter and verse to support his statement concerning one of my anti-Ross friends, 'He's a poorly tied pig's bladder, Ellen, and the wind is seeping out of him.' ([T]he old one is worse than Dan and Paul for using absurd Vermont farm language.)

"I could make no bargain. I would do as Cephas Wear wishes, get rid of the other man and the whole anti-Ross crowd if—yes, there is still that if in my mind—Dan would take me back. Even so, I fear the old clash would be renewed; Dan said that he had no intention of returning to New York or Vermont; and the Cherokees he is interested in still bore me.

"However, I shall not give up; as you have told me, the best bargains are made after long and persistent chaffering. I hate Dan for so many reasons that it must seem that I am insane for continuing to want him as I do. And it's not that I am determined to have my way. Not altogether. There is so much love and desire to care for him mixed up with it in my mind that I am confused.

"It will not be long, I believe, before the final test of strength between the pious Ross men and my friends occurs. When it does, and it is decided who is to govern, I shall feel free to loose my hold on the horns of the ox I have been attempting to lead. To be honest, I don't greatly care whether my ox wins or not."

Fifteen

It may not have been original with Ellen, but it was she who first suggested to Tassel the policy that was adopted by the anti-Ross party. It was explained in another letter to her father:

"I said to them, 'It appears that you are not strong enough to overcome Ross by force of arms. You have the ears of the Government at Washington, however. Why don't you persuade Washington to divide the Cherokee Nation between the two factions. Then set up your own tribal organization, represent it at Washington as speaking for the real Cherokees, and have the Government pay your treasurer the money that is owing to the tribe. Quickly enough, then, you will find the people deserting the Christers and coming to you. It would seem that Washington hopes for such a division, since only a little of what it owes has been paid into Ross' treasury.

"So Talley Tassel headed a delegation to Washington (forgive me, Papa, if I write like a Cherokee politician, and all of this may be Greek to you, but you asked for it!) to ask for separation.

"However, Ross arrived in Washington as soon as Tassel's men did, and managed to delay action. Our men must be content with the promise of a Government Commission that will inquire into the desires of the Cherokee people.

"I suppose the Commissioners, had they come, would have reported an 'overwhelming' sentiment for separation—as Jackson's ex-Christer reported the tribe's desire to go west in 1835, a desire which they failed to express, he said only because they were 'overawed by John Ross.' The Commission was not appointed because Ross let it be known that his supporters would not attend the hearings should they be held. Also, Ross had the audacity to forbid the Government at Washington to meddle in matters that concerned only the Cherokees, and it would appear that the Government has no wish to challenge Ross. Think of it, Papa, that homely little Christer, with only some twelve thousand followers, telling Washington to keep hands off. But, of course, Jackson is no longer there . . .

"I suppose, too, that Mr. John Howard Payne, who has lately been a guest at Ross' home, is still desirous to publish his history of Cherokee wrongs, and the Government is aware that further 'persecution' of the Ross following would cause it to be read everywhere and stir the anger of many people. Mr. Irving might also be tempted to turn advocate for Ross' 'martyrs'; I have been told that in his talks with Sequoyah and Ross, his sympathies were enlisted."

In one of her last letters, Ellen told how the separation movement died after showing only a flicker of vitality even amongst the Westerners. "With it," she wrote, "went all hope of effective resistance to Ross. All that remains is bitterness amongst the would-be secessionists. Many are determined to go to the South, and some have actually set off for Texas or Mexico. The rest engage in frequent brawls with Ross men which often lead to killings and the breeding of feuds that have little relation to the issue of leadership in tribal government . . .

"As I promised myself months ago, I shall now free myself from entanglement with the anti-Ross men. My particular friend, who has been in love with me for more than three years, talks about making one last desperate gesture, the nature of which is vague in his mind, in which he begs me to join. As nearly as I can guess, it would mean playing the role of 'Beloved Woman', but not as Dan used to use the term! Oh no, I would ape one Nancy Ward who took up a gun and stood beside her warrior husband to fight the enemies of the tribe and fell beside him and earned by that action the title and lasting renown amongst the Cherokees. When I understood this, I merely pointed out that history never repeats itself exactly—and anyway I do not know how to shoot a gun.

"I can tell you, Papa, that my gallant Cherokee will not risk his life either—not when he is sober.

"I mean soon to invite myself for a visit to Kate Acton. That will place me near Dan. I shall go once more to Oak Hill, and tell the venerable Mr. Wear, if he is still there with Paul, that I have 'got rid of that man,' and also of every 'if' in my vocabulary.

"I still have no idea of what Dan intends doing. He has not been idle, of course; I know that he has been working in the role of peacemaker, through Sequoyah principally. When that role is played out, I can imagine him setting up as a free lance missionary. Even that I could bear—now. I want to live with him again on any terms he cares to make. I seem to care less than ever before about uprooting him and having him in New York . . . Do you suppose, Papa, that he could forgive my infidelity? Surely a repentant sinner—and I am truly that! —would not appeal in vain?"

Ellen came to Oak Hill from Gibson too late for the talk she had promised herself with Cephas Wear. We saw a very old man whom we had come to love and revere go sweetly to sleep, and we could believe with him that his awakening would be in his heavenly home. He had lived almost twenty years beyond the allotted three score and ten. Near the end, he said to Dan and me, "God has been good to me. I have been permitted to serve Him as I wished, and to lie down for my last long rest in ground broken by my kin who also serve Him."

Three days before his death, Sequoyah and Hummingbird came to talk with him. Dan told him they were at Oak Hill, but would understand if it was explained to them that he could not see anyone. However, Mr. Wear would have them come in and sit beside him, and said, "I have so little breath left that I shan't waste it in talk, but I will gladly listen." Between them, Sequoyah using his fluent Middle Towns Cherokee and Peter putting it into hesitant English, they spoke to him of what they were doing to bring peace. Now and then, he approved, "Good, good," and twice shook his head and advised, "You would do better to follow Ross' lead in this."

Knowing that he was nearing the end, one of the school girls asked Miss Eula if she and the others might say good-bye. Miss Eula told him of their wish, but protested that they would overtax his strength. "What if they do," he said. "I know of no better way to use it. Have Paul bring the boys, too, if they care to come and wish me bon voyage."

They all passed by his bed, and each laid a hand in his as he whispered, "God bless you." They did not go out at once, but huddled in a close-packed group to sing "How firm a foundation," knowing that the hymn was a favorite one with him and Dan. As they ceased I saw tears on his cheeks, and his hand went to his beard as though he strove to find words to thank them. "God bless you," he repeated; and the girls were moved to tears also, and the boys hung their heads the way Indian children do when stirred.

Only Dan, Miss Eula, Catherine and Richard heard his last words, and the final sigh of release: "It is time; the trumpet of the Lord calls."

Dan took as text for the funeral sermon in Pease Chapel words from the Psalms: "He hath dispersed, he hath given to the poor; his horn shall be exalted with honor."

He went on, "David's words describe such a man as Cephas Wear whose earthly remains are with us in the Chapel today. Tomorrow they will lie in Oak Hill cemetery, where his gravestone will remind us of his very great understanding, his ripe wisdom, his courage, and his love . . . A valiant servant of God has passed this way. 'The righteous shall be in everlasting remembrance.' "

Ellen said, when she came to Oak Hill and talked with Dan in my presence, "Cephas Wear was the only man I ever knew who could tell the whole truth without getting angry or really offending. I'm sorry I could not have told him so." As if it could have mattered to him! But it was characteristic of Ellen to assume that her every thought must be important.

Dan listened attentively to her disavowal of what she called her mistaken faith in Tassel; and when, irked by his silence, she asked sharply, "Don't you believe me?" he answered, "Yes, of course. One thing you have never done, and that is lie to me."

She went on: "Now that what I conceived to be high political drama has turned to farce under my eyes, I want to atone for my error . . . Dan, I never dreamed that I would come to any man and beg to be taken, but I would get down on my knees to you if I believed I could move you that way. I want your love, as I have always wanted it, but more than anything else I want to live again with an honest man."

At length he said, "I shall have to think it over, Ellen."

"Of course, Dan," and her face lighted as though she were already sure of him. "I'll go back to Kate and wait."

He went on, "I can't say any more, except that I mean to go soon with Sequoyah to the South. He believes I can be useful in persuading the Cherokees in Texas and Mexico to return; he has waited for me knowing I would not leave Uncle Cephas."

Ellen stayed a week, and it was as though she had found sanctuary at Oak Hill. The nervous tension under which she had lived relaxed noticeably, the sharply drawn lines of her face softened, years seemed to have dropped from her. I began to see again the youthful, buoyant woman seated at Dan's side in the one-horse wagon as we drove away from Kingslake, her parasol tilted to protect her complexion from the sun, leaning close to provoke him to complimentary speeches.

I was indeed busy in that week. Dan wanted me to join Sequoyah's party, and I was eager to go. Before starting on the extended journey I must plan with Richard, Catherine, and Miss Eula for the conduct of Oak Hill, go over with them hundreds of details. Finally, I must report my intended absence to the Board, to the Cherokee authorities, and to Fort Gibson. Ellen rode to Gibson with me.

Of course, that other ride to Gibson was in our minds, but neither of us spoke about it. What had then been only a horseback trail was now a tolerably good road over which military ambulances rattled at speed and mail and passenger stages, each drawn by four tough Santa Fe mules, raced to maintain regular schedules. The trees were in full spring leafage; no vestige remained of the windows of parti-colored autumn leaves that had haunted my dreams in spite of my successful effort to banish them from my mind in waking hours . . . I wondered if Ellen would believe me if I would tell her that I was still a virgin man.

I thought of what The Runner had once said, that a "singing bird" often molts, sheds its fine feathers, stops preening to attract males, and becomes a worthy keeper of the fire. I was sure that Ellen had molted; her interest in the affairs of the mission station about which we talked at length on the way to Gibson was not feigned[.] I thought, She is like a candidate for station teacher and assistant eager for service. She is, too, like a bride-to-be intent upon equipping herself to help a missionary husband-to-be.

I made no excuses in my mind for what she had done to Dan, but if he could forgive her—well, that was his affair. In her talk with Dan she had said as little as possible about Tassel. I had seen him only once, at the Flint District court house, sober and subdued in manner, but I could understand why he had been described as something of a dandy with the figure of a Greek god and the face of a dark Anthony, devastating to women. I tried to make Ellen talk about him in her frank and vivid way, but she cut my suggestive questioning short, "Paul, it is as though I never knew him. I have put him so completely out of my life that I could not tell you the color of his eyes."

"Has he also banished you from his life?" I asked.

"I don't know," she answered, "and don't care. I owe him nothing, not a thought, not a moment of remembrance. If he believes that he owes me anything you may tell him, with my compliments, that the debt is canceled." With the words, she closed the door on Tassel.

She wanted from me details of Dan's life since that other day we had ridden to Gibson together. I was glad to supply them. I wanted her to see him going about his work of making Oak Hill useful to the people, unshaken by her desertion. I wanted her to realize that although she had caused his removal as head of the station his interest had not slackened, and to understand the bond that held us Wears together, Dan, old Cephas, and I; in our way, we had been as indomitable and walked as high-headedly as any Morin.

She surprised me by probing into my work with the boys, listening to little quotations I remembered from what some of them had written. One, by a twelve-year-old nephew of Richard, I had approved for inclusion in a story-tract which Catherine had written: "Vacation time will soon be here. The year that has passed we cannot call back; and in the future we ought to improve our time as much as possible and not spend our time in idleness. Our people will be glad to know that we are learning fast."

Hearing me recall the boy's words, Ellen did not dismiss them as "pious trash" as once she would have done, but said, "Why, Paul, that is good, as simple as a-b-c and written as a child ought to write. Did you show it to Dan, and did he like it?"

"Yes, and Catherine did, too."

"I like Catherine," she said, "and shall see much of her if Dan's plans will permit."

I promised Ellen to search out letters written by another scholar that reflected the troubled time through which we were passing more vividly, I believed, than the Government agents' reports. Here are portions of that fifteen-year-old girl's budget of gossip and grim facts that went to her father, an anti-Ross refugee living in Arkansas:

"Dear, dear Papa, I must send you the news before I forget it. Mama said she would send it in Cherokee, but I just know she will forget to . . . John Coon broke into Green's store and stole 200 dols, him and a negro; the negro's name is Teeny Raikes and he is Mr. Green's black. They had John Coon up before the judge and gave him 200 lashes, and tried to make him own up and he did, he went and got 130 dols of it and said the negro had the rest . . .

"Ned Wolfe is dead, poor boy I feel sorry. Uncle Tom's negro Zeke died the same day, he was killed, a boy by the name of Asa Blacksnake did the murder . . . Will Redbird has been arrested for killing Return Mason . . . The light Horse have taken Eli Spring, and run David Nelson off, they will either whip or hang Eli . . . Several others have run over the line into Arkansas.

"That boy they whipped for stealing is dead . . . They say it was James Laws and Hiliard Norman that burned the Parishs' house, but that is just a story . . . They hung Tim Peace for having a hand in killing Stand Olds, they say he made a long confession, I don't know what it was . . .

"Mama was disappointed when she got your letter and found you would not come home soon. It has wore out her spirit she says living this way. She is perfectly sick of the world, seems like she has lost all earthly friends and God Himself has said let her alone for she is joined to her idol (that is you, Papa) . . . I forgot to say they had Cooks up for stealing horses, sent him to Little Rock bound hand and foot—and they will send more over the same road if what they say is so . . . Reed-shooter and Ben Stooping are in chains for burning Mack Bread's house."

Other letters were in a lighter tone:

"Papa, I feel like I am the only heart free girl in the Nation, everybody but me is in love with some little fellow. But what do you think, somebody did write me four letters, and I sold his letters to Carrie Bond for a dress, I think that was a fine trade, don't you, Carrie wants to show the letters as if they had come to her.

"The other day Miss Eula asked for compositions, and I wrote one on lettuce. I will tell some of the things I said. I said there are various kinds of lettuce not too tedious to mention if I knew them all but it is no use to commence and then not finish. We have lettuce here sometimes but not as often as Miss Eula would like, she says it puts her to sleep if she eats it on school days but not on Sunday, I expect she stays awake to hear Mr. W[.] preach. Sue Runner loves potatoes too but not as well as lettuce. Edna Ross loves lettuce as well as she does the boys and Jane Wolfcatcher loves peas as well as she does me.

"Papa, how is that for a composition?

"You remember me grumbling over my old arithmetic, well I wish Mr. Ray that wrote my arithmetic had never seen a figure much less made up that book for me to study, but by the time school closes I will understand it if gymnastics will help beat it into me. Yes, you just ought to see us practice, we beat away on our chests as good as Capt. Wilson's drummers when the Gov. of Arkansas came to Fort Smith, remember?

"Carrie says she heard the legislature in Arkansas just passed an Act for an insane and deaf and dumb and blind asylum. Maybe they will get several blind and insane but no deaf and dumb, not in Arkansas anyway. I think it would look like an insane asylum if they got the legislature inside the Capitol and locked the doors."

Recalling as much of the girl's letters as I could, I said to Ellen, "The Cherokees have come a long way on the road to what we call civilization, when a girl of fifteen can write like that."

Ellen laughed, "That girl reminds me of myself at fifteen, curious and skeptical; and she probably writes better than I did at her age."

I told Ellen of Dan's intervention to save the lives of two innocent Cherokees from the fiery Wah-ti-ka who had denounced them as slayers of his cousin Cloud-eater. Dan had heard of Wah-ti-ka's threat to murder them, had sought the truth from Hummingbird, and had gone to warn them. She said, "Yes, Wah-ti-ka is too much given to shooting first and determining the facts afterwards. I could put up with his violence, however, better than—" she did not finish the sentence, but I knew she was thinking of Tassel's hypocrisy.

That was her last reference to a past which she had determined to blot out of her mind.

My business at Gibson and at the Government Agency was soon concluded. I was cheered to hear, at both places, the fervently spoken hope that Sequoyah's peace mission might succeed.

Sixteen

Sequoyah's party started the journey towards Mexico from his cabin early on a May morning. After we were mounted, his wife Sally came to stand beside Dan's horse and say, her eyes half turned to Sequoyah, "You take care my man; she not young now, hard to fin' things to eat that are good for him."

"We'll do our best, all of us," Dan promised.

Then Sally, with a daughter of eighteen and a son of sixteen, both of whom had been scholars at Oak Hill, went to Sequoyah and laid their hands in turn on his knee before he touched his pony's flanks with his heels and led off. I looked back, to see them standing in silence, with Sally touching her eyes with the hem of her apron.

With us rode Sequoyah's elder son Tee-see, a sturdy young man of twenty-five. The others, all young men, were The Worm, Broken Rock, Wildcat, The Path, To-he-ka, Jimmy, and Oo-lah-neh. All were fullbloods who wore their hair long. Among them was understanding of Spanish and various Indian languages, for they had hunted in western Indian Territory, Texas, and Mexico.

Dan rode at Sequoyah's side, flanked by Tee-see as interpreter. I stayed back with The Worm and Jimmy to help with the pack horses which carried camp equipment: a large oblong of tent cloth under which Sequoyah, Dan and I could sleep, brass cooking kettles, blankets, salt, sugar, coffee, and as much flour as could be carried, for Sequoyah ate little besides white bread and honey. The honey, I was told by The Worm, we would find in abundance wherever we went. The funds for the party were in Sequoyah's keeping, his savings from his pension from the Cherokees and earnings from his trapping and his salt concession. These, Dan had told me, had been supplemented by a substantial gift from Hummingbird. Both Dan and I also carried gold.

After a time, Dan dropped back to ride with me, and speak of Sequoyah's purpose. "I know little more," he said, "than you have already heard, although I can guess that it is more than a teaching and peace making mission. I am hoping that he will tell me."

Fording the Arkansas River, we bore southwestward through the

Creek Nation. The first trader's post on our course where we could replenish our supplies of flour and sugar, The Worm told us, was at Little River, "ten days ahead if we go slow like this." In reply to a question by Dan, he said, "No, Sequoyah she don' tell us nothin', only we goin' to them Cherokees in Mexico."

I had never before ridden for more than a few hours with Indians, and it was hard to comprehend the simplicity of their traveling routine. There seemed to be no organization, no plan. At any time of day, two or more of the young men might ride away without a word, to be absent until we halted, an hour before sunset, to make camp for the night. Some time before it grew dark, they would come in with game and honey, throw it down by the fire, then unsaddle and hobble their horses. Before sunset some one, whom I never heard designated for the duty, would prepare food, Sequoyah would limp from his shelter, and we would sit in a circle to eat. Before the stars brightened we were in our blankets, and were up at dawn. By sunrise we were in motion. We made long noonings so that the horses might get a mid-day fill of grass.

One evening, a week after our departure, I wondered why none of the Cherokees was busy at the cooking fire until The Worm, grinning, touched my elbow and said, "I think it you cook now." As we ate, the young men made a joke of my denseness, laughing at The Worm's imitation of my startled look "when I tell him, this one, we elect him cook!" Dan, laughing with them, asked, "Will it be my turn tomorrow?"

Sequoyah spoke to The Worm in Cherokee, and The Worm said, "She say you don' cook," and, with a grin, added on his own, "Maybe we get too sick if you do." That, too, was a joke that lasted for days; and each time it was repeated Sequoyah would join in the laughter, put his hand on Dan's knee and say, "No good, this one!"

Once accustomed to the routine, I found the journey delightful. The May days lengthened under a friendly sun, and the rains were refreshing. We slept dry, ate well, and rode no faster than an occasional jog trot.

Once, before coming to Little River, The Worm and Tee-see motioned to me with their chins to join them on a hunting detour. We ranged far from the course, skirted the timber of a creek that runs into Little River, and found a flock of wild turkeys. Tee-see stalked them, as The Worm and I sat immobile on our horses, and killed two. In the afternoon, we entered the timber, halting presently for no reason apparent to me, then The Worm, pointing, said, "That way."

He had seen bees, honey-laden, bulleting their way to a hive-tree. Lining the bees from another point, he led us to the tree. I helped them cut down the tree and, protected by a smudge fire, rob it of the dripping honeycombs. As he and Tee-see put the honey into rawhide carry-alls, The Worm smacked his lips and said, "We eat good this time," and gesturing towards me, "she don' cook it supper today." Tee-see laughed, then assured me, "She like to make it fun; we think you cook all right."

I thought, These men are wise. They have retained the simplicity and fresh-mindedness of children. To them the high purpose of Sequoyah needed no explaining. He is their leader; they follow and care for him as unquestioningly as Cherokee children follow and obey their mothers. I seem to have gone back to live in an age—call it primitive if you will—untroubled by such problems of civilization as getting ahead in the world, education, love. It was hard to believe that Dan could be thinking of what to do about Ellen, and wondered if he did not feel, as I did now, that the matter was of little importance.

Perhaps I exaggerated this impression of a world belonging only to men, as before I may have overestimated Ellen's power to bring happiness or misery to Dan; he had said once that I had too much imagination for my own good. I wanted him to talk about Ellen, but we went on day after day with scarcely a mention of anything we had left behind, and never a word concerning her. The day's incidents, trivial as they were, occupied us as completely as they did Sequoyah and the young men.

Keeping count of the days became a bothersome task. When we came to Red River, at the boundary between Indian Territory and Texas, where Sequoyah said he would rest, I had stopped saying to myself, Today is Monday, or Tomorrow will be June tenth, Miss Eula's birthday, or, Our school will close for the summer next Friday.

Sequoyah merely said that he was tired as he called Tee-see and The Worm to him and instructed them to go across the river to the towns of the Wichata Indians and ask if there were any Cherokees nearby who had come up from Mexico. If any were found, they were to be brought back to the camp so that he might talk with them.

They were absent twelve days. Four days they used in reaching the Wichatas, four days they spent in running down false rumors that Cherokees were to be found farther south, and four days were required for returning. Meanwhile our stock of flour was exhausted, and Sequoyah fell ill.

When The Worm reported that no Cherokees were among the Wichitas he went to his rawhide carry-all, saying, "We pass little while ago plum bushes. I get some ripe ones—good," and emptied them in front of Sequoyah, who ate them with relish. Spitting out the stones, he said, "These are good, but I need bread."

Tee-see said, "Then we go again to that town for flour."

Sequoyah nodded, and said, "When I can ride again we will follow your tracks." Then he went back to the writing at which he had been busy during our noonings and while in camp at the river.

Six days later we set forth again, crossed Red River, and rode slowly until we met The Worm and Tee-see with three bushels of corn packed on their horses; they had been unable to find flour. We hunted shade and good water and camped. The young men pounded corn in a mortar chopped in a log, and made bread and fine-grained hominy. This, with honey, greatly strengthened Sequoyah.

After eating, he told us that he had made a plan which would restore him to health: we would rest at this camp another day, go on for two days, rest again for a day, then travel on to the Wichitas. There Tee-see's and The Worm's jaded horses would be replaced by fresh ones. From the Wichata towns we would not travel straight south to Mexico, over the treeless plains of Texas, but swing eastward and keep to the timbered country where a variety of game, and honey could be found.

At the Wichita towns, their head chief gave Sequoyah a ceremonious welcome, provided a lodge for his use, and the special food suited to his needs; from some source, wheaten flour had been obtained against Sequoyah's coming. During the three days he remained, resting and writing, Dan and I and the young men explored the scattered Wichita settl[e]ments. On the fourth day, he called us to him and said, "It is better that only my son Tee-see and The Worm stay with me from this day—and also my friend the Straight Talker," he touched Dan's knee, "if he wishes to bear with me in my slow travels."

Dan said, "Yes, I will go with you."

"The others," Sequoyah directed, "will return to your homes." When I ventured to suggest that he, too, return lest he become seriously ill, he shook his head, saying, "I cannot turn back."

Next morning, therefore, six young men and I took the back trail, and I reached Oak Hill on a day of excessive heat in late July, resting badly in my bed after sixty-nine nights of sound sleep on the ground. Richard shook his head on hearing my account of the journey, and said, as though pronouncing sentence, "I know Sequoyah will not come back; he is old and lame and sick."

* * *

What I know of Sequoyah's journey beyond the Wichita towns comes from the notes Dan sent back to me from Mexico. Together with my own jottings covering the days before I turned back, I wrote out Dan's notes for Ellen, who was eager to learn every possible detail.

The notes yielded a chronicle of travel not unlike what I have written about our progress to the Wichita towns, except for certain mishaps which were serious enough but did not greatly delay the arrival of the four—Sequoyah, Dan, Tee-see, and The Worm—at the Mexican town of San Fernando in and near which lived the greater part of the Cherokees who had migrated beyond the Rio Grande.

Dan wrote of Sequoyah's increasing absorption in his writing, about which he would say nothing. "I guessed, however, that it was a history of his people, and that he could not complete it without the material he hoped to find in Mexico. This is pure speculation, but I believe it has to do with the theft, long ago, of certain sacred symbols of the Cherokees by the Delawares. I recalled what old Ta-ka-e-tuh once told me, that after their loss there was unrest and spiritual discontent amongst the people. Perhaps Sequoyah believes these sacred symbols—I have no idea of what they consist—are somewhere in Mexico, and that he may be able to recover them. I have felt, since coming to know him well, that a purpose even greater than his passion for teaching and for a reunion in peace of all the tribe dominates him. It is believable that he hopes to restore the faith of the Cherokees in their old god."

The last page of Dan's notes was written after five days in San Fernando, where the self-exiled Cherokees looked upon Sequoyah as a wise and revered leader and teacher:

"Sequoyah has just told me that he will set out on the last stage of his journey tomorrow morning, and will be pleased if I accompany him. I said that, of course, I would go. He will not take Tee-see and The Worm, nor any of the young men of San Fernando who want to go. He says we will go to a place in the mountains about which he is vague but which I suspect is the remote country of the Yaqui Indians. He said that if all goes well he will there conclude his journey and accomplish his mission.

("Now I must write briefly to Paul, and prepare these notes and the letter to be taken to him by The Worm, who is to return to Oak Hill.")

Here is Dan's letter to me:

"I tried to persuade Sequoyah to send by The Worm, along with my notes, that which he has been writing, but he refused, saying, 'It is not yet finished.'

"I cannot guess when we shall return, if ever. Sequoyah is in good health, and I am fit. You will tell Ellen as much, and tell her also that if I had the time before leaving I would send a letter to her and try to satisfy her as to my plans. It must suffice, now, to say that I have determined to include her in them if she wishes to be included. 'He that is without sin among you—' You will be able to set her mind at rest, I know. My love for her has not died; it has been stifled only.

"My personal papers, including all my journals covering the time between leaving New York and undertaking this journey, I left in The Runner's charge. They are to be turned over to you if I do not come back.

"To you, Paul, and to all the others at Oak Hill, I say, 'God bless you until we meet again.' "

Seventeen

It was almost a year after I got back to Oak Hill when The Worm delivered Dan's letter and notes. We were putting our scholars through the June examinations, and the corn in our fields was waist high.

In that time, Ellen had gone to New York to be at her father's bedside when he died and to assure him that she and Dan would again live together, "whether as man and wife, Papa, I cannot say." She had stayed only long enough to sign the necessary papers insuring the division of his considerable fortune as he had willed it. Ellen inherited by far the greater share.

She returned to live with us for a time at Oak Hill; and gave the necessary funds required for erecting for the accommodation of our boys the twin of the girls' fine building. Then she said, "Paul, I want to live in Dan's cabin, and keep it fit against his return." I agreed, of course, and arranged for Lucy Buck, one of our older graduates, to stay with her and for Lucy's brother Thomas to make a garden and do whatever other outdoor chores that needed doing.

Until The Worm's return from Mexico, Ellen existed, so to say, in a state of suspended animation. Nothing was of more than momentary interest, so constantly was Dan in her thoughts. Sitting in his favorite chair, a gift from Uncle Frank, she read his books and put his clothes in order. She urged Lucy to help her think of things that might add to his comfort and pleasure. They put up simple but expensive window curtains, spread a deep carpet on the floor of the sitting room, sent for the new window screening she had seen in New York and silverware of a rich, heavy pattern. She employed The Runner to add a room to the cabin for Lucy to occupy when Dan should come home. Once, flushing, she said to me, "Paul, I want to replace that very comfortable but narrow bunk of Dan's with a wide New England four-poster bed, but I dare not until—" Would he take her again as bedfellow? She could not know, of course.

She rode often to Oak Hill, spent much time with Catherine and courted, petted, and spoiled Catherine's children. Richard's print shop drew her, too; and she gave us the funds for hiring an extra printer and to purchase needed supplies when we undertook to publish in a single volume the Gospels in Cherokee. Our serious discussion concerning the exact wording of Mathew III: 6 confused her, and with a flash of the old scorn cried, "What does it matter whether John sprinkled, dipped, or washed with soap and water the children of Judea!" I explained that it was a matter of actual concern to our Board, under whose authority we were to issue the Gospels, as well as to our Baptist friends who were also circulating sections of the New Testament in Cherokee.

When The Runner told me that Tassel had come to the cabin, drunk, to talk with Ellen, and that Lucy Beck had run to him for help in getting the man out, I begged her to have Thomas Beck occupy the added room and at all times remain near for her protection. She refused, saying, "I appreciate your solicitude, Paul, but I'm sure that Lucy and I can take care of ourselves. We're not cowards, and we've both learned to use a pistol. We practice quite a lot."

Ellen was with me as I listened to The Worm's account of what he and Tee-see did after Sequoyah and Dan rode away from San Fernando:

"We wait at that place maybe two months, then Standin' Rock, she's man lives San Fernan', come an' say we mus' fin' this Sequoyah an' The Straight Talker. So we hunt up horses, me an' Tee-see an' that Standin' Rock, an' start out. We can' fin' no trail, so long them two been gone, an' we jus' go this way an' that way askin' about them men. We fin' out they go west good many days, an' after while no more people say they see them men.

"We come to that country where Indians live in the mountains, an' some of them speak Spanish, so we can talk with them. They say no they ain' seen them men. One man say, Maybe you go an' talk with them other Indians over yonder. She show the way, an' we come to that valley where they live. They are call' Lenapi. We can talk with them Lenapi only in sign language, but we think maybe they know about them two men an' don' want to tell us; they don' look straight in our face when they talk.

"So we ride on. We don' hear nothin', an' our horses get poor an' lame goin' over the rocks. So we mus' go back to San Fernan'. We wait a while, then Tee-see say for me to come back here an' bring this writin' while she will stay an' go again to fin' he's father if she can. So I come back with a man from San Fernan' that come to stay a while with he's uncle on Skin Bayou."

The Worm's talk ended, I looked again into Dan's journal-notes, and read again his tentative speculations as to Sequoyah's secret mission. I knew that at one time the Delaware Indians were known as Lenapi, "the real people," and that in the old days the Cherokees referred to them as their grandfathers. I, too, began to speculate: Had Sequoyah and Dan found in that remote valley the sacred symbols? Had the ancestors of their present keepers fled with them to Mexico, swearing to hold them, they and their children and their childrens' children, until men should write no more of their daring in the Lenapi "Walum Olum," the record of the tribe's years on earth? Had they killed Sequoyah and Dan after refusing to listen to Sequoyah's plea for the return of the Cherokees' Ark of the Covenant, and destroyed all traces of them?

I said nothing of these speculations either to The Worm or Ellen. I said to her, "I will copy for you Dan's notes and his letter to me, so that you may have all the information that I or anybody else has except Dan and Sequoyah if—"

"No!" she cried. "Don't say it Paul. I know that Dan is alive and will come back to me."

"Surely," I agreed, and wanted to believe that Sequoyah's wisdom and Dan's resourcefulness were adequate to save them. Yet I found it hard to account for their remaining away from San Fernando so long, or at least not sending word to the Cherokees of that settlement who, they knew, anxiously awaited their return.

Ellen said, "We must find them! We must send men who will not be stopped; and I," she seemed to blaze with the sudden, daring resolution, "will go with them."

"That," I told her, "is impossible. Besides, as The Worm told us, Sequoyah's son will make another search."

"If I could reach Sam Houston," she said, "he would make it possible."

"Don't forget," I pointed out, "that to the Mexicans he is an enemy."

"Did I say," she spoke sharply, "that I should expect him to go into Mexico with me? Paul, don't be stupid."

I reminded her. "There are already two better minds than mine, or yours, engaged on the problem, Dan's and Sequoyah's."

"Yes," she nodded, "that is true. I once thought Sequoyah a muddled old fanatic, but Dan believes in him, almost worships him, and I believe in Dan. Now, Paul, what shall we do?"

I dared not say that I believed it was too late to do anything to save them, dared not tell her where my speculations had led. The Worm's account of meeting with the Lenapi had not impressed her as significant; only Dan's warning in his letter to me that he might not return alarmed her. At length I said, "Probably Sam Houston could find means to have you escorted into Mexico, and to insure your safety. We can make inquiries."

She asked, "Why should I not go at once to Sam, in Texas, and set him to planning?"

"Because," I objected, "your negotiations would be known in Mexico, and you would do more harm than good."

"I suppose so." Then she promised, "I shall do nothing without consulting you. Dan always trusted you, Paul, although I have told him he had an exaggerated opinion of your ability."

"So he had," I admitted, "but his belief in me has helped me over many hard places."

She abandoned the plan to lead an expedition in the story-book manner not only because all of Dan's close friends—The Runner, Richard, Peter Hummingbird, and others—agreed that it would be fruitless, but also because she had lived past the phase when the grand gesture meant much to her. She did write to Houston, however, who promised to put the matter to Chief Bowl of the Texas band of Cherokees.

She did not show me Houston's letter. My imagination led me to wonder if, believing Dan lost, he might have asked her to join him in the rude cabin at Columbia that was the official residence of the President of the Republic of Texas. He might have asked her help in combating the cabals of Mirabeau Buonaparte Lamar and certain other "patriots" seeking to tear the laurels of San Jacinto from his brow. He might have sought her help to save himself from becoming once more a whiskey soaked caricature of a statesman, as she had done at Little Rock. Had he believed that her concern for Dan was only a gesture? However, another letter came telling of Bowl's great anxiety over Sequoyah and the steps he had taken to aid in the search.

I told her, "You have done all you can; now you can only wait."

"I know, Paul, and waiting will be hell. I feel that I was responsible for his going—and I have always loved him so!" It was a cry of anguish.

She was not alone in her grief. I saw Miss Eula's eyes grow tragically sorrowful and her face become bleak as the months dragged on. Her unacknowledged love for Dan was now a canker eating at her heart. But in no way did she neglect her duties. I thought, She has almost reached the end of her tether; strain and suppression will cause her to break if something is not done. So I ordered, "You are to go home on leave for a year when school is over next week. Rest, enjoy your family, and don't think about Oak Hill and its demands."

I expected objections, but she said, "Paul, it might help. I feel so tightly wound that sometimes I want to tear off my clothes and run screaming into the woods!" Then, unexpectedly, she asked, "Has Ellen suggested sending me away?"

"No," I answered. I was glad to be able to answer no. Once Ellen had determined to live as Dan's true helpmeet, she was no longer jealous of Miss Eula.

At the boat, I went aboard to see that her cabin was comfortable and to say, "There is only one thing I want you to do for me, see Mary Lyon and ask her to send out a Mount Holyoke graduate as teacher; she will know our needs."

"Yes, Paul. Are you sure that is all?"

Something I had never seen in her eyes before, a softness that was strange and inviting, led me to put my arms about her and whisper, "No, that isn't all, my dear. Keep me in your heart. I love you, and want you to be my wife. Will you remember that?"

"Dear, dear Paul," she put her face against my shoulder and wept. "I don't know what I shall decide about us, but I will remember—and I do love you. Why you want me I cannot understand, I'm only a confused, tired, nerve-racked old maid. God bless and keep you, my dear." She gave her lips for a moment, then, "Please go now; I don't want you to see me weep." Tears were trembling on her lashes as she smiled and pushed me out of the cabin.

Going back to Oak Hill, I thought, Already the tenseness that has hurt her is loosening. In the year ahead our anxious uncertainty concerning Dan will be ended one way or the other. Should he come back, as we hoped and prayed he will, he and Ellen will make a life in which Miss Eula can have no part. If he is indeed past all hope of earthly aid, a chapter will be closed and she might, as we used to say in Vermont, take the leavings without grumbling.

Catherine said on my return from the landing, "Brother Paul, I'm so glad you sent Miss Eula away. I expect she'll have you when she returns." She laughed, "You know, distance lends enchantment."

"And absence makes the heart grow fonder," I quoted. "We should have sent her away long ago."

"Or you should have stormed her as shamelessly as I did Richard. I shudder to think of what I should have missed by submitting to Mama and Uncle Obidiah and renouncing my Cherokee!"

"Yes," I said, "Richard is a fine man."

" 'Fine'? Heavens, you sound like Uncle Dan in his worst word-sparing moods!" Then, to my consternation, she burst into tears. When she could speak coherently, she said, "Of course, we loved him for that very austerity. Richard and I have been miserable."

"So have we all," I said, "even the scholars who seemed so in awe of him."

Catherine nodded, then, "Do you know, Brother Paul, that they hated you for a time after you took charge? I can tell you now because they were made to understand that you were in no way responsible for his dismissal; and they like and trust you . . . How I wish Richard could have that manuscript of Sequoyah's! Wouldn't his fingers itch to put it into type?"

"Who among the Cherokees," I wonder[e]d, "could do what Dan suspected Sequoyah was doing, write the history of his people, express their philosophy, put meaning into their old beliefs? Do you suppose Richard could?"

"No," she shook her head. "He came upon the scene too late to suck in with his mother's milk the reality of the old life. Dan's ancient friends, Ta-ka-to-ka, The Blanket, and Ta-ka-e-tuh, might have done a great deal. It might be that my own little son, Richard Junior, could do a good job if he will keep his eyes and ears open, go away to Harvard for his English, and come back a Cherokee."

"Yes, or some other of our boys or girls," I said. "At least, Dan and I have not tried to stamp out their reverence for the old beliefs. We have not tried to discredit their god, nor to mold them in every thought to our pattern. Dan used to say, 'The Christ ideal is sufficient to win the way to their hearts without coercion from us.' "

"What can we do for Ellen?" Catherine asked. "Would she come and help us at Oak Hill?"

"No. We have nothing to ease the pain of her anxiety; and, to be practical, I don't believe the Board would sanction her presence here as a worker—I should have to report it, you know."

"True, but for the moment I had forgotten. They leave us free as a rule to do as we think best; and our visitors from the Mission Rooms have seemed tolerant. Only Ellen has roused them to action."

"Yes," I said, "and it was indeed a notable rousing. Ellen is like that." I was remembering my first ride to Gibson with her, and thinking how nearly she had come to wrecking my life.

* * *

With the passing of time, peace between the Cherokee factions became a reality. Nearly all of the anti-Ross refugees returned and adjusted themselves to a regime that promised comfort for the people and education for all the children. Even before Ross' dream of establishing male and female seminaries was realized, it was said that the number of Cherokees above the age of six who could not read either English or their own language could be counted on the fingers of two hands.

Such boasts we heard with satisfaction, though we were careful at Oak Hill never to comment publicly on our work, as we were careful in everything we printed to keep out any trace of controversy over Cherokee policy.

We watched an orderly tribal government re-erected out of chaos. Schools, accessible to all; courts, with the able Bushyhead serving as Chief Justice; an efficient police; mills, blacksmith shops, wheelwrights, and stores; small farms and big plantations; passable roads, and river ferries; and one Cherokee-owned Arkansas River steamboat—these were material evidence that more than twenty thousand tribesmen were well on the way to hold their own in competition with the whites.

We were part of that onward surge, cheered to know that we were contributing practically and spiritually. From time to time, visitors from other missionary stations among the Creeks, Choctaws, Chickasaws, Seminoles, Osages, and the more western plains Indians came to tell us of their work. In nearly every aspect, it was like our own. Everywhere, pressure on mission facilities was severe, and mission problems were being solved by resourceful men and women who, in spirit, were brothers and sisters to Dan and me and Miss Eula and Catherine; and back of them all, Presbyterians, Baptists, Methodists, Moravians, Congregationalists, Catholics, stood the multitude of Christian Americans who, through their Mission Boards, declared their belief that the universal brotherhood of man is more than a theory.

Following Dan's practice, I invited Cherokee preachers to conduct services in Pease Chapel as often as possible. One I liked especially came from a remote creekside settlement and described himself as "a man that plow his fiel' an' make his garden early in mornin' an' Sattidy, teach school eight in mornin' til four o'clock in evenin', preach in little log schoolhouse two times Sunday, an' fin' time also for Sunday school an' temperance society meetin'."

He took as text the words from Mark X: 14, "Suffer the little children to come unto me," and for more than an hour told us of the boys and girls of his Cabin Creek neighborhood, their parents, family problems, their way of living, their creek-bottom farms, the walnut, plum, pecan and pawpaw trees bordering their fence rows, chattering squirrels that ran along the top rails of their cornfield fences, flashing redbirds in the early spring, and other details of the sylvan setting in which he labored by precept and example to teach "same as I think they teach you at this place."

As he and I walked to Richard's cabin for dinner, Catherine having asked us so that he might see her youngest, I wondered what Ellen of the Arkansas days would have said of Bear Timson's broken and dirt-stained fingernails, the earthy Indian smell of his person, his shabby old broadcloth coat and patched shoes. But now, I thought, she would not notice such details, but would look below the surface and recognize this solid man for what he is, a sweat-stained soldier of the Lord who has left his hoe and double-shovel plow to come to us. I wished that Dan could have heard his sermon, and his talk at Catherine's table, with her small Cephas sitting quietly and proudly on his knee.

Once during the meal, beaming on Catherine, he said, "This one is man now, you don' have to chew his meat first." I recalled Ellen's horror at the sight of Indian mothers masticating their babies' food then transferring it to their mouths. "Worse than beasts they are," she had shuddered. Dan had laughed, and said, "Let us say they are like the birds of the air that feed their nestlings as God intended they should so that their plumage shall shine, their flight be swift, and their song be a joy to hear."

"Paul," she had gibed, "we have a nature poet in our midst!"

We watched, with little apprehension because of the rapid advance of the tribe, the beginning of the movement to take from the Cherokees this last refuge which they had made attractive enough to draw the white man's covetous eyes. It started, of course, in Washington, where the land-grabbers' mouthpieces agitated for white control of Indian Territory. In the *Cherokee Advocate*, the tribe's newspaper, was printed the warning, "In five years, or sooner, something that will be called a treaty will be made with some people that say they represent the Cherokee, Creek, and other Indian Nations which will put our lands under white control—as fair a treaty as that of December, 1835, that robbed the Cherokees of their homes in Georgia and Tennessee."

North and south of the Indians' country white men were halting, facing round and asking, "Why must we be denied entry into this land? Let us set up over it a Territorial government." They said this openly, but the further thought, to evict the Indians and send them farther west, they did not voice—yet.

We watched their maneuvering, but it was not within our province to comment or protest. We could only teach our scholars the history of the world, and of America, as it had unrolled, and hope to plant in their minds the hard lesson that the strong and well equipped have always taken from the weak and ignorant.

Eighteen

I was riding to Dan's cabin one day in late spring, more than a year since The Worm had brought his last message, when I saw Lucy Buck slip out of the door of the lean-to addition and start running. I called to her, and she hurried to meet me.

"That man has come again," she cried. "He is crazy, an' say he will shoot her with a pistol!"

"Take my horse," I said, dismounting, "and go as fast as you can to The Runner. I will do what I can until he comes."

I had only two hundred yards to go, and I covered the distance in less than half a minute, but Lucy had ridden out of sight when I turned at the cabin door to look.

At my knock, Ellen bade me enter in a voice which she managed to keep under control. Inside, Tassel sat facing her with a cocked pistol across his knees, his right hand grasping its handle. I knew from his bloodshot eyes, the sparse bristle of beard on his face and his rumpled clothes that he had been drunk for days; and he was in the ugly mood of spree drinkers in whom the effects of whiskey begins to wane and sick sobriety begins to blot out rosy dreams. I thought, Probably he decided to come while the liquor was still filling him with the delusion that his attraction for Ellen was irresistible. That delusion is gone, and now he means to force her to go with him.

"Sit down, Paul." Ellen did not move as she spoke, nor take her eyes from Tassel. "I believe you know my friend?"

"Yes," I managed to keep my voice level. "How are you, Tassel?"

He shifted his eyes to me for a moment as he asked, "You are head Christer now at Oak Hill?"

Ellen answered before I could speak, "Yes, Paul is in charge. I expect you've come for Dan's notes on the translation of the Gospel according to John, haven't you?" she suggested.

"Yes," I said. "We are—"

"Well," Tassel interrupted truculently, turning again to me, "you had better go away now!"

"Just a minute, Talley," Ellen made as if to rise, "if you will excuse me, I'll get the notes for Paul."

"Sit still!" he ordered, and to me, "You can come back for anything you want here after we go."

I pretended surprise, and said to Ellen, "I had no idea that you were leaving."

"Nor had I," she contrived to laugh, "until Tally came with an urgent invitation to go somewhere with him. Just where," and I could see rising within her the familiar spirit of scornful irony, "do you propose to take me, my love?"

"Never mind now, you'll find out soon enough. And you," he addressed me angrily, "get away from here while you can!"

Ellen said quickly, as if to cut off any heated retort I might be tempted to make, "But I want Paul to hear your reason for thinking you have any claim on me. I have told him that you and I were quits a long time ago."

"It's none of his damned business; and I've warned him to—"

She cut him off icily, "Also, I want him to confirm what I have told you, that I mean to live with Dan again."

"That man?" he laughed sardonically. "You can't live with a dead man. But even if he was alive and would have you back, you couldn't live with a damn Christer."

She went pale with anger at that, but held her tongue in check. I knew that she was trying to hold him in talk as long as possible, having heard my shout to Lucy and guessed that I had sent her for help. Now, quietly, she went on, "Dan and Paul are Christers, yes, but they have never deserted their God, never renounced their faith. You, Talley, were a great disappointment to me."

"If you think I'm a traitor, or a coward—"

"Of course, you're a coward," she taunted. "I've known that a long time, and now I know you're a traitor to Wah-ti-ka and the other honest anti-Ross men. Now I know you're willing to lick Ross' boots if you can keep your hands on that precious register of claims and continue to live on what you can get from the Cherokee claimants who don't yet know you're only an empty pumpkin shell."

"That is a lie, circulated by my enemies!" Tassel cried.

"No, Talley," she was quick to prod him again, "I'm telling you the truth about yourself; I know how your mind works. In the drunken fog that is clouding your mind, you believe you can force me to go with you. Why? Because you believe you can get money from me.

You would threaten me with scandal, threaten to publish it and make it impossible for me to live with Dan unless I paid you to keep quiet. You're a cheap blackmailer, or would be if you could frighten me into going with you."

Her low-spoken words were like knife points, cruelly sharp, and he was writhing. His voice was high-pitched as he cried, "It is not true, Ellen!" Instinctively, he raised his hand from the pistol butt, and I was speculating upon the desperate chance of springing to knock the weapon to the floor when he resumed his grip on it and went on, "I can't live without you, Ellen, you are my Beloved Woman!" His voice rose to a shriek.

I felt with sickening certainty that these would be his last words, that he had lost control of himself with that mad cry. Murder and suicide showed plainly in his eyes, and I gathered myself to rush him. I had not heard The Runner's approach; and I jumped at the very instant the bullet from his rifle thudded into Tassel's body. Ellen, thinking that she could hold him longer in talk, had risen to restrain me. If she had remained seated, Tassel's one shot, fired before he fell from the chair, would have passed over her head. As she was rising, however, the heavy bullet burned a stunning gash across the top of her head. She fell, and as I leaped to her side I believed that Tassel had killed her.

The Runner rushed in, followed by Lucy, and swooped to secure the pistol even before looking at the jerking body of Tassel. Lucy dropped to her knees beside me and moaned, "Oh, she is dead!"

Then Ellen's eyelids fluttered, and she attempted to sit up. "Oh, she is alive," Lucy whispered with a gasp of relief, then to me, "I ride as fast as I can, and we come back both on your horse." She thrust her chin towards The Runner, and went on, "She make us get off back yonder an' creep up to the window. Oh, Sir, that man come an' surprise us, so we could not get our pistols." As she talked, Lucy took Ellen's head in her lap and with the kerchief she had worn about her head dabbed at the blood flowing from her scalp.

The Runner went to fetch Doctor Butram from Dunster. Before he came, we had lifted Ellen into Dan's narrow bunk, and Lucy had used one of Dan's clean linen shirts to bandage her head. The doctor said, as he bent over Ellen, "I sent The Runner to find the District Sheriff and report." Then, "Lucy, you and Paul seem to have done all that was immediately required, but if I can have warm water I'll bathe the wound. Infection is, I believe, the only danger we have to guard against." He fell silent, and a questioning look came into his eyes as he applied an antiseptic to the wound, and he asked, "Has she spoken?"

"Not to me," I answered. "Did she speak to you, Lucy?"

"No, she don' speak to me either."

"I see." Butram rose and, taking me by the arm, led me outside, saying, "I hope I'm wrong, but I believe there will be a partial paralysis that will prevent speech. It may be permanent, or only temporary —or intermittent. It is impossible to tell . . . Do you mean to take her to Oak Hill?"

"Yes," I answered. "It has been—it is her home; I couldn't let her remain here."

"No, but—of course, there are hospitals; and remember that you will be in for a certain amount of—shall we say trouble? There will be an official inquiry, and much talk, of course. The Runner will be tried in the Cherokee courts, and Tassel's friends—he still has some, remember—and the politicians—but you know as well as I do what will be said."

"Yes," I said, "but we shall have to face it. Dan would wish us to take her in, as we do. I shall do my best to convince the Board that this time the trouble was not of her making."

"I wonder!" the doctor shook his head. "You know, she would not have been living here alone except for Lucy Buck. Why wasn't she with her people in New York?"

"She wouldn't go while she still believes there's a chance that Dan is alive; and she insisted on living in Dan's cabin, waiting for him here."

"And she has always had her way! Well," Butram shrugged, "she seems to have had a genius for bringing trouble to others—and now to herself. Not that I, or any one else at Dunster, has wished to sit in judgment." Then, abruptly, "I'm sure she can be moved to Oak Hill tomorrow, but wait until I can see her again."

Next day Ellen seemed surprised to see Doctor Butram, and spoke for the first time since she was wounded, "Why are you here, Doctor? Why is my head bandaged? Why—" her voice failed her, only her lips moved with the effort to speak, and then she subsided into a blackness that blanked out memory.

I wrote at once to Mr. Tilley, at the New York Mission Rooms, explaining everything and asking that any action by the Board be deferred until all local investigations were completed, and that some one be sent to obtain at first hand full knowledge of the facts.

In Arkansas, where Tassel had made something of a reputation as a criminal lawyer, his killing caused some of the newspapers to revive the anti-Ross agitation. But their attempts to make the brief, formal trial of The Runner a *cause célèbre* failed because [Ellen] could neither appear to testify nor answer questions put by an agent of the court who came to Oak Hill. Bushyhead came to sit with the Cherokee District Judge, who held the examination of Lucy Buck, and mine, strictly to the facts, and directed a verdict of acquittal. Then, for the ears of those who crowded the courtroom, Bushyhead said, "Let there be no more talk about that man who has gone to his final judgment; and let no anger abide in any of you against him who was compelled to shoot, for he acted as a man should act."

An effort at Washington to use the affair as the basis of a fresh attack on Ross—as one agitator put it, "an illustration of the farce of Indian self-government"—fell flat when it failed to stir Ross to any other than the terse statement, "It was merely a case of one man killing another to save the life of a woman. The District Court has so decided."

To the Mission Board's representative who had come out at my suggestion Ross talked freely about Ellen and Dan. He said, "She is living down her past. We have a saying among the Cherokee, 'When the singing bird molts she is a better wife than ever.' Dan Wear knew it, and he would have taken her back to his fire. We would not have liked or trusted him less because of that Christian act. We believe in a God Who can forgive all to one whose heart is cleansed of evil . . . If your Board can ride out the storm of criticism in quarters where it is only an outcry against outraged morality by those ignorant of the facts, you will be stronger than before amongst the Cherokees by making no further changes at Oak Hill. I would have said the same thing had I been consulted before Dan Wear was dismissed."

I believe that Ross' words, circulated discreetly amongst the Board's supporters, saved Oak Hill as a mission station, and me from sharing Dan's fate. More than once, I asked myself what I should have done if I had been dismissed. Set up an independent mission and school, or go back to live out my time in Vermont with the farmer Wears? Probably the answer would have been determined by Miss Eula, whose letters were a great comfort to me.

Ellen became our permanent guest at Oak Hill. Her memory was soon completely restored, and at intervals her power of speech. When this happened the first time, her words were, "Is there any news of Dan?" and when I shook my head, "We shall just have to wait a little longer." Then she asked, "Paul, are the remittances from New York coming to you regularly?"

"As your guardian for the time being, yes," I told her.

"Are you using the money to help your work?"

"Only a little. We don't really need it; as Dan used to say, 'Every dollar we earn is worth ten in donations.' We are well organized to support ourselves."

"Surely there must be something I can do to earn my keep?"

"Of course," I agreed. "When Doctor Butram says you are fit, you can help Miss Every who is new to Oak Hill. Help her in the classroom, and in teaching the girls how to live like ladies."

"I'm afraid I shall lose that assignment when Eula Benson returns."

"Not if our plans work out."

"So she has consented at last, Paul? I'm so glad!"

"I have her promise," I said. "I shan't allow her to teach again. As mistress of Oak Hill, she will have her hands full."

"And when Dan comes you will have to do without me, of course."

"We shall be glad to lose you to Dan."

"Oh, Paul, he will come back!"

"Meanwhile, I shall count on your help—unofficially, of course. You understand?"

"Yes. I've been naughty, and must be stood in a corner—not with a dunce's cap on my head, but—Paul, do you happen to have an iron for branding on my forehead the letter 'A'?"

"The Scarlet Letter? No; we don't even brand our cattle. Farley says we have lost none yet; the Cherokees seem to have convinced the cattle thieves that it would be bad luck to steal from us."

"Suppose, Paul, that this paralysis strikes me dumb again; Doctor Butram says it may."

"Why, go on with the faculties that remain. To have four of the five senses and use them to the full is to be better equipped for our work than most of us are."

"Why, Paul, you are a philosopher," she gibed.

"I don't mean to be pretentious," I said, "only I have never doubted your intelligence, Ellen."

* * *

The Board willingly granted an extended leave when Miss Eula (for so I have always thought of her) wrote, "Yes, Paul, come as soon as you can." We were married in the parlor of the old Benson farm house in Far Cry Valley, fragrant with lavender and opened to the wind and sun for the ceremony. In the train with her on the way to a honeymoon splurge in Boston, I said to myself, Why it seems only yesterday that we were riding away from Kingslake in that big two-horse wagon and I was thinking how like the music of a Vermont trout brook her voice was. I suppose it would seem slightly ridiculous to one watching us now that I should be thinking the same thing at this moment. But I am, and it is true that my wife is as beautiful and desirable as she was then.

She slipped a hand into one of mine, smiling happily as she whispered, "A penny for your thoughts, dear." So I told her. She laughed, and said, "Mine are not worth even a penny now, they are so like yours. I'm sure that I have always been in love with you. I knew I loved you, but—"

"But what, Miss Eula?"

" 'Miss Eula' indeed! You might at least manage to address me as 'Wife', as grandfather did grandmother . . . Darling, what I was about to say is that I believed one must feel something more—I didn't know exactly what. It was only when I dared to kiss you on the boat and put my head on your shoulder that I suspected the truth."

"Catherine told me I should have stormed your maidenly reserve long ago."

"But it hasn't been bad, has it, dear, since we've been together so closely in the work we love? I mean—well, those last months at Oak Hill were rather terrible while waiting so anxiously for Dan, but all the rest I loved being close to you and him."

"I know," I pressed her hand strongly. "We both have loved him. No, our years haven't been bad, but now—I want to kiss you."

"And I want to kiss you. Do you think it strange, Paul, that I've never before wanted to kiss—I mean the way I want to now?"

"No, for it has been like that with me. Oh, once, when I was eighteen, I believed I was in love passionately, but—well, you have married a virgin man, Miss Eula."

"Thank you for telling me, dear. Once I thought that perhaps Ellen—she has not always been scrupulous."

"She might have," I confessed, "except that the thought of Dan came between us. It was when she believed she had left him forever. She said she hated him, and would have taken me to hurt him; and yet she never ceased to love him. Women are strange!"

"Women are human, darling; let's put it that way . . . Paul, do you want children? It's not too late."

"Yes, although I may be jealous of them. But—Miss Eula, talk like this should make you blush!"

"Should it, dear? But I've thought about having your babies ever since I knew I wanted you; and for an elderly spinster I know a great deal about babies and motherhood. I used to pray that Ellen might bear children for Dan. He would have been a wonderful father; and Ellen so lovely and vital. She was the most beautiful bride I ever saw."

"Look in your mirror tonight and you'll see a lovelier!"

"Why, Paul!" she laughed happily, then, "But, of course, I can't believe you."

"Can you believe that I like arbutus better than hollyhocks?"

"Nicer and nicer—go on, darling!"

"And character and purpose and Puritan beauty of soul better than—well, you know Ellen's attractions."

[* * *]

Our return to Oak Hill was delayed by many visits to our Vermont and Massachusetts kin, to New York, where Mr. Tilley told me how proud the Board was of my wife, by a brief stop in Tennessee for a look at Kingslake (no longer a mission station), to a round of visits to mission stations in Indian Territory and to the homes of Hummingbird, Bushyhead, Coodey, Vann, and Ross. Ross' new Rose Hill home had not long been completed, and furnished with French pieces brought up from New Orleans, and the young wife he had lately brought from her Quaker home in Delaware gave us cordial welcome, saying, "Thee are his good friends, and thy coming is a joy to me." We drove with her and the Chief to the Cherokee Capital at Tahlequah, and to the sites he had chosen for the male and female seminaries. His eyes shining, Ross said, "After we have our seminaries going well, and are able to collect what is owing to us from Washington, we shall build a fine brick Capitol in the center of this square"—we were walking about the tree-shaded square in which the temporary log structures housing the tribal government were scattered—"and outshine Oak Hill!"

He talked with Miss Eula again concerning the prospects of getting teachers for the female seminary from Mount Holyoke, and said, "Finding good teachers will be my responsibility. I shall make the rounds of Eastern colleges and seminaries—you know, Miss Eula, I found my Mary," his eyes dwelt fondly on his lovely wife, "teaching in a Quaker school."

Before coming to Oak Hill, we also made many visits to little cabins where former scholars lived. Everywhere we found all of the outward evidence of peace and plenty, yet unrest smoldered. The loss of their Georgia and Tennessee homeland, their betrayal by the signers of the spurious treaty of removal, the growing movement amongst the whites to force an invasion of Indian Territory all contributed to this unrest. It seemed to me that amongst the people there was a frantic yearning for something to symbolize the sustaining strength of their old beliefs. Could it be, I wondered, the things which Sequoyah had hoped to recover in Mexico, and in the quest of which I believed that he and Dan had lost their lives?

Our tour made us realize anew that we were living and laboring with a people hardly more than a generation removed from the hunter stage. They had come forward with almost incredible swiftness, but were still as capable of wrecking as of building a stable civilization. The young men especially needed a firmer anchorage than they had yet found . . .

As we came within eyeshot of Oak Hill, Miss Eula kissed me and cried, "Home again! I'm so glad, my darling."

She went at once to talk with Ellen, who came out of the schoolroom with Miss Every, kissed her warmly, and said, "I'm in luck, my dear, I recovered my voice again yesterday." Then to me, "Hail to the bridegroom, Paul. You're both blooming."

Catherine's first question, after embracing Miss Eula, was, "Aren't you going to have a baby?"

My wife answered, "How in the world did you know? I've not told anyone yet, not even Paul."

Nineteen

The Cherokees call the years between the reunion of the Easterners and Westerners and the War Between the States the decade of peace, although it was in fact an extended decade. For us at Oak Hill it was certainly a fruitful period.

Miss Eula bore a son whom we named Paul Daniel, and he was able to hold his own as he grew towards his teens with the stoutest Cherokee boys of his age. His closest companion, with whom at the age of six he solemnly exchanged pin-pricks of blood to signify brotherhood, was Catherine's third son, Kingsley. Our daughter, born two years after Paul Daniel, we named Prudence. Of her, Catherine said, "Some day a fine young man will tell her that these baby eyes are stars and this gurgling voice is like the ripple of water over the pebbles of Spavinaw Creek."

With Catherine's assistance, Richard conducted our print shop so efficiently that I scarcely needed to give it a thought. Now and again Catherine turned out a story-tract in the series she had started with the life of Catherine Swan, each glowing with life and zeal. In the last five years of our era of peace, her name appeared now and then in the story papers in the East as author of Indian tales, the characters in which we knew, by other names, at Oak Hill.

Miss Every married Willis Corn, a Cherokee protégé of Bushyhead who had taken his bachelor of arts degree at Princeton College, and afterwards rose high in the councils of the Nation. That marriage caused scarcely a ripple of comment in the New Hampshire village where they were united by her uncle, a Baptist minister. To replace her I secured the daughter of one of my Vermont cousins who had been schooled under Mary Lyon; and when the number of girls in our school increased so that one teacher and Ellen could not adequately instruct them, Miss Every's sister, also a Mount Holyoke graduate, came to us.

In that period, also, I replaced the two boys' teachers, who left us for positions in the East, with graduates from our Hebron Creek school who had afterwards gone to Dartmouth College. We were now, as Miss Eula pointed out with pride, staffed by an all-New

England-Cherokee family, and she exulted, "Dan would be so pleased!"

Farley lasted through the years of peace, becoming a competent farm manager after his working days were over and a friend of the successive relays of schoolboys who learned from him what thorough cultivation of the soil will produce, and that farm animals have individuality and character. Miss Eula lost Mrs. Ryan as housekeeper, and pleased Ellen by replacing her with Lucy Buck. A lame graduate of Hebron Creek took over the work of our shops when death ended our long association with Uncle Frank. The installation of efficient neighborhood grist and saw mills made it possible to dismantle our own, and turn millwright Taylor into assistant farmer and carpenter.

Uncle Frank's passing cut our last link with negroes under slavery; and though, in the difficult months preceding the war, we were at times referred to as "damned Yankee Abolitionists" we held to Dan's policy of remaining silent on that explosive subject. We saw what outspoken opposition to slavery could lead to when Eben Wright was expelled from his Baptist mission in spite of the years of effective work he had done and Bushyhead's loyal support.

If we erred in believing that our neutrality would save Oak Hill, it was because we put our work above any satisfaction we might have in expressing opinions. Dan had said, "Teach facts in the schoolroom. Let the scholars find the interpretations for themselves," and we strove to follow that formula.

In these years, Ellen led a curious life. I could never be sure that her conviction that Dan would sometime re-appear was altogether an illusion. She spoke of his return as confidently as she did of everyday happenings at Oak Hill. At times, I was tempted to believe that through a psychic sense not granted to us others she was able to communicate with him.

We others, of course, had given up hope. Colonel Pease drove over from his Arkansas plantation to request that the name of our chapel be changed to "The Daniel Wear Memorial Chapel," but when he understood how utterly Ellen believed that Dan still lived, he said, "Of course we could do nothing to shake her faith or wound her feelings. I regret this because Dan Wear was a man whose memory I should be proud to honor."

In deference to Ellen's faith, also, I refrained from placing in the Chapel the tablet I designed and inscribed with Dan's own familiar saying, "Our time in the service of the Lord is brief, but there will always be an Elisha to seize the mantle of the departed Elijah." Following her lead, we ceased to speak of Dan, even among ourselves and out of her hearing, as one who had passed; and I believe we gained strength and confidence from the assumption that we were shaping our work for his approval.

In the last two years of her life, Ellen's power of speech remained unimpaired.

* * *

The war between the States broke upon the Cherokees before the wounds opened by their forced exile and deepened by factional strife had quite healed; and almost from the beginning they suffered terribly.

I have no intention of writing a history of the Cherokees in those turbulent years, of the hard pressure brought to bear upon them by both Union and Confederate leaders to take sides, of the violence of some of their own leaders, of the organization by slave-owning Cherokees of the Knights of the Golden Circle and by Union tribesmen of the Loyal Leaguers, of the early dominance in Cherokee councils of Confederate agents, of the recruitment by both sides of Cherokee regiments, or of the events that led the tribal government to treat first with Richmond and afterwards to renounce the Confederate alliance. I shall speak only of what we at Oak Hill saw, and what affected us.

Close about us, we saw the whirlwind of destruction that is raised when brothers take up arms against one another. I would not say, however, that the savagery of the Cherokees who pillaged and burned and killed in the names of the Confederacy and the Union exceeded that of the white men who marched with Sherman through Georgia. Compared to what was now loosed upon the Cherokee Nation, the bloody feud which had inflamed the Eastern and Western tribesmen against each other was mild. The battles among our scholars of the Ross and anti-Ross families had been, by comparison, mere tussles. Twice, in spite of all we could do to drag them apart, they fought pitched battles with knives, stones, and clubs. Girls fought alongside their brothers viciously. One boy was seriously slashed, and a girl lamed for life. Scholars were taken out of our school by parents on both sides who believed us to be in sympathy [with either] the North or the South until only thirty of a hundred and eighteen remained.

All of us received threats against our lives, and only constant vigilance saved the buildings from destruction by fire. Our fields were ravaged, our cattle and horses driven off, and as the days wore on, as our granaries and cribs emptied and the shelves of our cellars and storehouse became bare, we were saved from hunger only because Ellen used her money—that which she had accumulated and what could come through from New York—to buy stores. These grew increasingly expensive and difficult to have delivered at Oak Hill before being captured by foraging troops and marauding guerillas.

Our distress was as nothing, however, compared to that of families we had long known as friends.

The Coon's eleven year old son, back from a short visit to his home, said to me, "Sir, the soldiers come an' make me go away; they say all we got to eat mus' be cook for them. They make my mother cook all day, an' they pass by the fire with tin plates an' take all that bread an' meat. They hit my mother an' curse when one fin' in the cellar a bowl of turnips my mother wan' to save for us. When all in the house is gone, they kill our cow an' make her cook it, too. Then they go, an' when I come in from the woods we have nothin'. So I go down to the creek an' catch some fish. We eat them fish, then some of the men come back an' make my mother go away with them. So I come back here."

"Where is your father?" I asked.

The boy answered, "My mother say to me some men come to talk with him, then take him away. My aunt fin' my father where them men kill him an' put him in a hollow log."

At a home that had been prosperous I found a scholar's grandmother alone; all the rest of the numerous family had either gone to war or fled, as they hoped, beyond reach of the raiders. She showed me how she had removed a portion of the ceiling from an upstairs room, hidden in the attic a store of flour, sugar, and salt, then replaced the ceiling boards. She told me how she divided the family's livestock into small bands and sent them into the woods, each band in charge of a slave whom she believed she could trust. Concerning the secreted food, however, she said, "I could not trust anyone to help me hide it. And," she added, "I do not know where any of my cattle and horses are now."

A young woman of another family said, "I mus' live alone now, an' I am afraid to go to sleep because I am afraid of men that prowl around. I hate all the sounds the crickets an' katydids make at night because they might not let me hear the sound of men that come to do me harm in time to run an' hide in the woods."

Another woman, once a scholar at Hebron Creek, whose man had been killed said, "Everything to eat in the neighborhood is gone, all the crops and cattle and hogs and sheep; all the game in the woods, too, seems like. Not even the wolves can find enough. They are like skeletons covered with mangy hides, and their hair falls off because they are starving. One day I found one at the corner of my chimney; it had tried to dig into my house to find something to eat."

Southward towards Texas fled the women and children of the Southern families that could find means to go, and northward into Kansas went those of Union men. Women drove the refugees in ox-wagons; they went on horseback or on the backs of scrawny mules; some undertook to go on foot.

So desperate became the hunger that women began digging up the dirt floors of smokehouses when some one suggested that a little salt and grease might be recovered by boiling the dirt; and it was whispered that if you buried any potatoes you had saved under the hearthstone they might escape the keen-eyed foraging squads.

When it began to be said that young women, maids or wives of men away from home and fighting on "the other side," were being snatched from their homes and forced to accompany "our side's" soldiers as camp followers, their men thought to leave a loaded gun when they went away so that a wife or daughter might use it either to drive away the ravishers, if possible; if not, to kill herself.

Once, as Ellen saw and reported to us, the loaded pistol was used in another but hardly less dramatic fashion when a squad of Wah-ti-ka's men came to The Runner's home. Ellen was there helping to care for Abigail, The Runner's lovely daughter of ten, who was recovering from a long illness. No man of the family was at home. Coming into the house, the squad leader looked closely at Ellen, and said, "I know you, see you long time ago when Wah-ti-ka go your house, so we don' take your horse. Everything else here we take," and he sent his men to search for horses, cattle, hogs, and poultry.

Abigail was watching from an open window when one of the men led her beloved pony out of the bushes in which her mother had hidden it. The little girl cried out frantically, "Oh, don't take Selim!" but the man only laughed. Then, desperately, she begged, "Please let me say good-bye to Selim."

"All right," the man grinned, "but you hurry."

Abigail seized the loaded pistol from the mantel, held it under her apron as she went out to hug Selim's neck and kiss its muzzle. She put the pistol to its head and fired; and as it fell to its knees, she ran screaming back to Ellen. The squad leader came storming in to shake his fist in Ellen's face and accuse, "You tell her to shoot that pony!"

"No, but I wish I had," she denied insultingly.

"You will pay for that pony," he warned, "you an' all your Christers. You will pay a big price."

She told us of his threat, but refused to take it seriously, saying, "I can't believe Wah-ti-ka would raid Oak Hill, or allow his cut-throats to do so, although he does hate me and blames me for the killing of Talley Tassel."

We had no protection for ourselves or the mission property beyond the good will of the people. The Ross government was unable to maintain order, and he had rushed to Washington in the desperate hope of convincing President Lincoln that Union soldiers must be sent into the Cherokee Nation. Confederate leaders, enacting the farce of deposing Ross, had set up a rival government backed by Wah-ti-ka's armed men, but it was equally powerless to suppress the anarchy that prevailed.

When Wah-ti-ka himself led the assault on Oak Hill, we could do no more than stand by, under guard on the playground, and watch the looting and then the burning. They had galloped out of the woods at dawn, a whole troop. Wah-ti-ka, whom I saw for the first time, rode well in front. I had just dressed and walked outside, having heard the clatter of hooves, when he pulled up within five feet of me scattering the fine gravel of the yard. I looked up into the face of a squat, very dark fullblood, a long and powerful arm thrust out at me as he rasped, "Get ever'body out!"

He and a squad of his raggedly uniformed men went with me as I summoned our staff and the few scholars that remained. The others swarmed into the building to carry out and pile on the playground everything that took their fancy, meaning to return with wagons to carry the loot away.

Miss Eula, leaving our children with me, ran to Ellen's quarters, and brought her to where the rest of us were standing. When I said to Wah-ti-ka, "We are all here," he stepped out to face us for a moment before going close to Ellen and demanding, "You know why we come here?"

"Must I guess?" her contemptuous smile was like a slap in the face. "Your man there," her eyes went to the corporal who had threatened her, "was vague, but he did say that we would pay for Abigail's pony—just why I can't imagine."

"You pay, yes. Like he say, you all pay a big price!" The corners of his mouth lifted in a wolfish grin. "Now you watch." He half turned his head to order the firing of the buildings.

It seemed a long time before they began to blaze up, one after another, the two big school and dormitory buildings, the chapel, my cabin and office, the shop, the granaries and cribs—all the solid structures that stood as evidence of our years of effort. It was long past sunrise before they were all alight, leaping pyres; and the incongruous thought came into my mind, After all, even these great fires seem pale in the sunlight. And then I wondered, Can he believe that he is destroying Oak Hill?

Satisfied that nothing could be saved, Wah-ti-ka stepped close to Ellen and ordered, "Now you come with us." A trooper brought forward a led horse on which a side saddle was strapped, and Wah-ti-ka said, "This yours; get on."

"No!" I stepped between them, but was seized from behind and dragged back. "Don't be foolish, Paul," Ellen cried, "you would only get yourself killed!" She went to the led horse, put her foot in the hand of the stooping trooper and mounted. She drew the reins taut and, looking intently at me, said, "Tell Dan that he will know where to find me; I shall be waiting for him."

Wah-ti-ka gave the order for his men to mount; and when they were in line raised his hand to signal them to move out.

Ellen urged her horse alongside Wah-ti-ka. I heard Miss Eula's gasp as Ellen's hand sought the handle of the razor-sharp and dagger-pointed butcher knife she had picked up in the kitchen and concealed in a fold of her skirt. Then, with the swiftness of a striking rattlesnake, as she pulled her horse closer, she plunged the knife into Wah-ti-ka's back.

He was near enough for me to see the look of surprise on his face as he turned his head, and hear his savage command, "Kill her!"

Miss Eula knelt to shield Prudence's eyes as the two men who rode nearest to Wah-ti-ka raised their carbines and fired.

By the time I got to Ellen, a trooper had ridden to support Wah-ti-ka in his saddle and hear and repeat his order to ride on. The double line opened to let me run between; and, carrying her back to the playground, I saw them ride away following the slow pace of their dying leader.

Ellen spoke only once before she died. Her eyes were on me, as Miss Eula and I bent over her, but she said, "Oh, hello, Dan!"

Notes to the Novel

10 *Horseshoe Bend in 1813* The battle of Horseshoe Bend was the final battle of the Creek War of 1813–1814. General Andrew Jackson and his Cherokee allies defeated the Upper Creeks, ultimately resulting in a peace treaty that ceded 20 million acres in what is now Alabama and Georgia.

11 *Chickasaw Old Fields* This area is located in present-day Madison County, Alabama. It was also known as Ditto's Landing and Whitesburg.

30 *John Looney* Looney was one of the three chiefs of the Western Cherokees during the 1830s.

48 *Ki-tuh-wah* The more common spelling for this group of full-blood Cherokees is Keetoowah. Oskison adheres to the alternate spelling of Ki-tuh-wah throughout the manuscript.

92 *Mr. John Howard Payne and Mr. Washington Irving* See Moulton, *John Ross, Cherokee Chief* (esp. 66, 69) for Payne's relationship with Ross. For more information about Irving's trip to Fort Gibson, see Irving, *The Crayon Miscellany* (chs. 1, 2).

93 *forced to emigrate* See *Cherokee Phoenix*, June 5 and June 26, 1830. Edited by Elias Boudinot, the *Cherokee Phoenix* was published in New Echota, Georgia, from February 21, 1828, to February 4, 1829, at which time the publication was renamed *Cherokee Phoenix and Indians' Advocate*. This latter publication ceased in May 1834.

100 *Only seventy signed the treaty* In addition to John Schermerhorn (the Federal agent characterized here as an "ex-preacher untroubled by scruples or conscience"), there were twenty signers of the complete Treaty of New Echota, 1835. Even if all of the Cherokee signers are tallied, including those who signed the draft before it was amended to its final version, only thirty distinct signatures appear. digital.library.okstate.edu/kappler/Vol2/treaties/che0439.htm. The treaties—originally "Compiled and edited by Charles J. Kappler" (Washington: GPO, 1904)—have been reproduced online by Oklahoma State University as *Indian Affairs: Laws and Treaties*.

112 *the decree of that council* See McLoughlin, *After the Trail of Tears* (esp. ch. 1), for a more detailed account of the murders of the Treaty Party members.

147 *Wichata Indians* The more common spelling is Wichita, but Oskison uses both spellings interchangeably.

Bibliography

Allen, Paula Gunn, ed. *Voice of the Turtle: American Indian Literature, 1900–1970.* New York: Ballantine Books, 1994.

Bays, Brad A. *Townsite Settlement and Dispossession in the Cherokee Nation, 1866–1907.* New York: Garland, 1998.

Blankenship, Robert. *Dawes Roll "Plus" of Cherokee Nation "1898."* Cherokee, N.C.: Cherokee Roots Publication, 1994.

Boudinot, Elias. "Documents in Relation to the Validity of the Cherokee Treaty of 1835 . . ." Document PAM012. Southeastern Native American Documents Archive of the Digital Library of Georgia, University of Georgia. dlg.galileo .usg.edu.

——. *The pious Indian, or, Religion Exemplified, in the life of Poor Sarah.* Newburyport, Mass.: W & J Gilman, 1820.

Callahan, S. Alice. *Wynema, a Child of the Forest.* 1891. Lincoln: University of Nebraska Press, 1988.

Cherokee Phoenix. New Echota, Ga.: Isaac H. Harris. Georgia Newspaper Project, as presented in the Digital Library of Georgia, under "Historical Newspapers," at dlg.galileo.usg.edu.

Corkran, David H. "A Cherokee Migration Fragment," *Southern Indian Studies* 4 (1952): 27–28.

Deloria, Ella Cara. *Waterlily.* Biographical sketch of author by Agnes Picotte; afterword by Raymond J. DeMallie. Lincoln: University of Nebraska Press, 1988.

Deloria, Vine, Jr. *God Is Red: A Native View of Religion.* Golden, Colo.: Fulcrum, 2003.

Dimock, Wai Chee. "Deep Time: American Literature and World History." *American Literary History* 13.4 (Winter 2001): 755–75.

Dippie, Brian W. *The Vanishing American: White Attitudes and U.S. Indian Policy.* Middletown, Conn.: Wesleyan University Press, 1982.

Duncan, Barbara R., and Brett H. Riggs. *Cherokee Heritage Trails Guidebook.* Chapel Hill: University of North Carolina Press, in association with The Museum of the Cherokee Indian, 2003.

Fenton, William N. *The Great Law and the Longhouse: A Political History of the Iroquois Confederacy.* Norman: University of Oklahoma Press, 1998.

Foreman, Grant. *Indian Removal: The Emigration of the Five Civilized Tribes of Indians.* Norman: University of Oklahoma Press, 1953.

Gregory, Jack, and Rennard Strickland. *Sam Houston with the Cherokees, 1829–1833.* Austin: University of Texas Press, 1967.

Hagan, William T. *Taking Indian Lands: The Cherokee (Jerome) Commission, 1889–1893.* Norman: University of Oklahoma Press, 2003.

Hill, Sarah. *Weaving New Worlds: Southeastern Cherokee Women and Their Baskets.* Chapel Hill: University of North Carolina Press, 1997.

Hoig, Stan. *Sequoyah: The Cherokee Genius*. Oklahoma City: Oklahoma Historical Society, 1995.

Irving, Washington. *The Crayon Miscellany*. Philadelphia: J.B. Lippincott and Co., 1870.

Johnston, Carolyn. *Cherokee Women in Crisis: Trail of Tears, Civil War, and Allotment, 1838–1907*. Tuscaloosa: University of Alabama Press, 2003.

Justice, Daniel. *Our Fire Survives the Storm: A Cherokee Literary History*. Minneapolis: University of Minnesota Press, 2006.

Kalter, Susan. " 'America's Histories' Revisited: The Case of Tell Them They Lie." *American Indian Quarterly* 25.3 (Summer 2001): 329–51.

Kilpatrick, Jack Frederick. *Sequoyah of Earth and Intellect*. Encino, Calif.: Encino Press, 1965.

Kilpatrick, Jack F., ed. "The Wahnenauhi Manuscript." Smithsonian Institution, Bureau of American Ethnology *Bulletin* 196. Washington, D.C.: GPO, 1966.

Littlefield, Daniel F. "Short Fiction Writers of the Indian Territory." *American Studies* (Lawrence, Kans.) 23.1 (Spring 1982): 23–38.

Littlefield, Daniel F., ed. *Native American Writing in the Southeast: An Anthology, 1875–1935*. Jackson: University Press of Mississippi, 1995.

Littlefield, Daniel F., and James W. Parins. *A Biobibliography of Native American Writers, 1772–1924*. Metuchen, N.J.: Scarecrow Press, 1981.

———. *A Biobibliography of Native American Writers, 1772–1924. A Supplement*. Metuchen, N.J.: Scarecrow Press, 1985.

Mallery, Garrick. *Picture-Writing of the American Indians*. New York: Dover, 1972.

Mankiller, Wilma, and Michael Wallis. *Mankiller: A Chief and Her People*. New York: St Martin's Griffin, 1993.

Marcus, Joyce. *Mesoamerican Writing Systems: Propaganda, Myth, and History in Four Ancient Civilizations*. Princeton, N.J.: Princeton University Press, 1992.

Marshall, John. *Worcester v. The State of Georgia, Reports of Decisions of the Supreme Court of the United States*. Edited by B.R. Curtis. Vol. 10. 5th ed. Boston: Little, Brown, 1870.

Mathews, John Joseph. *Sundown*. 1934. Norman: University of Oklahoma Press, 1988.

McLoughlin, William Gerald. *After the Trail of Tears: The Cherokees' Struggle for Sovereignty, 1839–1880*. Chapel Hill: University of North Carolina Press, 1993.

———. *The Cherokees and Christianity, 1794–1870: Essays on Acculturation and Cultural Persistence*. Athens: University of Georgia Press, 1994.

McNickle, D'Arcy. *The Surrounded*. 1936. Albuquerque: University of New Mexico Press, 1997.

Momaday, N. Scott. *House Made of Dawn*. 1968. Tucson: University of Arizona Press, 1996.

Mooney, James. *James Mooney's History, Myths, and Sacred Formulas of the Cherokee: Containing Full Texts of* The Myths of the Cherokee *(1900) and* The Sacred Formulas of the Cherokees *(1891) as published by the Bureau of American Ethnology: with a New Biographical Introduction, "James Mooney and the Eastern Cherokees," by George Ellison*. Asheville, N.C.: Historical Images, 1992.

Moulton, Gary E. *John Ross, Cherokee Chief*. Athens: University of Georgia Press, 1978.

Mourning Dove. *Cogewa, the Half Blood: A Depiction of the Great Montana Cattle Range*. 1927. Lincoln: University of Nebraska, 1981.

Perdue, Theda. *Cherokee Women: Gender and Cultural Change, 1700–1835*. Lincoln: University of Nebraska Press, 1998.

Perdue, Theda, and Michael Green, eds. *The Cherokee Removal: A Brief History with Documents*. Boston: St Martin's, 2005.

Peyer, Bernd, ed. *The Singing Spirit: Early Short Stories of North American Indians*. Tucson: University of Arizona Press, 1989.

Ridge, John Rollin [Yellow Bird]. *The Life and Adventures of Joaquín Murieta, the Celebrated California Bandit*. 1854. Norman: University of Oklahoma Press, 1955.

Robb, John E., ed. *Material Symbols: Culture and Economy in Prehistory*. Occasional paper no 26. Center for Archaeological Investigations. Southern Illinois University, Carbondale.

Ronnow, Gretchen. "John Milton Oskison." In *Handbook of Native American Literature*, ed. Andrew Wiget. New York: Garland, 1994.

——. "John Milton Oskison: Cherokee Journalist Singer of the Semiotics of Power." *Native Press Research Journal* (Spring 1987): 1–14.

——. "John Milton Oskison: Native American Modernist." Ph.D. dissertation, University of Arizona, 1993. AAT9322773.

——. "John Milton Oskison: Part-Cherokee Journalist, Editor, Essayist, and Novelist." *Encyclopedia of North American Indians*. college.hmco.com / history / readerscomp / naind / html / na_027000_oskisonjohnm.htm.

Ross, John. "Letter from John Ross, principal Chief of the Cherokee Nation of Indians: in answer to inquiries from a friend regarding the Cherokee affairs. . . . " June 21, 1836. Document PAM017. Southeastern Native American Documents Archive of the Digital Library of Georgia, University of Georgia. dlg.galileo .usg.edu.

Ruoff, A. LaVonne Brown. *American Indian Literatures: An Introduction, Bibliographic Review, and Selected Bibliography*. New York: Modern Language Association of America, 1990.

——. "Pre-1968 Fiction." In *The Cambridge Companion to Native American Literature*, ed. Joy Porter and Kenneth Roemer. New York: Cambridge University Press, 2005.

Silko, Leslie Marmon. *Almanac of the Dead*. New York: Penguin, 1991.

Smith, Melinda G. *Singer of His People: The Unification of Two Peoples in John Milton Oskison's* The Singing Bird. Master's thesis, University of Georgia, 2003.

Speck, Frank. *The Penn Wampum Belts*. New York: De Vinne, 1925.

Starr, Emmet. *History of the Cherokee Indians and Their Legends and Folk Lore*. 1921. Muskogee, Okla.: Hoffman Printing, 1984.

Strickland, Arnie. "John Milton Oskison: A Writer of the Transitional Period of the Oklahoma Territory." *Southwestern American Literature* 2.2 (1972): 125–34.

Strickland, Rennard. *Fire and the Spirits: Cherokee Law from Clan to Court*. Norman: University of Oklahoma Press, 1975.

Traveller Bird. *Tell Them They Lie: The Sequoyah Myth*. Los Angeles: Westernlore, 1971.

Vizenor, Gerald. "Native American Indian Literature: Critical Metaphors of the Ghost Dance." *World Literature Today* (Spring 1992): 223–28.

Wahnenauhi. "The Wahnenauhi Manuscript." In Kilpatrick, *Sequoyah of Earth and Intellect*.

Warrior, Robert Allen. *Tribal Secrets: Recovering American Indian Intellectual Traditions*. Minneapolis: University of Minnesota Press, 1995.

Washburn, Cephas. *Reminiscences of the Indians*. Richmond: Presbyterian Committee of the Publication, 1869.

Weaver, Jace. *That the People Might Live: Native American Literatures and Native American Community*. New York: Oxford University Press, 1997.

Wilkins, Thurman. *Cherokee Tragedy: The Ridge Family and the Decimation of a People*. 2nd rev. ed. Norman: University of Oklahoma Press, 1986.

Womack, Craig. *Red on Red: Native American Literary Separatism*. Minneapolis: University of Minnesota Press, 1999.

Worcester, Samuel. "Account of S[amuel] A. Worcester's Second Arrest, 1831, July 18." Document CH050. Southeastern Native American Documents Archive of the Digital Library of Georgia, University of Georgia. dlg.galileo.usg.edu.

Works by John Milton Oskison
(in Chronological Order)

"A Trip to Yosemite Valley." *Indian Chieftain*, August 8, 1895.
"I Match You: You Match Me." *Indian Chieftain*, May 27, 1897.
"Tookh Steh's Mistake." *Indian Chieftain*, July 22, 1897.
"A Schoolmaster's Dissipation." *Indian Chieftain*, December 23, 1897.
"Only the Master Shall Praise." *Century Magazine* 59 (January 1900): 327–35.
"When the Grass Grew Long." *Century Magazine* 62 (June 1901): 247–50.
"Biologist's Quest." *Overland* n.s. 38 (July 1901): 52–57.
"John Oskison Writes of His Visit in Europe." *Indian Chieftain*, August 9, 1900.
"Cherokee Migration." *Tahlequah Arrow*, May 31, 1902.
"The President and the Indian: Rich Opportunity for the Red Man." *Vinita Weekly Chieftain*, December 25, 1902.
"The Outlook for the Indian." *Southern Workman* 32 (June 1903): 270–73.
"To Younger's Bend." *Frank Leslie's Monthly* 56 (June 1903): 182–88.
"Working for Fame." *Frank Leslie's Monthly* 56 (August 1903): 372–82.
"The Fall of King Chris." *Frank Leslie's Monthly* 56 (October 1903): 586–93.
"The Quality of Mercy: A Story of the Indian Territory." *Century Magazine* 68 (June 1904): 178–81.
"Lake Mohonk Conference." *Native American*, November 4, 1905.
"Remaining Causes of Indian Discontent." *North American Review* 184 (March 1, 1907): 486–93.
"The Problem of Old Harjo." *Southern Workman* 36 (April 1907): 235–41. Republished in *The Heath Anthology of American Literature*. 4th ed. New York: Houghton Mifflin, 2001.
"Making an Individual of the Indian." *Everybody's Magazine* 16 (June 1907): 723–33.
"Young Henry and the Old Man." *McClure's* 31 (June 1908): 237.
"John Smith Borrows $20." *Collier's* 43 (September 4, 1909): 14.
"Exploiters of the Needy." *Collier's* 44 (October 2, 1909): 17–18.
"Case of the Western Slope." *Collier's* 44 (January 15, 1910): 19.
"Competing with the Sharks." *Collier's* 44 (February 5, 1910), 19–20.
"Lung-Mender for the Lord." *Collier's* 44 (February 19, 1910): 24.
"Institute and Treatment Frauds." *Collier's* 44 (March 5, 1910), 23.
"Koenig's Discovery." *Collier's* 45 (May 28, 1910): 20–21.
"Carlisle Commencement." *Collier's* 45 (June 4, 1910): 21–22.
"Carlisle Commencement as Seen by *Collier's Weekly*." *Red Man* 3 (September 1910): 18–22.
"Diverse Tongues: A Sketch." *Current Literature* 49 (September 1910): 343–44.
"Round-up of the Financial Swindlers." *Collier's* 46 (December 31, 1910): 19–20.

"Out of the Night That Covers." *Delineator* 78 (August 1911): 80.
"Spider and the Fly." *Woman's Home Companion* 38 (October 1911): 9.
"The Indian in the Professions." *Red Man* 4 (January 1912): 201–204.
"Cooperative Cost of Living." *Collier's* 48 (January 27, 1912): 48.
"Address by J.M. Oskison." *Red Man* 4 (May 1912): 397–98.
"Little Mother of the Pueblos." *Delineator* 81 (March 1913): 170.
"An Apache Problem." *Quarterly Journal of the Society of American Indians* 1 (April 1913): 25–29.
"Farming on a Business Basis." *System* 23 (April 1913): 379–84.
"$1,000 on the Farm: Some Answers to the City Man's Query: 'Can I Go to a Farm with a Small Capital and Make Good?' " *Collier's* 51 (April 26, 1913): 24.
"$1,000 on the Farm: Answers to a City Man's Query: 'Can I Go to a Farm with a Small Capital and Make Good?' " *Collier's* 51 (May 3, 1913): 26.
"Farm, the Thousand, and the Ifs." *Collier's* 51 (May 24, 1913): 24, and 51 (June 7, 1913): 24.
"Walla-Tenaka-Creek." *Collier's* 51 (July 12, 1913): 16.
"New Way to Finance the Vacation." *Delineator* 83 (August 1913): 10.
"New Farm Pioneers." *Collier's* 51 (August 2, 1913): 27.
"Hired Man's Chance." *Collier's* 51 (August 9, 1913): 24–25.
"An Indian Animal Story." *Indian School Journal* 14 (January 1914): 213.
"Acquiring a Standard of Value." *Quarterly Journal of the Society of American Indians* 2 (January–March 1914): 47–50.
"Apples of the Hesperides, Kansas." *Forum* 51 (March 1914): 391–408.
"Arizona and Forty Thousand Indians." *Southern Workman* 43 (March 1914): 148–56.
"Boosting the Thrift Idea." *Collier's* 53 (April 4, 1914): 22.
"The Closing Chapter: Passing of the Old Indian." *Indian Leader* 17 (May 1914): 6–9.
"Less Known Edison." *World's Work* 28 (June 1914): 180–85.
"Chemist Who Became King of an Industry." *World's Work* 28 (July 1914): 310–15.
"Road to Betatakin." *Outing* 64 (July–August 1914): 392–409, 606–23.
"American Creator of the Aluminum Age." *World's Work* 28 (August 1914): 438–45.
"What a Modern Fight Is Like." *World's Work* 29 (November 1914): 87–91.
"Why Am I an American?" *World's Work* 29 (December 1914): 209–13.
"How You Can Help Feed and Clothe the Belgians." *World's Work* 29 (January 1915): 275–77.
"Indian Kicking Races." *Outing* 65 (January 1915): 441–47.
"The Record of the Naval Conflicts." *World's Work* 29 (January 1915): 345–50.
"From John Paul Jones to Dewey." *World's Work* 29 (February 1915): 447–69.
"With Apache Deer Hunters in Arizona." *Outing* 64 (April–May 1914): 65–78, 150–63.
"The Man Who Interfered." *Southern Workman* 44 (October 1915): 557–67.
"In Governing the Indian, Use the Indian." *Industrial Management* 5 (January–March 1917): 36–41.
"In Governing the Indian, Use the Indian!" *Case and Comment* 23 (February 1917): 722–26.
"The New Indian Leadership." *Industrial Management* 5 (April–June 1917): 93–100.

"In Governing the Indian-Use the Indian." *Tomahawk*, September 20, 1917.
"Back-Firing against Bolshevism." *Outlook* 122 (July 30, 1919): 510–15.
"Herbert Hoover: Engineer-Economist-Organizer." *Industrial Management* 61 (January 1, 1921): 2–6.
"Hoover Message to Export Manufacturers." *Industrial Management* 65 (March 1923): 131–35.
"Other Partner." *Collier's* 74, December 6, 1924, 14–15.
"The Singing Bird." *Sunset Magazine* (March 1925): 5–8.
Wild Harvest: A Novel of Transition Days in Oklahoma. New York: D. Appleton, 1925.
Black Jack Davy. New York: D. Appleton, 1926.
A Texas Titan: The Story of Sam Houston. New York: Doubleday, 1929.
Brothers Three. New York: Macmillan, 1935.
Tecumseh and His Times: The Story of a Great Indian. New York: G.P. Putnam's Sons, 1938.
"A Tale of the Old I.T." Unpublished autobiography, n.d. Western History Collection, University of Oklahoma.